Donald Barr Chidsey

STRONGHOLD

TO ALBERT RICHARD LOESER

NOTE TO THE READER:

It seems that the proper pronunciation of Habakkuk is Hah-*back*-uk. However, long before I learned this I had been pronouncing it in my mind (as you probably have) *Hab*-a-kuk; and I decided (as you probably will) that it was too late to change. It doesn't matter much anyway.

THE AUTHOR

. 1 . . .

Habakkuk, snuggling closer to his friend John, felt a sadness upon himself that wasn't brought by the rain; for they'd both, though only sixteen, known a might of weather. They lay not breathing much, listening to the rain, which slammed the house confusedly, and clattered and tinkled, and then soggily thump-thumped, each drop like a handful of mud, and then clittered back to tinniness thin and sharp. They couldn't hear the wind, but they could tell from the rain how squally it was. Cold, too. This was March. They pulled the covers up to their chins, less, though, because of the cold than because Judge Watts would soon be in to say good night and they didn't want him to see that they were dressed.

"Thing I don't like" whispered John "is, we take 'em out there, right to the very edge of excitement—and then we turn back!"

"What else can we do?" whispered Hab, snuggling close, vaguely troubled. "We've got to come back. We're bounden, ain't we?"

The wind seemed to stop a moment, all breathless; it sent a splatter of drops against the window, making a tentative quick metallic sound; and then suddenly it began to lash the house in a regular frenzy, as though a madman was out there with a long many-thonged lash, swatting and flaying as hard as he could.

Habakkuk wondered why he was afeared. It wasn't the rain and wind, and it wasn't the job ahead, the possibility of being shot at or drowned. These things didn't scare him any more—or not much, anyway, and not beforehand. What troubled him now was a creepy fear that something terrible was going to happen.

He felt as if the sky was lower than it had ever been before. He felt as if the air was tighter.

"Keeps on this way we can soon buy ourselves off. Then we can go wherever we've a mind to."

"Sh-sh! No profit being silly, John."

"Who's being silly? Ain't we going to make another twelve shillings each tonight, and won't we go on making——"

"How long do you think this Embargo's going to last, telling people they can't ship goods from one place to another? If they don't get sense there in Washington, well, we'll just have to cut off from the rest of 'em."

"You reckon that'll happen, Hab?"

I

"I reckon *something*'ll have to happen right soon! It can't go on like this, no matter what. You and I're lucky right now, that's all. But it won't last. We'd never get the money to buy ourselves out . . . But that ain't the point, anyway."

They lay there, whispering. They were warm under the covers, and that was good; their bodies could store up some warmth, for they were going to be tarnation cold before this night was over!

John Rellison turned his head a little.

"What *is* the point, Hab?"

"Point is, you know as well as I do that we wouldn't either of us have the heart to walk up to Judge Watts, even if we had the money, clinky hard cash right in our hands, good fat eight-pieces—we wouldn't either of us be able to go right up to him and ask to buy ourselves out. That right?"

John shifted his ground.

"This is supposed to be a free country, ain't it? We're not niggers, are we? It's different with niggers, but we're not niggers."

"Never mind about niggers. *You* wouldn't go right up to the judge and look right into his face and ask him that, now would you?"

"No" John admitted after a moment. "No, I don't reckon I would."

"I reckon not. I reckon we both know he loves us too much" said Habakkuk, feeling choky but still scared about something.

They heard the judge go downstairs. They heard him moving about, taking a last look at things.

"All the same, it's a pity we've got to stay here in this little place and have everybody else sail away. We take 'em right out there—out to the gates of romance, you might say—and then we pocket our money and come back. Next morning we're in the yards swinging a maul, but *they*'re way out away somewhere having sport."

"I don't reckon they have such a heap of sport out there," somberly.

"Well, it'd be better than staying *here,* wouldn't it?"

Hab knew exactly how he felt, for indeed Hab felt the same. Only thing was, Hab seldom talked about it; he was not interested in hearing his dreams come out of his mouth, the way John was.

"I swum, it might be hard work and it might be risky, but anyways you'd being *going* somewhere! You'd have a chance of——"

"Sh-sh-sh!"

They heard Judge Watts shove home the great bolt of the front door, and heard him come up the stairs, and pause in the hallway, and then enter Deliverance's room. He'd be out in a moment, after the kiss, they knew; and sure enough he was. He came to their room. Big in the little place, he held his candle high, looking down at the boys. He was not a smiling man—it was said that he hadn't smiled in seven years—but he was a good one, forthright, just. He was tall, and his hair was graying, and he held his shoulders straight, his back stiff; nor was his complexion blurry, or his eyes gummed with rheum. Nevertheless you thought, looking at him: here is an old man. He was strong but had no joy in his strength. His step, though firm, lacked spring. He was tired —not just now but all the time, from first thing in the morning. His eyes would meet without fear the eyes of any other, but you didn't expect ever to see fire in them again.

He had served as a captain of infantry in the independence fighting, under General Putnam; but he never talked about it, not being much of a talker at any time anyway. He wouldn't put on his old uniform and go out and tramp back and forth with the Liberty Boys, the grizzled Liberty Boys, on July 4. He didn't even hang up his sword: the only martial note in the Watts house was the musket over the fireplace in the parlor, a musket he'd had from boyhood, but he had never shot anything bigger than squirrels with it.

Now he leaned over a little, his attitude, relaxed for him, going well with the almost gentle expression on his face. His nose was longish and hooked, jutting down, as his strong thick chin jutted a bit up. A stranger, glimpsing him, might think Jonathan Watts hawklike, a grasping man. Point folks knew better.

Seeing him walk, any sailorman would say "no sailor," while a soldier would claim him for the military. When he was motionless, however, he could readily be mistaken for a ship's master, with his tight bloodless mouth and his very deep blue eyes. His house, too, near the yard, overlooking the bay, showed like a sailing man's trim house, even to the railed walk on its roof. There was a glass in a leather case hanging beside the ladder which led up to the walk, and John and Hab, sometimes on a Sunday afternoon between services, would take this glass and climb up to the walk and lie there gazing at ships, commenting on them. The judge's house was on a high place, and sometimes they would turn the glass the other way and study clearings in the woods back by the old Indian village. They saw a heap of hugging and kissing in this manner, when the Sunday happened to be clear and warm. More often, though, the boys studied ships in the harbor, which seemed to them of greater importance. Now and then they'd even see a ship under way, from up there, and they could study her sailing qualities and estimate her speed; but mostly, on a Sabbath, the sloops and ships were simply at anchor; and weekdays of course the boys didn't have time for such doings.

Mrs Watts had never paced that walk, that roof, yearning for her husband, who, to tell the truth, had never been out of sight of land. He did own a few shares of a few schooners, or perhaps somewhat more than that—he was a secretive man—but it was not in anxiety about the return of any of these that the walk was built. It was built when the Wattses' only son Aaron went to sea.

Aaron never returned. For three years Captain Watts missed not a morning and not an evening on that roof, the glass at his eye. In every weather, even in a snowstorm, when obviously it was impossible to spot anything, he could be seen there for at least a little while. If it weren't for the notable sanity of his conduct in every other respect the Pointers might have thought him touched. (It was generally accepted by this time that Mrs Watts, a glum one, was not quite right.)

It was during those three years that whatever sparkle there might once have been in his eyes faded like far smoke, and whatever trace of a smile might have twitched the corners of his mouth disappeared.

After a while he had put the glass back into its case and never touched it again. He had never smiled again either.

It was in part because of this lonesomeness, for his wife seldom said a word, and Deliverance was frightened—though admittedly also this was at a time when apprentices were needed at the yard—that Judge Watts interceded for the waifs John Rellison and Habakkuk Jones who had walked to Stonington in the hope of getting on a ship. They would have been sent back home had he not stepped in and bound them to him, after the permission of John's father and Hab's father and mother had been obtained. Neither of the boys had wanted to go back. They had wanted to go to sea, but they were willing to work in the ship-yard, or for that matter to do anything at all—anything except go back!

Judge Watts, when he visited their homes, understood why the boys had been so vehement about this. The judge leased a piece of timber-land up that way.

What it had cost him to get these apprentices was his own business; but everybody knew that he was kind to them.

Now he leaned over them a little, as the flame of the candle swung back and forth.

"You all right? Warm enough?"

"Yes, sir. Thank you, sir."

"Said your prayers?"

"Oh yes, sir."

He straightened, nodding. He stepped to the doorway.

"Have you been sleeping well lately, both of you? I've noticed—I meant to speak of it at supper—I've noticed that you've seemed a mite peaked and dauncy at the yard. Do you sleep well?"

Oh yes, they slept very well.

He nodded again.

"Good night, boys."

"Good night, sir."

Still he seemed reluctant to go. He showed uncertain, hesitant. It could be that he was troubled by the same premonition of disaster that troubled Habakkuk Jones. He stood there at the foot of the bed (while the rain sang a high reedy song outside and from time to time slashed knifelike at the house as though slashing a mattress in the hope of

4

finding hidden jewels) and he held the candle rather low, so that his shadow upswooped clear to the ceiling where it bent over a little in a menacing attitude. These boys were a great comfort to him. Deliverance was a good thing; but it was boys a man wanted. He had worked these two hard, and whupped 'em too when occasion suggested, but he had fed them well, and he never raised his voice to them, and he believed that they loved him. It was good to see them there, young and so healthy.

On impulse he went again to the side of the bed and gave each one an affectionate pinch in the cheek. Even then, even through his amazement—for the act was as startling as though a figurehead had winked at a porpoise—Habakkuk noticed that Judge Watts pinched John's cheek a little longer than he pinched his own, Hab's. This in no way hurt or astonished Habakkuk. The old judge thought that he was impartial, and undoubtedly he tried to be; but he wasn't, and hadn't ever been. Hab, however, was used to this

More brusquely, as he really did go out: "Well . . . good night boys."

"Good night, sir."

They waited until they heard his door closed, waited until they heard his bed creak, and there were no other night-sounds excepting those of the rain. Then Hab squeezed John's shoulder, and John nodded in the darkness, and they began to count to five hundred by ones, not aloud but each to himself, each trying to make his count regular like the ticks of a clock and not too fast. It is probable that they were hurrying toward the end, but hurrying at the same rate of acceleration; for they knew one another extremely well, these two, and they not only thought alike but thought at the same speed; and in fact on this occasion they finished a scant couple of seconds apart, Habakkuk finishing first.

They pushed back the blankets and climbed out of bed, and got their rain hats.

John started for the door, and he was on tiptoe, tense and elated; but Hab touched his elbow.

Hab whispered "Let's pray again, just a short one. I feel funny."

John Rellison nodded, and slipped instantly to his knees at the side of the bed. Habakkuk knelt beside him. They knew well enough that they might not come back alive—Lieutenant Ferguson had sworn that he'd get them if he had to blow himself to bits to do it—and while this thought didn't sober but rather exhilarated them, still and all they could see that it was a good time for a prayer.

Not that they had lied to their master! They had said their prayers, as usual, before getting into bed. But another one never hurt.

It was short; and they rose at the same time, as though by signal, soundless like cats, and sneaked downstairs.

Deliverance was waiting for them at the window, and this irked them, and startled them too, for though they assumed that Deliverance

5

knew about their piloting, they had not supposed she knew which window they used. They frowned in the darkness, esteeming it not fair. Hab Jones felt as he sometimes felt when he caught her looking at him with a suppressed laugh. It didn't seem right for a female to look that way; but there it was, and who was he, an apprentice, either to do or to say anything about it? He had noticed that she didn't laugh when she looked at John Rellison; and she looked at John more often than she looked at Hab.

However, Deliverance Watts was not by ordinary a laughing person. Their age exactly, sixteen, she was as quiet as her mother, if not as glum. Oddly, for she was a pretty girl in the face, and had a fine and strong if somewhat square figure, there was nobody sparking her yet; and she didn't appear to be interested in ballads and glees and quilting frolics. It could be that she didn't have time for those trivialities. She did a power of work each day, not only in the house but also on the Watts farm property, which was several miles north of the village. She could smile sometimes, and cleverly and sweetly, but she was no talker. She probably didn't herself know just how much she remembered personally about her brother Aaron, the boy who never came back. His death could scarcely have caused her much immediate grief, at that age. Indirectly, however, it must have shaded her whole life. It kept laughter and light talk out of the Watts house, as it twisted her mother's mind. Deliverance was no slavey! She worked very hard, she worked pauselessly, and she'd take most orders; but when she thought her mother wrong she ignored her mother. She never stopped to argufy. She simply did the job her own way.

Now she showed white, in her nightrobe, in the hallway. She was vague and floaty, not the solid stolid Deliverance they knew at meals.

She whispered "He didn't sound right when he came in my room! He sounded worried about something!"

"What are you talking about?" gruffed John.

"Father, of course. His voice sounded worried and tired, and . . . and kind of scared. Does he know you're going out tonight?"

"Reckon he does. *Might* not, of course. *We* didn't tell him."

They didn't need to tell him. Everybody in Stonington knew that the skipper of the Good Harvest had for weeks been waiting for just such a night as this to slip out past the revenue marine sloop. Everybody knew too that Hab Jones and John Rellison would be the pilots.

The Point folk were not unaccustomed to smuggling, nor were they ashamed of it. But it was a new kind of smuggling they were called upon to undertake in that year 1808 after Mr Jefferson's well-disciplined Congress, sharing Mr Jefferson's belief that the only way to keep out of a European brawl was to keep out of everything else in the world, passed the Embargo Act which forbade commerce of any kind with any belligerent nation (and there weren't any neutrals). This meant not only smuggling goods *in,* but also, if the Point folk wanted to live, smuggling them *out.* It involved not only dodging the warships and revenue vessels of foreign countries but also those of your own country, both coming and going. A new technique being needed, then, a new technique was devised.

The first thing was to get the vessel loaded. Well, the brig Good Harvest had been loaded, and perhaps overloaded, with flour, potash, and dried eels. The next thing was to get her out past Montauk, out to sea, beyond the reach of the coasting cutters' cannon. This was a job for the boys.

"He wouldn't—— There isn't anything special tonight, is there?"

Here was not the Deliverance they were used to, the girl who so seldom spoke at all, and then only in a low voice, and who at table kept her eyes on her plate and her idle hand in her lap. There was a curious catch in her voice now, as she floated nearer to them.

They shook their heads.

"Nothing that might make him afeared after you?"

"Not that I know of" muttered Hab Jones.

"We're all right. Get out of the way" muttered John.

She air-drifted aside, a wraith, but she touched and held John's elbow for a moment as he passed her.

"You—you'll be careful, won't you, John? You won't get into any trouble?"

"No, we won't get into any trouble" John whispered in the low contempt-rich tone he used when he talked about womenfolk, old or young; but he seldom spoke that way to their faces.

She touched Hab's elbow too, though briefly.

"You'll be careful, won't you?"

"Why, sure" Hab said, surprised.

They cut around to the front of the house, across the lawn, under the great magnolia tree, and there they fell into step, heads low, shoulders hunched high, and for some time they walked in silence down toward the yard where their small dogbody was docked. In that boat, a cat-schooner, erratic and very fast, hard to handle if you didn't know her, they could go just about anywhere and do just about anything—provided they didn't venture out into the open sea. At times when no ships were making and there was no work to be done in the judge's fields north of the Point, Hab Jones and John Rellison, who of course could not be permitted to be idle, were sent out to fish. They knew this end of the sound perfectly.

The dogbody itself was called the Deliverance; and they frowned, both of them, as, walking through the rain, they remembered this. They had so named it—for it was their own property, not the judge's: he had given it to them outright—not to please the girl but to please the father, to whom they were duly grateful.

All the same, it looked now as if there was a little too much Deliverance around for a night like this.

Her ghostlike emergence from nowhere just before they reached the window had angered rather than troubled them. Her words didn't seem to make a great deal of sense, even to Hab, who had himself thought he noted something strange in Judge Watts's voice this night. What was she doing there? Why did she have to poke her face right up to the threshold of their little adventure? It was wrong, a false note, and they didn't fancy it. Not saying anything, they were thinking alike as they walked.

John Rellison and Hab had never had a chance to play much—either back on the farm, which they hated, or here in Stonington—but they sometimes got in little games in the course of their work. On Sunday afternoons they might take walks, horseplaying, occasionally even wrestling; or they would lie up on the roof and look through the glass at the motionless anchored ships and invent sea battles and brilliant pursuits. Summer nights after supper, if it wasn't raining, they were permitted to sit outside on the doorstep, or even to wander down past Oliver York's place, where they could overhear the jangle of voices from the taproom. For the most part, however, their lives had been dedicated to work.

They told themselves glibly enough that they piloted ships out through the Washington people's blockade in order to make money and for no other reason. Their conscience didn't poke them about breaking a law—not a law like *that*. They did it for money, they said. Well, they got the money, true, and they didn't spend it but had it hidden away in a fattening bag under a loose board of the floor of the room they shared. But there was more to it than this. They were doing the job cheaper than any other pilot available, which is why they were so much in demand; but if asked, they'd probably have done it for nothing. John had grumbled that they took ships to the very edge of excitement, the very gate of romance, and then ingloriously returned. There was truth in this; but it was also true that in just the taking-out, in each routine job of pilotage itself, there was a great deal of tremble and fun. Weren't they famous, practically? Hadn't Red Ferguson, a nasty-tempered man even when sober, shaken his fist in their faces the other day right out in front of Stiver's store, and shouted so that a dozen men heard him that if he ever got Hab and John in the sights of his swivel gun this God-damn lawbreaking den of Federalistic spies was going to find itself short of two members, by Christ? John and Hab had sidled away, giggling, embarrassed, but pleased too. For they weren't such old-timers as to know boredom; and even now, after having taken out two or three ships a week for several months, they quivered not from fear but from joy as they hurried down to the dogbody.

This was their fun, the game they played, the only game they had a chance to play; and Deliverance Watts had no business interfering with it.

The rain hit their faces, hurting.

"She ought to mind her own affairs" muttered Hab Jones.

"Say, that's the first time in a long while I've seen her in a night-dress" John whispered. "Say, she's really got some bumps, ain't she? About ready for a husband, I guess."

Hab was shocked. He knew well enough what John meant, and he had thought about such things; but thinking about the girls out at Eb Armstrong's public house and thinking about Deliverance Watts, who was virtually his sister, were two different things. Hab stumbled, shaken.

"She'll get one, one of these nights, without getting married first—she walks around dressed like that much more" John Rellison said savagely.

"She ought to mind her own business" muttered Hab.

They reached the shipyard and shinnied over the fence, and they made their way to the dock. The rain was dervishing here and there, crazy, flighty, almost hysterical. The night was dark.

On the beach, right near the dock where the Deliverance was paintered, stood a stumpy man in a long black greatcoat, a man who from his posture waited and waited, straining to see something, straining to hear something through the rain. Oh, sure, he was waiting for them. They knew it. He held a pistol in his hand.

. 2 . . .

THEY DROPPED BEHIND A PILE OF TIMBER AND PEEPED AT the man. Though he was cold and wet, and sometimes walked up and down the little dock, he kept good watch.

When he walked it was woodenly, with legs spread, as though wading through water. The collar of his greatcoat was turned up. His face was two blobs of dough shining white through the rain and stuck with a couple of raisins. Despite this, and despite the pistol, a large one, he didn't look sinister: he only looked unsure of himself. The pistol embarrassed him. It was a huge horse pistol, so big that it made the man seem even shorter than he was, and it must have been heavy to carry. Obviously it was useless in such a rain. Obviously he felt foolish holding it. After a while he looked at it reprovingly, and shook his head, and suddenly thrust the pistol under his greatcoat. As suddenly he drew it out again, and uncocked it before putting it back. This too was absurd, for the priming must long ago have become wet. When the man walked with the pistol under his coat he looked even more awkward than before: he was like a poacher trying to conceal a fishing pole.

Hab and John knew him. He was Joey Bludge, the deputy federal marshal of this district. He was not as big as his title; and indeed had he been a more efficient man he would not have dared to take such a position, for the people of this part of Connecticut were much displeased with the way they were being misgoverned and were ready to slap a suit of Massachusetts velvet on any damn democratic official who was too conscientious about trying to enforce any damn democratic laws—and especially the Embargo. The Pointers tolerated Joey Bludge just because he was a joke; and he knew it. The trouble was, he was as much afraid of Lieutenant Ferguson as he was of all the Pointers, and Ferguson was forever threatening to bring him in a prisoner. That is, Joey Bludge might at any time be called upon to act as a real deputy marshal, a prospect which dismayed him.

John and Hab knew immediately what he was doing by the dock. Ferguson had stationed him there. Legally Ferguson had no authority to do that; but though a law-enforcement officer, Red Ferguson refused to be bothered by legalities. He had told off Joey Bludge to watch the Deliverance, while he himself, a speaking trumpet in his hands, his guns run out, his matches lit and hooded, cruised in the vicinity of the brig.

Joey Bludge had no right to be here on private property without a search warrant, but Ferguson had doubtless calculated that John and Hab either would not know this or would not care to take steps, that night, to have the man thrown out. They'd be more likely, the lieutenant probably thought, to do one of two things: either sneak away without attempting to put out to the brig or perhaps be chased away by a showing of the pistol, or else brazen the thing out, defying Bludge to stop them. Ferguson probably hoped that they would choose defiance. In that event he would have Joey Bludge to testify afterward that he saw them push off in the dogbody at such-and-such a time—testimony which would go far to support his own testimony about their activities. It was all very well that everybody in town knew that they were going to pilot the Good Harvest out to Montauk that night; it was another thing to have a reputable if unloved citizen stand up in court and swear that he saw them *go* out.

Hab and John waited, with the patience of Indians, behind the timber. They did not need to confer, even in whispers. The only thing to do was wait and see what happened.

The deputy marshal began to move further from the dock with each turn. He was wet and badly chilled, and it made him feel good to stretch his legs. From time to time, walking away from it, he'd wheel around to face the dock again, as if afraid that those pesky apprentices of Judge Watts would snip right in behind him like a couple of deerflies. He would see nothing but rain and the little dock and the dogbody and the dark expanse of the bay. He'd walk on.

At any other time it would have been funny. Hab and John, however, had no inclination to laugh. Joey Bludge, something of a comic character, was slow, yes, but despite his shortness he was very strong. He couldn't have fired that pistol, but he could have used it as a club. If he saw them go out he might, under Ferguson's tutelage, get them into a heap of trouble. He wouldn't wait to see them come back, of course. They could return to any one of a dozen places, for the dogbody drew almost nothing.

The Good Harvest, on the other hand, loaded as she was, drew more than twelve feet, and she couldn't be brought up the channel: she was anchored, none too firmly, somewhere off Wamphassuck Point.

To get to the brig they would have to use the dogbody, and to get to the dogbody they would have to pass within a few feet of Joey Bludge, and Joey Bludge, treading his weary round, looked good for the night.

They watched him.

He had fallen into a half-circle, never out of sight of the dock, never more than a hundred feet from it; he watched the dogbody sideways as he walked, like an overeager trapper watching a trap; he walked back and forth from shore to shore, as though fastened around the waist by a rope the other end of which was tied to the dock.

This half-circle brought him within a few feet of the timber behind which the boys crouched.

They got to thinking. They couldn't see much for the rain and darkness, but they knew this shipyard like a man knows his own bedroom, and each began to check in his mind just what Joey Bludge was passing, just what he was stepping over, even, as he made his rounds.

They thought of the sawyers' pit at the same moment, each reaching out excitedly to touch the other. This was like them. They might have been one boy, when they were doing something together. They had been not only in daily but almost in hourly contact with each other since either of them could remember anything, and though they talked somewhat differently (John talked much the more, for one thing), and did not look alike, and in fact weren't kin however remote, their minds meshed neatly and nimbly.

So now they knew what they should do.

Joey Bludge had paused at the south edge of his half-circle; paused and stared at the dogbody; and then started toward them again. He passed the sawyers' pit, perhaps not even seeing it, not knowing it was there. He passed them. They didn't stir. The time to get him was when he'd come back, when he'd have his back to them and his face toward the pit.

It was the oldest and deepest pit in the yard, and there were a pack of stories about it, and there were even some of the shipwrights and gravers—though no sawyers—who wouldn't go near it. "How d'ye know what's under that stuff?" they would ask. "Why, you could push a man down into there and he might never come out again!" It was reported that a man *had* been so pushed once, though nobody remembered his name or the circumstances. It was called the Black Pit, probably only because the sawdust in it, being older, was dirtier than the sawdust in the other pits; and even this name helped to touch it with horror. Hab and John were too familiar with it to be afraid of it. Back in the days before they drank rum, at the cry "Grog-*ho!*" at eleven in the morning and four in the afternoon for the workers in the yard, John and Hab, if they had happened to find themselves near the Black Pit, used to amuse themselves by jumping into it ass-first, the way boys jump into water, holding their noses that same way too. In dry weather this was like jumping into a haymound, though easier on the eyes. Even in dry weather, though, it was a difficult place to get out of. The trick used to be to jump in with a shriek; scramble, all covered with sawdust, for the ladder; scramble out of the pit; and pull the ladder up before the other one could reach it. Then you sat and jeered at the other one.

In wet weather it was even harder to get out of the pit. The sides were slimy then, the sawdust of the bottom sticky and stinky as mud. Oh, it could be done! but it took time and patience.

Nothing could possibly have been more convenient, just then, than the Black Pit.

When Bludge had passed them and was about fifteen feet away, and somewhat nearer than that to the pit, Hab and John began to run. No doubt Bludge heard them coming. He tried to turn, he *started* to turn, but they struck him at the same instant, working perfectly together, as they always did. He couldn't have seen either of them sufficiently well to identify them later. Anyway, their heads were down. It was with the tops of their heads, in fact, that they struck him, John at the left buttock, Habakkuk at the right. They might have been two brisk frolicsome goats.

Shoved forward, Joey Bludge disappeared over the lip.

A moment later, and without exposing himself, Hab had reached over the edge and scooped out the ladder. It was a light ladder, made of rope.

A moment after that they were aboard the Deliverance.

The rain swished about and swept into their faces and jiggled crazily on the surface of the sound, making a thousand tiny silver spear-tips.

The Deliverance was so small a craft that skippers often gasped to see it and made a fuss about permitting John and Hab to return all the way to Stonington. It is true that the weather almost always was opposed to such return. The boys didn't take ships out on the good nights. They moved only in fog, snow, hail, or a howling gale, when the Deliverance would seem to spin like a drunken dancer. In fact the little dogbody, with its two preposterous masts, one far up in the bow, the other back by the sharply pinked stern, was probably a safer vessel, in these its own home waters, than the ships and brigs and schooners Hab and John took out. John at least used to say, as he'd drop back into the dogbody, that he was glad to get somewhere where he could feel safe again—and he didn't say that just for a joke, either. The Deliverance was as skittish as a goose, but it was fast.

They sat in the sternsheets, leaning this way, leaning that, both holding the tiller, Hab's right arm, John's left. The rain was frenzical.

John Rellison started muttering like an old man whose indignation will not die.

"Again and again, same way, we take 'em 'way out here, and then, who makes the money? Who sees the world? Why, you'd think——"

Hab pushed against his shoulder, putting the tiller over. He caught the sheets and payed them out a little, so that they wouldn't squeal.

"You'll be seeing the world from between prison bars, you keep talking as loud as that" he whispered, furious.

"Dreadful sorry, Hab . . ."

Hab took in a little sail, to keep the dogbody from changing course too abruptly. He'd begun to hear it speak—that is, shush at the bows. He straightened it.

The other boat wasn't speaking, and they didn't hear her at all, and only saw her sails, not her hull. The sails, ghostly white in the rain, slid by like a wisp of fog. This was directly ahead. They must almost have rammed the boat. Close though it had been, a moment later it was difficult to believe that the other boat had cut ahead of them. They had to look down at the wake eddies to convince themselves; and even those were soon battered out by the rain.

John Rellison made an "o" with his mouth.

"I *am* sorry" he whispered.

"Sh-sh-sh . . ."

They could not be sure that they hadn't been heard. It was not likely that they'd been seen. Sailing close-hauled, they had not presented much surface to the men in the other boat. Moreover, the dogbody, being a cat-schooner, carried no jib to flap and flutter and catch the eye, and her fore and main sails were tanned. This was a trick the boys had learned from acquaintances who had made the run down to the West Indies. Down there sails were tanned to keep them from mildewing in the wet tropical weather. Hab and John tanned theirs to reduce visibility.

"That was Red all right, too" whispered John.

Hab Jones nodded.

"The canvas . . ."

"Yes" said Hab.

Lieutenant Ferguson had lost an old and badly split mainsail the previous week whilst pursuing the Deliverance. The Washington government, stingy enough in other matters, had cheerfully replaced this; and it was the snowy whiteness of the new sail that had caught Habakkuk's eye.

A little later they came upon the Good Harvest.

They made the dogbody fast to a rope trailing astern, went right aboard, and mounted the quarterdeck. They started giving orders almost immediately, each in a low swift voice, without having conferred with one another or with anybody else. They had been expected. They were obeyed.

Once, not many months before, it would have frightened them to stand, sixteen years old, on the quarterdeck of a seagoing vessel and rap out orders—and expect to be obeyed. Once they had been accepted as the best thing available, had been snickered at, made sport of. That was because of their blushes and stammerings. Even John Rellison, not a shy boy, had been awkward and seemingly uncertain of himself then.

This hadn't lasted long. They had soon grown to know that they had no need for apologies. They might be small and slight, they might be young, they might never have gone beyond Montauk; but they knew their way.

These others, who talked such a strange gibberish, who sneered so readily, and rolled as they walked—they might be very admirable beyond soundings, knowing just what was going on, just what to do, and what everything was called. Their officers too, grim and squint-eyed, might have been flawless in their confidence and skill as the ship lay at dock or approached a familiar harbor. But they were all of them lost and confused and a little frightened at the prospect of creeping from under cover out into the open sea late at night or during a storm, all the time keeping watch for the revenue sloops. *Then* they wanted somebody local, an expert.

They had laughed at the boys at first—but only at first. The world of the sea that Hab and John knew was not extensive, but such as it was it was their own. They didn't need to ask questions. They didn't need to stammer or apologize.

Captain Wilson came up to them now, as they stood behind the helmsman.

"I'm glad you made it, boys. We might not've got another night like this in weeks."

"Yes, sir" said John. "A little more to larboard, you."

"Will you crack on more, sir?" Hab Jones asked; but it wasn't really a question, it was a command. "This has got to be a fast run."

"Don't you think it might be safer" Captain Wilson suggested "if we creep a bit, and maybe even send boats ahead to scout for Ferguson?"

"Don't have to scout for Fergy" Hab said. "We know where he is. Making for Watch Hill. He'll probably hook around Sugar Reef and come back outside Fisher's, hugging the shore all the way to the Race. Doing seven knots or better on the way to Watch Hill, but he won't make five when he cuts back."

Captain Wilson stared in amazement.

"We passed him, coming out."

Hab was laconic. John offered: "He must have somebody else watching between the Race and Plum Gut. Maybe two-three boats. He reckons we're going to sneak around Wicopesset and hug the south shore of Fisher's, and that's why he's making that run himself. If he misses us, he figures, then the sloop stationed at the Race will pick us up."

"But how in tarnation do you—— Even if you did see him, how can you——"

"We know Ferguson" John Rellison said. "We know the way he works. A touch more to starboard, please. And steer small."

"And couldn't we have more canvas, Captain?" asked Hab. "We'll want to scoon right along to get clear afore he's back from Watch Hill way."

"Seems to me we're going dreadful fast right now."

"Crack on everything you've got" said Hab.

They were silent a little while, the captain sometimes wetting his lips but not otherwise moving.

15

"I see" he said at last. "You had this course all plotted before you started out?"

"Didn't know where we were going to take you, till we saw Fergy."

"Oh . . . Then you had a conference, then and there?"

They stared at him. He was an earnest man, this Captain Wilson, strong, thick, not stupid; but he was a little hard to understand sometimes, on account of being a foreigner: he came from New York.

"No, we didn't do any conferencing" Hab said at last. "We just saw Fergy, and we could calculate the rest."

"But you mean you plotted our course without a chart? Then how do you know where we are now?"

"We know exactly where we are now" Hab answered coldly.

"See here, don't you think maybe you better come down to my cabin and look over a chart so's you can be sure that——"

"We don't need no chart" said John Rellison. "Helmsman, I reckon you must have rheumatism in that right elbow of yourn. You always let that wheel inch over. Hab, you want to go forward, or'll I?"

"I'll go" said Hab.

The deck was wet but it rolled very little and the footing was easy. Hab Jones walked slowly. He felt like being alone. Behind him he heard Captain Wilson address John again, this time in a tone not merely of respect but of admiration. John made some careless, too careless, reply. John was a handsome lad, with his sleek black hair and his bright dark eyes and his swift smile; he was easy and confident, if maybe a whit stuck-up, in his movements; and he took a boyish delight in impressing people.

The canvas above was taut and fine, and silent. The only sounds were the sound of the ship working, a tiny multitude of squeaks, and the sullen patter of rain. No light showed. Nobody shouted. There was nobody in sight when Habakkuk Jones walked along the deck.

This was good; it was as Hab wanted it. He and John in these circumstances were guided as much as anything else by their ears. You could *hear* your way through a storm, if it was a tolerably steady one. The surf made a different sound against each rock and reef and beach and point, and all you needed to do was hear and recognize it. But rain made it hard, made estimating the distances hard. Snow and fog too, though snow even more than fog, tended to dull the sounds you wanted to identify; but rain split and splintered them, and made them seem now deceptively near, now far away. He walked the deck very quietly, and probably his face wore a look of absorbing thought like that of a man sunk in the contemplation of infinity. In truth, while he was listening sharp enough, what he was thinking of was his—and Deliverance's—queer hunch that something was wrong, or would be wrong, this night.

16

A man appeared. He might have been a mate, more likely he was the bosun.

"Leads?"

He almost added "sir." He was glad that he hadn't.

"No" said Hab.

The man disappeared.

Was it the encounter with Joey Bludge? No, that had been a farcical episode, which could have serious consequences only if Joey had seen them—and assuredly Joey hadn't. Then the near-collision with the government sloop? That admittedly had been a close thing, and it had frightened Hab. But it was not an extraordinary thing; for after all they both knew that Ferguson would be out searching these waters for them.

No, it was something else.

He felt lonesome as he walked forward; and this was an unusual feeling for Hab to have. He almost turned, at one time there, and ran pellmell back to John, to the cheery insouciance of John Rellison, who got scared sometimes too but would never admit it to anybody but his friend. John would be back there now, standing behind the man behind the wheel, and confident in his stance, easy and bright, showing off.

Hab never could show that easy confidence, even when he felt it. He knew that he could never look and talk a John Rellison. His movements could be fast enough on occasion, but they were ordinarily rather slow. His head was thick across the cheekbones, faintly suggesting Indian blood, though he had none. His tight full face was ever so slightly flecked with freckles, of which he was ashamed. His eyes were the lightest conceivable blue. His hair, which was the color of red mud, was stiff and would never stay combed.

There was a lookout stationed at the bow, right square up between the wet anchor cables. He didn't stir when Hab approached. Hab stood beside him for a minute, listening, and then moved to the other side of him, but the man might have been frozen or asleep standing up. The rain shone dark on his face.

They were all right, they were on their course. He couldn't see anything, but his ear placed Latimer Reef, and in a moment John Rellison back there, if John wasn't too busy talking big to the captain, would also be hearing it. John would know when to change the course then, southing a bit toward the Seals. They never had to discuss matters like that.

Once well around Wicopesset they'd head due south. Then he and John would pocket their fees and slip overside into the dogbody. Then home—for a few hours' sleep and another day of hauling timber.

Hab looked up at the canvas, and sighed a little, smiling a little at the same time. He wondered whether he and John ever really would get a chance to make a voyage to the West Indies or South America or Africa sometime. He didn't think he wanted to go to Europe. Somebody in Europe was always fighting a war or getting ready to fight one, and every seaport there, he'd been told, was cram-packed with laws calculated to stun and strip and geld a sailing man. But Africa or the West Indies . . . He would ask Judge Watts someday, after things had settled down. Right now, as he well knew, they couldn't be spared. Not that anybody was ordering ships these days, what with the Embargo. But that couldn't last long. And if it ended with free commerce restored, or if Connecticut, maybe alone or maybe together with Massachusetts and Rhode Island, stepped out of the federal union, as seemed very likely, or again if the country got involved in the war in Europe, as also seemed likely, whether against France or England or both—in any one of those cases ships would be needed again, needed in a hurry. Meanwhile there was timber to be set out for seasoning, to be brought down from the judge's stand upstate. They were getting ready for the rush. Also there was fishing to be done, and piloting like this. And from time to time they'd have to go out to the country and help Deliverance with her father's fields. She was a strong girl and willing, Deliverance, but she couldn't do everything. John didn't like to work with her, but Hab did. Hab didn't like farm work, but he did like to move along next to Deliverance Watts, thinking about her, saying nothing. As often as he dared he would look sideways at her hair, which was full and thick and wavy, without being curly: it was a rich brown with tiny red lights in it.

He drifted aft, all the time looking up at the canvas. What would it be like to see that canvas every night and every day, to lie on the deck there and watch it in the snow, in the rain, in moonlight and sunlight, the fine fat sails bellied out so bravely, straining and straining with no sound?

"There's Latimer, John" he said softly as he returned to the quarterdeck, for he'd felt no change of course.

"Oh, sure! I was just going to—— A little starboard, two points, maybe three . . . that'll do."

"We'll be clear soon" Hab said, and sat on the taffrail.

"I reckon" John muttered.

Habakkuk Jones might well have looked an idle sailor as he sat there on the rail, his chin, a thick strong one, a bit high, his eyes staring at the canvas and at a starless sky beyond. He might have looked a dreamer. Matter of fact, he was working hard. He was listening, listening, his mind concentrated upon the waters ahead, while with the seat of his pants he felt the brig and rocked with it and estimated its speed.

It was because he was working so hard that he did not notice, for a while, that John no longer gave directions to the helmsman, and that both John and the captain, who had appeared to be striking up such a friendship, now were strangely silent.

Hab looked down at them.

"Huh?" he said stupidly.

They were both looking at him, and John showed embarrassment. Captain Wilson looked away, and soon he shuffled toward a companionway which must have led to his quarters.

"Hab," said John Rellison, "do you mind if I go below with the captain for a minute or two? He wants to show me something."

"Sure, go ahead" said Hab.

He stared after them, at the rectangle of darker darkness which marked the companionway, and as he stared he rocked instinctively with the movement of the brig and his ears never left off listening for shoal water.

The troubled feeling came back, stronger than ever, but now it wasn't as fuzzy as it had been. For the first time he began to know why he was scared.

He slipped off the taffrail.

"A little more larboard" he whispered.

There was no light of any kind to go by. The light the government had recently put at Watch Hill would in itself have been enough to go by here, for one of Hab's experience; but though the government had given, the government had taken away. The government, Mr Jefferson's government, had decreed that there should be no commerce, not even coastwise commerce, lest we get mixed in European affairs; and if there's no commerce, where is the need of a lighthouse?

The light at Little Gull was not on either, though he probably couldn't have seen it anyway in this rain.

There was no light showing on the brig, not even at the binnacle. Well, Hab Jones didn't need to see the compass. He stood behind the helmsman; and now he was strainedly silent, though troubled in his mind.

He believed that he knew what John Rellison was doing, and it caused an agony to go all through his body.

But he couldn't quit his post. This was the most ticklish part of the whole run, getting past Wicopesset here. Hab trembled, sweating.

"Now starboard a bit . . . just a little . . . *there,* that's good! Hold it that way. I'm going below for a minute."

His heart beating in great thumps, his outstretched hands atremble, he felt his way to the companion, all but fell down it, felt for a doorknob. He threw open the door.

There was a light inside the cabin, and he saw immediately that he had come too late.

. 3 . . .

JOHN RELLISON STOOD BESIDE A DESK THAT LET DOWN from the wall, and he looked at Hab for only a moment and then looked at the paper he'd signed and he laughed nervously.

Besides pen and ink and the paper, there was a bottle on the desk and a beaker. The bottle was half full, the beaker was empty. But it was the paper which held Hab's gaze.

He closed the door. He hadn't forgotten the light.

He saw that Captain Wilson, that large heavy man, was staring fondly at John, pleased with himself, even delighted, as though while netting for minnows he'd scooped up a bass. It was clear that already he liked John, who must have done some fine talking while Hab was forward. Folks did like John Rellison at first sight, and always had, if he wanted them to.

"John, *did you sign on?*"

"Well, you see, it's a pretty bad night for getting back, the wind the way it is, and Fergy's right across our course, and Captain Wilson here——"

"Did you sign on?"

"Well, yes. Look, Hab, when could we ask for a better chance to get out and see the world? Captain Wilson here says we can haul the Deliverance inboard and he'll promise we'll get more for her than she cost. He's willing to make us stewards, and we'll be able to learn navigation, he'll teach us himself, and all we're going to is just down to Martinique and then——"

Hab started for the desk, his arm outstretched.

"Give me that thing. I'll tear it up."

"Just a minute" said Captain Wilson, and got in his way. The cabin wasn't large. Captain Wilson could not stand upright; he hunched over toward Hab, and his face was shadowed. "Just a minute. That's a ship's paper."

John Rellison looked hurt, taken aback by Hab's tone, but his eyes still glittered: he was still a boy looking through a window at something splendid inside.

Captain Wilson was a New Yorker who was clearing out of his home port by the back way—through Hellgate and Long Island Sound—which, if longer, was safer: the front door, the Narrows, was altogether too narrow and too well guarded. He'd had very few dealings with

Yankees ashore, and he wasn't sure of himself with them. On a ship, his own ship, however, it was a different matter. On a ship he was not accustomed to being addressed in this way. He was a large man and slow-moving, and judging from his voice he was easygoing—Hab had never really seen his face clearly. But now he put a huge hand on Hab's chest. He didn't press. He simply held it there.

"Yes, your friend just signed aboard. You can verify his signature, if you want, but I'll not have you touching the paper."

"I tell you he *can't* sign!"

The captain rolled his bear's head.

"Well now, I think he did a very good job of it."

"He's bounden! So'm I! We're apprentices! He's got no *right* to sign!"

"Well now, I didn't know that. And I still have only your word for it."

"John, tell him the truth. Let's get this business over with and clear out of here! Tell him that——"

"Don't take it that way, Hab. I was counting on your coming with us."

"And leave the judge? After he's been so clever to us? You *can't* do that!"

It was the wrong tone to take, with John as with the captain.

"I can if I want to" muttered John, looking away. "Well, anyway, I *have* done it, so there's your answer!"

Captain Wilson had not removed his hand. His voice was not aggressive, but neither was it as affable as it had first been: the voice grated a bit now, like something heavy on rollers being shoved over a stone-strewn surface.

"It may not be my place to ask it—after all, I'm only the master of this vessel—but I can't help wondering, Mr Peppery, what you're doing down here when the man at the wheel hasn't any orders?"

Hab brushed this aside. He had scarcely heeded the captain, though he talked with him; but Hab was watching John's face, trying to catch John's eyes.

"He's got orders. Straight course. We're heading right out to sea now. I wouldn't have come down here while there were any reefs left."

"Oh" said the captain.

He said it softly, rolling it on his tongue, seeming almost to smack his lips over it. He said it ominously; and his hand tightened on Hab's chest, the fingers digging in. Hab for the first time, frightened, really looked at him. Hab couldn't see much. The man's face was in shadow. All the same, Habakkuk Jones could *feel* the difference in this captain's attitude once he had learned that his ship was safely through the channel.

Hab had heard of skippers who became different men the moment their feet touched a deck, and who, again, changed back to their former kindness and gentleness the instant they stepped ashore. That was the way it was with this Captain Wilson, this New Yorker, except that instead of merely a deck he needed to know that the sea itself, the open sea, was beneath him.

He heaved himself up, seeming to expand, so that his head thudded along the ceiling and his big shadowed face got close to Hab's face. His voice rose from a menacing rumble to a roar: it was as though he were trying to shout above a hurricane: the noise filled the cabin.

"Well, sir, I guess we've had enough of this! You"—he shoved Hab, so hard that Hab staggered and the back of his head hit the door—"get outside and make off in that tub of yours! Here's your twelve shillings! Go on!"

"I tell you he's bounden! He's not old enough to sign a contract anyway! He's only sixteen!"

"He looks eighteen to me. Go on!"

Hab glanced at John. John was scaring now. A moment before he had been ashamed of himself; a moment before that he'd been cocky, talking big. Now he was getting scared. He was a little boy again; and though he bit it, his lower lip began to tremble; his face shone with sweat in the candlelight.

"I—I reckon I'd better go with you, after all, Hab."

He took a hesitant step toward the door.

"You stay right where you are" shouted Captain Wilson.

The candle flame wavered and spluttered and sent up a twisting ribbon of thick brown smoke. It was a cheap tallow candle. The three of them stood there, very wet, rainwater dripping and dribbling off them to the floor, where it formed pools. The air was thick and odorous, everything, door and portholes, being closed and stuffed against the outshining of light.

"And you," Captain Wilson said, turning back to Hab, "get out. Your friend has signed on and he's staying, and it'll be a long while afore he gets back. As for you, if you're not headed for land yourself inside of three minutes, well then, sir, you're coming too!"

Hab kept talking, but it was not what he would have said had he been given time to study. Likely enough his speech wasn't impressive, either. He could hear his own voice, shrill and excited, not convincing.

"I'll have you arrested! This is kidnaping! It's against the law!"

Captain Wilson, with the hand on Hab's chest, pushed him sharply against the door. Hab's head slammed back, and it hurt: it made him dizzy. Captain Wilson withdrew a huge hamlike fist.

Hab's knees went greasy and soft. He felt himself slipping. He fumbled for the door handle behind him, and got it, and opened the door a little ways.

The captain's fist crashed against the edge of the opening door, and he cursed. He kicked Hab, who had fallen. Hab rolled out into the passageway.

He heard John scream, and he heard somebody tumbling down the companionway ladder. The captain filled the doorway, blocking off most of the light. Hab scrambled to his feet, rushed past somebody on the ladder, slithered to the deck on hands and knees.

"Grab that boy! Grab him!"

There wasn't far to run. The only person who might have intercepted him was the helmsman, who fortunately was a slow thinker. The helmsman took his hands off the spokes, but his mouth fell open and he only gaped at Hab when Hab scuttled past him to the taffrail.

Hab threw one leg over the rail, caught the Deliverance's painter with his foot.

"It isn't high seas yet, remember," he heard himself shrill, "and if you don't let John go——"

Three men came running aft, two with knives, one with a belaying pin. Captain Wilson loomed at the companionway hatch, cursing and cursing. He too had a sheath knife. They thought faster than the helmsman, these fellows. They closed in.

Hab threw his other leg over and dropped to the dogbody. It rocked like a canoe. Either the painter snapped from the force of the jump or else somebody cut it. At any rate, he was suddenly free, bobbing and whirling wildly, while the wake water boiled around him.

Clinging to the foremast, he looked up. There was not much more to be seen of the Good Harvest, which disappeared in a swirl of rain. He did see, momentarily, the shoulders and arms and faces of the seamen, who jabbered fiercely—though Hab couldn't hear a word—and the dominating figure of Captain Wilson. One other thing he saw, though this even more briefly. John Rellison appeared at the rail, his arms waving, his mouth open, evidently yelling something, his eyes bugging with fright. Captain Wilson turned and swung his fist into John's face, and it was such a big fist that it covered all the bottom half of the face, though Hab Jones still saw fleetingly the popping fear-filled eyes. Then there was only night, and rain, and an empty sea.

There was no sign of Joey Bludge at the dock or in the yard. The ladder of the Black Pit was still on the ground where Hab had left it. He remembered now, dog-tired, how he had giggled as he did that.

He was so tired that he had a hard time shinnying the fence.

Deliverance ran across the yard to him. It was almost time for dawn now, and there was no longer any rain, except doomed drops that hung one from each leaftip, but everything was still wet and the sky was dark.

She was in her nightdress and had a shawl over her head.

When he stopped before her he was so tired that he had to hold his feet wide apart in order to keep from falling; his head hung like that of a dog after too hard a hunt.

"What's happened? Where's John?"

"It—it wasn't his fault."

"What's happened, Hab? *Where is he?*"

"Sh-sh . . . He went with the ship, I reckon. Went out with her."

"You *reckon?*"

"Well, he went with the ship, yes. But it wasn't his fault. He didn't know. . . ."

He marveled at himself, dribbling off. Why did he talk this way? It was John's fault, of course it was! If John hadn't been so filled with crazy romantical notions, if he hadn't been so all-fired eager to look like a man to that captain . . . If John hadn't gone to the cabin and had a few drinks . . .

"But where's he gone, Hab? Hab, will he come back? Oh, he's *got* to come back!"

"He'll come back all right, I reckon. But not for a long time."

He tried to step around her and was so dizzy that he almost fell. She put an arm under his. He lifted his head with a great effort.

"You go in" he whispered. "I've got to wake up Judge Watts and tell him."

At the window he tried to help her up, but in fact she was obliged to help him. Her nightdress went very high, but he gazed at her legs without excitement. He remembered how he had felt about her when he saw her like this earlier, and remembered what John had said. . . . He got inside, somehow.

"Hab," she whispered, close to him in the darkness, actually pressing against him, "do you want me to go into Father's room with you? Do you reckon maybe it'd make it easier?"

"No, that's all right. You go on up."

"I'll do it, if you want me to, Hab."

"No, you go up. I'll do it alone."

She went up the stairs and into her bedroom, shivering, her feet wet, the bottom of her nightdress wet. She closed her door. She wasn't ready to cry yet, but she knew that she'd cry soon. She leaned against the door, letting the shawl slip off.

After a while she heard Hab Jones come up the steps. She heard him go to the door of her father's room, and knock. She heard her father's door opened. The voices were clear and low, not murmurous, and tolerably calm.

"What is it, Habakkuk?"

"I—I—— There's something I should tell you, sir."

"Come in, Hababbuk."

She heard the door closed, and she let herself slip to her knees, though even yet she wasn't crying.

"Oh, he's *got* to come back" she whimpered. *"He's just got to come back!"*

24

. 4 . . .

THE TREE WAS A RUNT OF A TREE AND LOCATED ON TOP of the highest hill for miles around—which yet was not a very high hill, any more than the tree was a big tree, though it was conspicuous. It stood alone except for the rocks by which it was surrounded and which almost engulfed it. There were no other trees nearby, not even any bushes, only tufts of tough harsh yellowish grass, sour-looking, short and thick and deep-rooted. The tree must have had deep roots too, and a good many of them, to hold tenaciously to this high place.

Why it had picked such a spot, the worst conceivable, no man could know. Clearly once it had started to grow there it had no other thought than that of merely continuing to live. It had the winds to resist, now from the north, bitterly cold, now with a salty bite from the south, from off the sound, or east winds from the open sea; and it was obliged to hold up against snow and rain and sleet and hail, and in summer for a little while scorching suns; while its roots found what clinging-room and what pitifully scant nourishment they could among the rocks. It had rock below, the poor scrunty thing, gray mossless rock all around, and above a murderous sky. Its career was simply being-alive, somehow; its career was hanging-on. To its twisted fantastic thin trunk only scraps of bark clung. Its leaves, you knew, would be born late and with a struggle, and for the most part would quickly be carried away. It would bear no fruit: it could never reproduce its kind, not on that high terrible place. Its branches, gray and sere like the trunk, writhed sideways rather than up, as if crouching as close as possible to the rocks. Perhaps it was an old tree, perhaps young, but it must always have *looked* old and gnarled. It would never grow much. On the mildest and wettest of days, sullen and suspicious as it was from long battle, it would scarcely dare to lift its arms and put forth large glossy leaves, to raise itself toward heaven, to spread itself, giving kindly shade. A tree should be gracious, as most trees are. This one looked a malicious hard-bitten midget with hurt baby-eyes and a long weedy dirty gray beard, a thing prematurely aged, packed by magic with all the evil of all the world. It might have been a tree from some Bavarian fairy story, which should have grown somewhere under the earth among the Little People.

The wind blew, and it stayed there. The sun came out and caressed

25

it, but it paid no attention to this, for it didn't know what caresses meant and didn't have time to learn, being too busy hanging on.

It had been there, looking exactly the same, Hab remembered, four years ago when he and John Rellison had made their frightened but determined way down to the coast. It would still be there, he supposed, years and years from now, still clinging, still fighting.

He gave the nigh-ox a wallop on the rump and started off again, going north, toward the farm.

Near noon, when the road was no more than a path through the woods, he found a brook and followed it up to its spring, and he ate the piece of Indian corn bread he'd brought and had a gurgly long drink, belly-down, and unyoked the oxen and permitted them to drink; and then he lay on his back under a tree. The oxen didn't do anything, just stood there.

He supposed that he should have felt worried. John was gone, and that hurt. There were embarrassing explanations to make. Life at the Wattses', never gay, had become gloomier than ever; for Deliverance, though she was kind, seldom smiled at him; the judge tried hard to show that he held him in no wise to blame and that he would stick by him, but the judge had been wounded and was suffering; and as for Mrs Watts, who had never made any secret of her preference for John, she was outspoken in her crazy belief that Hab had somehow killed his fellow apprentice or perhaps contrived to have him kidnaped. Yes, he should have been sad. The affair of the Good Harvest had infuriated Lieutenant Ferguson beyond his usual measure, and he was threatening vengeance in the form of a warrant for Hab's arrest, which was the reason why Judge Watts had decided to send Hab upstate to the white-oak stand just at this time. He was virtually a fugitive, then. He was going to a place he hated, and where he would have to do backbreaking work on starvation meals for a week or more; and worst of all, he brought the news about John.

He should have felt low. He didn't. The answer to that was in the air. For all the colors of the hills around him, and even of the nearby trees, he might have thought it was early fall, not spring; but the air on his cheek told the truth. Spring's air advises your face to take things easy, lean back, half-close your eyes. The air of fall, even when it's balmy, holds a sting of old-codger fussiness and impatience. There is so much to be done! is what Fall keeps telling your face; but Spring doesn't give a hoot.

So Hab stretched out, and put his hands behind his head, and yawned at the whispering trees, at the patches of sky. Egg-shaped sunspots quivered all over and around him, and the brook was chatty at his side.

After a while he smelled rotting whitefish. His eyes closed, he frowned, as a half-asleep man might frown at a buzzing-near fly. However, the stink grew stronger; and at last Hab sighed, and opened his eyes, and rose, his curiosity getting the better of him. He yoked the oxen, took another long drink, and returned to the trail, where he waited. The stink was very strong now, and kept getting worse. It made Hab's eyes water, and made him catch for breath as though he stood engulfed in a cloud of acrid gas.

There was a horse, the skinniest Hab had ever seen—bones everywhere, no sheen to its coat—which plodded without interest in anything, its eyes closed: it did not even twitch its ears or swish its tail against the flies. Most of the flies, though, were more interested in the load in the cart the horse drew. Ah, this was delightful! This was toothsome! The cart had high sides made of osier, and the load was a heavy one—much too heavy indeed for the poor toiling horse. It consisted of decomposing fish.

Behind the cart, reading a pamphlet, oblivious of the horse's struggles, oblivious also of the flies which sometimes attempted (always in vain) to pester him, there walked a scarecrow with orange hair.

The scarecrow stopped when it saw Hab's feet, and looked up with a quizzical open smile. The horse stopped too, head down, hoofs widespread.

"Good afternoon" said the scarecrow. "My name is Macgregor."

"Jones."

"Good, good! A beautiful afternoon, Mr Jones. A right chirky afternoon. May I ask your politics, Mr Jones?"

"About the same as usual, thanks."

"Ah, interesting! I'd sure admire to have a discussion, Mr Jones. You look a lad of probity and no harum-scarum." He wiped his forehead with a blue kerchief. Otherwise clean-shaven, he had an orange goat's whisker hanging from the under part of his chin: it waggled when he talked. He had the friendliest conceivable smile. Nodding to the load of fish: "Could we be going the same way? I'm headed for the West farm."

"I pass there."

"Good, good! Then if you would care to lend me the boon of your company, Mr Jones, perhaps we could have some enlightening conversation?"

It made Hab feel queer to be called Mr Jones. He kept staring at the load.

"Whitefish."

"I know" said Hab.

"Nobody wants to eat the things, of course, but the fishermen get a heap of them in their nets. They're good for crops, mixed in with the earth."

"Yes" said Hab, who had barrowed many a load of decaying whitefish and rockweed from the shore back to Judge Watts's fields, where Deliverance would hoe it in around the Injun.

"Four shillings a thousand, down there. West'll pay me six. Not a notable profit, but I disbelieve in big profits anyway, Mr Jones. I always say you can't get more cat than the skin'll hold. This is a humble business or trade, as you see, but it's one that permits a man a might of time for reading and for thinking about the affairs of the union."

Hab nodded.

"From your talk, Mr Jones, from your accent, if I may so express myself, I take it that you're a Pointer. That right?"

Hab nodded.

"Ah yes. An interesting place, Mr Jones. Edifying, too. There was a dreadful fuss going on down there when I left this morning. Man named Ferguson, a revenuer, was talking of arresting some lad who'd piloted an embargo runner out, and folks were right sore about it. There was a buzz of beating him. A right loud buzz, too. Pity."

Hab said nothing.

Mr Macgregor suddenly grinned at him. Mr Macgregor had a charming grin.

"A Pointer, eh? When I was a boy, when I was a Buckie, I would have called you a Fishtail. And we'd've put up our fists and fought, instead of talking."

"Oh. You come from Westerly?"

"I move around . . . I come from here and there . . . But I did live in Westerly when I was a lad and full of fighting and foolishness."

Hab grinned. He couldn't help it. It seemed wrong to be liking a person as much as this on such a short acquaintance: it didn't even seem decent: but he could not help enjoying himself.

"Sure" he burst out. "When the Buckies came down we used to fight with anything we could lay our hands on, and once John and I marched with a heap of others all the way to Westerly. We had a grand time. John almost lost the sight of an eye and I got my nose broke. Then to finish it up, old Judge Watts whupped us both for not sticking to our work."

"Quite proper, I'm sure. Optimo corrupta pessima."

"Oh, it was proper all right. He's always proper."

"I have never had the pleasure of meeting Judge Watts, though I've heard a power about him. They do say he's always fair and just and that he's a man of peace. I hope that's true. Because he seems to be involved in some manner with this trouble which is fomenting in Stonington, the threat to the revenue marine man. I hope he'll be able to control it. I am a man of peace myself, Mr Jones, as you perceive. I distrust violence. I never saw that it got you anywhere. And if I ever smelled trouble in the air it was at Stonington this morning, Mr Jones. Perhaps you noticed it too?"

"Aye."

"I have a keen nose for that sort of thing. That was why I only stayed there a few hours. It was not because I mislike your village—you understand that, Mr Jones?"

"Aye."

The man of peace belabored his spindly horse with a stick, shouting at it. He and Hab put their shoulders to the wheels, as though these were mired, and this got the cart moving, and the horse was able to keep it moving—but no more. Hab, who was going past the West farm anyway, offered the use of his oxen: the cartful of fertilizer would be a trifle to them.

"Well now, that's right clever of you, Mr Jones! That's right neighborly!" As Hab unharnessed the horse: "I should like to point out that it's a sort of symbolic act too, in a way. It's one of the many things that leads me to hope that we're coming into a better world, a world of peace, Mr Jones. For look: Here a Fishtail meets a Buckie, and what does he do? He helps him along—instead of trying to knock his teeth out. I think that's excellent, Mr Jones, excellent. I take it that you're a man of peace yourself, Mr Jones?"

"I guess so."

Mr Macgregor fingertwisted his goat's whisker, pleased.

"I take it, Mr Jones," as they started to follow the cart at the greatest advisable distance, "that, being a Pointer, your politics are more or less impregnated with federalism?"

"Why, sure" said Hab, amazed. It was as though Mr Macgregor had asked him if he was sure he wasn't a Chinaman.

"Good, good! Natural enough, in the circumstances. And the fact that I cannot force myself to admit that there's any truth or wit in that group constitutes no reason why you shouldn't be a convinced member of it. Non decipitur qui scit se decipi. You see, Mr Jones, I personally am a democrat."

Hab shied. He did not stop in his tracks, he kept walking, but he stumbled twice.

Mr Macgregor smiled.

"Never saw one in the flesh before, eh?"

It wasn't that. There were democrats among the Pointers; but they were either men who thought it wisest to keep their opinions to themselves or else they were office-holders like Joey Bludge, men incapable of earning an ordinary living, whose politics were dictated not by conviction but by regular pay, so that in talk they made light of their party affiliations, apologizing. Oh yes, there were democrats. For that matter, there were even a few Baptists out on the Point; but these, like the democrats, mostly kept to themselves. The great majority of Stonington folks, like the great majority of those all through Connecticut, would no more have thought of trying out some new-fangled republican everybody-equal system, such as Tom Jefferson was seeking to thrust down the nation's throat, than they would have thought of changing their wives, their noses, their diet. Federalism was the right thing, and that was beyond argument. They might rage and screech at the experimenting Virginian democrats in Washington, with their mad dangerous French ideas; but for the local democrats, when they thought of them at all, they had no hatred, not even any real contempt, only a sort of wondering pity of the sort you might feel for an idiot or a cripple.

"No, sir, I reckon I've seen democrats before."

"But not one who was proud of it, eh?"

He was perspicacious, this scarecrow. He chuckled at Hab. His eyes were atwinkle, his little whisker quivered.

"I reckon that's about it, sir. After all, it stands to reason."

"What does? Thousands of your fellow Americans voted for Tom Jefferson. You wouldn't say that they were all corrupt, would you, Mr Jones?"

"No . . . maybe not all. But a good many of 'em were. And then a lot were southerners. And as for the rest, I reckon they just went soft in the head from reading and hearing about your Tom the Jeff."

"You refer to one of the greatest statesmen this world ever knew."

"Oh, I guess he's got grand ideas all right. Only thing is, I wish he'd keep 'em home where they belong."

"He kept us out of war, Mr Jones. He did that."

"War ain't over yet."

"You imply that we might still be dragged into it? I don't think so, now that we have the Embargo Act. If we stay far away from Europe, at least until such time as they recover their senses, then I think that maybe we'll survive without fighting. We should do more. We should survive as the strongest and most admirable nation of all, an example to the rest. Don't you think so, Mr Jones?"

"No."

"You don't think that Tom Jefferson's admittedly somewhat extreme measures were justified when it was a question of keeping us out of war? But tell me, Mr Jones, is there anything in this world *worse* than war?"

"Wouldn't know. I ain't ever been in one. But it don't seem to me to make sense that just because we're afraid of getting in a tussle where we might get our hair pulled we sneak down the cellar with a razor and scalp ourselves."

Mr Macgregor refused to bridle. His good nature knew no bounds. He fairly beamed, delighted to hear an argument, any argument.

"You disapprove of the Embargo, I infer? Being a Pointer, you would. But after all, Mr Jones, Stonington isn't the whole United States."

"Only part I live in."

Mr Macgregor laughed.

"Oh, I know all the stories against it. I know what they call it—the

30

*dam*bargo. Ha-ha! And I know what it spells backwards. Do you know that, Mr Jones?"

"O grab me."

"That's right, o grab me! Oh, it's amusing enough, Mr Jones. But the point remains, after all the fun's been made, that the Embargo Act is only an experiment. I'm sure that it works an occasional injustice, but it was designed to do the greatest good to the greatest number, and I for one think it has succeeded. Ad sanitatem gradus est novisse morbum. At least you must admit that the Embargo has kept us out of war so far."

"Aye, so far. And when we die of starvation, Mr Macgregor, sir, won't it do us a power of good to know that at least when we decided to stop eating we saved ourselves from all danger of being poisoned?"

The scarecrow clapped his hands in joy. He stepped more briskly now, and held his head higher, for he believed so much in whatever it was that he believed in that he couldn't conceive of not bringing into the fold such an intelligent and amusing argufier as this.

Hab on the other hand was getting angry.

"We're choking ourselves to death, that's what it is! Just because a fancy southern planter decides he wants to play with politics instead of hunting foxes or fighting duels or what-not, then do we have to hail him as a genius? Are *you* flattered that such a high gentleman is paying attention to you? Well, *I'm* not." With great feeling, Hab spat. "He don't like cities, Tom Jefferson. He don't like commerce. He thinks we all ought to be farmers and then we'd be happy. You ever work on a farm in Connecticut, Mr Macgregor?"

"Well, no."

"I figured not."

"No, I must admit frankly that while my business——"

"Look: Bad enough forbidding us to have any kind of trade with any country at war, when everyone is, but he won't even let us deal with ourselves! There's no roads that are any good for travel, much less for moving produce, and yet you can't get permission to ship something from Mystic to here! Is *that* a noble experiment?"

"Ah, come, come now, Mr Jones! You know as well as I do that the law isn't directed against coasters. It's directed against men who'd clear as coasters and then go somewhere else. You can't trust 'em. Why, in the beginning there was ship after ship clearing from New York for Boston—and getting there by way of Cuba! That's the reason for the big bonds now."

Hab nodded. He was familiar with the trick. As often as possible a skipper who planned to run the embargo blockade would get clearance papers to some coastal city. Once out of sight of land he'd head south. He could always say afterward that he'd met with a fierce storm which blew him off his course. There were officials in Havana and Kingston and Fort-de-France who for a consideration would condemn his ship as unseaworthy, giving him a chance to sell ship and cargo for twice their value at home. Then the skipper could come back to the United States, armed with the proper condemnation papers, and sue for the return of his bond. What happened to the sailors was of course *their* concern. Why, even Captain Wilson of the Good Harvest had tried to get clearance from Stonington to Newport. Imagine taking dried eels to Newport!

"Course you can't trust 'em" Hab conceded. "Only thing to do with a law like that is bust it, and keep right on busting it."

"Isn't that something like treason, Mr Jones?"

"I reckon. Leastways that's what England called it, thirty years ago."

He told about a miller who had his mill some ten miles up the Thames, and who bought his wheat at New London and took it up to the mill in his own boat, later taking the flour back to the city the same way. He was now obliged first to go to the city and get a clearance for the wheat and give a bond to bring the finished flour to the city. Then he had to get a certificate from an inspector at the customs house to prevent forfeiture of two hundred dollars for each ton of his boat. After that he would go back to his mill and then to a magistrate six miles away, where he paid a stiff legal fee to get a certificate stating that the wheat had actually been landed at the mill. If he failed to get that certificate back to the collector in the city within thirty days his bond was forfeited. Well?

"Yes, yes, there are bound to be some misadjustments."

Habakkuk brought up the farmers of Greenwich, who sent lamb, veal, poultry, and potatoes to New York in small coasters—the stuff of course would go bad before it got there by road. Now Greenwich was in the federal district of Fairfield, twenty miles away, and the bonding trip to Fairfield had to be made both before and after every shipment! The august government at Washington had so decreed it. This was a hell of a way, Hab said, getting more and more sore, to run a country.

Mr Macgregor did not agree. He still thought Thomas Jefferson a great man. When they reached the turn-off to West's farmhouse, and Hab was unyoking the oxen, Mr Macgregor went into an impassioned peroration—to which Hab scarcely listened, he was so sore—on single-mindedness, on sincerity, and on seeing things in a large rather than in a small way. He was desperately in earnest. He fairly shouted his speech at Hab, who, he saw, might escape unconverted. His orange goat's whisker wagged vigorously and he shook a long bony forefinger like a schoolmarm shaking a ruler.

"Mr Jones, I believe that it comes down to a simple matter of motives and belief and faith——"

"Sure" said Hab, hitching the skin-and-bones horse to the cart.

"If you have faith in your fellow men, that's the most important thing of all. In fact, it's the only thing, really."

32

"Why worry about clearance papers at all then?"

"Mr Jones, I still think, I'll go right on thinking always, no matter what happens—I think that people would rather be good than be bad!"

"Well" said Hab.

Just before the crickets started chickering he arrived, alone, at the Rellison farm.

. 5 . . .

ABNER RELLISON WAS A THIN MAN, SCRAPED THIN, WORN thin by work. His neck was a scraggle of cord and the Adam's apple leapt as he drank. When he put the jug down he wiped his mouth with the back of his wrist.

"So he's gone away? Reckon he'll come back?"

"Oh, he'll come back! I'm sure of that!"

"Right fond of him, ain't you, Habakkuk?"

"Well, sir, I'm right *used* to him."

Old Man Rellison's dry derisive eyes flicked in the direction of his older son, Ab Junior, who sat looking expressionless. This one was no John! Oh no, Junior wasn't really big but he seemed massive, being oxlike in so many ways: he had much of the strength of an ox, all of the docility, and not much more intelligence. There had been three other sons but they'd died young. Also there had been four daughters, only one of whom survived to maturity and she was now married and giving forth children of her own: Old Man Rellison was five times a grandfather. The old man had no illusions about Abner Junior. He *liked* Junior; but he'd really respected his other son.

"God's will be done" he said unpleasantly, and lapsed into silence.

When he was silent his face was all closed-up. It showed as though something inside of him sucked the skin in between the bones at every possible place. His eyes were squirts of vinegar, his mouth a steel-toothed trap.

Mrs Rellison, John's mother, had been a very tired woman when she died. John's aunt Charity kept the house now, and she was the glummest of the lot, habitually disapproving. She showed no emotion at the news of John's going.

"Reckon he'd never have come back here anyway" she said.

"Reckon not" Old Man Rellison said.

After a while Hab rose. "Well, I'm going to bed, I guess." Nobody said anything, so he went to bed. He lay awake a long time, though he was tired: he lay listening to the crickets and to a pesky persistent close-at-hand whippoorwill, and he thought about John and why he loved John so much.

John came from these people without properly being of them. He was different from his brother and his equally doltish sister Sarah, and as different from his aunt Charity, that wasp. John liked to laugh. He liked

34

to play tricks, and try out things, and poke his nose into strange places. His father had none of that. Old Man Rellison, as far as his face was concerned, was John mummified; but he couldn't smile, couldn't understand. It was dreamable, Hab thought, lying there, that Old Man Rellison once had been something like John, a boy with a grin. It was equally to be conceived, and the thought gave Hab a slow shiver, that had John remained here on the farm he might have turned into something like that flinty taciturn drunkard downstairs.

It was no doubt from his mother that John had got the grin which made everybody love him. Hab remembered her better than he remembered his own mother, who with his father had died two years ago. He'd used to call Mrs Rellison Ma. He'd often come here, to this house, to see John and sometimes to take refuge in the kitchen over which Mrs Rellison presided. He'd linger too, even though it meant a harder licking, a longer whipping, when he did go home. Mrs Rellison sometimes gave him a drabble of rye-and-Injun he wasn't entitled to. His own mother never did that.

Once Hab had spent two whole days and nights in this house. He had spent most of that time in the kitchen, where he could be near the stove, for this was midwinter; and he'd slept with John. When Hab's father came for him that time he had a run-in with Old Man Rellison. "Don't you whup that lad too hard now, Ez Jones" Old Man Rellison, prompted by his wife, had called out. "I aim to bring up my own chick my own way" Hab's father had replied, his face horrid. There had been no further conversation. Mrs Rellison had whispered urgently to her spouse, but either he was scared of Hab's father, who was powerful het up by prayer, or else he didn't think it was any of his business. Hab's father was perhaps a little crazy, as some folks said: he was certainly crazy when he had a praying spell; and that day he'd been in a cold religious rage. The beating was the worst he ever gave Hab. It took place in the barn, where it was very cold, and Hab was stripped stark naked and spread-eagled over a sawhorse and tied there, and maybe this helped, maybe the coldness helped, that is, making him more or less numb; but even so, it hurt more than any other licking he'd ever had. His mother came down to watch it. She had on a blanket, which was wrapped around her, and she sat and watched Hab take his whupping, and her eyes were malevolent, so that she suggested an Indian squaw, sitting there with that blanket wound around her and her shoulders hunched high. Hab kept his own eyes closed most of the time. The blood froze as fast as it appeared, practically, the barn was so cold: he was all sticky with it afterward.

Ez Jones of course worked with Old Man Rellison in the fields, as he worked with other farmers from time to time. Hab's mother, however, never joined work with Mrs Rellison, spinning or preserving or soap-making. Hab's parents hadn't approved of the Rellisons, who drank.

35

Lying there listening to that danged whippoorwill, Hab reckoned that the folks downstairs were the same as ever. He wondered what they were thinking down there, if anything. They might have been just sitting, not thinking at all, just sitting stunned and stupefied by the applejack. He never did know how drunk or sober the Rellisons might be. They did not sing or jackass around, the way other people did, and they didn't talk any more than usual, or fall to looking for a fight. There wasn't a touch of ordinary sociability to their drinking, much less conviviality.

When he got to thinking about it, Hab remembered that there wasn't anybody around here who didn't do a little secret or open hating, who didn't nurse at least a few nasty searing grudges. There were women who refused to nod to other women even just outside church on Sunday, and men who, though they toiled beside them day after hard day, simply would not speak to certain other men.

The huskings and raisings, Hab remembered, customarily ended in wrestling matches which were meant to be sport, and might start as sport, but which like as not would develop into bitter fights. Some hidden hatred, unsuspicioned by the onlookers, and perhaps even by the contestants themselves, would flare up; and soon they'd be slogging each other and kicking in the wrong places. Likely enough too the spectators would be taking sides, so that the party would end in a free-for-all. There was no joy in this battling, and not even much noise. They fought with silent teeth-clenched ferocity, in slow cold anger.

Down to the shore, Hab had observed promptly, men, while they sometimes fought with their fists, more often went to the law. There were many disagreements down to the shore, and often enough they were bitter ones, each tailed by a wake of bad feeling; but they were paper matters. A lawyer there could always find work, as the judge used to tell Hab and John whenever he urged them to take up the study. Hab wondered whether there ever had been such disputatious folks anywhere as at the Point. But they would not fight hitting, usually, at least not unless and until the law couldn't or it may be wouldn't give them what they wanted.

Up this way there weren't any lawyers. There wasn't any money, that's why.

He wondered where John was and how he was feeling.

The whippoorwill called on and on.

Breakfast was pea porridge and a little hasty pudding. Hab knew that the evening meal—there wouldn't be any at midday—would be the same, though then there might also be some watery bluish milk or a broth made of the liquor of boiled salt beef or pork. The Rellisons would have fresh meat only when they shared in a killing, three or four times a year, and then only for a few days. They never had fresh fish. Salted cod, one of the few boughten things in the house, was a treat reserved for Saturdays.

It was at breakfast that they settled the matter of work. Hab was firm. He would work for the farm every other day; and every *other* day those of the farm, not including Aunt Charity, who was getting too old for field labor, but including John's sister Sarah and her husband, who were to come from their nearby farm, would assist him at the stand of white oak. Looking at the fact that Hab and the oxen would get their keep the while this arrangement lasted, the arrangement might be thought to be in Hab's favor. This was not the case. Old Man Rellison, who himself was getting on in years, drank a lot even in the daytime. Abner Junior was strong but inconscionably slow. Sarah Simmons was six months with child and nursing a baby at the same time, and her husband was a spindly coughing little man. On the other hand, Habakkuk Jones, as Old Man Rellison well knew, would work from sunup to sundown without pause or whimper, and work fast too. Even more important was the pair of oxen which came with Hab. Old Man Rellison couldn't afford an ox, never had been able to. All he had was a ramshackle old horse.

Old Man Rellison decreed, then, that they would start the first day on the stand of white oak. It was clear why he did this. Sarah and Gus Simmons had not yet been sent for, and because of the haggling at table breakfast wasn't finished until past dawn. Old Man Rellison, when he got a day's work out of anybody, wanted it to be a full day's work.

It was good to smell the clean white oak again, to hear the chips fall. White oak, Hab reflected, would always be his favorite, unless it was southern live oak, which was hard to get these days. Red oak stinks, and you have to watch out for pin-doze and sap pockets; but good mature seasoned white oak from the Connecticut upcountry—*that* was the stuff to use for frames and rub molds and rail caps, and in fact for just about everything excepting the decking itself and the spars and crooks. There was nothing gritty about white oak, nothing soggy about it either.

The stand belonged to Old Man Rellison, really, and not to Judge Watts, who had only leased it for twenty years. It was tolerably well known that Judge Watts had done this for the purpose of getting Old Man Rellison to consent to the bounding of John to him, and that he'd presumably been overcharged (he never did tell anybody what he paid, but then he never told anybody anything like that anyway: nobody ever found out, either, what he had paid Hab's mother and father, still alive then, but who, however, on their deaths left their only child nothing but a scrunty mean stone-crowded farm mortgaged rather higher than the hilt). All the same, it seemed as though the deal might prove a good one for the judge, traditionally a lucky dealer. White oak was scarce hereabouts, and wood from anywhere else, what with the

Embargo, was difficult to get. Farmers were cutting timber and breaking their backs to clear away stumps only to make fields, not to make ships; and they planted no saplings. You could see further, as a result; but what was there to see?—stone walls, and stones not in walls, pasture land, hayfields, kine squandered across the hillsides, and wheat and barley that was short, touched by the blast, yellowing spottily. The valleys were almost bare of trees, and if a few did cling to the hilltops it was in the way that small dry tough gray tree from a Bavarian fairy story clung to the stony earth, its branches bowed, its roots in the rocks, living—yes, living, but nothing more, not worthy of the attention of any man with an ax.

More than a few had been lopped off here since Hab's last visit. He saw stumps everywhere. Old Man Rellison, when he needed wood, came here, or, when a neighbor needed wood, sent him here, accepting payment in kind. This was a violation of the terms of the lease; but Hab said nothing. He was angriest to see the *kind* of trees that had been cut —growing trees not yet ready for the ax—but though he would tell Judge Watts, he kept his mouth shut now.

Supper was rye-and-Injun without butter, and salt-beef broth. Breakfast was the same. Hab had expected this. He had not forgotten life on the farm. He marveled that on the Point he had not been dazzled by the luxuries, which, however, he had learned slowly. Sure, he wore homespun, but it was better homespun than they wore here, and not made in the house where he lived; and on the Point he had often seen American broadcloth; and it was common there for a woman to have, in addition to her homemade drugget and crape, two or three camblet gowns and perhaps even a silk shawl. But then the shoes, the hats, everything here was different—and inferior.

There was never any wheat bread, only rye-and-Injun. There wasn't even much wheat, thanks to the Canada thistle and the Hessian fly and also to that mysterious disease called blast which Old Man Rellison insisted was caused by noxious fumes from the barberry bushes. There weren't many potatoes, which were not planted in separate patches but only along the borders of grain fields. There were few turnips or carrots. Manure wasn't used, just left to lie there. Hab liked tomatoes; but these superstitious country folks, as he reflected somewhat smugly, would have nothing to do with tomatoes, which they declared would make you sterile. Their tea wasn't real tea from China, such as John and Habakkuk and Deliverance were sometimes given: their tea was made from raspberry and blackberry leaves. For pepper, an expensive commodity even on the Point, they served the pulverized bark of the prickly ash. Their coffee they made from parched rye and chestnuts ground to powder. In the whole house, too, there was not a decoration, no bedcover, no rug. There was nothing to read, not even a Bible. There was no way to make music.

Next day, after a breakfast of bean porridge and hasty pudding, they went out to clear a field. Hab had expected this too. Old Man Rellison would attend to his fuel wants when no lieutenant of Judge Watts was around. The oxen couldn't be used in the kitchen. It was overearly for haying or spring planting. On the other hand, the first thaws had forced rocks to the surface, and the wind had here and there toppled a fence; and anyway, when you can't think of anything else to do in Connecticut you can always clear fields.

All day long, then, men and beasts and the one woman, sour-faced Sarah, who was incredibly John's sister, moved rocks. It rained some in the afternoon, a thick cold rain, but the horse was the only worker who seemed to mind. With the heavier rocks, the ones assigned to Hab Jones, the work was the harder by reason of the fact that Old Man Rellison wouldn't allow the use of an iron crowbar Hab had brought. Iron thrust into the earth would poison it, he averred. For the same reason he had steadfastly refused to buy or even to borrow one of those new-fangled plows with a blade of iron. You couldn't tell him that metal wouldn't pollute the soil! Not just for a few crops, either, but forever! He continued to push an all-wood plow, the kind the men in the Old Testament used to use, and his harrow had wooden teeth.

For supper, by the light of a spluttering tallow candle, they had salt-pork broth with Injun meal, and some hasty pudding.

Hab tried again to talk about John, and again he met silence. It wasn't that the others appeared to resent the topic, it was just that they were not interested. John was gone. Supper was here. And the jug.

This irritated Hab, who began to show edgy; but they paid him no mind. Hab wanted to talk about his friend, and even to boast about him like a doting father. He wanted to tell them how John could turn out as much work as any journeyman and almost as much as a master builder, when he'd a mind to; and how he had filled out, who'd been sickly as a small 'un; and how everybody spoke so well of him, and had a smile for him. He did say some of this. He might as well have talked to the shadows on the walls.

Hab felt very lonesome that night as he lay listening to the whippoor-will.

They had pea porridge and hasty pudding for breakfast, and a little milk. Getting into the swing of things now, they did a power of work at the stand. Still Hab was lonesome, what with nobody ever talking. Here, practically within sight of the farm where he was born and where he'd spent the first twelve years of his life, he was homesick. He began to understand, chopping, trimming, why men and women too in a place like this took to drinking or to praying. Personally Hab admired to pray a bit now and then. It cleared you out, made you feel better. But when a man like his father or a woman like his mother got to praying they might keep it up for days—and when they finished there was no telling what they might do. Drinking, except when you feel like it, with good friends around, he had never seen any sense to.

They had porridge and rye-and-Injun and hasty pudding for supper, and nobody said anything, and Hab, thinking of that damned whip-poorwill, was downright pleased when Joey Bludge appeared to serve upon him a warrant charging him with conspiracy to violate some Washington law. Joey Bludge added that if it was all the same to every-body they'd start back first thing in the morning.

. 6 . . .

THEY LOAFED AT THE SAME SPRING BESIDE WHICH HAB HAD
been lying when first he smelled the democrat, and they talked of this
and that in a lazy fashion, but after a while it was only Joey Bludge who
talked, for Hab, though he had not fallen asleep, had got to thinking of
other things. Bludge was confidential, earnest, almost obsequious in his
manner, very pronounced in his insistence that he was going to do
everything he could do for Hab, very eager to have Hab agree that duty
was duty, once you'd sworn an oath, and that friendship should not be
permitted to interfere.

Didn't Hab think so?

Hab said (remembering what he had seen of Deliverance when she
climbed in the window that night John went away) that he reckoned
he did.

Bludge was not in the mood of this clearing, of the leaves, the sunspots, spring. He sat up; and he talked about the universal need for
understanding the other man's problems. Didn't Hab think so?

Hab murmured that he reckoned he did. In fact he was reproaching
himself for having permitted his memory to retain that picture of Deliverance, who after all was too good a girl to be thought of that way.
He started to think about John, and about the fun they'd used to have
together, and he wondered if John was safe; but he reproached himself for these thoughts too, which were selfish—for it was hard to keep
clear of selfish thoughts on a day like this in a place like this; and he
thought about what he knew he really should think about—Judge Watts
and Mrs Watts, and how hurt they'd been by John's going-away, and
how distressed and even disgraced they might feel about the fact that he,
Hab, had been arrested. He did hope that the judge, in particular,
wouldn't find it too hard a blow. Hab wasn't worried by thoughts of a
whupping, which as a matter of fact he didn't believe he'd get; but he
was sincerely concerned about the judge's state of mind. Coming right
after John's going-away, the arrest seemed dreadful mean.

He supposed he should be afraid, but he wasn't. He was sure that
Judge Watts could get him free, sure indeed that the Pointers, even
without the judge, would not permit any such goings-on.

He popped open his eyes. He almost sat up.

Joey Bludge, that blowsy man, that twistical small moon-faced man,
talked on and on, argufying, waggling his white hands.

"Don't you reckon so?"

"I reckon so," listlessly.

The thought that maybe they weren't going home had struck Habak-kuk Jones, and it smarted. This man might take him to Mystic or Portersville, where he knew very few people, or even to New London, where he didn't know anybody. It would not be the same as in Stoning-ton. Folks in any of those places or in any other place along the shore might feel as the Point folks felt about the damn Embargo, but they wouldn't be likely to risk their health intervening in behalf of a pris-oner who wasn't one of their own. He might even be taken all the way to New Haven. Like John Rellison, he might not see Stonington again for months, years.

Here was a thought sure to dismay. He had trouble keeping his voice casual, his eyes slitted.

It was true that Governor Trumbull, as was only right and proper, had told those southerners in Washington, right to their faces in a manner of speaking, that no matter what disorders there might be he positively would not call out the State Militia to enforce an unconstitu-tional law. All the same, in a place like New London, say, or Saybrook, there might be more than a sprinkling of Joey Bludges, and, what was more disquieting, of Red Fergusons.

Yet while he lay there on the grass, when he looked up at Joey Bludge, Hab felt easier in mind; and soon the fright went away. For it was clear from what Bludge said that they were going back to Ston-ington. It was clear too that the deputy marshal was afraid to do so, and was eager to enlist the sympathy of his prisoner. Folks didn't under-stand, he said, almost sobbed, how when you were an officer of the law a duty was a duty, no matter what your personal feelings might be.

"You know, Habakkuk, I swouch it! It wasn't for nothing you read the law with Judge Watts, who's a fine man, a fine, fine man! You have read the law with him, haven't you, Hab?"

Hab shook a slumbrous head.

"Well, you aim to, don't you?"

"I reckon."

Yes, he had meant to for several years, he and John Rellison. The old judge wanted them to read the law. He used to say that unless you started rich it was the only way to rise in politics. If only his clients were to pay him, he used to say, he would be making more money out of his law practice than out of fishing, farming, shipbuilding, and all his in-vestments put together. He would see the boys through. He'd see them admitted to the bar. However, he had not at any time *insisted* that they read the law. He was a queer old codger in some ways, and while he'd make them do all manner of things around the house and in the fields and at the yard, and be all-fired mad if they didn't do 'em fast enough and right, in this one matter he did not press. He was wishing, and they

42

knew it, that they would go to him and ask his permission to read the law. He wouldn't drive them into it; he wouldn't even urge it upon them; but he had a powerful wish that they'd do it all the same. Now and then they had talked about it, the two of them, agreeing that they ought to do it. They could write tolerably well and read first-rate, but they both knew that to have studied the law was a great thing in the eyes of all who hadn't, and the best thing for you no matter what your business; and besides, the old judge had been so clever with them, and he obviously wished it so much. So they agreed they'd do it soon. Soon. It remained soon. And now John was at sea, and maybe he'd never read the law. He had always been more interested in ships, in sailing ships and navigating them, just as Hab had always been more interested in making them. Well, Hab was left, and it was up to him to go to the judge in that matter. He'd do it soon, he decided.

There was Joey Bludge, still a-talking, on and on, in his roopy voice. There was a whine in the voice. Seemed as if he was going to bust into tears; and his elbows were on his knees, and his pale pudgy hands flapped like sails in a scanting wind, while he talked and talked . . .

Maybe the man was so stupid that he had not even thought of taking his prisoner to some other town or village? It did not seem likely. All this boggling could only signify that for some reason—Hab didn't know what and didn't care—they were going to Stonington. Hab smiled a little, and closed his eyes. He would be all right in Stonington.

"Don't you reckon that's the truth?"

Hab didn't answer, being asleep.

The leaves over his face were smeared a strident, a virulent red, when he woke. It startled him. He sat up. Joey Bludge, watching him, nodded slowly, and the bags under his eyes shook and his little round chins shook too, so that he showed very sad. He rose as Hab did.

"Yep, I reckon we'd better stir our stumps. Be dark afore we're in. Didn't like to disturb you, though, Habakkuk. You looked so serene and—and sort of like an angel there."

Hab all but snickered, it amused him so, him a prisoner, to be compared with an angel. You let me sleep because you're itchy to get home late, you old scobhotcher, he thought. Because you're afeared to step out on the Point again while there's anybody abroad might see you with me.

Even then Joey Bludge wavered and hovered. There was nothing to do but go, no work; for to the delight of Old Man Rellison they had left the oxen behind.

Hab suggested, meaning it, but meaning it mostly for Joey Bludge, that they have a prayer. Bludge stared astonishment for a moment, then nodded.

"Might help" he muttered. "Might help. Can't harm."

They knelt side by side; and Hab didn't know what Bludge prayed

43

about but he himself prayed for Judge and Mrs Watts, for Deliverance too, and for John Rellison out there on the far hot sea. He prayed for a long while, without sound, and the crickets were speaking by the time he rose. He had not prayed for himself, partly because it didn't seem right when he was a prisoner like this, and partly because he wasn't much scared anyway.

Joey Bludge, on the other hand, *was* scared. He was standing when Hab rose, and seemingly he had been standing for some time, staring at his prisoner; and now he was letting on that he was all affability and condescension, and he smiled a smile made of suet; but there was fear in his eyes.

In the pale blink of the moon, some hours later, when they rounded Lantern Hill and gazed out on the Point, they saw that sundown had not, as it usually did, sent their fellow townsmen to bed. Stonington ordinarily was no place for night doings. Oliver York and Tom Swan might keep their public houses open late if there were sailing men to buy drinks; but the townspeople themselves seldom lingered there after dark. Sometimes a personage of consequence, say Judge Watts, might entertain some sea captain at a dinner which lasted until half-past eight or nine o'clock; or, if there was to be a late sailing because of the tide, there might be a last-minute bustle-with-lanterns at the Wheelers' loft or one of the chandleries. Since the Embargo, however, all such nocturnal activities had ceased. Since the Embargo ships had departed without cheers, without lights.

Now there was activity in Stonington. There were not many lights, but men were milling about in Water Street and Main Street both, around the big buttonwood they still called the Liberty Tree, in Town Square, and out on the public lands on the tip of the Point itself—practically everywhere except where Bludge and Hab stood, north of the stir, near the big solemn white meetinghouse. A whole fleet of ships, Hab thought, puzzled, could hardly have caused such a to-do. Yet he saw no vessel standing out or recently wharfed. Far out Wamphas-suck way, out almost as far as Mason Island, it looked, was a schooner he did not recognize. He saw her but fleetingly, for the clouds were erratic that night, coming and going on no schedule across the face of an uncertain moon; and now suddenly, as though a candle had been whuffed out, they stood in utter darkness, not even able to see the Pointers so near at hand, though they could catch the broken bumble of their talk. Hab had not been able to tell whether the schooner rode at anchor or was tacking, headed out for the end of the sound.

"What's that?"

Joey Bludge had no need to ask what. Pointers were to all intents and purposes islanders, and when they spoke of something without locating or qualifying it, the assumption was that they spoke of something in the water around, not something in the sky above or the land beneath. If you meant a non-ship matter you ought to so specify, lest folks get confused.

"Harp of Gold. I reckon she's aiming to get out tonight. Reckon she needs a pilot."

They had stopped. Bludge was looking at Hab, and Hab continued to look at the place where he'd glimpsed the schooner. Harp of Gold, eh? He had taken her out once, he and John, some four months ago, when they'd earned their three dollars apiece easily enough—or so it showed at first—for she handled easily and was well manned and fast as billy-be-damned. She'd been carrying flour and salt fish below, horses on deck. The thing had looked so easy, one of the first of their piloting jobs, and they'd been so proud of themselves after they turned over the vessel to her captain off Montauk! They'd chuckled, congratulating one another, *almost* all the way in—and then they had encountered Lieutenant Ferguson.

This had been off Bartlett Reef, Hab remembered, and the night a nasty one of heavy hurrying wet snow that *splapped* against your face. He and John had been warm enough by reason of the fearnoughts Judge Watts had recently bought them, the finest coat either had ever had; and they'd buttoned these high, laughing, pleased with themselves.

They had not actually collided with the government sloop, but it was a near thing. Ferguson had been cruising, his thought being to bottle Harp of Gold in the harbor, and seemingly they'd slipped him without even knowing he was there. He knew *them,* the instant he saw them, as both helmsmen, gasping, put sharp about. He had recognized their boat, and they'd recognized his, and he must have known that its return meant that the schooner had given him the slip. Such things enraged Lieutenant Red Ferguson of the marine revenue service. He could not have sworn in court that he had recognized the boys themselves—for he was honest, to give him credit—but certainly he recognized the dogbody Deliverance, and he had put about after it with no delay. He was a killer by instinct, and a noisy man when roused, and he had fired not once but half a dozen times at the dogbody as he chased. His bow gun made a murderous splintering sound, a dry sharp sound that even the snow couldn't soften. The water all around Deliverance had begun to lift white and choppety, and spray flew.

They could have run straight in, Hab realized as he stood alongside of Joey Bludge and stared at a Stonington he couldn't see. Had they known then what they knew now, had they kept their heads, everything would have been all right. But, inexperienced, they had tried tricks; and Red Ferguson was a crack sailing man, and if he hadn't quite overhauled them he had stayed breathlessly close, whipcracking that chaser all the while, keeping the sea asplash.

Yes, Hab remembered it well. They'd aimed her right, lashed the tiller, and slipped overside. What they should have done, of course, was

cast their fearnoughts into the water, so that they could not be identified; but they loved the fearnoughts, and anyway they were afraid of
a whupping. At first the water had not seemed notably cold. Their
legs and feet, yes, but not their bellies and chests. They had started to
to swim, while the government sloop sped past; and then they'd found
that they couldn't swim. It was the first time either of them had ever felt
panic in the water; and each had later confessed, in bed, to the other,
that he was sick with fright then, being sure that he was going to die.
Somehow they had swum, though. They were good swimmers. Somehow they had started for shore.

Neither of them would ever forget that night. More than once they'd
been ready to quit, so cold that nothing seemed to matter. The original
panic did not return; they were, after the first terrible minute, without
fright; but it was just too darn cold to keep struggling. More than once
John Rellison had shaken his head, turning it to face Hab Jones, and
had motioned with his hand for Hab to go on; and Hab had swum
closer and had pushed him in the face, shaking his own head vigorously, motioning that they must both go on. Even at the time Hab had
wondered why he did that. Like John, all he truly wanted was to relax,
to stop moving: when you moved all you did was hurt yourself more,
but when for an instant you were still, not even treading water, you
felt warm all over. Hab knew he never would have made it alone. Nor
would John Rellison have made it alone. Neither had helped the other
physically; but the grins now and then, grinning through agony, and
Hab's pushing John in the face—this is what had done it.

They never even caught the sniffles. They had kept their underclothes on and had taken their shoes and stockings into bed with them,
drying them by hugging them close; and as far as they knew, neither
Judge Watts nor his wife ever suspicioned that they'd been out.

The dogbody, as they'd hoped it would do, had gone quietly aground,
undamaged, at the mouth of Quanaduck Cove, where they claimed it
next morning. Presumably Ferguson had pursued it clear inshore,
firing at it, and finally boarded it only to find it empty. He'd been
drunk all that next day, roaring the most direful threats around town;
but he couldn't do anything about confiscating the dogbody, which
belonged to John and Hab, and which *might,* after all, have slipped
its moorings and got washed about a bit before drifting ashore. In
that case, Ferguson had yelled, why was all her canvas set? John and
Hab hadn't answered. They hadn't told any lie. They'd simply held
their mouths shut.

This had been the beginning of Ferguson's dislike of them, of his
own private war upon them.

Yes, Hab remembered Harp of Gold. So now she was back?

"She made a might of money on that voyage" Joey Bludge was
whispering. There wasn't anybody near at hand, but Bludge was a

whisperer by instinct. "She'll make a might of money on this one too, Hab, if she's just taken out there to Montaug all safe."

Hab said nothing.

"Jed Slocum's her skipper, and he's sure looking for a first-rate pilot, Hab. Jedediah Slocum. Noank man. You know him, don't you?"

Hab nodded.

"I reckon he'd even pay the price of *two* pilots, two like you and John Rellison, if he could get either of you" Joey Bludge said low, leaning sideways close to Hab. "Reckon it'd be worth six dollars to him, the way things are. Don't you reckon, Habakkuk?"

"Couldn't say."

"Now see here, Hab," and the deputy United States marshal hitched himself closer, exactly as though in fact they were seated in two separate chairs at a table. He tapped Hab's forearm with a fat finger. His voice went lower still, his manner became even more confidential. "I know this ain't just the right thing to do, looking at my official rank and so-forth, but a man's got to think of himself sometime, and after all there isn't anybody in this world I'd trust their word for anything any more'n I would yourn, Habakkuk. Naturally I aim to keep you at my house tonight, but all the same there's no reason why if you want to move around a little first—I mean, there's a job out there, and as far as I'm concerned if I wake up and find you in my house that's all I ask. It'd be quieter that way, too. Wouldn't be all those folks around. I'm sure you could get in without anybody seeing you, Hab. You're mighty spry that way, always have been. You wouldn't even have to pitch somebody into a pit of sawdust, eh?"

"You mean to say you're *asking* me to take that schooner out?"

The little man had the grace to avert his eyes. Nevertheless he persisted.

"Does seem strange, Hab, and I can appreciate your feelings, but after all a man must look out for himself. I'll be frank and open with you, Habakkuk. Truth is, I've got a small piece of this voyage on my own. Oh, not much! But such as it is, it means a lot to me. So of course I want to see that schooner get clear of Montaug, and there ain't nobody can do that like you. Now don't get sore! After all, I'm deputy marshal but I ain't a revenuer, am I? It's my duty to arrest folks if a federal officer orders me to, but there's nothing said about how I can't have a little business venture of my own on the side if I'm so minded, is there?"

"Reckon not," and Hab smiled.

"Well, there you are! With anybody else I wouldn't talk to them this way, but I know you, Habakkuk, and I know I can trust you. So—you want to do that for me, eh? Jed Slocum'll give you the six dollars himself. And it ought to be easy, a night like this. I doubt that the lieutenant'll even be out. He'll see this crowd and he'll come ashore to find out what's happening—for the lieutenant's one as dearly loves a fight, Habakkuk."

"Aye."

"Well—you'll do it, then?"

Hab looked at him, having almost to look down at him, though Bludge was three times his age. There was no question of the deputy marshal's sincerity. This was no trick! He would take Hab's word, he would welcome Hab back.

"What if I should get drownded?" Hab asked.

"On a night like this?"

"Well, what if Red Ferguson should catch up to me?"

"He ain't done it yet, out of a power of tries. Besides, the way I told you, Hab, I don't believe he'll be anywhere but ashore at the Point tonight, looking for trouble. But if he *should* stumble over you," Joey Bludge went on, his voice trembling, his face averted, "well, I can always say you escaped as I was bringing you in. *You* wouldn't have to say anything at all."

"I wouldn't anyway."

"I know that! I know it! That's one thing you do better'n anybody else, Hab—you keep your mouth shut! Well, going?"

"I reckon" said Hab, and started away.

He still couldn't see the Harp of Gold schooner, but he knew exactly where she was, and if this thing was to be done at all it must be done promptly. He was chuckling a little at the absurdity of it. He thought of dropping in to Judge Watts's house but decided against this. But he did decide that he'd save John's three dollars for him, along with his own, in the bag under the loose board, for the time when John came back. It seemed good to think of that. It seemed, for a second there, almost like working with John again.

Joey Bludge ran after him, grabbed an elbow.

"You understand, Hab, the back door. So's folks won't——"

"All right."

"And take the first room on the left, upstairs. The bed'll be turned down and all. And, Hab—just one more thing——"

"Yes?"

"If you snore you'd better put a pillow over your head, because my wife just can't abide snoring."

Hab smiled, slipping away.

"I don't snore."

"That's good. I'm sure glad to hear that, Habakkuk. My wife, she just can't abide snoring."

. 7 . . .

THE MOONLIGHT, WHEN THERE WAS MOONLIGHT, SHONE
on the sleek smooth buttocks of horses tethered head-in along both
sides of the schooner. They were close together, and they'd recently been
fed, and they were quiet. The sailors who tended them, and who of
course didn't like horses, sometimes, meaning to tone down a stir,
would slap some among those serried rumps; and this always caused
more commotion than it was meant to quell.

Hab Jones didn't like horses either. A man from Baltimore, a
visitor at the judge's house, to whom he once told this, was frankly
shocked, taking it as nothing less than sacrilege; and he hastened to
point out that Hab had presumably never seen a good horse. "These
skinny critters around here, I don't wonder you don't fancy 'em. Now
you take——" Hab still didn't like them, and especially he didn't like
them as deck cargo on a ship he was taking out. There was always that
danger of whinnying, for one thing. And there was the mess. He didn't
object to the smell of horse apples, but their urine was something else
again: it was a peculiarly *penetrating* stink, a *carrying* one, and if Red
Ferguson sniffed it coming from the south of his sloop on cruise, well,
Ferguson, no fool, wouldn't suppose that that came from horses clear
over on Long Island, now would he? However, tonight Hab was un-
worried. He gazed down over the long double line of backsides, and
shook his head.

"They can't get enough of 'em down there, can they? Why don't
they use oxen, you guess? Suppose they can't stand the heat as well?"

"Oh, they don't use 'em in the canefields, much. What they want
'em for is to eat—or anyway give 'em to the slaves to eat."

" 'Bout all they're good for."

"Far as heat goes, they do stand up under that tolerable."

Yes, it was hot in the West Indies, hotter all year around than
Connecticut in August, he'd been told. He had been told a lot about
the West Indies these past four years. He wondered again if he would
ever see them, feel them against his face and under his feet. He
wondered what John would think of them or already was thinking of
them.

He got moony when he thought about John, so he renewed talk with
Jed Slocum the skipper.

Nodding to the beasts, "Make much on them last voyage?"

"Made a pretty sum on the flour and fish but nary a penny on the critters. Struck it still, off the coast of Cubie, and a boat put out from somewhere there, some bay or something, that I didn't like the looks of."

"Pirates?"

"Could've been. I didn't wait to find out. She carried sweeps but we had to depend on our canvas, and it was pretty nigh a dead calm. So we lightened cargo. I'd've chucked out the flour too, if I'd've had to, but we were well clear by the time we got down to that. You could see 'em swimming back there for a long while afterwards, swimming round and round, crazy-like."

"A pity."

"Yes, they'd have fetched a good price."

Hab asked for and got six dollars, double the amount he was accustomed to but even then less than an adult pilot would be paid. He pocketed this. He looked around, taking advantage of a splash of moonlight.

"That's fine" he said. "Just keep it right on this course for another two hours and you'll be full to sea."

"Say, I thought you were going to take us clear out to Montaug!"

"No need. You couldn't scrape anything now if you tried."

"Now see here, Hab, you know tarnation well that it wasn't because of the danger of grounding that I hired you so much as it was to keep clear of that revenue mariner. Why, you know that, Hab!"

Hab threw a leg over the taffrail and started to pull in the Deliverance. He glanced back at the neatly arranged, gleaming posteriors, and he touched the coins in his pocket.

"Don't you worry about him. He's to the village. Saw him put in just before I put out. Saw him get ashore, to find out what's going on."

"You didn't tell me that before, Hab!"

"You didn't ask me. 'By."

He docked the dogbody at its usual place, not fearing detection. There was nobody in sight, but from the village, from Main Street, came a bumble of angry voices, and there was a gleam there too of lanterns and red torches held high. Hab had a scared scrapy feeling in chest and throat, and his stomach wambled. He ran up to the house. Mrs Watts came to the door.

"So you're back? Well, damage's probably been done now. While you were away hiding."

She didn't move to admit him, but Deliverance peered over her shoulder, crying excitedly: "Hab, Hab!"

"Aye?"

"Father just went to Joey Bludge's house . . . Don't know what it is but they were dreadful worked up when they came for him!"

"Told us to stay here" said Mrs Watts. "Didn't say anything about you."

"You'd better get to there, Hab, and see if——"

"I'll go there. That's where I'm supposed to be anyway."

He had not seen her, only heard her in the darkness, when he turned and sped away. He wished he'd had a chance to see her.

"If they arrest you, you tell 'em the truth about what you done to John Rellison" Mrs Watts screamed after him.

Water Street was strangely deserted, even for this hour of the night, and there was nobody at or even near the taverns, but in Main Street, which was not the main street at all, there was a prodigious crowd. It was not an obviously angry crowd, not noisy. The men—and there were no women—did not wave their lanterns or torches or weapons—most of them were armed—but neither did they stand around irresolute, but instead pushed slowly and with a terrible certainty of purpose toward the home of Joey Bludge. No shouts rose from this crowd, only a low bitter hum. It was without frenzy: it had passed the frenzical stage.

Hab glimpsed some faces, and his very gizzards felt to freeze. These were men he knew, or had known, his neighbors, his friends. But were they? He had never seen such hard mouths, such cold eyes. There was murder in the soul of each of these men, of even the gentlest, cold deliberate murder. The disputatious Pointers had tired of the law. They were setting forth to kill.

Hab was never to forget the looks on those once-familiar faces as he pushed and wriggled his way through the crowd.

It was not hard to get ahead of other men, at first. They were not hurrying. They were converging with the stupid insistence of ants upon a single spot—the front lawn of Joey Bludge's house.

Now this was one of the best houses in Stonington. Joey's father had built it, with the aid of neighbors, and it was a good house, not showy but roomy, of two stories. Joey himself kept it up well. You could always say that for him: he took pride in the way his grass and shrubbery looked, and the way the house itself looked.

They didn't look well this night. Palings had been knocked out of the fence. The hedge was trampled, the grass too. The front door hung open. Like a startled confused ghost, curtains moved now out of and now back into a window from which all the glass panes had been smashed. Other windows too, upstairs and down, had been broken.

This much Hab saw as he struggled to reach the house—for the crowd was thicker here and he had a hard time getting through—but from the upraised voices he could guess what had happened or was about to happen. He heard the shrill pleading babble of Mrs Bludge, always a shrill woman anyway, hysterical now. He heard Lieutenant Ferguson's profanity, his hoarse rum-thickened blasphemy. He heard

Judge Watts's temporizing yet mighty voice, the courtroom voice, the voice not of an old soldier, not of an angry man, but of a good citizen, a moderator. Sometimes too there was a thin high bleating, as though you had pulled a lamb's leg, and that would be Joey Bludge.

An upstairs window was thrown open, so that more glass fell tinkling to the lawn. A man looked out, a man Hab knew, Simpson the sailmaker. But this was not the fuzzy-grinning Simpson of Water Street. This man was red in rage, and despite the cold air his eyes were hot and the sweat stood out in a sheen on his face. He waved his arms.

"He is not in this house. I swouch it, we've searched and he's not here!"

Then where the devil *was* he? was what Red Ferguson demanded, evidently of Joey Bludge, who burst into renewed wailing. The crowd muttered low, surging forward very slowly like a wave made heavy by seaweed. Hab, fairly fighting his way now, heard Judge Watts pleading for silence, for a hearing.

They had a rope there was the first thing he noticed when he did break through the crowd. They had a long piece of rope, unknotted, and four or five of them held onto it, not like mountaineers who are prepared each to help the others but rather like political assassins who have agreed that somehow each shall have a hand on the knife when it kills, sharing the responsibility for the deed. The rope might have been a bluff, a bit of playacting calculated to intimidate Ferguson or to terrify Joey Bludge into telling the truth. Most of those who held it shamefacedly asserted, later, that it was never intended to be anything else. But bear in mind: they were different men later, as they had been different men before. The rope was real enough, strong enough, long enough, when they held it on the Bludges' front lawn. If indeed they were playacting, then they were very good actors, who convinced everybody, even themselves.

None of them was an old-time Liberty Boy. If there were some of those in the crowd, and there probably were, they were quiet. Yet the men who held the rope had the Liberty Boy spirit. Their uncles and fathers, if not themselves, had burned barns, had cut the throats of Tory cattle, had ridden Tories on rails and covered them, screaming, with hot sticky tar.

Mrs Bludge was a heap, albeit a throbbing heap, on the lawn. She had a blanket over her shoulders but underneath that only her nightrail; and her feet were bare. She sobbed wildly.

The Bludge tabby, Stephanie, sat in the doorway washing itself.

Bludge—and be sure that the rope was real enough in *his* eyes!—fairly groveled behind Judge Watts's legs like a whipped mongrel. His face was ashen. His eyes were huge and watery, bright with terror, and great greasy pear-shaped tears rolled out of them unheeded down his cheeks. His mouth worked, and he never ceased to make some manner of sound, but it was gibberish. He was so badly frightened that he couldn't even plead for his life. He looked as if he might vomit. His hands plucked piteously at Judge Watts's breeches.

The judge and the treasury man, those were the only two admirable ones, the only men there who knew just what they wanted and what they might have to pay to get it. They're the two bravest men in the village, Hab thought with awe, proud of his master, somewhat proud too, in a curious way, of his sworn enemy.

The judge and the treasury man stood between Joey Bludge and the men with the rope. The whole thing was perfectly clear in a flash to Habakkuk Jones, who paused only for an instant at the edge of the crowd, where he took in the shattered glass, the tangled red lights of torches, the washing tabby, the heaving sobbing Mrs Bludge, the rope . . .

"Where the devil *is* he, then?" and Red Ferguson kicked Bludge, kicked him hard, two or three times. Bludge seemed unhurt, almost unaware of the kicks, though he kneeled closer than ever to Judge Watts. Red Ferguson showed sober, but he was very sore just the same: he was in one of his worst rages. "You tell me where that boy is, or by God, Bludge, I'll—— And *you* keep back!" he snarled, suddenly remembering the men with the rope, the men behind him, who were edging closer. "This is my business, and I'll take care of it the way I like, damn all of you!" He drew his hanger, a short, ugly, cutlass-shaped one. "This man is an official of the federal government, and anybody touches him has got to fight me first!"

Judge Watts had had his arms raised, palms out, in a gesture intended to placate. Now he appeared to decide that the time for argument was past, and that the time for action was here, willy or nilly. He lowered his hands to his hips, where he fisted them. Old though he was, he looked mighty strong as he stood there with his feet widespread, his chin jutting forward. It was odd to see him standing thus, standing right next to Red Ferguson.

"This man is a citizen of Connecticut and he's entitled to a citizen's rights, and anybody who lays hands on him has got to fight *me* first too!"

It might have succeeded had not Simpson and the others of the searching party come out of the house at this moment. The men with the rope were motionless in their tracks, and were even beginning to resist with shoulders and elbows the pressure of the crowd behind.

"Well, where is he, then?"

"Don't you suppose I want to know just as much as you do!" the judge flared. "Isn't he my own boy, you fools?"

"Yes, where is he?" cried Red Ferguson, kicking Bludge again. "By God, you'll tell us or else——"

Then Simpson came out. He was carrying in his fist a long old-fashioned cavalry saber, his father's perhaps, bright enough, sharp enough. He tried to kick the tabby cat, which left off washing and scampered out of the doorway and then, after giving him a resentful look, upped its tail and stalked across the lawn, paying no attention to anybody.

It might have been better if Simpson had succeeded in kicking that cat. It might have taken some of the ferocity out of him. Little things like that often have such big effects! As it was, missing the cat made him, if this was possible, even more blindly angry. He walked very fast.

Behind him, also walking fast, were three other men. Each held some kind of weapon. Two had horse pistols, which were cocked. These men didn't hesitate or hang back. So far from fearing violence, they sought it.

"He's had the half-hour we promised and he still hasn't told us. Well, you know what we agreed, don't you?"

Simpson strode down the steps and made straight for Joey Bludge.

Lieutenant Ferguson raised his cutlass. Judge Watts didn't move: he just stood there, directly in their path, his hands on his hips.

It was then that Hab caught control of himself and started to run. *"Don't fight! Here I am!"*

He slipped and fell hard, and when he sprang to his feet blood was gushing from his nose, slobbering over his mouth, but still he kept calling as he ran that they shouldn't fight because here he was.

How much they had talked about him, and how they'd threatened to avenge him! yet now that he stood in their midst it appeared that he had stirred up additional trouble by his coming, increasing the crowd's unreasoning rage. If they were glad to see him they showed it in the oddest fashion. Men waved lanterns in his face and jabbered at him questions he couldn't make out, all talking at once. Men grabbed his shoulders and whirled him around, now this way now that. Some even shook their fists at him. He did not have a chance to talk to the judge, nor did the judge, busy trying to keep men away from him, have a chance to ask his own questions.

The sight of the blood that streamed from his nose could have been in part the cause of the excitement. They thought at first that he was injured, that he'd been manhandled, and they actually started kicking and punching the prostrate Joey Bludge themselves. Hab had to shout, again and again, that he'd been bleeding only for a moment and only because of an accident. He shouted that he often bled from the nose like this in moments of excitement, sometimes even without any precipitating shock. Judge Watts, likewise shouting, and windmilling his arms for attention, confirmed this.

Perversely, then, the crowd turned from solicitude for his welfare to resentment of his appearance—or rather, of his original disappearance. Where in hell *had* he been, damn him? It was not only Lieutenant Ferguson who demanded to learn this, but every one of them.

Every one, that is, excepting Judge Watts.

They shook him, they screamed at him, and spat on him, but he said nothing whatever, didn't even open his mouth. He just looked at Judge Watts, who nodded in grave affectionate approval.

"You are absolutely right, Habakkuk" the judge said when at last he could make himself heard. "You don't have to answer any questions at all."

There were cries of rage at this, and Lieutenant Ferguson fairly bellowed his indignation, but the judge stood firm, as always; and Hab just kept looking up at him.

"No man can make you say anything, if you prefer to keep quiet, Habakkuk."

"I'll make him say something when I get him alone!" Ferguson stormed.

"About that," Judge Watts said seriously, "I think it might be well for everybody if the deputy marshal should see fit to parole the prisoner in my custody. You have my word for it, of course, Mr Bludge," he spoke down solemnly at the frightened little man who still groveled at his feet, "that he will be produced on demand. Don't you think this is best?"

Joey Bludge did think so, promptly, thankfully. Lieutenant Ferguson would have protested, but the judge looked at him and he looked at the crowd. Lieutenant Ferguson would have fought them all, but fighting them all and Judge Watts besides was another matter. He nodded his head curtly, turned away, strode off.

That sort of ended the meeting. There were some who went on muttering and mumbling in corners, but most of the men, suddenly tired, drifted home, feeling, as they looked, a little foolish. Several—the whole village was to do this within the next few days—approached Judge Watts and sheepishly apologized for having seemed at any time to defy him. Some congratulated him with warmth and assured him that in the event of a fight they had been prepared to take his side. A few even stayed around to ask the Bludges if they couldn't help straighten things up. A few out of sheer nervousness went to one of the taverns and got drunk.

Hab Jones and the judge walked home, the judge with a hand on Hab's shoulder.

"You did absolutely right, Habakkuk" he repeated. "Every freeborn American is privileged to keep his mouth shut when he's a mind to —though not many of them seem to know it."

After a while he asked "Was it the Harp of Gold, Habakkuk?"

"Yes, sir."

"Did she, um, you reckon she's away all right?"

"She's all right."

"That's good. I, um, I have a small share of that voyage myself, Habakkuk. No need to mention that to Mrs Watts or Deliverance, though."

"Yes, sir."

He sat up with the judge for an hour or more that night, fetching rum and hot water from the kitchen and putting cold compresses on the judge's forehead. The judge's heart was going like mad. He was older than he thought; and it had been a strain.

His wife—who attributed this and almost every other disturbance these days to something Hab had done, she was never clear what, on the night John Rellison went away—was helpful though scarcely cheering: she resented Hab's presence. Deliverance, who worshiped her father, was a miracle of nursing efficiency. All the same, it was Hab Jones who finally quieted the old man.

"You know, sir," he said one time when nobody else knew what to say and there wasn't anything to be done, "I'd like to start reading the law someday, if you think you could find time to help me?"

The judge almost smiled; certainly there was a smile in his fine blue eyes if not on his lips. And he relaxed. And his heart got normal again in a little while. And pretty soon he was asleep.

. 8 . . .

THE GULLS HUNG AND ROCKED OVER THE SHORE, OVER THE water, sometimes dipping a little, sometimes rising; and now and then, too, one would swoop for a snippet of seaweed or garbage afloat in the bay. They scarcely ever flapped their wings. Their little heads were far out, their sleek small necks stretched, as with tiny bored red eyes they kept watch, rocking, drifting with the wind. They made a thin shrill sound, negligently, languidly talking to one another. It sounded like ee-eep, ee-ee-ee-ee. It came from high up, very far away.

Obe Lent stepped back from the fire and wiped his forehead and raised his head to blink smoke-reddened eyes. He had been knocking stubs of wood from among the rocks, piping hot now. He scowled at the gulls.

"They're still around when we put the vegetables on they're liable to drop something on 'em" he muttered.

"Do 'em good maybe" somebody said.

"I prefer mine without" said Obadiah.

Hab Jones wheeled up another barrowload of clams and dumped these beside the table where the women worked. He grinned at the women. Some were hunkered down, sorting the clams, which were all small, thin-shelled, not quahogs, not littlenecks. Deliverance was one of these women, and Hab always liked to watch Deliverance work. He knew, sometimes, that she knew he was looking at her, and didn't care. Deliverance and the other squatters opened the shells they had selected for chowder and strained the juice through a piece of cloth. They removed the bellies and passed the rest of the meat up to the table to be ground. The women standing at the table ground this meat, and they diced potatoes which had been soaked all night, and chopped up very fine some fat salt pork, which they fried slowly. They chopped up some onions brought from Bermuda—a local onion would have been too strong—and fried these in the pork grease.

"That enough?" Hab asked.

"That's too much."

"Well, it's proper right then. We're supposed to have too much."

The women began to hang pots over the fire, their own fire, and to dump in clams and broth, and to season with salt and pepper and a little sage. Hab wasn't wanted. He drifted away, feeling good. He helped the men at the big fire for a while.

With pitchforks, with rakes and shovels, they knocked the unburnt wood pieces from among the rocks. The rocks were so hot that you couldn't stand near them for more than a few seconds at a time. The men didn't knock out all the wood. They left some ashes in, "just for flavor," as Obe Lent put it. Then, using pitchforks, they piled on the first layer of rockweed. This was the part Hab liked most to watch. The weed had only recently been pulled off rocks under water, and it was wet with brine and hissed angrily when placed on the hot rocks, so that a great turbulent column of steam rose into the darkening air, causing the gulls to ee-ee indignantly and veer away.

"Here comes the *cla*-ams!"

In baskets, in basins of every sort, the men hauled from beside the table the clams the women had discarded, the larger ones, though in fact they were notably small clams, small and dainty and delicate, with thin shells. They dumped these on top of the rockweed, hundreds of them, perhaps thousands. They chucked on more rockweed, and then another layer of clams. The seawater from the rockweed trickled down through the clams to the hot rocks, which sent it back as steam. The great column thickened at its base. It swayed a little in an early evening breeze, which, however, was not strong enough to break it. The steam hissed furiously as it came up through the rocks and clams and seaweed.

They put on white potatoes in their jackets, and sweet potatoes, and fillets of fish, and onions, and unhusked corn, and cloth bags filled with savory stuffing. They put on another layer of rockweed, another layer of clams, more wet rockweed, and then the lobsters. Finally they put on still more rockweed and covered the whole ponderous mass with a sail which they weighted at the edges with rocks. It was a great protuberant belly of a thing, this sail, swollen like a belly too, and straining hard as it held back the steam. Some steam escaped under the edges of the sail, between the rocks; but this was a trifle; the column no longer reached high toward the gulls. The sound of spluttering juices had been smothered by the sail, but there was still a great agitation going on under that canvas, which rose and fell gaspingly, and the steam that did manage to escape under the edges swirled hastily away, evaporating.

"*Chow*-der!"

The women had set out wheat bread and rye-and-Injun, and also tomatoes, apple quarters, onions, pickles, vinegar, ketchup, salt, pepper, drawn butter, jam. They began to ladle the chowder into bowls, and the men lined up to get it. There was a great deal of talk and of laughter. Folks were feeling good. Hab Jones had never known a party so gay. Everybody seemed prosperous and lighthearted. Even Mrs Watts smiled a rather sweaty smile at Hab when she ladled out his fourth bowl of chowder. She wiped back hair with a hooked thumb. She blew upward. "Good?" "It's dreadful good!" "Well, you're not taking much." "Saving up for the real meal." Then she became morose

58

again, and looked down at the pail and stirred it vigorously with a long wooden spoon. "Well, there's God's plenty, if you want it" she muttered.

They sat at long tables, boards laid out over sawhorses: Hab had fixed them that morning. There was a great deal of talk, in which Hab did not join—for he was never much of a talker, though he liked to hear others talk if it made them feel good—and for once it had nothing to do with either politics or religion. It was not contentious talk. It was neighborly, intimate, even rather light. Later, when they really got to eating, they wouldn't be able to talk like this; and when they were *through* eating they wouldn't be able to talk at all for a while; but it was easy to talk with chowder. It was the friendliest all-around conversation Hab had ever heard, and he delighted in it, beaming left and right between mouthfuls, clucking his tongue in approval, playfully shaking his head. There had never been any unnecessary talk back to the farm, excepting when men were drunk, when it was better to keep away from them. The shore men were more sociable, though Judge Watts himself had always been a silent one, and Mrs Watts too. Hab in passing would hear a power of talk from the two public houses, but that was not for him. The talk in the yard, the talk in the streets, such of it as he overheard, was seldom about neighbors on the Point, not often even about affairs in Hartford or in Boston, but rather about the prices of things in the West Indies and the political situation in faraway Washington where the Virginia clique was stronger and less scrupulous than ever. Today, however, noisily sipping chowder, men chattered about things nearer to hand, and even included the women in the conversation, those who weren't hurrying around carrying things.

Well, it was over. They were free now, temporarily at least, of the worst restraints on shipping. This was April in the year 1809; and the thing that had been coiled around and around them, and had been killing them, not strangling them but rather crushing them to death like some fabulous jungle snake, getting tighter and tighter, more and more taut—that thing was dead, cut down a few weeks before by Tom Jefferson's own hand, though not by any means at Jeff's desiring! A few days before stepping out of the White House he had, sighing, signed the repeal of his pet Embargo Act. The fact that Tom Jefferson was out, after eight years as President, in itself gave no satisfaction to the Pointers and the other people of Connecticut; for the Virginia dynasty was well established by now, and Jeff's neighbor and fellow party boss, Jemmy Madison, succeeded him as President, while a third of that ilk, Jemmy Monroe, was being groomed to succeed Madison when the time came: he was the vice-president. Politically you couldn't tell one of these men from either of the others. The Pointers could look to none of them for relief; for everybody knew that Tom Jefferson would simply run the country now from his own comfortable home instead of from an official

59

residence in Washington. No, what was pleasing was the indubitable fact that the Embargo had failed—and failed so conspicuously and so raucously that even the Virginians were obliged to admit it.

It had run for a year and four months, and the people of the country had simply refused to have any part of it.

This legislation hadn't died without a fight! The democrats controlled both houses of Congress, and Tom Jefferson controlled the democrats, and after the passage of the original Embargo Act, and when it was seen that this wasn't working out, the subservient legislators had passed one enforcement act after another, each more drastic than the last. They had cut the voyage-completion time—the time Congress allowed a skipper to get back to his original port with a certificate testifying that he had landed such-and-such cargo—from four to two months. They had prohibited all land trade with Canada and Florida, imposing staggering penalties—confiscation of all goods, wagons, horses, sleds, and up to ten thousand dollars fine for every person involved, howsoever remotely. They had given the collectors of the port extraordinary powers—unconstitutional powers, the Pointers contended —and permitted them to superintend all lading, to arrest a vessel or her owners on mere suspicion; and at the same time they had made it almost impossible to sue these officials for false arrest. They had authorized the commanders of all public armed vessels to stop and search any American or foreign vessels in United States waters or on the high seas on mere suspicion that it was violating the Embargo Act. They had created an army of clerks and enforcement agents, most of them no good, many of them thieves. They had boosted the bond required from twice to *six times* the value of ship and cargo. Seeking sneaks, they had offered informers one-half the amount of the staggering fines on conviction. They had empowered the President to use any part or all of the land or naval forces of the nation or to call out any state militia in order to try to enforce this abomination of a law. They had appropriated money for the construction of thirty new revenue cutters.

And what had it got them? For all the laws and preparations, for all the revenue mariners and smirking democratical clerks in port offices, the public just plain didn't want the business and wasn't going to take it. As fast as the federal government found and plugged up one hole in the law, the men of the ports and the sea opened another. Thousands of citizens smuggled or assisted in smuggling every day. They'd have starved if they hadn't! Prices went mad. Nobody trusted anybody else's money. Nobody dared to build anything or to make a long-term contract.

And with it all, we still teetered on the verge of war. It began to look like a question of whether we should enter the war—Europe's war, not ours, but we were being sucked into it—whether we should enter it rich and strong and willing, or half-starved and utterly destitute. Men on the Point and in the surrounding country were saying outright, when perfectly sober too, and in the hearing of any number of others, that if we did get into war they wouldn't fight. What's more, they wouldn't risk a shilling in government bonds. Not when the government was being run by a passel of power-thirsty Virginians.

However, the Embargo had shaken itself out of existence by the very force of its own foolishness. Even Tom Jefferson was obliged to admit that it had failed. It might have been an experiment noble in purpose, as Mr. Macgregor told Hab that afternoon in the country, but as far as the Pointers were concerned it was a tarnation outrage, besides being unconstitutional; and they wondered why it had taken the rest of the country so long to realize this.

Well, it was finished now. There were still restrictions, of course, but they were nothing like the old ones. The man of the sea, still in almost every case a smuggler, at least could call his soul his own again, whilst the man on the wharf knew approximately, now, how much his dollars were worth.

Ships came and went openly, in fine weather, while Hab toiled night and day in the shipyard. He should have been in bed right now, getting some rest, for his muscles ached and his eyelids were weighty, but he wouldn't have missed the clambake for anything in the world, and besides it gave him a chance to look around the harbor. Yes, ships came and went. . . . Only a little while ago, beating the dusk in, a schooner, a fine high-sided vessel, empty or in light ballast from the look of her, had dropped the hook a short distance from the tip of the Point, and her officers and hands were coming ashore now in boats. Hab watched them, smiling.

The repeal of the Embargo Act, which touched every one of them so closely, was the reason for this clambake. It wasn't the *announced* excuse, and perhaps some of the eaters didn't even realize that it was a *real* one; for the idea of the bake had risen, it seemed, spontaneously, with no one group or set in charge, except that by general agreement Obadiah Lent was master of the fire; there were no banners, no signs, and nobody was going to make a speech; but all the same, nobody would even have thought of the event if everybody hadn't been feeling so good, and so prosperous, as a result of Tom Jefferson's failure.

The Pointers drank their chowder, laughing, talking, talking, talking, talking, for they all felt light and fine and generous.

Hab Jones held himself to four bowls. Besides the corn and lobsters and all the rest, there was a power of clams a-coming—he ought to know, who had dug out so many!—and at the moment when the sail was lifted he wasn't going to be caught with a full stomach. He ate no more than four or five slices of bread, too.

He took his bowl to the washing table and left it there. He asked Judge Watts if there was anything for him to do at the house while they waited for the meal, and was told that there wasn't. He went to Deliverance, who was slicing apples.

"Thought I might take a little walk out to the tip of the Point" he said. "See the lights. See the moon come up."

She straightened, turning. She looked at him with a little smile.

"All right" she said.

"Well?" he asked.

"Well what?"

"Reckon you might come along with me?"

She smiled the broader then. It was not a derisive smile, not a superior smile, but she did shake her head in affected sadness.

"Habakkuk, if you were going to ask me to walk out with you, why didn't you say so right off? Why do you come here and slip all cater-corner around it?"

He said "Well."

Impulsively she laid a hand on his forearm, which made him jumpy.

"I just wondered why you think you have to be *sideways* like that with me, that's all" she said. "I'd admire to walk out to the tip of the Point with you, Hab. It's going to be a mighty fine night. But I promised Mrs Robinson to do through these apples. Fifteen-twenty minutes maybe. You didn't eat much chowder."

"No."

"You go ahead, Hab. I'll meet you out there."

He nodded and moved off, at once happy and ill at ease. She could make him feel so tiny sometimes, and yet she was kind to him. He really didn't know much about her—that is, about the way she was thinking. He had no idea what she would answer when he proposed to her. He was prepared for a refusal; for after all, his common sense told him that Deliverance could do better, even right here in Stonington, than an apprentice with no land and very little savings.

On the other hand, if he wasn't rich, why, neither was anybody else, really, here on the Point. It wasn't a place that developed rich men, like Boston, like Newport with its monstrous slave trade, like New York or Philadelphia. He didn't think that Deliverance was one to haggle over a few dollars, more or less. There was the possibility too that she might fancy him a heap. She'd been smiling at him more warmly these days. And even if she refused she'd do so gently. Hab was not afraid of being laughed at.

Hands in pockets, he loafed over to the fire. He was uncertain whether he would propose tonight after all, and decided to wait and see how she treated him when she joined him. *He* knew what *he* was after, all the time; but Deliverance might not be set yet in her mind, and he didn't want to hurry or jostle her. He stood sniffing the smells that slipped under the edges of the sail. There wasn't much of them, which made them the more tantalizing. They gave such a mite—but promised such a glory-be! Each wisp of steam, before it evaporated, told eager noses about all that Indian corn, all those lobsters, and the fish, and the savory, every morsel of it permeated by the delicate odor of baking clams; for a miracle was happening beneath that sail, which strained like a tent in a wind, where under the pressure of the steam each kind of food was giving to each of the other kinds a hint, a suggestion of its own taste, while keeping its essence to itself. The sail bellied tighter than ever, tugging at its moorings. *"She's a-blowin'!"* Hab with others leapt to the breach and caught the loosened flapping corner of sail, which lashed savagely this way and that. It was sailorman's work, really, in a way; though sailormen were not customarily obliged to face steam. For the steam, too long imprisoned, was pouring out, and it was impossible to hold the struggling canvas-corner for more than a moment. Faces turned away, using now this hand and now that, screeching in pain and excitement, somewhat like the gulls above, they fought the sail back to the earth and piled additional rocks upon it. There were always plenty of rocks around.

Hab stepped back, running his hands through his hair, and laughed, partly from excitement, partly from sheer pleasure. The steam billowed and swirled, rising, uptwisting, and the odor of it was unbelievably good. The gulls, annoyed, ee-ee-ee'd huffily and swooped and soared away. This was just as well. It was time they were going anyway; for night was coming, rinsing the dregs of sunshine, and the shadows had grown so long that they were running into one another to make everything dim. The birds ee-ee-ee'd off, then, and no doubt found those night resting-places gulls do find, on sloping rocks whitened with brine, on sandy shingles protected by some reef where the shush of the sea was soft.

Hab glanced over toward the tables, but Deliverance was still slicing apples, so he walked out toward the end of the Point himself, stepping carefully from rock to rock. This was good: to feel the wind in his hair, to hear the slap of wavelets on the rocks and the low gurgly shoo-oo they made when they tumbled back into place for another small rush, and to watch the lights go on. For there were lights now, now that Americans were permitted to deal with one another again and sailing a ship was no longer a crime. Stopping in his walk, standing erect at the very end of the Point, Hab could lift his head and see the pinspeck on Little Gull, the quick jumpy blink of Watch Hill, even the new light they'd just built 'way out on Block Island: he couldn't see Block Island itself, not at this hour, but he could see the light as it started its night's work. He was pleased by that. Someday they'd have a lighthouse right here, maybe, right where he stood. They could use one here. A sailing man can't get too much guidance. There ought to be a lot of lights, and maybe there would be from now on, now that politicians had stopped saying no all the time and had started to try to help. Seemed as if anybody, no matter what political ideas they had, ought to approve of lighthouses. A lighthouse didn't ask where you came from or where you were going to or what you were carrying or why. It just told you where you were. You might be a federalist or a republican-democrat or even an old-fashioned Tory who believed in a king; you might be a Chinaman or a Greek; it still didn't do anybody any harm to let you find out where you were.

" 'Scuse me, Mister Jones."

This unexpectedly was the negro boy, a Jamaican, who worked for Oliver York. A ship had brought him only a few months ago, and supposedly he was a slave: even Oliver York himself wasn't sure of this. He was a serious quiet lad with a low respectful voice. He was hatless here, but he touched the place where his hat would have been had he been wearing one. He spoke in a queer grave accent which was almost courtly and which was unlike anything Hab had ever heard before.

"What is it?"

"Gentleman at the public house, Mr Jones, sir, says he would like very much to converse with you. Sailing man, sir. An officer. From this new schooner."

Hab frowned a little, turning, looking back along the Point. Even here he could sniff the steam and he could see men clustered around the straining piping canvas. Deliverance would be coming soon. She'd promised to.

It was going to feel fine to stand here on such a night and gaze out over the water, watching the moon rise, and propose marriage to Deliverance. For he had about made up his mind that he would ask her the question tonight, provided everything went well. She wouldn't be astounded. If he didn't ask her tonight he'd ask her soon. She knew that. Everybody knew it—just about everybody in town, he reckoned.

"If he wants to see me he can come here."

"Yes, sir. I shall convey that suggestion to him, sir. Thank you, sir."

"You're welcome" said Hab, and turned back to the sound.

There was nothing remarkable in this. Habakkuk Jones at seventeen was much pointed out. Now that ships could come and go more or less as they pleased instead of picking the worst possible times, and now that the lights were operating again, his services as a pilot were not much in demand. Still, seafaring men, and especially officers, had got into the habit of approaching him obliquely, surreptitiously. The federal government, with a rush of good sense to the head, after the near-lynching had transferred Lieutenant Ferguson to another, equally responsible post; and this was wise, for the man was hotheaded, and a foreigner, came from New Jersey, and he never had been able to get on with the folks along the Connecticut shore. While the Embargo had lasted after that the new local head of the revenue marine, a Providence man, had been almost as strict and conscientious as Ferguson, though he'd been by no means as offensive. The popular story—which was not at all true—had it that Ferguson had been removed because the blockade-running exploits of Habakkuk Jones had made a fool of him and of his democratic backers. Hab then was a hero, especially among newcomers and among Pointers who returned after a long absence. His fame had traveled far. They talked about him—not exclusively, or even much, but sometimes—in the smoky cafés of Lisbon, in Santiago-de-Cuba, in low hot moist New Orleans, along the waterfront of Philadelphia, off the Grand Banks, in New York, in Nassau, in the sealskinners' camps of Patagonia. It was not unusual for a foreigner or a returning native to ask to meet him. This officer might have been either. The Jamaican hadn't known him; but then the Jamaican had only been here a few months.

Even though the Embargo Act was a thing of the past there were always men who supposed that Habakkuk Jones might be talked into participating in other illegal activities. His services as a pilot had sold much higher just before the end, going up as high as ten dollars a night, and it was popularly supposed that he had hundreds and maybe even thousands of dollars hidden away and was only waiting to find the right shady deal to invest in. Naturally those whispers brought him strange callers.

Another thing. Maritime Connecticut appeared to have gone speed-mad. Will she sail well? they used to ask. Will she take anything? Does she handle easily? Now all they asked was: How fast will she go? For all the violations of the Embargo Act there were still high piles of cargo in the warehouses of all the coastal cities, there was still in the sugar islands a loud continuous demand for flour, lumber, horses, dried beef, salt fish. The skipper of the vessel that got there first was the skipper who named his price. What's more, most owners were expecting war with France at any time, or maybe even with England, and had plans to convert their vessels into privateers. More than anything else what a privateer needed was speed. The Watts yard had a reputation for building fast vessels. No matter what their size, no matter what their rig, if they came off the ways in Stonington they were knots speedier than anything else of their class. So men said anyway, whether they were right or wrong. It was known too that the Watts yard already had taken contracts for the building of ships two-three years in advance and wouldn't consider another order. Now Hab Jones wasn't anything of the sort but it was believed by many that he was the unofficial superintendent of the yard. All he was, really, was an apprentice; but that he had far more skill than most apprentices, that he'd had as much experience as some master builders, was generally acknowledged. When Judge Watts was in Hartford attending the sessions of the Legislature, as he so often was these days, Hab Jones the apprentice was perhaps the real superintendent. He had the prestige of a crown prince, an heir apparent. It was believed that Judge Watts would formally and legally adopt him someday, and that even if he didn't he would leave him the shipyard or a sizable share of it. Even if *this* didn't happen, they whispered, Hab might still marry the plant. In consequence when they wanted to get something in a business way out of the superintendent of the yard, or in a political way out of its owner, it was to Hab Jones that they went first. It didn't make any difference how many times he told them that he could not help them: they kept coming back.

Now he stood watching the moon rise, watching the lights come on, and enjoying the wind in his hair while he waited for Deliverance. He supposed that he should resent those lights, but instead he welcomed them. It was better this way. Once taking out ships had been fun, when he'd had John Rellison with him, and when good old Red Ferguson was there to give them a chase; but it was nothing but work now. And he had enough work in the shipyard. Even now, even with the days getting longer, he was through breakfast and down to the yard by dawn, and all candles were lighted before he got home to wash up before supper. It was understood between him and the judge that any money he made from piloting was his own; but he knew he couldn't do both jobs, not the way work was at the yard these days. He was strong, but not that strong. It would not be fair to the judge for Hab to drag around groggy all day, like a man with a hangover, dropping things. So he never took a pilotage job now unless it was an emergency or to help a friend.

Let the lights come on! That was fine. There should be more of them. He drew a deep easy breath, his legs spread wide apart. He stretched his arms high and stiff.

"Uh—Hab——"

He turned, knowing that it was John Rellison even before he saw him. Under the black varnished hat the face was not clear, but it was John all right.

"Oh."

They stood looking at one another, and after a while John asked if he was all right, and Hab said he reckoned he was.

"And you?"

"Never better!"

"That's good. I—uh—I've saved all your money, same place we had it before. You can take it any time you want it."

"That's good. That's fine."

Then Hab reached forward, his fingers moving, and clutched his friend, and John slid his arms around Hab's shoulders, and they both cried for a little while. With the moon coming up they stood there crying like a couple of women.

66

When they backed away from each other they had turned around. Hab noticed that there was rum on John's breath. Hab grinned.

"You came just the right time. We're having the biggest clambake anybody can ever remember. The judge'll be tickled to death. Why didn't you go to him first, John?"

John shrugged. He was a mite taller and certainly he stood straighter, stood firmer, his feet spread apart; but he had a singular trick, and a new one, of not looking straight at Hab. He shrugged a lot too, like this. He spread his hands, and shook his head, and in the moonlight Hab saw with amazement that there were rings in his ears, gold rings that swung back and forth.

"Thought it might be best to see you first. Didn't know how the old man——"

"Why, he's going to be the happiest person in the world! He's going to—— He's going to blubber and weep, I swum, just the way I was doing there myself a little while ago."

John smiled in embarrassment, moving his head to one side. They had turned after their embrace, so that now John faced down the Point. His head steadied, his eyes grew large and bright. He put his varnished hat back on, and smiled, and stepped around Hab. Hab turned.

Deliverance was coming toward them, picking her way carefully among jagged rocks. She wore a white dress and looked white as an angel in the moonlight.

Far overhead a gull screeched very thin and high, and it seemed frantic, lost, seeking its fellows.

John Rellison swept his hat off and bowed a deep fancy bow, his left hand on his hip.

"Evening, Miss Deliverance. May I be allowed to remark that you look lovelier than ever?"

She looked up, stopping. Hab saw her sway. There was no expression on her face, no horror or joy, not even recognition. The voice had stunned her before she saw the face.

Her knees gave, and she pitched forward in a dead faint.

. 9 . . .

THE JUDGE UTTERED NO REPROACH. THAT HE WAS GLAD to see John again was plain, and he said as much, though he didn't go on and on about it. Waving toward the piled food, from which they were beginning to peel off the tarpaulin: "We don't happen to have a fatted calf a-cooking, John, but we do have some mighty delicious clams!"

His hand trembled; but it often trembled these days anyway. The little blue lines on either side of his neck leapt wildly: this was the only real sign of his excitement Hab could see. The judge pushed John gently to the bench at his side.

"Sit you down, sit you down. No, no explanations now! This is no time for exclamations. This is a time for eating."

Thus he was jovial, in a restrained way. He summoned Hab.

"You on my other side, Habakkuk. I'm sure you're just as eager as I am to hear where John has been and what he's seen, but that can wait —and clams can't."

Mrs Watts made a considerable fuss about the prodigal. She wept, she threw her arms around him. Everybody smiled uncomfortably. The emotion was too noisy, the tears too big and bright, to appear authentic; but it was the accepted thing, in the judge's presence at least, to treat Mrs Watts and to speak of her as though she was a perfectly normal woman. After a while, very tenderly, the judge shooed her away.

"What about Deliverance?" He peered among the hurrying women. "You'll be wanting to say hello to her, John."

"I met her, coming here, sir."

"Oh . . . Well, sit down. You sit down on this side, Habakkuk."

Hab would have preferred to go to Deliverance, at least be near her, and watch her, and be ready. This was foolishness! Deliverance was all right now. She had not hurt herself, only a few bruises. She hadn't been long in the faint; and when she came out of it she made them promise never to tell anybody. At no time had she wept; so that now, as she threw herself back into the work of preparing food and serving it, if a bit dazed, and utterly silent, she was smooth-faced, clear-eyed. Nobody ever expected Deliverance to say much anyway.

Men came over and shook John's hand. Men and boys both, but

68

mostly men. They treated him like a grownup. They clapped his back. They asked him questions which fell into two classes: one, where had he been and what had he done? two, what was the latest price for herring, mackerel, flour, in Surinam, Havana, Montego Bay? and especially what could you get for lumber there? and what did you have to pay for molasses? for coffee? for rum? To the price questions he had prompt answers in detail. To the other questions, those about himself, he'd reply, with his old-time laugh: "Oh, everywhere . . . everything." Yes, he still had that laugh. He could look right at a man, and smile or laugh, and make that man feel happy; but a moment later John would be looking the other way.

He had changed ships several times. He wouldn't say why, but he intimated that it was to better his condition. On this schooner here now, Northern Constellation, he was third mate.

Somebody opened a bottle of rum and shoved it across the table.

"Drink to your return, John?"

"Thankee." John lifted the bottle, but he swiveled his eyes toward Judge Watts. "You have some, sir?"

The judge shook his head.

"Oh, I'm sorry, Judge!" cried the man who owned the bottle. "So stewed up about seeing young Rellison here again——"

"That's all right. I just don't like it with clams. Spoils the taste."

John, however, took a hearty gulp and bobbed his head.

The clams came then, great toppling basinfuls of them, and the men began to eat. Nobody called on anybody else for a while, nor slapped anybody's back, and there wasn't a conversation. Once Hab overheard John whisper to Judge Watts that he would like to talk to him about buying himself free. The judge almost frowned, though he did not look up from his basin.

"Time enough tomorrow" he whispered.

"I've got a certain amount of money now, sir, and if you'll——"

"Tomorrow."

It was odd to bring up a thing like that at a clambake, Hab thought. Hab himself throbbed inwardly with excitement; and though he was not at all sick, and though the clams were perfectly done, at first he could not eat more than thirty or forty of them. He was fretted; for this might draw attention to him—that is, draw attention away from John on this very night of his return, which would not be fair. He went light on the corn and lobster and fish and bread and potatoes and apple pie, since nobody ever noticed how much of that stuff you ate anyway; and this permitted him to accept another basin of clams.

After a while men began drifting or in some cases staggering back to this table. John Rellison had always been popular, with his quick flash of teeth and his ready answers, and he was popular now; though it was noteworthy—and Judge Watts noted it too, as Hab saw by his profile—

that many of them could hardly wait to get out their questions about prices in the sugar islands.

Indeed Hab was disappointed, as he realized slowly throughout the bake, and as he sensed that Judge Watts was, in the smallness of the stir created by his friend's return. To *them* it was a great and exhilarating event, and it caught at their throats and filled their chests, making them dizzy and weak. Others didn't take it that way. Folks were polite; but the men seemed too much interested in prices, and the women in seeing that everybody had enough to eat, to make much fuss about another boy back.

For after all, here in Stonington what was there so extraordinary about a lad of sixteen sailing away on no notice and returning, a mate, thirteen months later? They were doing that all the time. Still, Hab resented their comparative lack of interest. He wished that he could be alone with John. No, first he wished that the four of them could be alone with John, just the family, at home. He ate his clams hastily, scarcely savoring them, chucking the shells impatiently aside, as though he thought such speed would end the bake the earlier.

It came to him with a start, after a while, that to a good many of the feasters, to most of those from nearby farms and villages indeed, not John but he himself, Habakkuk Jones, was the chief attraction—after, of course, the clams. Group after group of Pointers escorting kinsfolk or friends from upstate or from some town further along the shore approached this table with corner-of-the-mouth talk, and Hab was surreptitiously pointed out. They greeted the judge, these Pointers, and introduced him to their friends or relations, as they greeted Hab and John, and they congratulated John on his return; but the fact remained that Hab was the reason why they had come to this table. A pity, he thought. This night should be John's. It was John who'd come back. All Hab had ever done was stay home.

Not that John Rellison chewed his nails in a corner! He put his forearms on the table, palms flat down, and laughed at everything that was said, throwing his head back, showing his teeth. He did look older, yes, though he was still boyish; but then, Hab reflected, maybe I look some older myself? No, John wasn't suffering from neglect. If he overheard or guessed the whispers about Hab, he gave no sign of this. He was in fact having one hell of a good time. He answered questions heartily, if evasively—excepting the price questions, and his answers to those were glib and unhesitating: he gave the impression that he had an immense store of trading statistics tucked away in his memory, and he was not a whit secretive about them.

He was thin in the face, though he looked a trifle fuller across the shoulders. His chest too might have been a touch deeper. Certainly his hair, blue-black in the lamplight, was longer, finer, thicker than ever. Running fingers absently through his own disobedient red locks, which went every-which-way and in fact refused ever to go anywhere else, Hab envied his friend that hair. It looked as if John brushed it nightly for a long while, and from time to time rubbed pomade into it. It was perfectly straight. It was clubbed in a neat plain blue silk sack, which was jerked back and forth as John swiftly, with the abrupt small movements of a bird, turned his head this way and that. His varnished hat was on the ground under the bench. He was something to look at, for he wore a blue and white striped jersey, a short blue roundabout jacket, flaring trousers, and varnished black shoes with silver buckles. When he threw his head back to laugh his teeth shone strong and fine, and the rings in his ears swung brightly.

Though through most of the talk John kept his glance skittering back and forth, never holding anybody's gaze for more than an instant, as a man might juggle from hand to hand a potato that was too hot for him to hold, on three occasions he deliberately leaned past Judge Watts and looked right at Hab, smiling his old straight warm smile. "D'ye remember, Hab, the night we——" Each time this happened Hab Jones's heart curled up in a hot tight quivering knot, and his eyes misted.

Inevitably the story about Joey Bludge and the night of the fracas came out. It was news to John, who put back his head and fairly bellowed in delight when he learned about the discomfiture of Red Ferguson. Four or five men told the story, breaking in on one another, sometimes two or even three of them talking at once, and they told it with more verve than accuracy. They made it funny, they made it exciting; but they didn't worry overmuch about the truth. It was more than a year since the lynching party had assembled; and though everybody present insisted that he remembered it as though it had happened last night, in fact he remembered, or believed that he remembered, something that had never happened. They were ashamed of that party. Proposing to break the law was not a matter which would have caused any one of them to hang his head; but a public display of passion, a leaving-taking, however brief, of all common sense—this was something else again. Because they were ashamed of the affair, but at the same time couldn't forget it, they tried to make it seem farcical. It got more so with each telling, and this night's was the worst Hab had ever heard. They *believed* this, the tale they told! They were certain of the details, even more certain of the spirit in which they had gone forth that night. By this time they had forgotten how they'd really felt. It may be that Joey Bludge had not forgotten; but who cared about Joey Bludge?

Hab had not forgotten either, and he squirmed in his seat, wishing that he had the ability to break forth with the truth and to make them believe it—or at least the courage to try to do so. This farce-version, which John was hearing, had it of course that nobody had ever really thought of hanging anybody; and because of this it took all the nobility and heroism out of Judge Watts's resistance. The judge had done a highly courageous deed that night, and Hab wished that he could shout this fact aloud. It was all very well for them to say now that they hadn't meant business, but Hab wasn't likely soon to forget the brightness of cruelty in their faces when they closed in on the miserable bundle that was Joey Bludge. It took courage to stand against that impulse, as the judge had done.

As it was, as they told it, Judge Watts was scarcely mentioned, Joey Bludge was the butt of an extravagant and hilarious practical joke, while Hab, because of Ferguson's subsequent transfer, was the hero.

"That wasn't it" Hab struggled to say. "He would have been shifted anyway. He was so unpopular nobody dared to be an informer for him, and so how could he hope to enforce that law? That's why he was transferred! He was too honest! I didn't like him, but that's the truth."

But nobody paid attention. They were finishing their favorite story, the Point's favorite story, and they roared with laughter.

John Rellison laughed too, but he looked at Hab in a new way. Nobody ever suggested that anything John had done had helped to bring about the removal of Red Ferguson. That's the way it was, that's the way people made up things and believed them. It wasn't Hab's fault.

Though he laughed so well, at least for the moment John Rellison was not happy.

When the laughter had subsided and bottles had been shared, John pointed to himself, stabbing a dramatic forefinger at his own chest.

"And now what about *me?* From what you tell me there's still a warrant out for *my* arrest. Maybe I'd better go scramble back on that ship out there and cut for some place where there ain't so many Jeffersonians!"

They laughed—lightly, though, this time, pooh-poohingly. He needn't worry. The Embargo Act was a dead letter, and nobody, not even a Washington appointee, would be so rash as to poke up an old charge at this stage of the game.

"And Hab?" He leaned over and looked at Hab. His smile was quizzical; and as a man who has met many he spoke lightly of a danger he had missed. "I can't yet understand why they didn't clap you in irons."

Judge Watts inclined his head to Hab.

"Explain it to him."

They all beamed on Hab, for they knew the little piece he would speak and they never tired of it. There were more listeners now, many of them women, who had finished with the basins and things. Hab made his voice parrotlike, mincing, and he rolled up his eyes.

"Well now, it seems this Lieutenant Ferguson of the United States Treasury Department revenue marine service, he swears out this warrant charging that to the best of his information and belief one Habakkuk Jones, apprentice, of the village of Stonington, Town of Stonington, County of New London, State of Connecticut, together with one John Rellison, apprentice, of the village of Stonington, Town of Stonington, County of New London, State of Connecticut——"

"U.S.A.?" somebody asked.

"U.S.A.," Hab went on, "did willfully and deliberately and with malice aforethought conspire and devise together to violate the second section of Chapter vee of the laws of the United States as passed by the first session of the Tenth Congress of the said United States, namely and to wit: 'An Act laying an Embargo on all ships and vessels in the ports and harbors of the United States,' the third section of Chapter vee-eye-eye-eye, namely, 'An Act supplementary to the act entitled "An Act laying an Embargo on all ships and vessels in the ports and harbors of the United States,"' section three of Chapter Ex-ex-ex, namely, 'An Act for extending the terms of credit on revenue bonds in certain cases and for other purposes,' section four of Chapter ex-ex-ex-eye-eye-eye, namely, 'An Act in addition to the act entitled "An Act supplementary to the act entitled 'An Act laying an Embargo on all ships and vessels in the ports and harbors of the United States,'"' and sections one and two of Chapter el-ex-vee-eye, namely and to wit: 'An Act in addition to the act entitled "An Act laying an Embargo on all ships and vessels in the ports and harbors of the United States" and the several acts supplementary thereto, and for other purposes.' Have I left any out, sir?"

"Not yet" the judge said gravely.

"And also sections one, two, seven, and eleven, of Chapter el-ex-ex-eye-eye of the laws of the United States of America as passed by the *second* session of the Tenth Congress of the said United States, namely and to wit: 'An Act to enforce and make more effectual an act entitled "An Act laying an Embargo on all ships and vessels in the ports and harbors of the United States" and the several acts supplementary thereto.'"

He breathed again.

"My, my" said John, smiling. "I should think they'd at least *hang* you for all that, Hab."

"Maybe they meant to. Judge Watts here, he let them go quite a ways. They were picking a federal grand jury, and they actually had me travel all the way to Mystic to stand up in front of the United States Commissioner there. Oh, Judge Watts he let 'em go as far as he thought safe! Then when they got me up before that commissioner, Judge Watts steps forward and points out that John Rellison, apprentice, of the village of Stonington, Town of Stonington, County of New London, State of Connecticut, U.S.A., wasn't present. He didn't know where you were, and neither did anybody else. Well—you see?"

"No."

"Red Ferguson, when he swore out the warrant, didn't believe you weren't around somewhere. He thought Judge Watts was hiding you, the way he sent me back to the white-oak stand, and he made out the warrant against both of us. He didn't charge me with violating section so-and-so of chapter this-and-that and all the rest of it: he charged *both* of us with *conspiring* to violate all those sections. Well, there you are." He touched his chest with the tips of his fingers, his thumbs raised high. "I couldn't conspire all alone with *myself* to violate even one section of just one law, much less that many, now could I?"

After the laugh—for they loved this finale—John shook his head.

"But why couldn't——"

"They could, sure! They could wait for you to come back, if you ever did," Hab added, and swallowed hard at the thought, "and then arrest you, if they had the warrant right here, and then arrest me again, and then get Red Ferguson back up here from wherever he is down south, and then get the two of us before that same United States Commissioner and start the whole rigamarole over again. The law allows it, the repealer last month. Section twelve specifically applies to such cases. But Judge Watts here, he told 'em that if they did that he'd argue that I had been put in double jeopardy or something like that, and he'd already made such fools of them that I guess they decided the best thing to do was try to forget the whole business. They must have known that they didn't have a chance in the world to get a jury anywhere around here to convict in a case like that anyway. See?"

"I see now" said John. "Another thing I see is that you've been studying law."

"Just that one case," and Hab grinned. "Too busy for any more. Too busy building ships to even have time to recite all those laws much less conspire to violate them again."

They rose, pushing the benches back, loosening their belts, and John took a final pull at a bottle somebody had left. Hab Jones went to look for Deliverance, whom he found apart from the other womenfolk and staring out over a breath-takingly lovely, moonlit sound. She looked very pale, but calm. She wasn't scowling or anything. He touched her elbow.

"Are you all right?"

"Of course I'm all right" she said rudely.

"Well, that's good. I just wanted to know. We—uh—— We're going home now."

She turned and strode past him without a word.

Well, certainly at home John Rellison played no second fiddle. There was chill in the night air, and Hab went out back for an armful of wood and started a blaze in the fireplace, and all this while, and for more than two hours afterward, John talked.

The odd thing was that he didn't say anything. He spread his hands, showed his teeth, threw up his chin. He answered the questions put to him with apparent candor; but his hearers didn't know what he meant. He described vividly ports he had visited, and all but made his listeners smell those far places and sink under their heat and feel their dust and the dazzle of their color against throbbing eyeballs; but he never told in what *order* he had visited these cities, nor what vessel he was with at the time and in what capacity. It seemed that he had served on no less than four different vessels. He named them readily enough, named their skippers, mentioned meeting a Pointer here and there, but he never did explain why he had left the Good Harvest in the first place, nor where nor in what capacity he had served on that vessel. When Judge Watts asked him whether he had endeavored to take any criminal action against Captain Wilson—charging abduction, say, since the crime had occurred inside the three-mile limit—John laughed and shrugged his shoulders: he was quick to shrug his shoulders these days. "I knew better than to try that" he said, and immediately started to describe Spanish Town.

Mrs Watts sat beside him, staring up at him adoringly. She was very short, a dumpy woman. Judge Watts looked into the fire. Deliverance sat a little back, saying nothing. Hab went out for more wood.

"Well," the judge said at last, and they all knew that he was announcing the end of the conversation, "for all we know now, it may have done you good after all, eh, John?"

"Why, uh, yes, sir."

The judge went out back to relieve himself, and the womenfolk went into the kitchen to fetch cider and doughnuts, and John looked at Hab and chuckled. John felt good now. He liked attention.

"Say, it must be worse than ever here."

"I find things to do."

"All the same, I'll bet you miss Red Ferguson."

"Well, yes, I do, I suppose. But I'm so busy—— Look: if you want to come upstairs with me now I'll get you that money."

"Fine! I've got a heap," he touched his chest, causing coins in a bag under his shirt to clink, "but it never does any harm to have a little more. I'm thinking of taking a few shares in the next voyage, besides my lay as mate."

Hab opened his eyes a little, but he said nothing. They went up to his room, the room he had shared with John Rellison for four years, and while Hab got out the money John stood in the middle of the room, fists on hips, and looked around; he nodded whimsically.

"Same old place!"

"Yes" said Hab. "Well,'here's the money, just the way you left it. I guess the judge is going to call prayers any minute now. Don't you want to get your bag or chest or whatever it is up here first?"

"No. That stays on the ship. The way I do."

Hab only nodded, though he might have sighed a little inside. He picked up the candle.

"Better break that easy to the judge."

"Oh, I will."

Over the cider and doughnuts the prodigal explained that as youngest officer it was his duty to stay aboard the ship at night. He wished it wasn't so, he said. He took a sip of cider, and when he saw that nobody else was looking at him he made a wry face at Hab. He said that that was what he had to pay for being an officer now. He said he didn't know how long this would last. Not very long, he hoped. Mrs Watts cried a little at the thought of John being so near and yet not sleeping under their roof, but the judge said nothing.

After prayers John said good night to each of them, and he kissed Mrs Watts. There was a glint of moisture in his eyes. He turned and went very swiftly, as though saying good night was too painful to be prolonged. The judge shook his head, and closed the door and bolted it and then closed the back door and bolted it. Both doors had ponderous bolts which always made a noise. The rumble and clack of them each night as the judge ceremoniously shut them formed as solemn and steadfast a part of the household routine as the call to dinner, as evening prayers.

They said good night, and that was all, before they went upstairs.

From his window Hab saw John Rellison going down the hill toward the village. His arms swung free and brave, and the moon smashed into a million diamonds upon his hat. His step had spring, his head was up. Wherever he was going, he was in a hurry to get there.

. 10 . . .

WHATEVER JOHN'S DUTIES IN THE DAYTIME, THEY DID not confine him to the schooner. He was in the village, at the yard, at the house, talking and laughing, spinning a might of yarn. He would not only talk with a person but he'd work at the same time, doing his share and maybe a mite more. But he wouldn't stay. Soon he'd be off somewhere else. He was a great one for getting around.

The Northern Constellation—it hailed from Newport—had put into Stonington partly in order to pick up any available cargo, chiefly in order to get its masts restepped in the hope of developing more speed. It needed no careening, and the restepping job was one the Watts yard could have done quickly and well. Judge Watts, however, refused to give this job preference, even when the skipper, one Northrup, through his third mate John Rellison, offered three times what the work would ordinarily cost. The judge had his previous commitments. The Northern Constellation, if he handled it, would have to wait its turn. The skipper fumed; but John was not astonished. John was careful not to press the old man too hard. Give him the impression that you were trying to bribe him, and the judge might fly into a rage and refuse to touch your work for all the money in the world.

So the Constellation, after a few days at anchor, came alongside Willison's wharf to have her masts restepped. There was a waiting list at Willison's too, but the waiters went on waiting. The Constellation skipper and crew also waited. They had tolerably good workers at Willison's but they didn't have the equipment the Watts yard had. The loading was finished the first day, and it was no secret that the schooner would clear as soon as they could clear it. The crew was made up largely of Europeans—Englishmen, Scots, Scandinavians—but there were a few Yankees, and these grumped and grumbled because they were so carefully watched, because when permitted to leave the vessel at all they were forbidden to go far from the waterfront. There was no fear that the foreigners at least would desert. They were well aware that American pay—some a.b.s got as much as twenty dollars a month —as well as the food and officer treatment on the worst American ships, was superior to that on the best European vessels. No, they wouldn't desert. But the skipper wanted them handy for a sudden departure.

The third mate himself, however, made little trips to other towns, Mystic, Portersville, Westerly. Once he even went to New London; and on his return he stopped at the yard to chat with his friend Habakkuk Jones.

He talked above the thud of gravers' mauls as they crashed on the wedges, and though this was a familiar sound in a familiar scene, and though as he talked he was helping Hab about his work, he was nevertheless somewhat self-conscious and had difficulty in keeping the pride out of his voice. Neither of them had ever been to New London before, and they had often talked of it. New London and Providence. They had not even dreamed of Boston, Philadelphia, New York; but Providence and New London, and especially New London, had once occupied a great deal of their thoughts. Now John Rellison had been there. Even at home he traveled more than his friend! True, he had been to many distant and colorful cities, cities of glitter and fame; but somehow, just for the moment, it was more important to have been to New London.

"Whatever'd you go for, anyway?"

"Old Judge Haviland's there now. He's a notary. I went to him to get a certificate saying he'd known me all my life and that I was American born. Good thing to have, in case a British warship stops you."

Now Hab knew this. Everybody knew it. England, facing all the might of Napoleon, with most of Europe against her, had a short-handed navy. The more her sailors deserted the more harshly she treated them, and the more harshly she treated them the more they deserted, most of them to take service on American ships. Her right to take them back, even on the high seas, was undisputed; but sometimes, not too choosy, she sucked in an American or two or twenty. That was likely to be the last ever heard of those Americans. To be in the British Navy was to be in a subterranean dungeon. Shore leave was denied. A man might spend years aboard ship, or if he was transferred to another ship it would be under heavy guard. He probably never got his pay, and if he did he gambled it away or lost it or spent it on extra rum rations: British tars didn't have to go ashore to get drunk.

"But you got a certificate only the other day from Judge Watts himself!"

"That's right. And I've got three others from other places too, where I know a magistrate." He took five papers from a pocket and spread them in his hands like playing cards. "No reason why I shouldn't get as many as I can while I'm home. One of them I'll probably keep, matter of fact."

"And what'll you do with the others?"

John opened his eyes wide. There was nothing sly about him.

"Why, sell them, of course! You can always find Britishers who'll give two or three dollars for one, provided they come anywhere near your description—roughly the same height and age and so-forth. They'd have to pay a magistrate ten dollars, and they can't even be sure of getting it then. Some of the magistrates are like Judge Watts here—they won't do it if they don't really know the man, no matter how much they're offered. And there are others who don't like to sign a paper like that when the man they're issuing it to's got such a Cockney accent that you can't even understand him: they think it looks bad."

Hab started to say something, but he forbore. He went back to work. John worked with him, humming.

"So I thought I'd take advantage of being here. Never does any harm to make a little money."

"Thought you said you had plenty of money."

"Well, I have. But it never does any harm to make more. And besides, it's really helping those Englishers. They'd give anything to get out of going back to their own navy and having to fight the French and Dutch and Danes and Spaniards and everybody else, on empty stomachs and striped backs. So it's really doing them a favor."

"I see" said Hab.

He was at all times amazed by John's acceptance of the life at sea. Indeed John not only made no plans to break away from ships but he extolled that career as a great one. This was a new note. Hab and John had always been interested in the sea, even before they ever saw it, and ships, these past five years, had been closer to them and of more immediate concern than trees or food or even people. They never intended to go back to the farm, no matter what; they never meant to get out of sight and sound of the sea; but though they had always planned to sail they'd never talked of sailing away their lives. A few voyages, yes. To see far places, to learn business methods in other countries, to learn too how a ship handled in all weather—this had always been part of their future, as they discussed it. They might make ships, repair them, pilot them, and occasionally sail them for a voyage or two. They might own ships later, whole or in part. They would assuredly keep up a lively interest in all ships and shipping. But it had not occurred to either that he might ever become a professional sailor. The truth is, they had both rather looked down on sailors, as Hab still did. Sailors had always been the scrum of the earth, the great kicked-arounds. They were the restless, the misfits, the drunks and dullards. They were the men who couldn't make a decent living on land and had to be cuffed and beaten into it at sea. They were the forelock touchers, the grovelers. They were underpaid and underfed, and they lived in a crowded sty. When one was lost—and admittedly it was a hazardous occupation—perhaps a few men shrugged, perhaps not. Ashore they were undesirable guests or customers, for they didn't have much and what they did have they spent quickly and noisily. They drank. They quarreled and fought. They were dirty, they were loud. Nobody wanted them, except the tapsters, the prostitutes, and the crimps; and after they'd been stripped nobody wanted them at all. Robbing them was always fair. They had virtually no rights, like ordinary citizens. Most of them were Europeans anyway, but the Yankee sailors had developed an outlandish lingo of their own, forgetting the language they had learned when young; so that if one went inland more than a few miles—the waterfront folks of course were bilingual—he would need an interpreter. Even the officers were not highly thought of—that is, the full-time, professional officers. Even a skipper was not much more, really, than a stagecoach driver with a little extra dignity and responsibility. Sailing a ship was all very well for a while, for a young man who had lots to learn. To make a regular thing of it seemed to Habakkuk Jones weak and perhaps even somewhat shameful. Hab was shocked by the way John talked.

For John loved the sea and he was going to stay on it, he said more than once. He loved sailoring; and he was a good sailor too, he averred with no pretense at modesty. He thought that he was being shrewd by studying navigation. He believed that there was a good future in this profession. He would become a second mate, a first, soon a skipper. They needed Yankee officers. The Britons and Scandinavians were strong and willing and they'd had experience; but they couldn't give orders, they did not know what to do with responsibility, the very thought of which frightened them. A Yank of twenty, who had made a few voyages and kept his eyes and ears open, and who had read a little Bowditch, nine times out of ten would make a better officer than a European salt three times his age who'd been crossing the ocean all his life.

John even went so far as to urge Hab Jones to join him.

"It's no frolic in the forecastle, but I'll be there to see you get special attention. And in no time you'll be a mate yourself. I tell you there's money in it, Hab! We're going to get into the war pretty soon, ain't we? Don't everybody know that? Well, all that needs to be done to the Northern Constellation out there when that happens is to put in at the nearest port and get it pierced for guns. You don't need many. And then a double crew, for manning prizes. And then—— Why, there's thousands in it, Hab!"

Hab shook his head.

"You may be right, but I reckon I'll stay here."

Certainly there was no doubt in John's mind about his own future. He had told Judge Watts about it promptly enough, the very day after his return. The judge had called Hab into the conference, from some sense of justice probably, for Hab hadn't opened his mouth. John had stated simply and in a manly manner that he was sorry he'd gone away so abruptly, that he realized that he was still bound to Judge Watts, to whom he would always be grateful, but that he believed that his life should be spent on the sea, to which he wanted to return. He had pulled a heavy sack of coins from his shirt and offered to pay Judge Watts whatever the judge calculated to be a fair price for the loss of his bounden services while he'd been away and for the five months his servitude still had to go.

The judge had shaken his head. The judge hadn't tried to argue with John. It hurt; but he accepted it with docility.

"No. Put your money away. I'll not hold you to anything. You and Hab have been good boys. Any time you want to go away, either of you, you can do it. And any time you want to come back, you can do that too."

Tears had filled John's eyes, which still were wet when he left with Hab.

"Brimstone! That was right clever of the old man to do that, wasn't it? It was right sweet of him, don't you think?"

"Aye."

"Didn't it knock you all whichways, when you heard him?"

"No."

"He's really a right kind old codger, when you stop to think about it, ain't he?"

"Aye" said Hab.

John somewhat avoided the judge after that—not a difficult feat, since the judge was in Hartford much of the time and a very busy man when he was at home. It was otherwise with Deliverance and with Mrs Watts. John sought them out. He would sit in the kitchen, helping them peel potatoes or what-not, any old chore, and without a thought for his dignity, while he'd talk and talk. He seldom saw Deliverance alone, Hab noted. He seldom had an opportunity. But when Deliverance went to the fields, then John would sit and spin yarn to Mrs Watts, who hung on his every word. John would lounge then, legs outstretched, and twirl his varnished hat on a forefinger so that the ribbon stood out straight as a stick. Now and then he'd take a surreptitious nip of rum, winking at Mrs Watts. But he never stopped talking.

"I declare I thought I'd never get to sleep last night, thinking how close that was that time John almost got et by the monster."

The others gazed in astonishment at her.

"Told me about it yesterday. Didn't he tell you?"

"I don't believe so" Judge Watts said carefully.

Her lips trembled from the force of her earnestness. Her eyes bugged far out. Her hair was all wopsed up, and she hadn't touched her breakfast.

"It was down to a place I can't pronounce the name of, and they had sent a couple of boats ashore. To get water, I think. Anyway they were four-five miles from the beach, and John was in one of them, coming back, and they were going right fast, just a-booming, when all to a sudden this serpent come up out of the water smack in front of them. John says they couldn't stop the boats, they was going so fast. The other boat was a little ahead, and that one crashed right into the serpent, which was rising up out of the water and then going down again in different places. The critter seemed to feel it and get mad, and it turned its head so that the scales sparkled like glass in the sun, John told me, and it snapped up that whole boat and all the men in it. There was four men. They never saw a one of them again.

"John said the serpent was never all out of the water at one time and so of course he couldn't tell how long it was, but he'd be ready to swouch it weren't less'n thirty feet. He said he got a real good look at the head because of his being only about the length of this room away from it. He said it had long saggy greenish whiskers, or at least he thought they were whiskers, though they might have been seaweed clinging to the critter's mouth: it looked something like seaweed, he said. He said there weren't any horns, but the mouth was as big as the whole head and there were three long rows of nasty yellow teeth, every one of them as long as that bread knife. He said he looked right into the mouth, so he ought to know. He says the scales were three-cornered and very big, and some of them were bright red and some were purple but they all glittered like glass and they clacked together when the serpent moved. He said that what it sounded like, like thousands of pieces of glass clacking together. John was in charge of the second boat, and he said that the only reason they got a chance to change their course before the critter could snap them up too was because it seemed to have some trouble with the boat it had already swallowed. Must have stuck in its throat or something. Anyway, John said it thrashed around something fierce, lathering up the water like it was soapsuds. But they stayed afloat all right, thanks to the way John handled it—though he didn't tell me that part—he's a very modest boy, you know—and anyway they started lickety-split for the ship, and the serpent, that had got the other boat all swallowed now, or practically all, he started after them. John said they just barely made it, with only inches to spare. He said he never saw anything move as fast as that serpent. It took great big up-and-down bends, he said, not sideways like a snake on land, and it would be humped up in six or seven places at once, and the parts between those bumps would be under water. He said some of the humps were so big you could've sailed a fair-sized sloop right through them—if the critter'd only hold still long enough. It frighted me, I tell you. All I could do to sleep last night."

Nobody made any comment, and after a while, after looking into each of their faces, Mrs Watts took up her spoon. Hab was furious. He saw the little blue lines on the side of Judge Watts's neck jumping, and he saw from her profile that Deliverance too was sore.

"John said the critter swam after that ship three-four miles but after a while it sank. Strange, ain't it?"

Somebody agreed that it was.

"John says he's a-going to sail away again day after tomorrow. Well,

I worry about him when I think of him in places like that. I'm going to pray for him longer, after this. Maybe we ain't any of us prayed for him enough."

If Judge Watts ever said anything to John about this, Hab didn't learn it. Hab himself meant to speak to John next day, but Deliverance got before him; and when he came back for supper, and saw them returning to the house after what could have been a long walk, he knew from their faces and from the shrieking silence that Deliverance had been giving him what-for. John was uncommonly quiet at that supper. Deliverance was quiet too, but then she usually was.

John sailed next day. They were down at Willison's wharf to see him go, and Mrs Watts gave him a neckpiece she had knitted for him, and Judge Watts gave him a bottle of rum, and Hab gave him a notebook. Deliverance, unexpectedly, gave him a kiss. At any rate, she permitted him to kiss her. It seemed to surprise him as much as it did the rest of them, but Deliverance said nothing and scarcely blushed, only stood there with her eyes downcast. A little later the Northern Constellation sailed.

Hab let a whole month go by then before he proposed marriage to Deliverance Watts. He hoped it might help. The magnolia tree on the front lawn was in blossom by that time, and they sat under that, on a lovely clear afternoon, when he proposed to her; and she refused him.

. 11 . . .

He walked over to the edge of the grass, to the fence, all white and trim, and he reached up and grasped a branch of the magnolia tree and stood there looking down over the harbor where there were three ships loading. He felt bad. His throat was lumped and his eyes were hot. He stood there looking down at those ships, which were each trying to get loaded and get out before the others. Everything was speed these days.

So he wasn't going to have Deliverance? Maybe he had spoken too soon; but probably not: Deliverance wasn't flighty, and when she said a thing she meant it. It was going to be hard, being right in the house with her, seeing her, helping her work, and all the time wanting her so much—and knowing that he'd never get her. It was going to be tarnation hard.

He squeezed the branch and perhaps yanked it a bit, for a dozen blossoms were dislodged and fell turning and twisting like tiny white-and-pink petals, until presently they lay in a prim pattern on the grass at his feet.

"I—I'm sorry, Habakkuk."

"So'm I, I guess."

A breeze picked up the blossoms and spun them in a single sedate circle, and dropped them, bewildered. Hab lifted his head, feeling on his cheek and neck that the wind had changed and was coming from the southwest, which at this time of the year was likely to mean fog, though right now the day was a beauty, the sun bright. Hab did not think this consciously, not being in the least interested in the wind. He did it somewhere in the back of his mind. He couldn't help doing it; he would have done it if he'd been about to die.

In fact he felt like hell, and his eyes stung, and he didn't trust himself to turn. The bay down there, the ships, the men on the wharf, were swimmy and blurred to him. The ground seemed to move a little, not to rock like a boat but to move horizontally back and forth as if he was standing on a board and somebody shoved it away and then pulled it back. He took a firmer grip on the branch over his head.

"I guess it's only fair to tell you why, Habakkuk."

"No, you don't have to. It's because of John."

"Yes," she said quietly there behind him, "it's because of John."

84

"Well, I knew that much. I guess I did. Only thing, I didn't know you loved him so much."

"No, you're wrong there" she said quietly. "I don't love John and I never have."

He didn't spin around. He turned slowly, letting go of the branch but still holding his hand high, so that his palm was outturned as though in a gesture of astonishment. He gawped, dumbfounded. Deliverance made a pretty picture, prinked out in her green homemade drugget, so clean it was shiny, sitting very straight, her back straight, her knees together, feet together, while her hands rested palms-up in her lap. Only her head was averted, and this was unusual with Deliverance, who had a proud way of holding her head ordinarily, as she had a proud way of walking.

"I *thought* I was in love with him, at one time there, but I know now that I was mistaken. I was only a girl then, after all. That was more than a year ago, and I was only sixteen."

"But—but then if——"

Had he said those words, himself? If he had, he couldn't say any more. However, she understood. She didn't raise her head. Her hair was a very soft fluffy light brown, and she had a pile of it, and there in the shade of the magnolia it showed rich and warm with light: a vagrant blossom settled upon it but slithered off when Deliverance, thinking some thought, shook her head.

"Yes, I told you that it was because of John that I can't marry you, and that's right." Her hands began to flutter. "I—I hate to say this, Hab. I hate it so poison much I wouldn't do it for anybody but you. I guess you deserve it, though. I guess you've got a right to know."

"You—*can't*—marry—me?"

He repeated it slowly, for that was as far as he had got. His mind had stopped at that sentence.

"Yes. You see, Hab, back there before he went away, when I was only a girl and sort of giddy, I reckon, I let John do it to me once. I let him have me."

"Oh."

"I was scared, of course," looking at her hands, trying to keep them still. "I knew it meant I might have a baby and in that case I'd have to tell Father and Mother, and John would have to marry me, and I didn't want him to marry me if he didn't want to. He wouldn't talk to me about it. He was scared too, and he wouldn't even talk about it. That's why he ran away, of course. I had a feeling he wasn't going to come back that night. That's why I spoke to you before you went, and that's why I met you when you came back—you coming back alone, no John. I'd had a feeling something like that was going to happen."

She looked at her hands but she no longer tried to control them. She watched their turnings and twisting as though they were things separate from her, say a couple of strange birds feeding on the lawn at her feet.

"Well, I didn't have a baby, and that was God's almighty mercy."

He shivered a little. The breeze was getting chiller, matter of fact. It had a wettish feel on his cheek now.

"When he came back——" She was having a hard time saying this, he could tell from her voice. "When he came back, and when I first saw him there, so sudden, it was such a pain inside me that I couldn't stand it. That was why I fell down, because I was dizzy with the pain. But I got over it, Habakkuk. I still get kind of weak sometimes, when I remember it, but I'm over it all right. John tried to make love to me again, but I wouldn't let him. He even wanted to marry me, this time. But I wouldn't. I don't love him, like I thought I did. Anyway," and for the first time she lifted her head, and her eyes shone, "even if I did love him I wouldn't have a man who'd run away."

Hab nodded. It flabbergasted him to learn not that John had done a thing like that but that he'd done it without him, Hab, knowing it. John must have been almighty scared, to keep it a secret from Hab himself. However, it wasn't of John that he was thinking. That had been a jolt; but he'd take it up properly in his mind later on. He was only thinking of Deliverance now. Looking down over the bay:

"If it hadn't been for that—for what you let John do to you that time—would you have said yes to me just a little while ago?"

She answered promptly, her voice steady again.

"I would have been proud to. You should know that, Habakkuk. I wouldn't have told you what I just did if I didn't—if I didn't feel that way about you. I wouldn't have told anybody else in the world."

He gave a little start, as though stuck by something sharp. He ran fingers through his hair, which seemed to crackle and spit like a cat's.

"Anybody else had asked me to marry them, I'd have simply said no and nothing more. But with you it was different. I reckon you had a right to know why. Naturally no man's going to marry a woman who—who's had somebody do that to her."

Hab ran fingers through his hair again. He still wasn't facing her.

"That might be up to the man to say" he suggested.

After some silence, "You—you don't mean you think you might come to *forget* a thing like that, Hab?"

"No, I don't. Man'd be a fool to try to forget it. But I could promise you never to mention it, not only to anybody else but even to you. I'm pretty good at keeping my mouth shut."

Then he turned, rather briskly, and held his arms out a little.

"Look at here," and he started toward her. "If that's the only thing against us getting married and if *I* don't make any squawk about it I'm danged if I see why *you* should. Kiss me."

Then her eyes abruptly were crowded and overcrowded, and tears as

86

big as tadpoles rolled down her cheeks, and she gave a glad little cry and rose from the bench right into his arms.

He wept too. It felt good; and anyway they were both laughing at the same time. They kissed and kissed, hugging each other, fumbling with each other, laughing and crying and feeling very wonderful and foolish too. This went on for some time. Finally he held her at arm's length for a moment, cocking his head, gazing fondly into her face: he was only a wee bit taller than she was.

"Look at here" he said. "You didn't tell me why if you felt that way about John you went up to him and let him kiss you, that day he sailed."

"I did it just because I *did* feel that way. I wanted to show him I could let him kiss me right before everybody and not get to trembling. I didn't want him to think, when he went away, that he owned me—or even any little part of me. So that's why I did it. And I think it worked."

He shook his head, not comprehending.

She said, "Maybe a man wouldn't understand that. I reckon you'll have a lot of things you'll have to learn about me, Habakkuk."

"I reckon I will."

And they laughed, and came together again for kissing, and tried to sit down on the bench without letting go of one another, so that they almost fell down, jarring the magnolia tree with their shoulders, and a great pink-and-white shower of blossoms fell all around them and on top of them but not in between them, for there wasn't room.

Jonathan Watts was a busy man and a man who liked to see others busy too, for he sometimes remarked that the devil would find work for idle hands. Once its postmaster, he had twice been mayor of Stonington. He had the biggest law business in the eastern end of the county. He was active in the affairs of his fellow war veterans, trying to get them all that was coming to them; but this of course he did without fees. He was a notary public and a justice of the peace. He served on a score of committees, and informally was called upon to settle all manner of neighborly disputes. He did a little trading, he did a little fishing, or had his boys do it, and he saw to it that the womenfolk did not neglect his little farm back of the village. He was financially interested in any number of local and maritime enterprises: probably nobody but himself knew how many. Though his shipyard was his greatest source of revenue he gave it little time, being in fact a land-minded person who never ceased to marvel at Hab's absorption in the building of ships. The judge did a great deal more law business than ship business in his office at the yard, which seemed natural enough to his clients, who, being Pointers, were accustomed to settling their affairs in an atmosphere of spars and sails and planking. The judge had taken over the shipyard for a bad debt, meaning to sell it at the earliest opportunity, and he was always astounded when it made money.

Recently he had been elected to the House of Deputies and he had to spend a lot of time in Hartford, which was a long trip away. He didn't greatly like the work; he had no ambitions politically and was indeed too straightforward and outspoken a man to make a good politician anyway; the coming and going was hard on him, who was no longer young; but he did it because he took it to be his duty. He was always a great one for doing his duty.

He was returning from Hartford this night and would get back the next day. This was the reason why Deliverance and Hab Jones did not immediately announce their intention of getting married. They would have to ask the judge first, of course, and though they had every reason to believe that he would approve the decision they knew how much importance he attached to his dignity as head of the house. Deliverance's mother would probably disapprove; but she wouldn't go contrary to the wishes of her husband, and this was another reason for keeping the understanding a secret until the judge came home.

All the same, it was a hard thing to do. They felt like shouting the news, they felt like singing and dancing and kissing and hugging right in front of everybody. A more observant person than Mrs Watts would have noticed that Hab all but jigged as he brought in stovewood, that Deliverance mixed and stirred rhythmically, humming a gay tune, and that the two of them were always exchanging swift secret smiles. At supper they sat opposite each other, as always, and they didn't dare look up for fear they'd start to beam. They didn't talk much: Mrs Watts did most of the talking. Si Wainwright broke the strain when he appeared unexpectedly and asked if he might see Hab. If it hadn't been for Si even Mrs Watts might have begun to notice that there was something unusual in the air.

He was an old friend, Hab's senior by half a dozen years but very intimate with Hab for all that, perhaps Hab's closest friend after John Rellison. Silas Wainwright had inherited a sizable brig, and since the best way to see that this vessel was operated right appeared to be to operate it himself, he took up sailoring, never, of course, meaning to make a permanent occupation of it. Except when he drank, he was a dour silent cautious young man, a hard one to bargain with, but reliable, a word-keeper. He was smallish and had a rather ratty face, but he did have warm green likable eyes that grinning at you made you forget his thin lips and prematurely yellow teeth.

He and Hab went out front, under the magnolia tree. Hab knew what was coming. Si might as well have made his proposition right there in the kitchen; but like so many other Stonington skippers he was accustomed to whispers when asking Hab to pilot.

"Coming up to fog" he said.

"Figured it would, when the wind shifted this afternoon."

Up here it wasn't bad, though it was damp, but the lights of the village showed fuzzy, and a low slow-writhing mist hung over the bay.

"I aim to go out tonight, Hab, afore those other ships do. Wasn't for the fog I'd take her out myself, but the way it is I'm scared to. You're the only man I'd trust to that, Hab. You do it?"

Hab, elbow in hand, pulled out his lower lip and let it snap back into place. He wasn't pleased. He was tired, though he'd forgotten this fact, and his muscles ached, and he had been looking forward to bed—not to sleep, for he was much too excited to sleep readily tonight, but to stretching out in the darkness and feeling his tiredness course all through him and thinking of Deliverance. He wanted to be fresh when the judge came back and they asked his permission.

"I'd admire a heap to have you. Folks say you get as much as ten dollars for the run nowadays sometimes. Well, I'd pay you that. I'd even pay you more. I'd pay eleven."

"Would you pay twelve?" Hab asked quickly.

"Twelve's a heap, Hab."

"I'm thinking of getting—— Well, anyway, I'm likely to need money soon. I'd want twelve for a night like this, Si."

Si exhaled, and none too graciously thrust his hands a little deeper into his pockets. Hab expected him to refuse. But he didn't.

"Well, if it must be twelve then I reckon it must be twelve. But you will do it, Hab?"

"I reckon."

"We'll be finished loading in another couple of hours. I'd like to clear out right off."

"I'll be down" Hab promised.

He said the prayers, as he always did when Judge Watts was away, and he read from the Book, but he did this at his own place, not at the head of the table where the judge used to sit. It was at his own chair, too, that he knelt. He turned his back to Deliverance so that he wouldn't be tempted to peek between fingers at her. He leaned low on the chair.

He locked front door and back door, making noise. He felt a little guilty doing this, the same as he'd felt when he read from the Book, as though it might be thought that he was trying to set himself up as another Jonathan Watts. But somebody had to do it.

He said good night gravely and without expression, got in one swift merry smile-exchange with Deliverance, and went upstairs to his room. He even moved around, making the sounds of a man undressing, before he lay down, fully clothed, to wait. This was silly; yet somehow it seemed right, like some ancient ceremony which, though it had lost its significance, retains a sentimental value. It was silly because both Deliverance and Mrs Watts knew perfectly well that he was going to pilot Si Wainwright's brig out past Montauk tonight. Nobody had *said* this at the table, but what else had Si come for? All the same, this was the way it was done. What's more, he would go out by way of the same old window too—though there was more sense here, since the opening of either door might wake the womenfolks up.

He lay thinking about things and being very happy. Happiness fairly surged through him, up and down, as if it was his blood.

He prayed a little.

The clock in the steeple struck nine.

He went downstairs without a sound. He was a cat for quietness in any clothes, on any sort of night, when he started out for a job of pilotage or when he returned. Deliverance had not made any sound either, when she came down. She was waiting for him at the window.

"A good wife should always kiss her husband good-by, even when he's only going for a little while" she whispered. "I'm practicing to be a good wife."

"You'll be the most wonderful wife in the world!"

A little later, half disengaging herself, she looked up at him—he could scarcely see her, it was so dark—and her whisper was even lower than before.

"Habakkuk, you really do mean it when you say you want me even after what I told you, don't you?"

"What?" he asked.

"Why, what I told you about John and me."

"What?" he asked.

She smiled then, closing her eyes.

"All right" she whispered. "Kiss me, Habakkuk."

He did kiss her, several times, at considerable length. Not until the clock in the steeple struck the quarter did he release her. He hurried out of the window without looking back. He didn't even close the window. He left that for her to do.

It was foggy sure enough, foggy as all-get-out, even up here where fog seldom reached. It had only recently invaded these precincts, it was still capturing articles. At a tree, for instance, it would fall back upon itself as though in bafflement; but in a moment it would slither in again, slide cautious clammy fingers around both sides of the tree, and then, having blotted the base from sight, writhe on. When Hab walked his legs created small sluggish whirlpools of fog.

Si's brig, the Horace T. Wainwright, was alongside the dock at Willison's, but Hab sailed there in the Deliverance quite as though the vessel had been anchored offshore. He had to have the dogbody anyway, of course, to get back in.

The fog was low, covering the water like snow covers flat land, and the Deliverance pushed through it like a snowplow pushing through dry snow, piling it to right and left only for a moment, leaving it essentially unchanged. There sometimes came from due north, or from north a bit northeast, an erratic ominous breeze which lifted the fog

90

oddly in streamers, obliterating everything from sight, and then departed, leaving the disturbed fog to settle coil by lazy lacy coil.

Hab had to feel for the rope ladder at the brig's stern. He paintered the Deliverance to this ladder, then climbed to the quarterdeck. Si was waiting for him. They were ready to sail.

A year ago Hab had been taking ships out in every fog that appeared. Skippers then had waited for fog, and even prayed for it, as now they waited for clear weather. All or virtually all of them were smuggling anyway, but they were smuggling only at the other end now, they needed to fear only English and French and Dutch and Spanish warships, besides of course pirates. They no longer needed to fear their own nation's patrol vessels. It might be necessary to sneak into harbor down there, but it was no longer necessary to sneak out of harbor here: they could kiss their wives and wave to their friends and leave like honest men in broad daylight, with pennants flying if they wanted 'em, with music playing. Most skippers, Hab knew, wouldn't have dreamt of going out on a night like this. They'd have waited two, three, four days, a week if need be, for clear weather. Si Wainwright was different. He was eager to make his pile and get out of sailoring and into a respectable profession; and besides he had recently suffered a series of exasperating if unavoidable delays.

Si didn't say much. He stood behind the helmsman and permitted his mate to relay the orders Hab gave. Now and then he'd talk a little about Point folks with Hab; and Hab, knowing that this vessel would be away for months, had difficulty refraining from telling Si about Deliverance; but for the most part it was a silent job. Even when sounds were made, in handling sail, for instance, they had a gruesomely short life. The fog had that quality, that it would gulp any sound almost before it was formed, leaving no echo. Anyway this was a night to inspire silence.

It was quiet work then, and nerve-wracking. Hab Jones, more restless than usual, moved from rail to rail, cocking his head, listening, listening. He had Si post leadsmen in the forward chains, both sides, and he often went forward to confer with them. Now and then he'd look over the taffrail, but he couldn't even see the wake they made, couldn't even see the end of the rope ladder, much less the Deliverance, because of the fog.

He got nervous, was irritable. He had known jobs as hard as this one, but he'd always had John Rellison with him in those days, and John had been the perfect companion, giving him strength just as they'd given each other strength that night of the long swim. Hab moved back and forth, frowning, listening, not often giving orders. Once, sometime after midnight, Si went into his cabin and made up a mug of flip; and that helped to keep Hab alert. He wasn't sleepy but he was very tired. He wasn't as sure of himself as he had been on all previous jobs. He was unaccustomed to this twitchiness. He wondered, was he getting old?

After a long while, though there was still no hint of dawn, he nodded to Si.

"All right, it's yours. You can't see it but," nodding a-starboard, "that's Montaug over there. About six miles, I'd say."

"I'll get your money" said Si, exhaling in relief.

"Yes" said Hab.

Si had to go to his cabin to fetch the cash, which he kept in a good safe place. When he'd returned and given the money to Hab, and Hab had pocketed it carefully, they shook hands, these two friends. Hab wished him a good voyage, a good profitable voyage.

"Strange thing to me, Habakkuk, you don't never want to go on past Montaug some night and keep rolling, the way John Rellison did."

"Maybe I do" Hab said. "But I reckon my place is here."

He leaned over the taffrail and grabbed the rope ladder that trailed astern, and he drew it up toward him. It wasn't until he held the wet end of it that he realized what had happened.

Si Wainwright realized it at the same instant, and bawled for hands, who came running, and set them overside in bosun's chairs to see if by any crazy chance the Deliverance after slipping her painter had caught in the rudder or upon some trailing line. Nothing like that had happened. Nor would there have been the slightest sense in searching for the dogbody, in this fog. It might indeed be near at hand, or it might be 'way back in Stonington harbor. The fog, drifting past, told nothing.

Hab glanced once, wildly, at the moses boat. But Si shook his head.

"I couldn't possibly let you have it. I've only got it and the longboat, and we'll have a heap of offshore work. It ain't as if we were going to some big city, openly, where I could buy another gig."

"I know" said Hab.

He still held the wet end of the ladder.

"No, I reckon you're just going on down to the islands with us."

"I reckon I am" said Hab.

. 12 . . .

Hab awoke feeling that something was wrong. He did not try to sit up, for he knew that he would hit his head. There were the usual snores, and, when he moved, the scuttling sound of cockroaches. The lamp smoked, as always, lending its stink to the steamy stink of wet clothes and of sweaty-wet dirty bodies, and to the stronger harsher stink of bilge. But something . . . The lamp wasn't swinging: that was it! For the first time in three weeks there was no motion in the forecastle. He rose hastily and went up on deck.

The rain had ceased—Hab would have slept on deck but for that rain—and everything was clean and shiny in the dawn. It was good to breathe real air, after the forecastle, where there was no port. It was one of the things he disliked most about life at sea, he had decided: this lack of fresh air. The men who handled sail or held the wheel, *while* they actually performed these duties, were clear enough—unless they happened to be stationed to leeward of one of the great crates of pigs and chickens which cluttered the deck of every outgoing vessel. But you had to sleep below; and there was a lot of work to be done down there too, especially if like Hab you were a carpenter; and below you weren't anywhere able to escape the sickening smell of bilge. The regular ship's carpenter, along with many of the sailors, was seasick most of the time—it had been a rough voyage—and Hab substituted as best he could; and in fact his best was excellent, for while he'd never been to sea before he was familiar with hull and rigging and knew just what to look for and where to look for it. On the brig Horace T. Wainwright what he sought chiefly were leaks. She was an old vessel, crank, not very fast, and she leaked a lot. This gave Si Wainwright particular concern because his cargo was all flour, eight hundred barrels of it. He kept Hab pretty busy, which Hab didn't mind as long as he could come up on deck now and then for a breath of air.

Mr Riley was on the quarterdeck. The mate, a glum lumpy man, very strong, a hard worker, he greeted Hab gravely. Hab's position was a curious one. He wasn't the regular carpenter, hadn't been signed on. He slept in the forecastle, but only because there wasn't a bunk for him aft. He ate with the officers. Nobody sirred or mistered him, nobody touched a forelock to him, but he was generally treated with a good deal of respect. This position troubled him less than it troubled the others; for sailors are conservative men, neat men too—aboard ship, at least—

93

who like things properly labeled and in their right places. However, Hab spoke their language, as of course every Pointer had to; and that helped; and another help was his reputation as a crack pilot and block-ade runner. He was thought of and treated rather as a "ship's cousin," that is as a paid hand who, however, was closely related to the skipper or the owners. Si Wainwright especially made much of him, which greatly increased his importance in the eyes of Mr Riley and the other mate, Mr Sanders.

"Beautiful morning."

"Well. How does it happen we're so still? Wind fail?"

Mr Riley opened his eyes very wide.

"Why, we're in! Don't you see that land over there?"

The dawn was early and thin, though already the air was hot, which seemed unnatural. Hab, too, had been sticky-eyed from sleep. Now he saw that the brig, as a matter of fact, was almost entirely surrounded by land. It was high land, nearby. Though it was so dark in this little horseshoe-shaped bay that you could scarcely see the water and you couldn't see the base of the cliffs at all, the cliff-tops were sprinkled with sunrise; and even as Hab watched the sun began throwing javelins of light down into the bay, making the water glitter; and he could see where he was.

It didn't help him much, though the land fascinated him. There was no house, no sign of human habitation, no smoke, no animals except-ing presently some high-wheeling gulls which uttered thin querulous squeaks, *ee-ee-eep, ee-ee-ee-ee*, reminding Hab of the gulls at the Point, though he reckoned that these, though they looked the same, must be a different kind. Certainly everything else was different. Though clearly these were cliffs, very little rock showed. The rest was jungle, a tangle of trees, climbing vines, ferns, flowers. Originally this had been sheer black, but as the bay lightened Hab saw that in fact it was green, a very dark deep wet green, in patches almost a bluish green, where it tapered off again into black. It was a scary sort of place, so quiet. Soon Hab smelled the vegetation there, wondering why he had not smelled it at first. It was a very heavy, dank odor. He was sensitive to odors, and this one frightened him even more than the appearance of the jungle had done. It was an ominous sort of odor, a threatening odor, which made you uneasy.

The watch were taking in sail. The foresail, still spread, bellied negli-gently in a breeze-wisp Hab couldn't even feel on his cheek, and then slapped back, and the reef-points rat-tatted like raindrops on water. The gulls scree'd on, high above. Hab ran fingers through his hair.

Si Wainwright came above. Young, and the owner, he was a consci-entious skipper, who not only stood a regular watch himself—the brig carried but two mates—but insisted on being summoned at every slight-est deviation from routine: he probably never slept more than three hours at a stretch, though the voyage, so far, had been uneventful. The wonder was that he did not reprimand Mr Riley now for taking the brig in at night without first summoning him, Si. It must have meant tricky wheelwork. However, Si was in high good humor, and clapped his hands together and rubbed them. He beamed on the mate, on Hab, even on the helmsman.

"Good morning, Mr Riley."

"Good morning, sir."

Mr Riley saluted. He was strong for nautical etiquette. "Drop the hook, sir?"

"I think so. We don't want to drift in too close." He turned to Hab. "This is your first sight of the tropics, isn't it? Well, what do you think?"

Hab shivered. Here was a hot morning, the day would be a scorcher; but he shivered all the same. He was still looking at the shore.

"Where are we?"

"Northwest coast of Martinique. Above St Pierre. See those three spikes away back there over the top of the cliff?—you can just barely make it out now, with the clouds around it—well, that's Carbet. Mont Carbet. Used to be a volcano. They've got one further north on that coast, Pelée, Mont Pelée, that they say still does sometimes cough up fire and so-forth."

Hab nodded.

"And this bay itself?"

"Oh, I wouldn't know what this is called, if it's even got a name."

"Why come in here, then?"

"Because for one thing it's too shallow for most warships but just right for us, even when we're loaded. If we was to be blockaded here we could last for weeks until we had a dark enough night to run out. There's plenty of fresh water ashore, and plenty of food."

"Wild berries? Snakes? Skunk cabbage?"

"No, no! You can't see a sign of it from here, but right over the lip of that cliff and a little ways further on through the jungle there's a huge plantation, biggest one at this end of the island, owned by my friend the Count de Pontalis. Well, he's got to feed his slaves somehow, and feed 'em cheap. The British Navy's stopping most of the French ships, and the French government won't let the colonists trade with any others, so what's he to do? Why, he keeps a boy stationed up there all the time, up in a tree, with a telescope. Soon as a ship puts in, with flour or horses or dried fish, why, my friend the count comes right out and makes a dicker. You'll see him any minute now."

Sure enough, almost as an echo to the words a boat put out from the shadows of the shore and made with fine confident strokes toward the brig. In the stern sheets sat a man with the biggest mustaches Hab had ever seen—but indeed they were also the only ones he'd ever seen—

95

and dressed all in white, with a white straw hat with a tremendous brim, the crown encircled by a brave scarlet silk ribbon. This personage waved cheerily.

"My friend the count" Si said, and waved back. "I was only the mate when I last put in here. Oh, he'll want the flour all right. Tell you what, Hab, what I'm hoping is that we can sell him the whole cargo, right here and now, and then turn around and beat back home. You'd like that too, I bet!"

"Well" said Hab.

"I don't mean on the ship here, because Count de Pontalis wouldn't do business that way. None of them would. They've got to invite you home first, and introduce you to their womenfolks, and have a few drinks, and spin some yarn. They're almost as eager to get news as they are to get food."

He was waving to his friend the count all this while, and his voice sank: he was talking from a corner of his mouth.

"I think I'll ask you to go along with me when I do go ashore, Hab. It'd be interesting for you to see the place, and we may not be here very long. Besides, I want to be sure to get a straight forty-five dollars a barrel, and I mean coins in a bag too, and the count can be pretty goosegreasy sometimes. If you was along, Hab, I'd feel a might safer about it."

Hab looked sideways at him, astonished. He had not supposed that Silas Wainwright would ever need anybody's assistance in striking a bargain. Could be, Hab reasoned, that the sheer *amount* of the proposed deal touched Si with panic. Forty-five was a lot to ask. Hab knew what had been paid for the flour at the mill—a breath above seven dollars. Hab did some rapid figuring. If his friend got forty-five cash, even after the supplies had been bought and the crew paid off, he would still pocket something better than twenty-seven thousand dollars, at least three or four times what the whole brig itself was worth. Evidently this islands trading was an even more interesting thing than Hab had previously supposed. He cleared his throat.

"Why, I'd admire very much to go."

The Count de Pontalis was tall and strong, and his features were very sharp and suggested a hawk. His chin jutted out, his eyebrows hung low. The ends of the mustaches, superbly waxed, went up almost to the eyes, which were small, dark, alert, highly intelligent. He had very small hands and feet, and there were rings on some of his fingers. There was a black silk sash around his waist, with nothing stuck in it, and he carried a fat red silk umbrella, which he waved. He talked quickly, explosively, and all the time. He showed overjoyed to see Si again, and it was true that he remembered Si's name, remembered his previous visit. Right there in front of all of them—for practically all hands had come topside by this time—the Count de Pontalis, shouting ecstatically, threw both arms around Si Wainwright's shoulders and kissed Si loudly on both cheeks.

Somebody forward snickered, and Mr Riley, that disciplinarian, glared at him. The count seemed not in the least abashed. He went right on talking. He spoke English with a funny accent.

Habakkuk Jones never felt like snickering. This was no man's fool, this one! Though Hab knew nothing about French, and not even very much about English as it was spoken outside of Connecticut, he instantly and instinctively distrusted that accent. It was a part of the man's very volubility. He wasn't talking because he wanted to say something but because he wanted to hide something. When he talked his features leapt and his eyes glittered and he made men laugh, and then he didn't look so much like a hawk. Hab had a notion that he knew this himself. It was no *more* than a notion; but Hab trusted it the way he'd never trust figures written down on paper.

When you stopped to listen to what the count actually said—something Hab didn't do at first, being too interested in the man's eyes and voice and his twistical mouth—you learned that he was right comical. His voice carried, as perhaps it was meant to do, and in no time at all, and despite Mr Riley's frowns, he had the hands laughing aloud; and in a little while even Mr Riley himself was laughing; so that the whole bay rang with laughter, to the amazement and indignation of the gulls high above. Still no sound came from the shore, however; and the count's boatmen, very dark negroes, sat silent, never stirring.

Si Wainwright suggested wine in his cabin, and Hab noticed that he didn't say a drink, he said wine. Si was ordinarily a rum drinker, but now he suggested wine. It was good madeira too, Hab noted with growing wonderment. Unless it was a gift, it must have cost Si plenty. It certainly cost more than the rum he customarily drank—though he wasn't much of a drinker anyway aboard ship, not the way he was ashore. He made considerable of a fuss about "Monsieur le Comte," calling him that. Hab sipped wine and watched him sideways. That gave Hab two strangers to watch.

"Well, we're carrying eight hundred barrels of the very finest flour, Monsieur le Comte. I knew you needed it, so I didn't try to make room for anything else. Forty-five dollars a barrel is all we're asking."

The count brushed this aside, and even Hab thought it a little early to start talking business when they hadn't even finished their first drink. Si quickly realized his mistake, and flushed. He was very nervous. He asked the count to stay for breakfast. This invitation the count refused, but with the utmost politeness, pointing out that he'd left before dawn, without a proper opportunity of greeting Madame la Comtesse, who would doubtless be worried about him, and moreover that they were at the end of a voyage and doubtless weary of the limited provisions, whereas he, as Monsieur le Capitaine well knew, was able to offer them great variety. He included Habakkuk in this invitation, but not Mr Riley because Mr Riley was not there. There wasn't room for a fourth man in the cabin. It was low, and the count was a tall man, and the bowing and scraping all this involved, and the hoisting of drinks, and all the rest, were difficult there; but he carried himself well. He used less accent than he'd used on deck. He finished, as he had started, smiling graciously.

"Well" said Si Wainwright.

"Ah, that is so good! And—you, Monsieur Jones?"

Hab finished his wine and smacked his lips and wiped his mouth with the back of his hand, and never having had such good wine before, he looked up at Si, hoping that Si would offer him seconds. Captain Wainwright, however, kept staring at Hab, and made no move for the bottle. He looked as though he was afraid of something, perhaps afraid that Hab would go back on his promise to accompany them ashore. This was odd. Si Wainwright wasn't a man who scared easily. Hab had never seen him look like this, his eyes fairly begging. Hab gravely inclined his head.

"I should admire very much to go along with you, Count. It's right clever of you to ask me."

Stepping out of the boat was like stepping into a tunnel. The sun was fully up, and the bay was bright with it; but when they stepped on land, thick and giving, they might have passed into a sealed-tight house, except that a sealed-tight house presumably would be dry, whereas this place was wet against the face as well as underfoot. Hab turned, sweating, half fearing that a door had in fact been closed behind them, confining them forever in a subterranean world; and it hardly comforted him, and it did smart his eyes, to see the round dazzle of sunlight that was his view of the bay, like a thousand bright lanterns at the mouth of a cave. He turned back, blinking. He knew that it was going to take him longer than the rest, now, to get used to this gloom.

"You have not been here before, Monsieur Jones? May I be the first to welcome you to the only island in the world made famous by the beauty of a woman?"

Hab didn't try to figure that out, though he recognized the voice. He was remembering, in spite of himself, and most unexpectedly, a sermon by a visiting preacher at the old meetinghouse. It was winter and almighty cold. Some folks had brought tiny braziers of coals and put these on the floor near their feet, but the judge and Mrs Watts didn't hold with such worldliness. Hab sat upright, John Rellison on one side, Deliverance on the other, the judge and his wife at the end of the pew, all of them gasping, their breath a flutter of steam. Before the sermon Hab sometimes rolled his eyes to see who was in the galleries around three sides of the meetinghouse, but once the sermon had started he was a statue. The sermon turned out to be about Hell. For an instant Habakkuk Jones had known a stab of joy, which was not commendable and might even have been irreverent; and afterward he calculated that a good many other folks there that morning must have felt the same way; for even to think of Hell at such a temperature might ease the pain a bit. The newcomer, however, a smallish fierce-eyed man, looking extra small high in that pulpit with the huge sounding-board suspended above it, had some new ideas: he told them about a different kind of Hell.

For he asserted that there might conceivably be other Hells or parts of Hell than the one with which they were familiar in Scriptures, that roaring seething pandemonium of brimstone lakes and everlasting laceration of the flesh. Such other Hells or parts of Hell had been talked about and written about, he said, and though admittedly the reports might be false, since we had only the word of men for them, never the word of God Himself, all the same it might be good for them all assembled here this Sabbath day to give a little thought to these other places as well.

Leaning over, waving his arms, shouting, he described some of the other places. He was an intense little man with a very strong imagination. He told about the one which was all cold air through which the disembodied souls of those who in life had turned from the Lord drifted and floated about, endlessly shivering, unable to see one another, colliding with great pain and agony; and the one he said was written about by an Italian, and it was where men and women were frozen in ice right up to their necks, and they just stayed there forever, in that ice, suffering and suffering; and he told about others too, each of them with something cold in it, for it was his point that to think always of Hell as a hot place, and especially such thinking in wintertime, was foolish and even over-indulgent, for it was surely foolish indeed, brothers and sisters gathered here together, to suppose that the Lord in His Wisdom hadn't foreseen wicked and evasive thoughts of *all* kinds and acted to offset or forestall them. But the description which made the deepest impression on Hab—possibly because it was the first and frightened him so that he didn't rightly hear the others in all their details, for he was still thinking about that first place when the sermon ended three and a half hours later, which perhaps was slothful—was of a limbo where the souls of the erring dead stumbled about as solid feeling bodies: they could come and go as they wanted, but in utter darkness in which they were afraid to cry out, so that they slid and stumbled about in that horrid cold place, where there was not even the slightest fugitive gleam of light, and no breeze blew, and the air was clammy, and the earth slick and slippery, and sometimes they splashed through cold greasy little pools in which unseen serpents coiled in anger; and though there was no laceration of the flesh, and certainly no fire, the place was utterly and unchangingly dark and cold, and utterly and always silent, except when two souls, despite outstretched arms, collided with one another—this was the most horrible part of it all, as the visitor described it—in which case each would suddenly scream at the top of his lungs, and they'd turn and run, screaming, stumbling, slipping.

There was much discussion of this sermon, and most were inclined to agree with Judge Watts that it was unnatural and maybe even sacrilegious to expiate on cold Hells which are not found in Holy Writ; and it was clear that the little visitor—he hailed from New Haven, where he taught at the college—would never be invited back. Habakkuk Jones hadn't done any of the discussing, even with John. He just hadn't wanted to talk about that place; but he knew now, here in Martinique, that he wasn't ever going to forget it.

There were men around him. He could hear them move, their feet soft and squodgy in the muck. He could hear them talk, some language he didn't understand, in velvet voices. Now and then a man would brush against him, setting his teeth on edge; but there were no screams; only the other man would murmur "Pah-*don*, monsieur." Hab heard too the faint creak of leather, a tinkle of small bells, and far above a thin unsteady desultory drip-drip-drip where the rain of an hour before struggled to get down through the jungle.

After a long time he began to see things. He saw the men whose voices he had heard, though their shirts (when they wore shirts) were visible before their faces were, and this turned out to be because their faces were so dark, some of them downright black. He saw five or six asses, tiny and toylike, and exquisitely saddled. He saw Si Wainwright, who like Hab himself squinted this way and that. The Count de Pontalis was easiest of all to descry, because of his size and because of his white clothes. He had been watching Hab; and now he bowed, swinging his hat gallantly.

"It startles you, monsieur?"

"Well, it's different from the woods back home."

He kept looking around, though his eyes avoided the cave-mouth of the bay. He saw a great many trees and they seemed to be extremely tall, though he couldn't be sure of this because he couldn't see anything above him, not even small slivers of sunlight at third- or fourth-hand. At first he didn't gather that those things were trees anyway; each looked like a small, thickly bushed mountain. Ferns were banked around their bases, not hand ferns but great jagged things, as high, some of them, as a man's head; and they reached out in all directions. The roots of the trees too here and there lurched up from the mud in great gawky knees and elbows, as though striving to escape, and they were covered with moss and creepers. Lianas were draped around the trees, dangling out of the gloom above, looping back again, some of them supporting their own little clumps and wet pockets of ferns, moss, flowers. Vines twisted and rioted among the trees, squeezing them tight, so that no part of the trunk itself remained visible, only black patches, clusters of ferns, gaudy masses of flowers. All of these things, the vines and lianas, the roots, the ferns, even the flowers and moss, strained silently to get up to where the sun was, the sun you couldn't even glimpse. That feeling of terrible strain was everywhere. Hab smelled it, along with the odor of death and decay, in the sodden gulping air.

"You can almost *hear* things rot!" he cried.

Pontalis smiled, his teeth flashing.

"Who was it who said 'Arboribus suus horror inest'? Was it Horace?"

Hab looked at him.

"Could have been."

He was always to remember that climb up to the plantation. After a short while he gave up the ass to which he'd been assigned, explaining that it hurt his back. His real reason was not that. The count offered him another ass; but still he refused; for there was a negro with each ass, and each negro had a stick, and every-so-often, without warning, the negro would thwack the ass over its rump and the ass would leap and wobble, which frightened Hab and made him dizzy. He was seeing better now, and he saw what he'd known anyway—that they were climbing a narrow winding path on the side of the cliff. He did not want to restrain the unpredictable negro. That might be taken as an impoliteness to his host; and he thought of Si and of the eight hundred barrels of flour, and also of the fact that the sooner those barrels were sold the sooner he, Habakkuk Jones, would get back to the Point and to Deliverance. He had not been seasick, though some two-thirds of the crew had been, even including for a little while the two mates. But if you're seasick you're just sick in your stomach, and he supposed that he could stand that. Others saw you and perhaps felt for you. If you were homesick there wasn't anything anybody could do. That was in your heart. Of course you could talk to folks about it; but he had never been much of a one for talking anyway.

It was partly physical fear, too, that prompted him to walk. In that dim world there was not much to tell you that you were going up. There wouldn't really be much danger of toppling off when the negro smacked the ass, and of falling far enough to break a bone. As he'd seen from below, and from the ship, the cliffside was well wooded. A few yards at most you could fall, and then you'd sponge into softness that would wrap itself wetly and nastily around you and all but suffocate you. *That's* what he was afraid of: not hurtling down the side of the mountain, but tumbling ignominiously into an infinity of rotting vegetation. Why, he'd as lief have run the risk of falling into hogs' swill! Thank you, but he preferred to have his feet on the ground—if you could call it ground.

Walking, too, as it turned out, gave him a better chance to look at this narrow procession. At its head was an enormous and scrupulously silent man who carried a long whippy stick, evidently a sort of badge of office: he could have been part negro, but it was hard to tell in this light: his clothes were better than those of the negroes, and he walked with an air of authority, if somewhat grimly, planting each foot with care; and Hab wondered why, if he was a white man, he didn't mount one of the asses, of which there were four unused. Directly behind him was Si Wainwright. Si was happy. His legs reached almost to the ground on each side of an ass, and he was singing, and sometimes he'd wave his arms and turn to shout something at Hab; and when the negro for his ass would use his stick, and the ass would lunge forward, Si would only laugh the louder. Hab was troubled in his mind about the captain. Already this was not the Si Wainwright Hab had known in Stonington. Hab had the conviction that Si was drunk. He couldn't be drunk on the drinks he had swallowingly *had*. Si was known to take more than he should ashore; but he was known also as a man who did not show the rum until at least the seventh or eighth; and today he'd had nothing more than the one drink of wine in the cabin and one drink of brandy before starting the climb. All the same he sang and waved his arms, and laughed. Could it be that he was drinking drinks he knew would be offered to him, drinking them in an alcoholic imagination, and feeling them real in his belly and head? Hab wished that Mr Riley had been invited to come along.

Hab himself was halfway down the column, trudging now before and now behind the beast he refused to ride, but mostly before it. Then there were three other asses, with a boy for each, and at the foot was the count, with a white man in pretty fancy clothing who could have been a very light negro but who acted like a servant—and he didn't ride. The count sang sometimes and sometimes called pleasantries to Hab and to Si. His hat was tipped far back on his head. He appeared to be having a wonderful time. But he wasn't drunk! Not that one! Hab thought again of Mr Riley, a very temperate and reliable man. He wondered if Mr Riley had ever been up to this place.

The trip wasn't long but just seemed long to Habakkuk Jones. Mostly he watched the negroes, of whom there were perhaps a dozen. He had only seen a few negroes and had never been able to understand whether they were real persons or whether they had been born to slavery as they were. It had been hard to figure a thing like that in Stonington, where when you saw a negro at all he was probably a boy from Jamaica or St Kitts, a sailing man, and not at all sure himself whether he was slave or free—and apparently not caring much. Such negroes as he had met, however, were cheerful fellows. These before and behind him now were quiet, and walked with their heads down. He guessed they were slaves all right.

He would not think so much about it, not on the memories of Stonington, had it not been for that Guineaman. They had raised only three sails on the run down, and that had been a blessing, since anything you met these days was likely to take at least your cargo and conceivably your life along with it—the cargo quickly, the life not so. Two they had lost readily: the Horace T. Wainwright being what it was, likely enough those two had been striving at the same time to lose *them*. That the third, the slaver, encountered just a little north of the Cuba coast, could outsail them or anything like them had been clear in the first hour; and it had given them a troubled morning. At last Si Wainwright put down his glass and smiled wanly. "With that rig, and when it can walk like that, a Guineaman. Nothing else. *They're* not looking for trouble. They're looking for water or their position or something. We'll just let 'em catch up to us. That's all we can do anyway." "At this distance, with it upwind of us like this, we should smell it soon, if it is a Guineaman" Mr Riley offered. "We will, soon" Si said. And they had. Most of the afternoon, thanks to a light wind.

The Guineaman in truth had wanted only water; and they'd sent it to her, not reluctantly, for they had plenty, but as hurriedly as they could manage the job. You didn't stay near a Guineaman. They had even informed that they were getting around to windward—to make things easier for the boats, Si had shouted through his speaking trumpet.

"Y'don't fancy us, eh?"

"NO!" Hab himself had shouted, though it is unlikely that they heard him, for his voice wasn't strong then.

Si had scolded him halfheartedly, and Hab had made no response, not caring; and the fact remained that of the whole crew of the Horace T. Wainwright, Hab Jones was the only one made sick by the experience. The reason was that each of the others had gone below now and then, with or without permission, for a good clean lungful of bilge stink; but Hab, fascinated, had stood staring at the Guineaman, cursing everybody aboard her. (He had prayed afterward, asking God's forgiveness for some of the words he'd said, but carefully not asking God for power to refrain from saying such words if ever again he came close to such a ship.) He had stood there, dizzy—for even to windward it was almost unbearable—and watched the dirty men bringing the blacks up for exercise, watched them waving, sometimes using the lash. . . . Twice while he watched a double row of negroes had hauled a prone negro from out of the hold and tossed him overside. One of the gang, the second time, had made some sort of protest, and the mate with the lash had knocked him down and kicked him in the belly five or six times. The ones who did this work all had chains on ankles and wrists, but the two thrown over were cleaned of irons and of course naked. *That* wasn't so bad, though. It was far enough away to seem almost impersonal. When Hab Jones lost control of himself was when Si came over to him where he stood at the rail quietly cursing, and Si, trying to be kind, had advised him to go below. The other boys had all seen this, or something like it, before. It was all right if you just didn't look any more than you had to. There was nothing you could do anyway. The Guineaman had a Long Tom astern, and no doubt it was shotted. You could only go below. Hab hadn't stirred, or even stopped cursing. He had vowed to himself, right then and there, that if he ever met a slaver face to face he'd launch right out at him. Nobody had ever liked slavers, including Hab, who until now, however, had known about them only by hearsay. This was different. This explained why most seamen looked upon slavers or even ex-slavers with such great abhorrence that they wouldn't stay in the same tavern with them.

"They've brought up at least forty for exercise. They must be repeating 'em, Si." The slaver was a much smaller vessel than the brig, a very small vessel, a sloop. "They couldn't have that many below?"

Silas Wainwright cocked his head, studying the lines of the Guineaman.

"I should say about seven hundred and fifty——"

It was then that Habakkuk Jones left the lee rail, where he'd been watching, and went to the windward side, which is not the best place to vomit.

"—or maybe eight hundred" Si said. "These days they——"

Afterward, miles away, when he'd washed his mouth, though he still had a splitting headache, he overheard several of the hands talk about the way one of the Guineaman's officers, as the vessels were separating, sat astern with a musket and took shot after tired shot at the breasts of one of the bodies (it happened to be a woman, and floating on her back) which had been tossed overside. The officer just shot quietly, and reloaded, and shot, and shook his head, and reloaded and shot again, they said.

The courteous count, observing Hab's preoccupation, now rode up.

"These are what we call marabous. They have one-sixteenth white blood. Or some are even sacatras, one-eighth white blood. The Englishman calls them both sambos. He calls the one-quarter-white ones that too, which we call griffes. You Americans just call them all niggers, eh?"

"They, uh, they're slaves?"

"But certainly! Any person with any African blood at all is a slave. Unless somebody has manumitted him. I don't approve of manumission myself. It simply makes them unhappy."

Hab reflected that these negroes he saw didn't look over-cheerful.

"Now Pierre, my valet back there, he's a mamelouque, what the English would call a mustee, fifteen-sixteenths white. So is the headman up there, Hubert. You need sharp eyes to tell the difference, monsieur. Up where you live I daresay that Hubert and Pierre would pass as white."

"I reckon they would."

"We keep closer watch, down here. We are more exact with our gradations, for these mean much to us, you comprehend? It is easy enough if you have a record of the parenthood. The offspring of a white and a black is a mulâtre, a mulatto, as you know. The offspring of a white and a mulâtre is a quarteron, you would call it a quadroon. A white and a quarteron give birth to a métis, or octavon, which the English call octaroon, seven-eighths white, and from one of *those* and a white person comes the mamelouque. Such, of course, work in the house, not in the fields. In the fields they are marabous or sacatras or just plain blacks fresh-over. We have a few Eboes and Angolans, who are slow but safe. But we have more Mandingos and Senegalese, strong men, monsieur, and dangerous men." He darkened. "Lately we have been obliged to take what we could get, you comprehend? We even have Dahomeans, fierce men, fighters, who hate to work. They do not like to be slaves."

"Can't blame 'em, in a way."

He switched the talk back to the lighter mixtures, observing that it must be tricksy to keep track of the various fractions when they got it down as fine as sixteenths. The count said not at all.

"We have a further degree. If a white man has a child by a mamelouque, you conceive, monsieur, that child is thirty-one thirty-seconds white, and we call it a sangmêlé, which means mixed blood."

"Ought to be pretty *well* mixed by that time!"

"But still a slave, you comprehend, monsieur? Often enough an uncommonly lovely and lively and intelligent one, too. The girls I will give you and Monsieur le Capitaine to sleep with tonight, they'll be sangmêlés."

Hab stumbled.

"The girls——"

"I have two who speak passable English, in addition to their other accomplishments." He laughed. "Not that you're likely to do much *talking*, eh?"

"No" muttered Hab. "No, I don't talk much any time."

The count chattered on, a brook. He had started something about the language of love and how it was superior in matters grammatical to other languages, being all verbs—when the rain came. Instantly the count opened his umbrella and proffered it to Hab, who declined: Hab would have felt silly trudging along in this mire with a great red silk umbrella over his head, and besides he didn't really need it, for the rain didn't come down on them, where they were, except in the form of fugitive shattered drops of which it was not necessary to take heed, but it did thud and clatter on the roof of the jungle with such ferocity as to make conversation impossible. The count fell back. Hab Jones stumbled on. Hab, who had never before had a chance to do so, thought that he ought not to lie with a woman, because of Deliverance. He was practically married, he reasoned, which would make it practically adultery. But he wasn't sure whether he'd feel that way later.

The rain had started loudly and all at once, as if God had turned on a tap in Heaven; and it stopped with this same abruptness. One moment it was roaring and slashing at the treetops, the next there was only the multitudinous but irregular and quiet drip-drip-dripping of what it had left.

The Count de Pontalis rode forward.

"We were talking about love."

"Were we?"

The negro just ahead of Hab sprang backward with a squeal of terror. He started to strike at something on the ground before him with his stick. The Count de Pontalis, shouting something in French, ran around Hab and got his left foot on the thing. It was a thin snake with a small head, green with dark spiraling. It must have been six feet long. It whipped and fought furiously. The count, however, had planted his foot very near the head, and he was wearing jackboots, riding boots. Coolly he permitted the snake to lash itself into momentary exhaustion. He looked around this while, and saw, as Hab did, that there was no rock and that the earth was much too soft to crush a snake on, given no matter how heavy a stick. When the snake settled for a moment, writhing still, struggling, but relaxing a little, the count stooped swiftly and picked it up by the middle. He lifted his foot and swung the snake in a circle, holding the middle, batting the two ends, head and tail, against the side of his jackboot. He did this unpausingly and very fast, so that you could hardly see the whirling snake. After a while he straightened, and held the thing up. Its head and tail were so bashed and battered, so pulped, that you could scarcely tell the one from the other.

"A fer-de-lance" the Count said. "This is a rather small one. But big enough to kill you."

He tossed the mangled thing aside. It fell at the feet or perhaps *on* the feet of that same negro boy who had first seen it, and the boy, who seemed possessed of a rather more than ordinary human aversion to reptiles, even dead ones, sprang backward with another squeal of alarm. He bumped Hab Jones, and Hab slipped in the muck and fell to his knees.

"Tarnation!" Hab cried, though he did not customarily use hard words.

It all happened very quickly. Count de Pontalis, shouting something to the headman, was picking Hab up, was solicitously brushing mud from his knees, offering his spotless kerchief. By the time Hab got to his feet and realized what had happened, the headman Hubert was beating the boy.

Hubert beat him over his bent back, swiftly and with great force, using a stick light and whippy enough to cut. The negro did not stir, didn't even lift his arms: he simply stood there, humped over, and accepted his punishment. He wore no shirt, and blood began to show on his back after the first few blows, though it didn't show readily because of the color of his skin. He moaned a little, but he didn't move.

As for Pontalis, he did not even turn his head. He must have heard the blows, but he continued to cluck and tut-tut around Habakkuk Jones.

"Say, quit that! He didn't mean any hurt!"

The count said something to Hubert, who held his stick in mid-air. The count bowed apologetically before his guest.

"Monsieur is sufficiently mollified?"

"Well, I guess so."

A few minutes after that they came suddenly out of the jungle and into the plantation proper.

. 13 . . .

THIS WAS AS DRAMATIC AS THE ENTRANCE TO THE TRAIL had been, though in the opposite way, for this was coming *out* of a tunnel.

Hab's first sensation was that of blinding light, so that his eyes hurt. The sun shone vehemently, there wasn't a cloud in the sky, and everything was open, everything glittered turquoise and green with fallen raindrops.

His next sensation was that of great space. He did in fact look upon a well-cleared plantation, which because of his previous cooped-in-ness seemed even larger than it was, and which in any case was far wider and longer than anything he had ever seen before, excepting of course the sea. In Connecticut you never see far in any direction: too many hills. The sky too, the sheer, shamelessly blue, tropical sky, appeared further away than he had ever seen it before, remote yet at the same time hot.

Then (and these thoughts, if they could be called thoughts, were going through his mind very fast, fairly humping along) for a little while he was disappointed. It was too—well, *quiet!* too *domestic!* While not for an instant did it suggest home—it was too vast, too flat, and the mountains which half-ringed it were much too grand—and also of course there were no stone fences—all the same it had an air of neatness and of studied routine industry, a rural air, as of a garden filled with sunshine and the sound of bees. It wasn't wild and fantastic at all. It was rather comfy.

Soon he learned that this too was a delusion. It might not be wild, this scene spread before him, but fantastic it assuredly was. Near at hand was a clutter of stumps, great piles of tree trunks and heaped-up underbrush, all burning smudgily, resentfully, with no flame but a great deal of heavy blue smoke which hung low over the ground. Negroes were attacking the jungle here, hacking it with axes, slashing it with machetes, piling it, setting it afire. There was a white man in charge, or perhaps he was another sangmêlé. Anyway he had two pistols in his sash, a saber at his side, and he carried in addition a musket. This personage came over and spoke to Count de Pontalis, who didn't dismount. Their talk was low and urgent, and brief; from their gestures and looks Hab deduced that it had something to do with the axes the slaves were using. An ax was missing, could it be? One was unaccounted for?

Two negroes came over and looked at the foreman, then looked down at a neat row of pitchforks on the ground, five or six of them. The negroes had axes. The foreman nodded, and they put the axes carefully alongside the pitchforks and picked up two pitchforks with which they went to work turning over the smudgy ponderous fires. The foreman, though talking to the count all this while, watched them carefully.

The smoke got into everybody's eyes. The count finished his talk with the foreman, and the party moved on.

Past the cleared space were cane fields, and these definitely did disappoint Hab Jones. The stuff looked like wheat! It was thicker and tougher, and certainly taller, but even when you got near it the young cane looked like wheat. This was just a series of the biggest wheat fields Habakkuk had ever seen. Somehow he had supposed that a sugar field glistened.

The fields were separated by roads along which moved pedestrians and horsemen and little wooden-wheeled carts drawn by asses. Everybody and every animal moved slowly, and this added to the drowsiness and easygoing domesticity of the scene. Some of the pedestrians carried great baskets or bundles on their heads, making them show grotesquely, impossibly tall. All were bright with color.

The mill, located near the center of the plantation, which was virtually all in view here, and upon which most of the roads converged, was low and gray, and from the tall black chimneys of its boiling-house the languid smoke rose white. *That* might have been New England smoke. The smoke they'd just left, the thick turgid heavy blue smoke, could only have been in the tropics.

They found a road, where they could ride side by side. Hab consented to use an ass here, though it did make him feel plaguy foolish. The tiny bells on the harness tinkled, a sound clear and thin and musical on this fine clear morning, and not soggy, as it had been before.

They overtook two of those women who carried baskets on their heads. Count de Pontalis, talking, waving his umbrella to illustrate what he said, paid them no attention; but Hab unabashedly turned to stare back at them.

The count was quick to notice this. For all his chickering, he didn't miss much, that Frencher! He asked, was Monsieur interested? Here, he said, was another porteuse. They would stop her.

She was not alarmed. She halted like a well-trained animal, but there was nothing servile in her attitude as she let them examine her. She was not a large woman and not heavily built. She was young. Her posture was the most notable thing about her: she stood beautifully erect without strain: just to see these women walk, Hab reflected, kind of caught at your throat, like watching a deer run. She was barefooted, barelegged, and her arms too were bare. Her skin was ruddily swart, like the metal of a statue. Her lips were thick, her nose somewhat flat, and her large liquid eyes, reddish-purple in color, were humorous. The breasts that bulged her chemise were large but without flabbiness. She didn't sweat or gleam, but shone quietly as she stood with feet together, her arms straight at her sides, an obedient if somewhat amused servant.

"It is a profession." The count might have been exhibiting a machine at the mill. "We have great distances and there are no real roads, only trails. The nearest harbor is St Pierre, and that is where all our goods from the outside world come—well, very *nearly* all, you comprehend, monsieur?" He nodded to the porteuse. "She probably started from St Pierre early yesterday and slept a few hours last night by the side of the road."

Hab studied the woman's face without seeing any sign of fatigue. There was no slump in her position, no sag. Though so near the end of her journey, she didn't seem impatient to get on.

"How far is this St Pierre?"

The count did some mental calculation for the benefit of his guest.

"About thirty-four or thirty-five of your miles. But it is not road like this, it is mostly rocky and steep. But she has friends along the way. She passes villages, huts, groups of field hands, and talks with them, exchanges gossip. She sees everything, though she doesn't move her head, only her eyes. She stops and has a banana now and then with an acquaintance, or a glass of goat's milk through a straw. Always standing up, you comprehend. She is filled with news now. She all but bursts with it! When she gets to the slave quarters here she will have all afternoon in which to gossip. She will be greatly in demand. And she will take and store, as well as give. Just before dawn tomorrow she'll start back with another load, and when she gets home she will be the center of attention for hours on end. They are a childish people, you perceive, monsieur. This one, she is very happy."

Yes, the woman did look happy. Hab stared at the basket.

"All sorts of things" the count said, answering a question before Hab could ask it. "Things from France, one hopes. Gowns for Madame la Comtesse, perhaps some shirtings and pistols for me, a book or two, pans and skillets . . . many things. And it would be added to on the way. Possibly half a lamb from the plantation of my friend Maîtrejean, who knows I like his lambs. It may be some oranges from the Lefèvre plantation just over the mountains, where they did not get that last big-blow which ruined my orange trees. Such things. One knows when one sees. Would you like to look into the basket, monsieur?"

The count spoke to Hubert, who called two negroes, and they lowered the basket. It was all they could do. She helped only by balancing it with her hands.

Relieved, the porteuse did not lie down. However, she did lift her hands to her head and took off a small thin pad of gaily colored cloth: all yellow and green and brown it was, and she patted it carefully back into shape, and then with demure fingers straightened her hair.

The basket was filled to the top. Hab didn't poke around. This was other folks' property, after all. But he did try to lift the basket—and couldn't. He could move it, he could rock it, but he couldn't get it off the ground. The two negroes, this time with the truly muscular assistance of the porteuse herself, were needed to replace it. Hab would have helped and instinctively started to do so, but the count begged him sharply to desist. That is, the count *said* that he begged him: to Hab it sounded more like a command. The count was deeply in earnest. It was of the greatest importance, he told Hab, after asking Hab's pardon for the sharp and hasty tone. A white man out here must do no physical labor, not in public anyway. That was of the *greatest* importance, he repeated gravely.

They left the porteuse behind but not alone, for two others they'd previously passed had overtaken her, and the three, as Hab saw when he looked back, were walking side by side, three enormous baskets perfectly balanced on their heads, talking animatedly, rolling their eyes to one another, giggling. They're probably talking about us, Hab thought, and about what queer people we are.

The house did not show until they were within less than a mile of it, and this was odd, for it was by far the biggest house Hab Jones had ever seen, a palace, and it was unremittingly white. Approached from the mountains which made up three sides of this plain, it would have been visible for many miles. Approached from the fourth side, the jungle and the sea, it was for a time hidden by a not readily discerned fold in the plain. No matter. It was something to gasp at, viewed from whatever angle.

Along three sides were fat white pillars, and behind the fourth side a covered walk led to a large white kiosk behind which there were sheds and smaller kiosks. The large kiosk had several chimneys, which looked as if they'd been stuck through the roof like sticks rather than built up from underneath, and from each of these smoke was rolling. Boys and girls, carrying things on their heads, moved back and forth on the covered walk. There were a great many balconies on the house proper, and the windows were as big as the doors, and indeed many of them *were* doors.

Hab at first supposed that this was at least a five-story building. He had once talked with a sailor from Edinburgh who told him that there were five-story buildings there, and of course everybody had heard about the four-story one in New York. When he got closer, however, he saw that there were only two stories of the Pontalis mansion.

There was a great deal of bustle at the main door. Many of the servants looked white to Hab, but even those, though they did no work, watched the work of others, and watched the Count de Pontalis too, nor did they speak to him or to Hab or Si unless and until they were spoken to. It was bewildering. They swarmed out of the house, took the bridles—two men to handle each meek tired jackass!—they helped the riders to dismount the full two inches, they brushed, they bobbed, they babbled pauselessly among themselves. A great fuss was made about the mud on Hab's knees. Dry now, it was elaborately scraped off.

The Count de Pontalis bowed to his guests.

"I sent a runner ahead, as soon as I learned how many we'd be, so breakfast is ready—once we've bathed and paid our respects to Madame. But first, shall we not have a soupçon to mark journey's end?"

Hab was noting these foreign words, making it a point to remember them once he'd caught their meaning. A soupçon turned out to be a wineglass holding about four ounces of a brandy so smooth you could scarcely taste it. This brandy didn't burn your throat like rum; at first it didn't even burn inside of you; but after a moment, when it did, it spread, fiery, to all parts of you, and you could fairly feel the fumes mounting to your head.

Guess I'd better take it easy with this, Hab told himself.

He looked around the entrance hall. It was difficult to see much, for they had only just come out of the sunlight. The hall was vast, as big, he estimated, as the whole inside of the meetinghouse at Stonington, until now the largest building he had ever seen. The floor was made up of tiny smooth shiny pieces of colored stone or porcelain, somewhat slippery to walk on but he reckoned it'd be cooler than wood. The ceiling was all but out of sight. There were no rugs or carpets. There didn't seem to be much furniture of any kind, and what there was was against the walls, which showed dimly white. There were a heap of negroes around, back by the walls, and they left the three men alone, left them holding the center of the hall the way three actors might hold the center of the stage. Even Si Wainwright, who had seen it before, was awed by the place.

"Shall we be washing?"

Preceded as well as followed by servants, they mounted a spectacular white staircase and went along miles of dim high-ceiled tile-floored corridors.

Walking very straight, still feeling the soupçon, Hab Jones thought of his little room under the eaves in Judge Watts's house, the room he had shared with John Rellison. He tried not to think of this because he didn't want to think of John because whenever he did so he thought of John and Deliverance. He could understand it happening—it might happen to anybody once—though it had never happened to him—and even though he didn't like to think about it, he could forgive and had forgiven Deliverance. What he couldn't understand, and what whenever he thought about it hurt him so poison much, was that John hadn't told him and had tried to sneak away. That would be harder to forgive. All the same, Hab knew he'd do it. He knew that the next time he saw John Rellison and caught the flash of John's old merry grin, he would be ready to forgive anything, if not to forget it.

Right now he shook his head. He was at a branching of this interminable great corridor, and from a chair a strong young negro had sprung to his feet.

"This is René. He or another will always be just here, monsieur, and he will guide you downstairs when you have washed, or, since your room is so near, he can be called at any time. Just this way, please . . ."

He led Hab a few yards down the off-corridor and flung open a door, "Thanks" said Hab, stepping in. The count said "I shall welcome your company again very soon, to greet Madame," and closed the door.

Hab looked around and saw a beautiful woman coming toward him with her arms outstretched.

He was afterward to think of her as golden. Honey might have been more accurate—she was more that color—but though honey is sweet it is also sticky. Hab thought "golden" right away, as much as he thought anything at all in that first stunning moment. He had never known that yellow could be so many colors. The room was large, and as she walked toward him she had her back to what light there was, which came from between the jalousies over tall door-windows opening upon a balcony and slid across her naked shoulders and the top of her outstretched arms. She was a smallish woman but firmly built and complete, nothing wrenched from place, nothing stuck on as though by afterthought. She walked slowly, swaying a little, with the indescribable grace of a cat.

He stepped back. He thought of summoning that negro at the end of the corridor, René, for help. But that would have made him ridiculous: the others, still within hearing, would hurry back to laugh at him.

The woman stopped when he retreated. She dropped her arms. She put her head a little to one side. He could not see her face well, because the light was behind her, but he could see that she had been smiling and that now the smile was gone; she looked puzzled.

"I—am—Suzanne" she said in a low singsong.

"Well." Hab moved sideways. He wanted to see her with the light on her. But he kept his distance. "I'm, uh, pleased to meet you, Suzanne."

She turned with him.

"You—do—not—like me?"

"Oh, I didn't say that!"

She spoke very slowly, spacing her words with care, pronouncing them like a person who had studied English well but hadn't had much chance to practice it. Her voice, however, was a lovely thing. Its sweetness was not cloying. It held, delicately, like a bell-echo, a note of concern for him and for his comfort.

He raised one of the jalousies a little. He was clumsy about it, for he'd never worked one of these things before, had never even seen one; but he didn't dare to take his gaze from her; he might have thought, if he thought anything then, that if he looked away for a split-second, or even if he blinked, she would strike with poisoned fangs—or would vanish.

The sunlight streaming in knee-high—that was as high as he could raise the thing—touched Suzanne indirectly but with fondness, as though proud of her. Golden, yes, that was the word. She stood facing him, facing the light now, her arms at her sides, one leg a little bent, the knee out.

"You—think—I am—pretty?"

He couldn't have said anything if a musket was pointed at him. Pretty? Tarnation, she was the loveliest thing in the world! He did not forget Deliverance, but it never occurred to him to compare this girl with her. Deliverance he had been brought up with, and knew, and was going to marry. What faced him now had nothing to do with Deliverance Watts or with Stonington.

Suzanne wore a dress which was little more than a chemise and reached only to her knees. It was of some light linenlike material and giddy in pattern, all crisscrossed yellows and greens and reds, as turbulent as a Scottish tartan, though lighter, brighter, gayer. Her feet and legs were bare. She had thrown back her foulard, another bright garment of the same material as the dress though it contained somewhat more green, so that her shoulders like her arms were bare. The greater part of her breast too was exposed. Her skin was smooth and clear, the color of honey, yes, but of very light honey. Hab reckoned that it would bruise easily, and also that it would always be warm: he found it impossible, even after having seen her for no more than a minute, to think of Suzanne as ever looking or being cold. Over blue-black straight hair she wore a turban of that same parti-colored stuff. It was wrapped in such a way that one end, stiffly starched, stuck up in front like an aigrette, a roguish cockade. There was nothing negroid about her features. Her nose was thin and delicate, slightly tip-tilted, but aristocratic by the standards of any white society. Her eyes were narrow and long, the irises green flecked with gold; they were liquid eyes, somewhat feline, somewhat pointed at the outside corners, suggesting a lynx, and of an agate iridescence. The cheeks were smooth, neither sunken nor plump, clear, rather light. She had no dimple when she smiled. The chin was small and round, and there was no dimple there either. The mouth was painted red. Now this was the first time Habakkuk Jones had ever seen a painted mouth, but it didn't disgust him as he would previously have supposed it would. On Suzanne, in this place, it even seemed proper.

She wore a great deal of jewelry, this golden girl, which caught the light admitted under the jalousies and smashed it, prismed it, shot it here and there around the walls and across the ceiling in wee scuttling polychromatic specks. In her ears she wore small, very light, thin, gold rings, and around her neck, the only thing on her breast, was a rope of golden blobs which rolled back and forth a trifle, catching and throwing light, as she breathed. Stuck here and there in dress and turban were many small trembling-pins. That was what Hab always called them in his mind, trembling-pins. He supposed that they had a real name in the patois or in French, but he never did learn it. They were very small, made of some thin wire studded with infinitesimal chips of glass, and they shivered and quivered with every movement, with every breath of air. It was difficult to look at those trembling-pins without getting twitchy.

She came. This time she held her arms not out toward him but more humbly up a little at her sides, the palms forward.

"You—came—here—to—take—me?"

Behind him were only the jalousies and the balcony. . . . It might be possible to slip sideways . . .

"Tell the truth," fidgeting, "I came here to get washed up."

"Mais certainement!"

Moving swiftly for the first time, a warm shadow, breaking a spell, she darted birdlike to the washstand, so that Hab was able to let out his breath.

"Monsieur—must—forgive—me—I—have—been—forgettingful."

"Forgetful" said Hab, who was beginning to like her.

"For-get-ful."

She lifted pitchers and poured water, first from this, then from that. They were heavy pitchers and the basin was huge, but she seemed effortless. She's strong, Hab thought. She got out towels and clothes and soap and brushes, and she got out all sorts of curious bottles, and presently the scent of perfume was pungent in the air.

"Voilà, monsieur! You—will—take—your—clothes—off, please?"

"Oh, we don't need to go as far as that."

He did take off his jacket, and she was right there behind him to lift it away and to fold it over a chair. He took off his stock, which she accepted reverently. He rolled up the sleeves of his shirt. He started for the washstand. It was a long walk, and on the way he passed the bed and for the first time, having until now looked at nothing but Suzanne, he noticed it. It was of a size for this room. Not only its posts but its head and base as well were elaborately carved and painted, cupids being predominant. It was quilted with blue silk lavishly embroidered, and over that rose-point. It was a high bed, and there was a damask-covered stool for climbing up to it.

The water was perfumed, despite protests. The soap too was perfumed. It wasn't yellow soap but an off-white and marvelously foamy to the touch.

While he washed he watched her back as she undid the buttons of a shirt the count had caused to be sent up for him. He would have refused the use of the shirt, and had feebly started to do so, but he couldn't deny that his own, though it had been clean that morning, was limp with sweat. He hadn't labored hard, but the air had been so hot and close and wet on that trail that shirt and stock alike, though still clean, were all but starchless. So he consented to the loan. But he didn't have any underclothes on, and Suzanne was still there, and about to turn to him, and he wondered what he ought to do. Ask her to go out into the hall? Or just ask her to turn around?

She came to him presently, and started to undo the buttons of *his* shirt. "That's all right" he gruffed, stepping back a little and undoing the buttons himself. He even pulled the tails out. He looked at her, wondering whether she'd have the decency to go somewhere else, but she just smiled and came toward him with the clean shirt, so he yanked his own damp shirt off swiftly, half turning away from her as he did so.

She slipped around in front of him and ducked under his elbow, and there she was with one hand resting lightly on his chest, which made him jump as though she'd placed a white-hot iron there, and her head averted so that the upsticking thing on the turban brushed his chin from beneath. She drummed her fingers very delicately on his chest, then ran them up and down. She lifted her head, and lifted her eyes to his, and then suddenly lowered them, the eyes, keeping her head back. Looking down at her then, in that position, he saw that she didn't have any underclothes on either.

Through lips that scarcely moved: "You—like—Suzanne?"

His eyeballs stung. He couldn't feel his heart at all, but his temples banged steadily, not together but alternating, as though two madmen with padded clubs stood one on each side of him, slamming, slamming rhythmically. He seemed staggered back and forth too, as if that were being done. He retreated somehow, grabbing the clean shirt, dropping the damp one.

In dismay: "But Monsieur is so hard and cold!"

"I come from a stony state" Hab said.

He got the shirt and stock on alone, though she managed to spray him with some kind of scent. He shrugged into his jacket. She polished his shoes with a dry cloth, and hastily he combed his hair.

There was one more thing. He had meant to ask about it when first he arrived but he'd hesitated to mention such a matter in so splendid a mansion. Now, however, thanks in part to the splashing of the water when he washed, his need was even greater.

He looked around.

Suzanne, watching him solicitously, divined his thoughts. With a little cry she ran to a cabinet by the side of the bed and drew something from it, and with this she started for him. She evidently supposed he was willing to use it then and there. He certainly could not see any place to hide.

Nobody could have used the thing for such a purpose anyway, or at any rate nobody *should* have. It was twice as big as the usual one—everything was big here—and it had two handles, which were gilded. The container itself, inside as well as outside, was glazed and gilded and painted pink, blue, yellow, with sylvan scenes, waterfalls, pretty shepherds and shepherdesses, peasants jigging. It didn't even seem decent, it was so over-decorated.

Suzanne cleared a corner of the washstand and placed it there, at a convenient height.

"No, no" cried Hab, and ran out into the hall.

The negro René sprang to attention at his approach, but it was clear from Hab's first words that the man didn't understand any English. And Hab hadn't yet learned the name for it in French.

Desperate: *"Where is? You understand that—where is?"*

Hab pronounced the words very clearly and distinctly and loudly, exaggerating with his lips. René nodded, bowing a little.

"Where is——" and Hab pointed.

René found it difficult to believe. He looked at the place to which Hab pointed, he looked down the off-corridor to the bedroom door. He bowed again, a little. "Pah-*don,* monsieur." He went down the off-corridor, opened the bedroom door, looked in; and his face cleared. Holding her by a hand, he drew Suzanne outside. Where, he wondered, had she ever been, that the white man had missed her? Hiding under the bed, playfully? Beaming in triumph, he pointed to her.

"La voilà, monsieur!"

Hab did not run away, for he was afraid to run, but he walked as rapidly as he dared. Of his own accord he found the place outside, coyly hidden in a clump of hibiscus, and though it was very large there were no pink shepherdesses anywhere and the hole at least was the conventional size.

Unguided again, he got back to the house and found the reception hall; but though no doubt he presented an impeccable appearance, he had been sadly shaken and his knees were trembling when he rejoined the Count de Pontalis.

. 14 . . .

THE MASTER OF THE HOUSE WAS IN AN UNAMIABLE frame of mind when Habakkuk stopped just outside the entrance hall. His lips worked, his accipitrine brows were low, he scowled at the floor as he walked back and forth. He looked no clown but an angry man and a dangerous one. However, the moment he saw Hab he started to smile, started to talk, to ask questions. Had Hab found everything satisfactory? Hab replied that he sure had, civilly thanking his host for the shirt. It was nothing! And Suzanne? Did he think that she would be acceptable? When Hab paused, not knowing what to say, his host was desolated, crying "Ah, it is so much I regret that I haven't another who speaks English! I had supposed——"

"No, no, that's all right" blurted Hab.

He had been about to remark that maybe he could get along without any girl whatever, having done so all his life, and he was coming onto eighteen; but the count's offhand manner, as though he was talking about a pillow or a washbasin, embarrassed Hab, and he wished to speak of something else.

So, as it happened, did the count.

Laughing, "Monsieur le Capitaine surely made a—what do you call it?—a slip-of-the-tongue when he mentioned the price of forty-five dollars a barrel for that flour, eh?"

Hab said nothing, only shook his head. The count raised mattressy brows.

"But if one were to buy it all, all eight hundred barrels?"

"Same price" said Hab.

The count shrugged, and his eyes darted here and there in search of something to inspire a change in the conversation. He was not one who could be silent and motionless at the same time. He was all action, a steel-spring man, who talked only to fill in lulls—and perhaps to conceal his emotions. Hab had an idea that right now he was feeling sore. He caught sight of an oblong box, and he ran to it, and bore it toward the door, where the light was better. A servant slid a small table under this box.

"You understand, Monsieur Jones, that when *this* arrived from France two months back I didn't have *it* brought by a porteuse. I went and got it myself."

He opened the box.

118

"They've never been used" he said wistfully.

There was the light of a lover in his eyes, and when he reached out to touch the things his fingers were a lover's fingers.

There were two of them resting in the crimson velvet, pointed in opposite directions, the bottom one upside down, while between them, each article placed like a jewel in its setting, were nippers, molds, a chased silver powder flask, cleaning rods, a silver box for flints. A silver plate on the back of the top of the box gave the maker's name, LE PAGE A PARIS. But the pistols themselves were the show.

They were exactly alike and must have been a foot and a half long. The octagonal barrels, themselves dull, were gold-mounted and had front and rear sights. The breech linings and vent linings were of gold. The trigger guards, of chased gold, were flat and exquisitely curved. The pistols were ball-butted, and each ball was a large one of solid ivory. The grips, made of Circassian walnut, were crisscrossed with gold filigree.

The count lifted one as though he were picking up a newborn kitten.

"Have you ever seen their equal, monsieur?"

"No."

Hab knew that they were beautiful, but he knew that they were terrible as well. It couldn't have been only their great size which made him know this. His unpracticed eye saw that, despite the fanciness, these were perfectly balanced, perfectly made. He couldn't feel about them as the Count de Pontalis did, but he knew something rare and lovely when he saw it.

"Never used . . ." The count closed the box and replaced it. "I had offered them for tomorrow, but——" He patted his mustaches with the underside of his fingers, somewhat like a man who genteely stifles a yawn. He glanced sideways at Hab. "Later, monsieur, if you are interested, we will perhaps inspect the mill and the kitchens and the slave quarters. But if you should care to get up early enough tomorrow, perhaps you would come out with me to watch a couple of my friends adjust their differences?"

"Adjust their differences?"

"Not, hélas, with those," and he glanced at the box he'd placed high on a shelf. "No, with épées, my friend, with the stickers of convention. I am not representing either of them, as it happens, but they are neighbors and have asked to use my property as neutral territory. It is not likely that you'll see great sport, Maîtrejean is by so much the better swordsman. But tame though it may be, monsieur, one sees so little of it nowadays out here. We are not like those at home, we habitants. Is it the hot weather which renders us so unbellicose?"

"Could be, I suppose."

"But this would be very, very early, monsieur! If other pleasures should engross you——"

"I never mind getting up early."

"Eh bien, I'll call for you. Before dawn. And now, would you like a soupçon of brandy, monsieur?"

"I'll wait a little while, thanks. That first one was pretty stiff."

"Your friend the captain has not thought it worth his while to wait, I gather?"

Hab remembered that there had been a decanter of brandy on his own bedside table, and he assumed that a similar bottle rested on the table in Si's room.

"He could be doing something else" Hab innocently ventured.

"True, he could. He could be leaping the matelotte I provided him."

The count didn't like it. His jaw twitched a little, and his eyes swiveled angrily toward the staircase; and somehow Hab knew that this strange violent man, who gave away women as though they were pieces of pie, nevertheless was offended when he thought that a guest was thus engaged before he had made his devoir to the lady of the house.

Probably wouldn't do it with one of 'em himself, even, without he said hello to his wife first, reflected Hab.

When Si did come it was obvious that he'd been at the bottle. His breath devastated, his smile was fatuous, and he no longer had that exaggerated snobbishness of manner toward his friend the count. Indeed he went so far as to wink at the count.

"Say, you sure can select 'em!"

The host said tartly "Shall we be getting upstairs?"

Si was not really drunk but he was feeling good, and his step coming down the staircase hadn't been notably steady. He looked a shade annoyed at the prospect of going back up again, after all that effort, without another drink; but the count started up, impatient; and Hab took his friend's elbow. Si leaned far over and whispered into Hab's ear, and fortunately it was a true whisper, not a liquorish one.

"She's old. Must be all of fifty. He married this, you know." Si rolled his eyes to indicate the surrounding grandeur. "A widow. But clever."

It was as well that he'd been warned; otherwise at his first sight of the countess Hab might have gasped, which would have been impolite. Fifty? She looked nearer sixty! Twice the age of her vigorous husband, and a minute thing, very pale, all in white, almost a white dot in that thronelike chair. Her complexion scared him. She must have some kind of disease, he reasoned. It wasn't possible for even an old woman to be as pale as that if she was really healthy. Her face looked not merely chalky but *chalk,* as though you could scrape it away with a fingernail. She wore a lace cap, and he couldn't see the color of her hair but it must have been white. Her eyes were a clear dark blue, intelligent, amiable. Hab liked her, right off.

The count went to her, taking long ceremonious strides, and bowed to her, and kissed her hand. It was the first time Hab Jones had ever seen this done, and he watched with interest.

"Madame, will you permit me to present friends who are American? We will speak in English, if you will be gracious enough?"

"But of course! And I always like to meet Americans."

The voice was fluty and thin, but it was musical. Any sound coming from that small body startled.

It was a long walk there; and when they arrived and Si was introduced all he did was shake hands with the lady; but when Hab was introduced—"Monsieur Jones," the count preferring to take no chances with that "Habakkuk"—he took a deep breath and swooped over the hand and gave it a good kiss. It wasn't showing-off. He liked Madame la Comtesse, and he wanted to kiss her, and if that's the way she liked being kissed, on the hand, well then that's the way he'd do it. Si looked taken aback. The count was impassive, utterly serious now. The countess twinkled at Hab.

"You come from far away?" in her sweet flute's voice.

"From Connecticut, ma'am."

"Ah, that is interesting. It is a fertile country, like this?"

"Well."

"The soil is not so good as here, perhaps? What a pity!"

"Oh, the soil's all right—when you can find any."

"Ah?"

"Well, maybe it'd make it clearer, ma'am, if I told you about how one time I was walking along a road back to home where I was borned, and all of a sudden I came across a rabbit sitting on a fence."

"Rabbit?"

She glanced at her husband, and he said, almost entirely with his lips, almost silently, "A hare."

"Ah."

"And this rabbit was weeping and weeping as if his heart would break, and I stopped myself up there and said to him that I reckoned I wasn't dreadful brainy but if there was any way I could help him I'd admire to try. 'Well, sir, you see this land roundabout here?' he says, sobbing so hard he could barely talk. 'Well, sir, I just inherited two hundred acres of this, and nothing else, and I've got to live on it, somehow, for the rest of my life.' And so I said, well, I hadn't known it was *that* bad, and I said I certainly couldn't do anything for him, so I went on."

There was a brief silence, and then the count laughed. He really laughed. Madame laughed too, when she heard him, but she was just trying to be polite, as was Si Wainwright, who joined in, for of course Si knew the story.

After that they talked for a little while of the voyage, crops, the weather. Then Madame cried "But you have not had your breakfast, you men! Away with you! You must forgive me" she said to Si and Hab, but especially to Hab, smiling. "I move about so little, I seldom leave this room. You will be happier without me surely."

They protested, she smiled. She smiled especially to Hab.

"You will surely say farewell to me before you go, monsieur?"

"Cross my heart."

They bowed themselves out.

Breakfast in a grand place like this you might expect to consist of berries, grapes, flippers with butter and syrup, eggs, bacon or maybe sausages, warmed-up gravy-bread, preserves, biscuits, milk, pie . . . Well, what they had, after a preliminary soupçon in the entrance hall, was pots and pots of thick rich heavy ropy chocolate, a kind of sweet fluffy biscuit that you spread with butter like a roll, half a dozen different kinds of jam and marmalade, at least ten different kinds of fruit, an omelette, whitefish with a peppery sauce, rice with chicken, and a great deal of chilled white wine. It was really breakfast and lunch combined, the count explained. They were hungry, and they did a tolerably good job of it, but they couldn't possibly have eaten a tenth part of what was set before them. What's more, little negro boys and girls kept coming from the kiosk in back with additional trays and bowls, heaped.

Wine for breakfast, or even for breakfast-and-lunch-combined, was a novelty to Hab, as it was to Si Wainwright, who took plenty. There were three or four different kinds, all white, all light.

Afterward they went out on the veranda and had rum and lime juice.

Though he remembered his manners, the Count de Pontalis paid little attention to Si Wainwright, on the whole giving himself over conversationally to Hab. There was even a hint of contempt in his eyes when he turned to Si, who, unnoticing, placidly continued to get drunk: Si indeed was pretty well along by the end of breakfast, and on the veranda he drank a heap of rum.

They could see the rain as it approached, see it march time and again right across the plain toward the place where they sat. They could estimate almost to a second when the first drop would strike the mansion. It was that definite. Hab was accustomed to rain which either was a drizzle, half a rain and half a mist, or else edged in apologetically, fell sullenly and without excitement, and went away beaten. Except in the summer, and sometimes even then, the rainclouds he had seen were indefinite, unreliable, slow-coming things, ominous perhaps but not fierce. You were never afraid of the rain in Connecticut. It could be a danged nuisance; usually was; but it inspired no terror. Here in Martinique the rain came like a demon in bright armor. It hurled itself upon a place, raged madly, and galloped off, leaving never an echo. You sat affrighted, unable to move for a while. Then you drew a long breath, and leaned back to wait for the next one. It rained five times while they sat on the veranda that afternoon, and each storm was as clearly marked, as neatly and exactly bordered, as a cookie cut out with a cookie-cutter: it was a precise measure of pandemonium.

Of course it was impossible to hear talk while the rain was falling. The count was an artist at bringing his narrative-of-the-moment to a climax as each separate wall of rain approached them, silver-shot mist marching across the plain. He would finish just on time, and then lean back and let the hell-from-heaven take over. Also, he was a master of the dramatic trick of snatching attention by starting the conversation anew, with a fresh topic, immediately after the storm had departed and before anybody else could catch his breath. His voice, coming clear out of those silences, arrested all ears.

For instance, just before the arrival of the second rain he finished on a high note the description of a chase of four runaway slaves back in the mountains, which chase largely took place during a storm, so that the real storm when it enveloped them at the end of the story sounded almost like a continuation of the tale the count had been telling. And then when that storm, the real one, had swept away and they sat a moment stupefied by the fury so suddenly removed, the count turned swiftly and unexpectedly to Si Wainwright.

"Monsieur le Capitaine, you will not discuss a lower price, eh?"

"No" said Si. "Forty-five's it."

"Even if I purchase it all?"

"Same thing."

Si wasn't very polite. He sat low, holding his glass of rum-and-lime far out on the chair's arm, and staring moodily over the plain.

The count sighed.

"Hélas, then, monsieur, I fear I shall be obliged to pay you in part with an order on my bank in Marseille."

"No bank orders" said Si. "Cash."

He took a sip of his rum-and-lime, and afterwards gazed at the glass resentfully, as though accusing it of playing him a dirty trick.

"I took a big risk coming in here. I've got to be paid for that risk. And what good is a French bank order when I'd have to run the whole blockade of the English navy to get it cashed?"

"There are those in St Pierre——"

"D'ye think I'd poke my head into St Pierre after having been out here? Don't you suppose those customs men would know how to make me tell what I'd done with my cargo?"

The count was silent. Si swallowed the rest of his drink. He slammed the glass on the arm of his chair.

"No, there's the price, and it stands. If the Britishers nab me after I leave and can prove I've been here, I lose brig and cargo both. If your own warships catch me here, or leaving here, brig and cargo again. Or if any of your colonial forces catch me here, it's the same thing. Do you realize that, Count?"

"Yes, yes," the count said slowly. "I realize that if you are caught here it would be very unfortunate—for you."

"Well, that's why I've got to ask forty-five, cash. I've got to get paid for that risk."

He did not wait for comment but without excusing himself rose and went out back. The Count de Pontalis looked after him, his jaw muscles twitching, in his eyes loud hate. Even when he turned back to Hab the count made no effort to hide his annoyance.

"Could you change him, Monsieur Jones?"

Hab shook his head.

"You see, though I need this flour badly, I do not have enough money here, nor do I have the sugar ready for exchange."

Hab nodded. He had already figured that.

"But cannot you—— You will forgive me, monsieur, but I have not had it made clear your position on this ship. You are the supercargo, eh?"

"No. Si's his own supercargo. I'm just a mistake."

He explained.

Attentive throughout, Pontalis cried aloud at the conclusion. So here was that Monsieur Jones of whom he had heard! Here was the incomparable pilot who had so many times outwitted the blockaders! Ah yes, his fame had spread. In such exploits they had an especial interest here, as Monsieur could readily comprehend, and more than once had the count heard from seafaring men the tale of how Monsieur had fooled and misled that lieutenant—what was his name?—ah yes, Ferguson—how Monsieur had triumphed over him by means of the rotten fish. The count, who after all did love to laugh, fell back in his chair and roared with laughter. But it might be that part of the reason for this was that he heard Si's returning step and would not have Si suppose that he, the Count de Pontalis, was worried about money or anything else. However, he really did know the story, one of the most bandied-about, and he persuaded Hab to tell it, professing delight to hear it at first hand, and warmly thanking Si Wainwright for having done him the honor to bring such a famous personage to his house. Si nodded, pleased, and sat down and took a fresh drink.

It had happened in Embargo days, when a New Orleans skipper, finding himself bottled in New York harbor, had escaped by way of Long Island Sound, first picking up a cargo of salted fish with which he hoped to run down to the islands. The eastern mouth of the sound, roughly from Watch Hill to Montauk, was the dangerous section, and the New Orleans man had accepted the advice of acquaintances and engaged through an intermediary the services of Habakkuk Jones and John Rellison. They had boarded the schooner in their usual way, trailing the dogbody Deliverance, on a night of darkness and nasty cold rain. Red Ferguson was loitering somewhere near at hand—they didn't know just where, but they were watchful.

Now this New Orleans skipper had bought some fish that was not good. A dozen or more of his barrels had already begun to stink, the fish having been insufficiently salted; and Hab, always sensitive in the nose, had pointed out irritably that Red Ferguson, though he couldn't *see* them at a distance of more than say two hundred feet probably, would be able to *smell* them two miles away. This reasoning being sound, hands had been told off to sort out the stinking barrels and heave them overside. Meanwhile the schooner had made for the Race; and it was just outside the Race that the worst had happened. Ferguson had got wind of them, properly speaking, and had begun to fire his bow gun. Since they couldn't see Ferguson they had assumed that he couldn't see them, but twist as they might he had little trouble following them. The schooner was a slow sailer, and Ferguson, firing blindly but savagely in the hope of frightening them into surrender, was overhauling her and soon would have her in sight, when the last barrel of bad fish had been hoisted out of the hold. It was John Rellison who had thought of what to do with that barrel. He had thought of it fast too, John had. Before they could heave the barrel overside he had convinced the skipper that Ferguson would overtake him anyway unless led astray. He had offered to do this leading-astray, with Hab, for two dollars each, besides their pilots' fees. They would simply take the last barrel back with them, and since Ferguson obviously was following his nose they should be able to draw him away from the schooner he couldn't yet see.

"It was John thought of it, it wasn't me."

They pooh-poohed this, begging him to continue.

There wasn't much else. The stratagem had worked perfectly. Instead of drawing a red herring across the path they had drawn a barrel of rotting fish. The schooner had disappeared into the dark and the rain, never to be seen in those parts again—which was just as well for the suppliers of the bad fish. Ferguson, still following his nose, a forthright man, had chased the Deliverance, glimpsing her sometimes but never making her out clearly enough to learn that she wasn't a schooner. Firing after her repeatedly, so that the water around her was all aleap, he had pursued her right into Stonington harbor, where the boys arrived in time to roll the barrel out of the dogbody and up to the Black Pit, there effectively to bury it in sawdust before getting to bed a scant half-hour ahead of the dawn's arrival.

"We sold it next day for fertilizer" Hab finished. "Didn't see any sense letting it go to waste."

During the laugh a slave refilled Hab's glass. This is the way it was all that afternoon. An indefinite number of negroes hovered in the shadows of the entrance hall, ready for a hail or a clapping of hands, now and then darting out even when not summoned, to refill a glass, to light a segar. The count drank a great deal, but steadily and without haste. Hab calculated his. He did not know how much he could stand, never having tried to find out, but he sensed that this was a time to walk with special care. Si Wainwright drank on and on, gulpingly, greedily. His speech was thick, when he did talk. Most of the time he stared out over the plain. He seemed to have wanted this, to have known that he was going to get it, to have hurried toward it; yet surely he was not happy in his stupor. Hab watched him from eye-corners. Hab had never had much to do with drunken men, and it was difficult for him to believe that Si would knowingly make himself this way. He knew that Si was getting drunk, and getting drunk swiftly and eagerly, but he couldn't see *why*. No matter. It was going to be up to him, Hab, to keep that flour price fixed.

The count excused himself, and when he had gone Si turned to Hab.

"Maybe he hasn't got the coins, but he ought to be able to raise 'em. I don't know. This is a big property and he's almighty far out, pretty much a king all by himself here. He can get cash if he wants to. If he offers you a girl to take away with you in part payment, don't you accept her, Hab."

Hab gasped.

"Well, it ain't so outlandish. He's offered me mine. To have and to hold—as long as I could hold her. To take back to the Point with me, I suppose. Can you imagine me at the Point with a gal like Helene?"

"I—I haven't seen her."

"You should. She's worth looking at. And she's something to romp with too, I can tell you, Hab! She knows her business, that one! How's yours?"

"Well, I—— As a matter of fact——"

Si was not interested in the answer, if any. He threw himself back in his chair, and again he was gazing across the cane field.

"He can find it" he grumped. "Or if he can't, I guess I won't come here any more. The poor count, in some ways I feel sorry for him. Invalid wife. British fleet right outside somewhere, just as likely to step in any day and take over the colony, the way they've done before. Don't very often get a ship from France with stuff he really wants. Had those crazy revolutionists for some years, and he never knew where he stood with them. They were always yammering about freeing the slaves—telling the slaves themselves about it, that was the trouble. Then Boney came along. He must have liked that—as much as a man like him can ever like a man like Bonaparte. Anyway, he's pretty sure now that he'll be permitted to keep his slaves—if the English don't step in and take them away from him."

"Or if the slaves don't do like they did in St Domingo."

126

"Yes, if they don't do that. Well, anyway, the count here, he wonders how many of these almost-white foremen and overseers he can depend on. And he's got to get practically everything from smugglers like us, who make our own terms. Oh, I feel sorry for him all right," Si finished, "but at the same time the price stays at forty-five, cash."

Another storm was coming in from the north, a moving curtain of rain, but on their right, back of the gray foothills, Mont Carbet was all blue-and-silver in the sun. What did the field hands do when it rained? Go right on working, Hab supposed. Working on empty stomachs right now, too.

"Si——"

There was a grunt.

"The law here say the same as it used to be with us, anybody who turns in a smuggler gets half the goods seized?"

"Same thing. Why?"

Hab did not answer, for at that moment Pontalis returned. That volatile planter was in high spirits, and he devoted himself to the task, not a hard one, of being entertaining to Hab, Si Wainwright having relapsed into the stupor from which he had so lately emerged. The count recalled to memory the rabbit story Hab had told in Madame's boudoir, and he laughed heartily. At that Si Wainwright sat up and began to blubber. Si always had been the kind who when he heard anybody let a whopper fly had to chip in his two pennies. His blurt was astonishing only because they had supposed him unconscious.

It would have been better if he was. All the rest of that afternoon, intermittently drinking, he regaled them with tall stories. Most of these Hab had known; none of them, though he laughed exactly, did the count care for. But Si didn't pause. Mumbling so that much of the time his words couldn't be made out, he went on and on.

He told about the Yankee Bogle, the bird which led all the shad from the Gulf of Mexico to the Connecticut River every season, in which he admitted that he half believed himself, though he had never seen it.

He told about the laziest man in the world, who when he was waited upon by a committee and informed that he had just been voted a five-dollar prize for being so lazy rolled over and asked them if they'd put it into his pocket.

He told about the pants that Jeminy made; and about the hen that was fed on hemlock sawdust mash in an attempt to break her from setting, and whose chicks all had wooden legs; and about the absent-minded man who was whittling and who finished the stick and went right on whittling his own fingers off until somebody called his attention to the blood.

On and on Si went, right through another rainstorm, not raising his voice except and until he heard Hab and the count whisper, when he got sore. He droned on right through the storm, though he couldn't even have heard himself. He didn't laugh and didn't seem to expect laughter from his audience. What he was doing it for wasn't apparent —maybe to remind himself that he was still alive, Hab thought. Hab and the count sat silent.

"This man Obe Willis, he was the best chimney maker in the world. I knew him well, used to watch him work. Trouble is, he made 'em *too* good. Got so that when Obe built a fireplace it had such a strong draft that it pulled up not only the smoke but all the fire and the wood too. Got so that that didn't pay, and it was dangerous besides, so people wouldn't go to Obe any more, and he starved to death. Yes, sir!" Si slammed a hand on the arm of his chair, upsetting his drink. "He *starved to death!*"

The count was looking at him, and Hab was looking sideways at the count, watching the muscles leap in his neck, for the count hadn't liked the sound of those last repeated words and the reminder they made for him; and it must have been a full minute before the skilled polite laugh came.

Soon afterward the count was handed a note on a silver salver, and he excused himself and read it, and then he announced that Madame la Comtesse regretted that she would not be able to join them at dinner, being indisposed.

"Shall we go in?" he asked, and rose. "You must give me ten-fifteen minutes first, if you'll be so kind. Something I must do."

From the shelter of the hibiscus, whither he had gone for another purpose, Hab saw his host go back to a building halfway to the quarters for the house slaves, a sort of storehouse. A file of blacks, under the eyes of overseers, went into that building, each with an armful of machetes, the Count de Pontalis counting every machete at the door and jotting the sum in a tablet he held. Each slave—these were field hands, very dark, very ragged, and sulky—came out with empty arms. Afterward the count himself locked the door with a double padlock, and shook it to test it, and put the key into his own pocket. When a minute later he rejoined his guests he was bubbling with jocular smalltalk.

This talk was lost on Si Wainwright, who was like a man dazed by a blow on the head, and who sat silent, all mumbled out. As for Hab, he too was mostly silent, and the greater part of the count's talk was wasted on him too, though he made an effort to seem to be listening and he asked some questions he hoped sounded intelligent. He had been up since before dawn, and the climb, the rum, and the weather combined to make him drowsy. The meal itself was an ally here, for they had many things: they had onion soup; crusty cap bread; four different kinds of wine; duck stuffed with oysters, eggs, chestnuts, and truffles; three different kinds of fish, one of them being called, according to the count, Le-Bon-Dieu-manié-moi, which is to say God-handled-me, a name Hab esteemed irreverent, though Hab conceded that the fish itself was tasty; and they had a mushroom omelette; a leg of lamb lapped with mint sauce; roast hare with currant jelly; peas, parslied yams, stringbeans; a mouth-stinging salad; and they also had, for wind-up, a tall porous cake saturated with rum, and fruits of all sorts, and brandy, and coffee, and candies.

Captain Wainwright did not get as far as the rum-soaked cake. He rose with some dignity, and even tried to bow, and blubbered something which they took to be a request for pardon, and teetered off. The count inclined his head toward some servants, who hurried after Si, not touching him when they reached him but walking just behind him, ready to catch his elbows if he started to sink, while one of them went ahead with a lighted candle.

The count himself handed Hab a candle, when they had agreed to say good night. Would Monsieur require a servant? No, he could find his own way. He was, as a matter of fact, pretty dizzy, having for courtesy's sake sampled each of the wines, and he didn't want a slave stalking behind him to see him reel—if he did reel, as he thought he might. No, he could find the way, and thanks a heap. Monsieur, it had been a great pleasure and a delight to have the company of the celebrated pilot Jones! Hab said sure. They bowed to one another, Hab bowing pretty low, for him, but cautiously.

The boy René was there at the branch of the corridor, and he sprang to his feet and bowed as Hab passed, and Hab affably tossed him a good night. Then Hab opened his bedroom door and went in.

It was quite natural, a natural thing, after such a meal.

A motion of the air, possibly caused by the opening of the door itself, made the flame of his candle wamble and then die; but Suzanne had a candle by the bedside, in a sort of lamp chimney which protected its flame. The candle lighted her as she lay on the bed, and it lighted little else as far as Hab was concerned. Except for her earrings she was naked. The skin of her body, like the skin of her face, arms, and breast which he had seen, was the palest honey-color: just now there was also a hint of scarlet in it, in this light. Her hair, blue-black, was spread all over the pillow in wanton confusion. She moaned a little, and turned toward him, so that her breasts squodged softly together. She held out her arms, wiggled her fingers.

"I—am—glad" she whispered. "Come—to—Suzanne."

He turned around first and bolted the door.

Later he slipped quietly off the bed, so as not to waken her. The candle was out but there was some moonlight sliding between the jalousies which rested tenderly on her body, slatted silver on the pale luminous gold. He swallowed pretty hard when he looked at her there, but for all the swallowing a lump remained in his throat. He felt warm but not hot, and wide-awake, and extremely happy, tingling all over, swallowing, wetting his lips a bit; he knew that maybe later he would feel bad, and he certainly hoped that he would feel ashamed, but just now he felt very good, light-limbed; he felt like smiling to himself there in the moonlight. He went to the balcony, lifted aside the jalousies. Now her body was all lighted, her face was touched with small yellowish hollows of darkness. She stirred, but she didn't open her eyes.

He looked outside, sighing. The moonlight was bland, simply stretching over things, not troubling itself to pack into corners. The moon itself was enormous, magnificent, pulsating, and he supposed that it too was the biggest *moon* he'd ever seen. He really did smile then, standing there, feeling good. Everything in this place was big, everything excepting Madame and Suzanne, and Suzanne was smallish and dainty everywhere, and delicate to the sight; but she was strong! He had been amazed at her strength!

Back over the fold of the plain, back where the jungle was, and the cliff, and the sea, and the brig, the way home, was a fitful red glow from fires themselves invisible. Those fires had survived all the rains, and continued to burn smudgily, helping to make the plantation even bigger. Big, big . . . it made him a trifle dizzy, and he was startled to find from the feeling of his face that he still smiled.

The smile went, like some cloth deliberately taken away from his mouth, when he saw the Count de Pontalis, who prowled, a musket in the crook of his arm.

The count went to the storage shed, and tried the door carefully, felt the lock. He shook a man seated there, spoke angrily to him, though in a low voice. He slapped the man's face, hard. Hab could hear the slap. The man rose, mumbling excuses. He picked up a musket and began to encircle the shed, the count looking harshly after him. Soon the count went down toward the slaves' quarters, and he was lost to Hab's sight for a while. Everything was still, sleeping. The count when he reappeared walked warily, instinctively cautious, looking this way and that, the master of a vast property but afraid . . . afraid. Watching him, Hab too felt scared. The count re-entered the house by a door almost immediately under the balcony where Hab stood. Hab shivered, and turned back, letting the jalousies fall without sound. The night was beautiful, yes, but it was scary here. It *wasn't* beautiful! But Suzanne was beautiful. She stirred, the moonlight all stripes on her again, and this time she opened her eyes. She did not open them wide, but she saw him. She smiled.

"Come—to—Suzanne" she whispered, so low that he could scarcely hear. "Come—to—me—again."

So he went to her again.

. 15 . . .

The hands were filing out to the fields in the first light of a dawn flagrantly opalescent, when Hab and the plantation master returned. The hands were silent men, very dark, fat-lipped, sullen, their clothing rags, their eyes shifty; and they moved at a begrudging shuffle, heads down. The overseers, whether mulatto or near-white, bowed and doffed hats, but the hands had no salutation for the gentlemen on horseback, not even a scowl. Hab was surprised by their numbers. There were scores, there were hundreds.

Some had cropped ears, ugly, dirty, reddish splotches, swollen stumps. Hab saw two with slit noses, which mutilation, a punishment, lent to their hideous faces a grinning, grimacing expression. Some were branded on one shoulder or on both. There were some who limped, the cords back of their left knees having been cut in order to teach them not to try to run away again: these had been obliged to leave the slave quarters very early, before dawn, in order to get to work at the same time as their fellow slaves. All looked hungry.

The owner of these creatures, though he acknowledged the greeting of the overseers, paid not the slightest attention to the blacks. In excellent spirits, he cut air with his riding crop and caused his horse to prance.

"A pity there was not better entertainment. It was over so soon."

"Yes, before I knew it'd started."

"Maîtrejean is quick, though unless he makes his touch immediately he'll press too hard. I have fenced with him. This, this morning, was nothing to him."

"Why'd he go out, then?"

The count shrugged.

"Oh, there was some sort of quarrel. Something about which had the better fighting cock, or the more ravishing mistress."

"I should think in that case they'd let the cocks fight it out, or else the women."

Hab was serious, but the count laughed. The count seemed not at all concerned with the fact that two of his friends, a few minutes before, in his presence, had attacked one another. Presumably he had come along just in preparation for future gossip, or it might be simply in order to entertain the only one of his two guests capable of rising from bed.

There had been a flutter of preliminary work by the light of torches. They had paced the field, trampling grasses, picking up sticks and stones, studying the place where the sun would soon rise. They had taken the swords out, long bright blades with bell guards, and hefted them, and measured them. They had conferred, each second with his principal, then the seconds with the referee, de Pontalis, and with the surgeon. They had walked the field again. They had placed the principals thus, and then after long discussion changed that rule and placed them so. At long last, when the dawn came—it was all they'd been waiting for, really—they backed away, all but the principals, each armed now, and the Count de Pontalis, who carried only his riding crop. The count had made a doubtlessly eloquent speech in French—he later explained to Hab that this was a formality, a last-minute plea that the quarrel be settled by peaceful means—to which nobody paid the slightest attention. Pontalis had then called them to the center of the field, close enough so that the tips of their extended swords just touched, and he'd placed his riding crop underneath those two points, and said something else, and then sharply stepped back. The two men had dropped into a catlike crouch, and one, Maîtrejean, had instantly lunged, and the other, whose name Hab never did learn, stepped back, dropping his sword with a quickly stifled yip of pain. And that was the end of it—except that they fussed a great deal about the cut the loser had received on his right forearm, and bandaged it solicitously. There hadn't been much blood. Hab had seen men at sea, yes and in the Watts shipyards at Stonington too, get as bad or worse cuts and never even stop working.

All the same, it couldn't be denied that somebody might have been killed. A little longer lunge, and that sliver of steel would have slipped through a heart instead of merely the skin of a forearm.

Hab certainly didn't approve of such goings-on, but he had been impressed. Not so the Count de Pontalis, who laughed and made jokes. Yet brief though the fight had been, and though he pooh-poohed it, clearly the count had enjoyed it. He would have enjoyed it as much and perhaps even more had he been a participant, Hab suspected. He just seemed to like violence for its own sake. Hab couldn't understand that. Hab could understand fighting, if you had to, but he couldn't understand liking it.

Another thing Hab could not understand was why he had ever belittled the horse as a spiritless beast. He knew now that it was as that visitor from Baltimore had said: he'd never seen a good horse before. The only horses he'd ever ridden were plow horses, and not even very good plow horses. This was no such animal he was astride now! Despite the fact that the count held himself and his own steed back, curbing his impatience and his wish to gallop, in order to keep with his guest, Hab had all he could do to stay in saddle. The truth is, it had never before occurred to him that he was a poor horseman, or even that there were degrees of horsemanship, just as it had never occurred to him that there might be better beasts than the old, broken, fattened ones Connecticut shipped as deck cargo to the sugar islands. On foot, he would have watched the count with sincere admiration. As it was, he didn't dare to watch anything except the back of the horse's neck and the high decorated pommel, to which he clung. He was badly scared.

However, this fear at least did keep him from thinking about what he had done last night. He still wasn't ashamed of himself, as he should be, and as he knew he would be soon: remorse would arrive, and with a crash, searing, tearing remorse, sometime later in the day, he believed. As when he had been a boy and had a whupping coming to him for something he'd done or failed to do, so now, though a little sickened at the thought, nevertheless he wished the thing would be finished, the pain endured and passed.

Yet it was not Hab's physical fear and resultant confusion of mind which made the count's question sound startling. The question *was* startling, voiced casually as it was.

"Have you made any decision yet in the matter of that flour, monsieur?"

Hab swallowed, clinging to the pommel, not moving his eyes.

"Decision was made before we came."

"Captain's orders, eh?"

"Captain's orders."

Still Hab didn't look up, yet he somehow knew that the count had shrugged. Hab could almost *feel* that shrug. The count never made any further reference to the flour. He talked on as gaily as before. All through breakfast he talked—not a big breakfast this time, just chocolate and brioche and marmalade and butter and fruit and an omelette— and when the meal was ended Hab tactfully suggested that since it would seem that they weren't going to do any business maybe he and Captain Wainwright had better get moving. The count was horrified. He wouldn't hear of it! They must stay at the very least a few days. Why, they hadn't yet looked over the plantation!

"I could do that today" Hab pointed out.

When he went up to Si's room, to see how Si was, Hab left his host in the library writing a letter.

Si's room was near Hab's own, though off another corridor. It was much the same sort of room, but the woman was different. Hab didn't like her. She was a beauty sure enough, but a sulky one, with none of the gravity and catlike deliberateness of Suzanne. Her mouth leapt sarcastically when she spoke, and her laugh was a shade too shrill. Moreover, when Hab called she was somewhat drunk. Si himself was wholly drunk, asprawl on the bed, half dressed, snoring venomously. The woman giggled. On a tray on a table there was a full cup of chocolate, the crumbs of a brioche, and an empty glass. This matelotte had breakfasted on brandy.

"He no good" she said, and giggled again. She came over to Hab and stood so close to him that he could look down her nightdress and see her breasts. She raised her eyes and swiftly dropped them, with a malicious little smile. "No good" she repeated. "Not big, strong, like you, eh?"

Hab stepped around her and made for the bed. He shook Si hard.

"He not even try" the matelotte complained. She waved exquisitely kept hands. "He come in dronk, he fall down, bipp! like that! Not even try."

Hab regarded his friend. Hab had known drunkards all his life but never intimately. He couldn't remember when he had had his own first drink of grog, not any more than he could remember when he had his first drink of water, and though he liked the taste of rum, some rum anyway, and some brandy and some wine, he never had liked the searing heat it imported to the innards, the giddy tingle it gave the brain. It was just this, he gathered, that your real drunkard *did* enjoy, rather than the taste. A man who got swacked absent-mindedly, drinking too much flip while argufying with companions in some public house, and regretting it, with a headache, next day—this man Hab could understand. He could even imagine occasions—he had never known one—when it would be right to be at least a little drunk, and wrong to be sober. But this business of settling down to saturate yourself with alcohol, so that you knew nothing, he couldn't comprehend. The Rellisons, John's folks, had used to do that out in the country, and no doubt still did. Si Wainwright had done it yesterday, drinking and drinking like a man obsessed, without real companionship, without encouragement. Surely he'd had no fun? He had been glum throughout, virtually senseless for the last few hours; and when, lighted, and perhaps part of the way supported if not actually carried by negro slaves, he had made his bedroom, he had lacked the strength to undress and had been incapable of making use of a girl put there for that very purpose. Why did a man do that? Hab shook his head, ran fingers through his hair.

One thing at least was certain. Si Wainwright still had a lot of sleeping to do, and it would be necessary to keep him away from the bottle when he did wake up. Not that there was much left. The sangmêlé, disgusted with Hab, doubtless disgusted at the moment with all Yankees, was grumpily pouring herself another. Hab, thoughtful, went out on the balcony.

Below him the Count de Pontalis was talking to Hubert, the mamelouque. He gave a letter to Hubert, who tucked it into his saddlebag— for a fresh, saddled horse stood by the side of the veranda, and Hubert wore riding boots. Even as Hab watched, the count, his face very serious, clapped Hubert on the shoulder, and Hubert mounted and was off. He rode at a long easy loping gallop, and he headed south, toward the mountains, toward St Pierre. Hab wished that he could ride like that. Hab did not, however, wish that he could see the letter. In the first place it would be written in French. In the second place he believed that he knew its message anyway.

Thirty-five miles away, the count had said St Pierre was, but over jagged mountains. A porteuse took a day and a half to make the journey. Such a horseman as Hubert, mounted as Hubert was, might do it in four or five hours. The question was, how long would it take for a whole troop of horse to make the return trip? Or would they send foot soldiers instead?

It was a matter of time; for Hab Jones had no doubt now that they were being betrayed. This jovial and aristocratic host could do arithmetic as well as the next man, and even though there might not be a French language equivalent of the old saw about half a loaf, the Count de Pontalis could easily calculate that half a cargo of flour was assuredly better than none. He might not fancy the idea of betraying his own guests to that common enemy the customs men; he might shudder at the thought of the reputation this act would give him when the news of it got out among Yankee skippers; but the facts remained that he needed the flour and that he didn't have the money to pay for it.

Hab turned back. His friend, his captain, was motionless, open-mouthed, snoring. The sangmêlé addressed herself to half a water glass of brandy. There wasn't much left in the decanter. Si would need a pick-up: that was only fair. Besides, to empty the decanter into the slop jar, as for a moment he had thought of doing, would be ungracious. Their host might be plotting the blackest treachery, as Hab believed, but he never forgot his manners; they might be teetering on the brink of ruin, he and Si, and about to be pushed over, but certainly they were obliged to admit that so far the hospitality had been without flaw.

And anyway, that woman was just as likely to polish off the rest of the brandy herself before Si woke up.

Downstairs the count overwhelmed him with smalltalk. Monsieur le Pilot must see this place in which he found himself, and see all of it, and none other than he, the master himself, would conduct Monsieur on the trip. Voilà! Should they start with the quarters of the field hands?

There was nothing remarkable about the slave quarters except their size. The count was evasive when Hab tried to learn how many slaves he had, but it was certain that they must have been crowded. They'd hardly have room to turn over, was the way Hab thought of it. However, they were sheltered from rain. If they had no bunks they had dry board floors. The sexes were not segregated, but they did have separate privies, which were comparatively clean. There was no dining room, no table of any sort. Each slave, male or female, had a bowl; and the

bowls were stacked high at one end of the ground floor; some had
crude markings to identify them to their owners, but most were identi-
cal. Old women, pregnant women, and children prepared the food and
kept the barracks clean while the able-bodied, men and women alike,
were in the fields. There were not many old women, not many pregnant
ones either. They died too young, these damned Dahomeans, the count
complained. And when one did get with child, he added, she was likely
to take it up with some one of their own witch doctors who would
perform an abortion with le bon Dieu knew what. Most of these operations ended in death, but no one ever consented to inform on the
surgeon, and woman after woman, despite the record, was willing and
eager to take this chance of ridding herself of the child conceived
within her.

"They just don't *want* to have babies!"

They got two meals a day, having no meal at the noon rest unless
they had saved part of their breakfast. On Sundays, however, they had
a third meal. They were fed local fruits and vegetables, bread made
from imported flour, and horse meat if horses were available. On Sundays they were also given salted fish, when the count could get any.

The count was outspoken in his distaste for these field hands. A
polite and even kindly master indoors, he was harsh outside. The house
servants—and he always referred to them as servants, not as slaves—
he didn't overburden, didn't curse; he treated them with consideration
and good humor, and it was obvious that they were fond of him and
proud of their places. But the blacks, he said bluntly, were sub-human;
they should be treated like cattle. This visit today, though it was partly
in order to permit his guest to see the living arrangements, was also a
routine inspection trip for the count, and he made it in precisely the
same spirit in which he might have checked on the condition of a
stable or a sty.

There was a small hospital in charge of an obsequious mulatto. It
was clean, but a depressing place. There were eighteen or twenty
patients, suffering from sundry tropical diseases, and they were utterly
silent, apathetic, as though they were lying there *trying* to die. They
scarcely glanced at the visitors. There was one man who had been so
severely lashed that he would be unable to work for several days. He
was lying on his belly, his back, blurrily visible through a gauze thrown
over it to keep the flies off, resembling raw beef that has been minced
in a grinder. *That* one wasn't apathetic! He said nothing; but the fear,
the screeching terror, that shone in his eyes when he saw the Count de
Pontalis enter was proof enough that he thought he was going to be
taken out and triced up for another flogging. The count never looked
at him.

The house servants' quarters were luxurious by comparison. They
used the big house's kitchen, in which kiosk, as a matter of fact, a good

136

many of them worked. They had their own dining room, their own plates and knives and forks and spoons and cups and glasses. All excepting the youngest had individual rooms, and the married couples were supplied with double beds: they were all Christians, the count said, and though it wasn't strictly legal, since they had no civic rights to enter into contracts, they were sometimes married by the priest who visited the plantation once or twice a month, and who was a liberal man. Yes; the field hands—it was one of the things the count held against them—for the most part resisted conversion; but the house servants were all Christians. A few, Pierre the head valet, the butler, Madame's favorite among her five maids, even lived in the big house itself. These and their like formed the aristocracy among the house servants, the almost-whites, who tended the very persons of Monsieur and Madame. The lesser servants, and the overseers, clerks, couriers, were as well housed but they tended to occupy the back rather than the big-house side of the house servants' quarters, and they were wont to congregate in a small court back there—a courtyard, the count said, in which a valet or lady's maid wouldn't be seen. Forming one side of this court was a small neat house which was reserved explicitly for couriers of color from other plantations or from the government, and for porteuses. It was the overnight house, a resting place for transients. At this hour it was occupied by one person only, a porteuse, who sat on a bench in front, her huge basket on the ground at her side, and regarded them with large solemn dark eyes.

The mill came next, and this first bored Hab Jones and then gave him a headache, the heavy unavoidable sweetness of the air being too much for him. He saw the cane crushed, he saw the sugar boiled, but he just couldn't get excited.

The kitchen, now, was something else again. The kitchen was not just a place where somebody went from time to time to prepare a meal. It was occupied every daylight hour and many of the night hours as well with men and women and boys and girls who were baking, roasting, cooking, basting, broiling, scouring, sweeping with large gawky palmetto brooms. It was an unremitting but friendly bustle. Everybody there worked hard, but everybody smiled, and they were delighted by the visit and strove to show off. Hab wished more than ever that he could talk the language, though the count was patience itself in the matter of interpreting. Hab asked all sorts of questions. He wanted to be able to remember everything, so that he'd be able to tell Deliverance. He cried out over the ash wood fires, the pots and pans in a bright row, the biscuits beaten with a three-pronged stick, a Dutch oven very similar to the one in Judge Watts's house, the roasting irons they called rabbits, the long metal-handled wafer and waffle forms, the round rice pot hung from a crane, the broiler designed to go right over live coals with its four iron feet and its long handle and its gravy grooves. . . .

As in the big house itself, everything here was on a large scale. You might have supposed that at the other end of the covered walk, back and forth on which dusky boys and girls constantly scampered, an endless banquet was in progress. In fact all this was for two of them, for Hab and the count, Si being presumably still asleep, while Madame had recently sent down word that being indisposed she regretted that she could not join them at dinner and wished them a good appetite.

"Shall we have a soupçon, monsieur?"

They repaired for this purpose to the wine cellar, which was not truly a cellar at all but rather a scooped-out, tunnel-like cave made of packed earth shored up by timbers. It was dark there, and oddly chilly. Extensive, the place wasn't filled. The lowest bins were several feet off the earthen floor, for fear of floods, and most of them were empty.

The count put down his candle and made a gesture of despair.

"These wars! You see how it is, monsieur? Less than a thousand bottles."

"Well, I guess you can hold out a little longer. Maybe the war will end."

The count opened brandy that was even lighter in taste than the brandy of the previous day and not as hot inside; but it was insidious.

"You don't like it?" anxiously. The count had never before seemed so touchingly distressed. So might Judas have felt, Hab thought. So might Caiphas have felt when he kissed his Lord. "Perhaps if I opened anoth——"

"It's fine" blurted Hab.

He drank the balance very carefully, and with real regret refused a second glass.

They must have lingered in that low chill place longer than he'd supposed, for almost immediately after they left it, as though waiting for just this signal, night came. It came abruptly and with no intervening twilight. It was as though somebody had blown out the sun as you whuff out a candle before going to bed.

The clouds were low over the western horizon, the direction of the jungle and the sea, and the red glow of brush fires lit their bunchy bottoms.

Hab's mind was made up, his plan was complete; but as a man of peace he would make one more peaceful try. He nodded toward the glow in the skies.

"Count, you've been mighty kind and I want to thank you a heap, and I'm sure Si would thank you too, if he was able, but don't you reckon we ought to be getting on? It's working against your interests to have us down in the bay there. Another ship might start in, and see us, and skeedaddle back out."

The count said immediately, and rather brusquely for him, that it wasn't to be thought of.

"I've seen the plantation and it was very interesting" Hab pointed out. "Si saw it before. I thought if we started out tonight——"

An overseer had appeared and the count excused himself to talk for a moment with him, and then the count excused himself again, saying that he had an important matter to attend to. Hab knew what that was.

"I'll go along."

"I am delighted, of course, monsieur, but this is only a routine duty."

"I like routine duties."

There was a certain tenseness about the counting of the machetes as the blacks brought them to the storehouse, both the overseers and the count himself being uneasy and very earnest, while only Hab, hands in pockets, showed no strain. The count supervised the whole thing, as he surely did every night, and he was too preoccupied to be approached again, then, on the subject of departure. Even so, it seemed to Hab that he took more time than was needed. Afterward he laughed, and placed a hand on Hab's shoulder as they started toward the house, and began to talk with animation on a subject he believed would interest Hab—the dinner they were about to eat. Hab, however, returned to the matter of leave-taking.

"But your captain's condition! Forgive me if I mention it, monsieur, but do you think it would be wise to take him back looking as he must look now? Do you think, even, that he would be able to make such a trip?"

"Might. Sleep does a lot."

It began to rain, and they ran, arriving at the house breathless, brushing aside the servants who had started forth with umbrellas.

"Shall we not have another apéritif, monsieur, before we wash?"

Hab fully intended to ask for a litter; but the sight of Si changed this. The owner-captain had finished his sleep and was in the middle of the entrance hall, on hands and knees, barking, woof-woofing playfully to chase away the servants who surrounded him and who were trying to get him up. The servants were gentle about it, and respectful, themselves giggling sometimes, but really trying to lift him without offending him. He would turn, woofing at them, and they'd pretend to be frightened.

"Woof" said Si Wainwright. "I'm a dog."

"You're a danged fool" Hab said sadly.

"Woof-woof-woof-woof! Gr-r!"

At a word from the count one of the slaves scuttled kitchenward, to return with a beef bone, which he tossed to Si. The slaves laughed. Si, also laughing, pounced upon the bone, pushed his face down to it, and pretended to chew and worry it. Hab went over and picked the thing out of his mouth. He caught Si under the armpits.

"All right, come on now. This is enough."

The count instantly was a penitent. It had been a *stupid* thing to do,

139

it had been *vulgar!* Would Monsieur find it in his heart and graciousness to forgive an unthinking act like that? He was desolated! And from his voice, from his eyes, he really did feel bad.

"Oh, that's all right" said Hab. "Come on, Si. You're going back to bed."

"Woof!"

"Shut up."

The servants were a little frightened, seeing the swift change in their master's manner, and a few sidled near, endeavoring to help Hab; but he shooed them away. The Count de Pontalis had the good taste not to interfere. Si struggled a little, and tried to burble some objection, but he hadn't eaten in twenty-four hours and was not strong. Hab got him to his room and shut the door on pop-eyed attendants.

The matelotte was no help. She was asleep, stark naked, starfished on her back, legs this way and arms that, her hair askew; still, and for all of it, if only her mouth were closed she would have been beautiful. There were lighted candles in a branch, and somebody had refilled the decanter.

Si disengaged himself. He was grinning, but not sheepishly, rather proudly. The sight of the woman had tingled his vanity. He started to undress, shaking off Hab's offer of help.

"You watch! I'm all right now! Had just enough!"

"Listen, Si, maybe if we started to leave here right now——"

"You watch! I don't mind anybody watching. I was kind of weak there, when I first woke up, and she got sore. But you watch us now."

Bare excepting for his stockings, he went to the bed, kneed himself onto it. He didn't take the trouble to blow out the candles. He clawed the inert lovely form, fell across it, got an arm under it. Hab left.

Hab almost hated to go to his own room and see Suzanne after that scene, but he was sweaty from the carrying. As it happened, Suzanne was quiet and attentive and very sweet, helping him to wash, handing him the towel, not pushing against him but smiling a shy smile now and then. When he was ready to go downstairs she came close and asked, with an upturned face, for a kiss.

He kissed her, somewhat distantly at first, but then he kissed her again and it was better, and she clung to him for a minute until without haste he took her arms from around his neck.

She stood with her head still tilted back, her eyes closed, her arms at her sides; and she swayed a bit.

"You—will—come—back—soon?"

"First thing after supper" he promised.

He wondered, as he walked down the corridor and nodded a greeting to René, why that feeling of shame hadn't set in yet.

. 16 . . .

DE PONTALIS STOOD AT THE FOOT OF THE STAIRCASE, right where Hab had last seen him, but now he was in other clothes, very trig and trim, all starchy at the throat. He apologized again, in a low earnest voice, for the bone episode. Hab tut-tutted. They drank some stuff which was unlike anything Hab had ever tasted, not wine and not liquor but something between the two—but not very strong— and then they went in to dinner.

It was a good meal, and Hab took his time and enjoyed it, trying to remember every dish so that he could describe it to Deliverance. They had a green turtle soup with bits of lemon floating in it; fried sheep brains with brown butter sauce, garnished with onions, peas, parsley, and bay leaf, and dipped in grated breadcrumbs; a dry white wine with the brains; oysters broiled in their shells and served in piping hot sand, along with champagne wine; a larded roast fillet of lamb stuck with cloves; a somewhat tongue-cutting red wine Hab didn't like much; and more other things than he could remember or even recognize. They talked of this and that. The count made no further reference to Captain Wainwright and none to flour, and he did not utter an objection when with a rich pudding, some fruit, and two cups of coffee and two glasses of brandy, Hab smoked one segar and then asked to be excused. Hab really was tired. He had slept little the previous night, and wouldn't dare to sleep tonight; and though he was accustomed to late work he knew that he needed at least some rest. He accepted a second segar but pocketed it. He and the count bowed to one another, and Hab said thanks but he could find his way alone. Then they bowed again, and Hab went thoughtfully upstairs. Suzanne was waiting for him, smiling a happy dreamy smile.

He reckoned it was well after midnight when he slipped off the bed, though he had no exact knowledge, for he had not heard any clock strike. Suzanne was asleep. He had listened to her breathing for a long time, while meticulously measuring his own. It had taken much to put her to sleep, for she was strong and for all her air of languor very alive and alert. After all, he supposed, she didn't have much to do in the daytime, so she could store up energy. But now she was asleep sure enough.

He got off the bed with elaborate care. He knew where his clothes were, he knew where everything he wanted was.

It hadn't rained often and wasn't raining now. Dressed except for his shoes, he knelt at the set of jalousies furthest from the main door downstairs, and lifted it half an inch. There was no moonlight, so there was little to be seen; but the shadows packed underneath the balcony, the veranda shadows, deep and dark, troubled him. Though he could hear no breathing and could see nobody down there—he could see nothing at all there—he hesitated. Well, he might wait for moonlight. But suppose the moon didn't show? If there was a man down there he might be asleep, but even a sleeping man could be awakened by the thud of Hab's stockinged feet as he dropped to the veranda. Hab lowered the jalousies.

When he passed the bed on his way to the door, his shoes looped around his neck, he tried in vain to keep from looking at Suzanne. He was afraid that if he looked at her hard enough, feeling the way he did, it would wake her up. He could scarcely see her anyway—in his real eyes. In the eyes of his mind and memory he saw her in detail. He stopped, trembling. He felt himself beginning to sweat, not just in the face and on the backs of his hands but all over. He swallowed. He ran his fingers through his hair.

He opened the door, peered out. There was no light in this branch corridor, but by a light apparently situated at the far end of the main corridor he could see René, seated, asleep. On his knees Hab crept out. He closed the door carefully.

Unable to see the floor, he crept over, he moved slowly, one hand outstretched low. Soon his fingers met a cord, no more than a thread from the feel of it, possibly an inch above the floor. He sucked in his breath. Nothing moved, nothing sounded, he hadn't set it off. He stepped over the cord and crept on, feeling for more, but there weren't any more.

René stirred. Hab rose, his right fist pulled back. René's lips moved a little, his eyelids fluttered. Slumbering in a chair at the branch of the corridor, the back of his head a scant two inches from a sharp wooden corner, René had no weapon that was visible; but he had a voice—and no doubt he had his orders. Hab hoped he wouldn't have to punch him. Making it hard enough to stun the man might kill him at the same time, and Hab didn't want to kill anybody if he could help it. René's eyelids fluttered butterflylike a moment longer. Some dream? Then they were still. Hab watched him long and steadily, and at last Hab lowered his fist. He was sweating badly.

The grand staircase was easy, being so big and so well carpeted. Also, there was a night light in a glass chimney in the entrance hall, which helped; though Hab, having placed it with precision in his mind, could have found the walnut box even in pitchy darkness. His one fear was that it might be locked. The count had not locked it when he put it away yesterday, but he might have come back to do so afterward, worried as he was about weapons. Well, it wasn't locked. No doubt the count took it for granted that nobody would venture to touch anything so personal to him. Then, too, there wouldn't be any powder in the flask: powder would be put there only immediately before these pistols were to be used. Hab shook the flask at his ear, and even unscrewed it and tipped it up, but no, there was no powder. He replaced the flask. A pistol under each armpit, he went back up the grand staircase.

There was nobody stationed at the door of Madame's boudoir, though there was a night light at the end of the corridor, and Hab, not wishing to scare her, placed the pistols on the floor and put on his shoes. He tried the door, and found it unlocked, and opened it and went in.

The maid must have been a very light sleeper, or perhaps she had been awake. She was off the pallet and standing before him, between him and the bedroom door, wide-eyed, trembling, frightened, but firm, almost before he could blink. He sensed that she was about to scream. There was light in the room and he could see her clearly: her neck muscles jumped.

He put a forefinger over his lips.

"M-Monsieur——"

He caught the glint of incredulity in her eyes, and knew what it was she was starting to think, and he smiled and shook his head. It was fantastic, that the maid should have thought such a thing, even for a split second.

"Madame" he whispered gently, persuasively. "I must see Madame."

The girl didn't move. He knew that she did not understand any word he said excepting "Madame," but he spoke further, very softly.

"Tell Madame I want to see her. Me," and he hooked a thumb at his own breast. "Tell her Monsieur Jones wants to say good-by. What's that in French?"

The girl was well trained, nobody flighty. She did not scream. She wheeled suddenly, with a whispered "Attendez," and went into the bedroom, shutting the door behind her. Hab waited.

Unexpectedly soon the maid reappeared. She stood aside in the doorway and motioned for Hab to go in. Fear still shone in her eyes, but she was obeying her mistress, whom she trusted.

Madame la Comtesse was such a little woman, so dainty and so old, and when Hab saw her seated there in her nightrobe and a lace shawl and a frivolous and probably very expensive lace nightcap, he knew that she suffered a great deal. There were lines of suffering in her face, at the sides of her mouth. It must have been a tiny life she lived in this enormous place, he thought. She must be like Job, he thought, and her stroke is mightier than her moaning. Yet she smiled at him, serene. He crossed the room and bowed over the hand she held out, and kissed it.

"It is a large pleasure, monsieur."

"I oughtn't to've come so late. But I promised I'd say good-by."

Genuine dismay filled her eyes: it was like a warm bright liquid running over them, though the woman did not truly weep.

"You go? At such an hour!"

"It was a sudden call, a messenger."

He could tell the truth: he didn't need to say who had sent the messenger, or where, or why.

"But at this time—— My husband——"

"Everything has been arranged, ma'am. Everything will be all right."

She smothered another protest, and smiled, and her little light-blue eyes twinkled fondly. She was so sorry, she said. She was desolated. But it was kind of him to come. Would he not sit down for a little while, and talk with her? She patted the edge of the bed.

"Thank you, ma'am," and of course he sat down.

They talked of divers things. Hab did not have to keep reminding himself that this was a countess: he only had to remind himself that he had not known her all his life. While he talked he thought some about Deliverance, and he intended for a while to tell her about Deliverance and about how much Deliverance meant to him, who had never had much of a mother he cared to remember. He thought afterward that he could have told her that and it would have been all right. But he did not.

Why shouldn't he sit and talk with her? An hour more or less wasn't going to make any difference to him tonight—unless Suzanne woke up. But it did mean a lot to Madame. There was not so much pain at the ends of her mouth now. She twinkled at him as she exclaimed softly that she hadn't known, when she first met him, that he was a celebrated pilot. Her husband the count, she said, had informed her of some of his exploits. Her husband had said that she would do well to hear from the pilot's own lips the story of the warship and the bad-smelling fish. Wouldn't he tell her? Well, it hadn't been exactly a warship, he said. Well, it was hard to explain. But he did tell her; and of the many times he had told that story, the story about Red Ferguson and the barrel of rotting shad, Hab had never got such happiness from it. She laughed delightedly, the laughter of a child, but not loud.

After a while he begged her pardon, and stood. She did not try to detain him, but she smiled regretfully, and thanked him for calling, and extended her hand, which he kissed. He kissed it harder than he'd meant to do, and worried afterward whether he had hurt her. It was a small and slender hand, warm, the bones delicate and crushable.

He went to the door of the boudoir, which opened before he got to it, for the maid of course had been snooping. He turned in the doorway.

"Bon voyage, monsieur" she called softly. "If ever you come again to Martinique you must call on us."

"I sure will, ma'am" he said, and made a low bow, the lowest he had ever made for anybody. "Good-by."

In the dim hallway he took his shoes off again and hung them around his neck, and he picked up the pistols. To get to Si's bedroom he did not have to pass René, though he could see half of the back of the seated slave, who was motionless, twelve-fifteen feet away. Si's door was unlocked. Two candles guttered, all but out, on the table. The woman was still asleep: that was the first thing he noted.

Si gave no response to shaking. Hab didn't shake vigorously, for fear of waking the woman. He picked up Si's shoes and tied the laces together and looped the shoes around his neck with his own. He put down the pistols and scooped Si's clothes from the floor. Scooping up Si himself was another matter, but he did it, and got the captain over his left shoulder, on top of the clothes. He picked up the pistols. The woman never moved, never made a sound. He hoped that Suzanne slept as heavily.

That morning as they'd ridden in from the duel the Count de Pontalis discoursed upon what they'd seen. Simple though it had been, and brief, it contained a point for discussion. "So straight, so clean, you comprehend, monsieur? When a man fears you and fears your skill, he awaits guile. He is taut. He dies the thousand deaths of the coward, because he is not sure what you will do, and his muscles are—how shall I say it?—all-which-ways." Hab had made no answer, for he'd been wondering whether that road down there was hard enough to crack a skull on if you fell from such a height as this. "So what is it that Maîtrejean does? He lunges direct, with no engagement or disengagement. You comprehend, monsieur? No underpass, no slipping over the blade, no beating, no waggling, no counter, nothing—only a straight beautiful lunge. And because of that he wounded! Oh, I'll not say that Maîtrejean could not have outfenced him any time, but this was more logical, and safer too. The other was a bungler, and that can be dangerous, to meet such a one. The best swordsman in the world, monsieur, is not afraid of the second best swordsman in the world— but he is afraid of the *fiftieth* best. Something wrong might happen, something that perfection can't cope with, you comprehend? And that is why Maîtrejean was sage, just now. He did the simplest thing that any man could do with a sword, which was the last thing his opponent expected him to do, and for that reason it succeeded, you comprehend, monsieur?" Well, Hab hadn't comprehended at the time, being more concerned with keeping in the saddle; but it came back to him now, the way things often did that he hadn't rightly known he'd heard. When men waxed subtle (the idea went) the most obvious thing was the best thing. All right. Hab left by the front door.

He didn't know what doors might be guarded, or even if any of them were, or if they *all* were; but the main one would be safest. "If a man fears you he awaits guile." Well, there wasn't any guile about just walking out, was there?

No sound was made, no shadow moved. Not pausing, he walked through the garden a good two hundred yards. Si was heavy on his left shoulder, and the two pairs of shoes pressed him on either side of his neck, but he strove to walk like a man who knows exactly where he is going and why. Any humping-up-and-down, any furtiveness, or jay-like start, might catch the half-opened eyes of a sentry. If there were sentries. He didn't know.

It was an effort holding the pistols, one in each hand. They were heavy.

He cast a glance of regret to his left, to where the murky brush fires lighted the clouds. He would have liked to go there without deviation, now that he was clear of the house. There were two reasons why he didn't. He could not be sure that his strength would hold out, toting a thing as weighty as Si Wainwright, from whom no moan issued, who might have been a corpse. The second reason was that he might not be able to find the entrance of that tunnel-trail down the side of the cliff to the water. If he were to fumble for that, and not find it until broad daylight, he might be too late. So he stuck to his original plan, fully knowing that the most perilous part was ahead.

The home of the house slaves was dark and silent, even the kitchen, and Hab gained the little courtyard behind it without incident. It was almost too lucky, the way he was going without an encounter, without challenge. The courtyard was paved with slabs of stone which tilted this way and that. There was one huge basket before the house for transients, the basket of one porteuse. He doubted that others had arrived, or any couriers, since he and the count had visited this place late in the afternoon. He had to take that chance.

Silas Wainwright of Stonington, Connecticut, fitted with reluctance into that basket, seeming all limbs, gawkily flapping and bending like some broken mechanical doll. But he did fit in, after a while. Hab piled his shoes and clothes on top of him. Then Hab went into the transients' house.

The door was unlocked, and indeed he would have been amazed to find it otherwise, for who'd lock a door on a far plantation like this? In the darkness his hands told him that there were two rooms without doors, a thin partition separating them. Male and female, no doubt. On the right-hand side he heard somebody sit up. He went in there, the pistols straight before him.

"All right" he said quietly. "I've got a load for you."

He knew she couldn't make out the words, but he counted accurately on the fact that she'd be half asleep and that she was accustomed to being wakened at unusual hours.

Well, as he knew by the sounds, she sat up without hesitancy or fright, and began to do her hair. It was a small place, and he could reach out and touch her—which touch did nothing to disconcert her—

and he was pleased to have his hand tell him that she was dressed. Her shoes? No, of course not: none of them wore stockings or shoes. But she did take quite a while with her hair. He waited in silence, not risking another word. There would be time enough for her to take alarm when she saw outside that he was a foreigner, and when she learned that they couldn't converse. The tone of voice had been enough here. It wouldn't be enough outside. But Hab had the pistols.

At last she was ready.. He mumbled something purposely unintelligible and went to the door, feeling that she was following him. Outside, he collided with a man who had been about to enter.

This was a man he had seen several times that day and the day before, an overseer or superintendent of some sort, young, tall, and strong, a taciturn man who had often been in conference with the count. He had a small stony mustache which looked chiseled out with the rest of his face. He was handsome; and he had small dark intelligent eyes. Hab had not previously seen him without a hat, but he knew him right away.

The overseer knew Hab too, and he was as startled as Hab. But he didn't think as fast. The only weapon he carried was a wooden club about two feet long, which hung from his right wrist by a leathern thong. He had started to lift this, but had not started to step back, when Hab struck.

Hab hit first with the barrel of the pistol in his left hand, swinging it up short, feeling the ivory ball-butt turn in the sweaty palm of his hand. The barrel hit the man in the forehead. Then Hab swung the pistol in his right hand, this time higher and wider and with more force, striking the man again in the forehead.

The man toddled back on his heels. He began to bleed. But he didn't fall down. And there was fight in him; for he started to lift his club.

Hab, standing spread-legged, pointed a pistol.

"If you yell," he whispered, "I'll blow your gizzards all over the yard." It was a still night of heavy oppressive wet air. It was almost too still. There wasn't as much as a cricket.

"And maybe further" Hab added.

He half-turned, seeing the porteuse in the doorway. She was a tall broad strong straight woman with no flabbiness. Both her hands were high when she loomed in the doorway, for she was still arranging her hair. She had fine large eyes. She was startled; but she took it well. She took it as though she had always expected something like this to happen to her sometime anyway, and didn't greatly care. Spanish ancestry, Hab reflected. He motioned with a pistol to the basket. She went dutifully, but with dignity, not in a hurry. She didn't look to see what was in the basket. She tried to lift it, and feeling that it was too heavy, she straightened and looked right at Hab.

147

"You" he said to the overseer, and waggled a pistol. "You get it up there."

It was plain what he meant, and the overseer did not plead his ignorance of English but went to the basket. He and the porteuse got it up on her head. Hab would have helped (being twitchy now about time) but he didn't dare. He had those long pistols to think of. He would have liked to command the overseer to drop the club which dangled from his wrist, but he didn't dare to do this either. It might take too much time, too many signs. The marvel was that some head hadn't yet been stuck out of a window, that somebody had not yet begun to scream. It was all too easy. It was eerily easy. When Hab motioned with his head toward the red glow in the sky, and whispered "We're going that way . . . all right, march!" the obedience was perfect, the silence they left behind them complete.

For the first slime-slick half-mile he had all he could do to keep from turning his head, and he thought of nothing except what would happen if the overseer became inspired to risk it that the pistols weren't loaded. Or rain—that would have destroyed the illusion by wetting the priming. The overseer still carried his club, a lighter, longer, and hardier weapon than the empty pistols. But the overseer walked on. Once he paused and began to turn, but Hab positively growled, advancing with both pistols raised, and the overseer shrugged and hurried again to his place by the side of the erect dignified trudging porteuse.

After that first half-mile Hab slacked his muscles and gave himself over to contemplation of the porteuse's back. They could certainly walk, those women! It was a very wonderful thing, the way she held herself. Studying her from behind, he was able to feel better. He was very tired, and he could only hope that the overseer wouldn't attack. He found time to hope too that Si had not recovered consciousness, because if he had he would be danged uncomfortable in that basket, stuffed in upside-down. Hab didn't worry about Si being stifled. The basket looked porous.

Before they reached the smoke he remembered his shoes and put them on over mud-clotted stockings. His feet hurt. But then everything hurt. It was hard to keep moving.

The smoke was thick and low, and it scraped his nostrils, stinging his eyes. He coughed—and then had a struggle to keep himself from coughing on and on in his weakness. He had never in his life fainted, but he felt he was near a faint now. Like a woman. Or didn't women know when it was coming? He got closer to the porteuse and the overseer, for it was harder to see them now in the smoke.

The overseer went to the entrance of the trail without question. There Hab called to him to stop. Hab didn't want him to go into the jungle where even in daylight it was difficult to see a man more than a few feet away.

They were a slight distance above the fires now, on higher ground, and the air was clearer, and it was coming up dawn over to eastward. They couldn't see the house, even through breaches of the smoke, because of the fold in the plain, but Hab did glimpse the mountains several times, and at the foot of the mountains, where it seemed some trail debouched upon the plain, he caught a glint of horsemen, of their accouterments. He didn't see them long and didn't see them well, and he could not estimate their numbers, but they were horsemen all right. Military horsemen. Cavalry. Coming from the direction of St Pierre, they were, and moving toward the center of the plain, the de Pontalis house.

Habakkuk Jones grinned tiredly.

"Well, we made it in time" he announced to the captain-owner of the brig, who being upside-down and still aslumber made no reply.

Anyway Si, container and all, was out of sight now. The porteuse, hearing no contrary command, had entered the jungle trail; shadows had gulped her and her burden. The overseer, however, had been halted by Hab's voice. He stood waiting, wondering, fearing. The blood on his forehead already had clotted and it looked as black as his mustache against a ghastly pale face.

Hab motioned with the pistols.

"All right, you go home. You can't get there in time to make any trouble now. Go on. Go home."

The man didn't move. He kept his gaze fastened on the pistols. He was petrified with fright, paralyzed. He thought—the thought was loud in his face—that Hab was going to shoot him in the back as soon as he turned.

Hab nodded to the path again. He lowered the pistols.

"Please go. I won't hurt you. Just go, that's all."

The overseer edged away, stumbled, went to his knees, got up slowly, all the while watching those pistols. He kept walking backward. Impatient, Hab raised both pistols. The man whirled around, ducking his head, and started to run. He ran a zigzag course, his head very low, his arms over it, and he was still running when he disappeared into the smoke of the fires. He would keep right on running, Hab calculated, for a long time. Hab went down the jungle trail.

He slipped and slid a lot, and once caught himself at the very edge of a sharp gooey precipice; but though he hurried he didn't get to the bay before the porteuse.

She was not alone. She had a crowd around her, four gaping members of the crew of the brig, including Fortman the bosun. The sun was up now, crashing over the cliff's corner to the bay, and there was light enough at the landing for them to see the porteuse and for Hab to see them.

"Good thing! Who sent you?"

"We was worried about you, sir. Mr Riley's had somebody waiting here with a boat ever since yesterday afternoon. Where's the captain?"

"Upstairs. If you'll give me a hand——"

The porteuse was placid, not understanding, not resisting. Perhaps she too expected to be slaughtered, as the overseer had. If so, she was ready. She regarded them gravely. Hab looked at her empty basket, after Si Wainwright had been dumped into the boat.

Hab put the two dueling pistols into the basket and hoisted the basket back up on her head. After all, there was no need to steal things like that from the count, who certainly loved them. Maybe because she came back with them the porteuse would not be punished. He hoped so.

The porteuse continued to stand there, waiting for something. Hab searched his pockets. He had no coin. Neither did any of the sailors. But Hab, still searching his pockets, found the segar he had recently accepted from the Count de Pontalis, and with a happy cry flourished it and thrust it into the porteuse's mouth. She had large strong white teeth, which she opened a little to receive the segar. She grinned massively, a happy woman. Hab pointed to the basket and made a sign to to indicate great bushy mustachios. She grinned on, because of her burden not daring to nod, but nodding with her eyes. He waved her off. Absurdly happy, the segar jutting at a sharp upward angle between her teeth, she started back and soon was lost in the shadows, her bare feet making no sound.

Hab got into the boat, sat in the stern sheets, pulled the recumbent captain toward him. He covered Si's nudity as best he could with Si's clothes.

"He'll be all right tomorrow morning" he sternly told the sailors. "And by that time we'll be far, far away. All right—pull."

. 17 . . .

Whenever he'd wake and because of the smell find it impossible to sleep again—though he badly needed the sleep—Hab would borrow oilskins and go up on deck, to stand in the lee of the cabin, feet braced, and watch the sea, and maybe chat with Mr Riley or Mr Sanders, whichever was on watch. These mates were capable mariners but neither had ever been a skipper and they were unaccustomed to so much responsibility; they were troubled in mind and short of temper now, and twitchy, which did not make for a pleasant gam.

Hab would have slept on deck if it were not for the rains. If the rains were as fierce here out at sea, they did not sound so. With no jungle, no cane fields for them to thunder upon—only the sea and the brig—and you couldn't even hear the rains on the deck for the thrumming they made against the unpushable sea—they had a sameness that detracted from their savagery; so that when you had heard three or four pass you were no longer afeared but had even begun to feel a mite sorry for them. Beating the sea, indeed! What would that ever produce?

What made it worth while to stand watching them and braving them time after time was the magnificence they left when gone. You could see them go as you could see and hear them coming, as clear a sound as that of thousands of birds, though infinitely greater in volume, and as definite a sight as would be a sky-high bedsheet swiftly swept toward you, swiftly swept away. Yes, you could see them go, mark them with the eye; but you didn't take the trouble. Instead you turned your head and watched that part of the Caribbean the storm had just quit, and you stood heedless of the receding roar as of the rattling and clittering and gurgling around you, the water sluicing off the cabin roof, sleeing flat over the deck, and humping and pushing and leaping frantically with throaty sounds in the scuppers. *There* all was brilliancy and a fine bounce. The sun would be back abruptly, almost with a pop, as though it with its very rays had shoved the storm aside; and the sea would be all a dazzling blue, softening to silver in the distance where it merged with a silver-white sky. Wavelets burst eagerly through the surface of the water, which had been flattened like a sheet of silk by the rain, and these caught the sunlight and glistered gaily, subsiding only to leap up again. Everything was most scouredly bright and marvelously *clean*. It seemed ridiculous, the notion of an ocean being *cleansed*, but that's the way it looked after the passing of each storm, a sight as astonishing as it was joyous, the colors so lovely that it almost hurt Hab's eyes to look at them. Each time the world was born all over again.

"Pretty, ain't it?"

Mr Riley, however, before answering glanced not at the sea and the unbelievable sky but at the after hatch. Mr Riley had been unable to get a word out of a captain who hadn't stirred since they left Martinique more than twenty-four hours ago.

"I reckon" he muttered.

Well, they had not truly left the island of Martinique at all, though they'd pulled out of the Pontalis domain fast enough! Orderless, Mr Riley had elected to move north with four or five miles leeway. On the one hand he didn't wish to keep too close to the coast, from the bays of which pirates might at any time appear. On the other hand he was afraid to get out of sight of Martinique, being uncertain of his own as of Mr Sanders's navigation; also in the event that a warship chased them, those very pirates' bays, small and shallow as they were, might come in handy. Mr Riley had turned north rather than south toward St Pierre partly because the wind was favorable for a northerly run but even more because from what Hab Jones told him he reckoned it possible that besides a land force the customs people at St Pierre might see fit to send a cutter north for the Pontalis plantation. St Pierre would be a good place to move away from, Mr Riley reasoned.

Soon he regretted his brusqueness. Had the ship's cousin been a proper sailorman, Mr Riley would have spoken in no other way, if he'd spoken at all; but non-sailors of whatever calling habitually stirred up the smallness of a snob in Mr Riley, so that now he essayed sociability.

"Well, what do you think of life at sea?"

"Don't like it" Hab answered without rancor. "Never reckoned I would, far's that goes."

"No, it's a hell of a way to live" agreed Mr Riley, glancing again at the hatch, shaking his head.

By all apparent logic Mr Riley was doing the right thing; but he knew, as Hab did, that few skippers act strictly according to logic and Bowditch, most of them trusting rather that very instinct, that indescribable unpointatable assurance, by means of which they *are* skippers: it was known as proceeding by guess and by God. Mr Riley would never be a skipper, Hab decided as he watched the mate. At least, not for long. It wasn't a matter of seamanship or even simply of the ability to command men: these qualities were taken for granted. It was not inner confidence but as in religion an outward *appearance* of inner confidence that counted. The ship's captain who always looked as if he knew exactly where he was and what he was doing, and why, regardless of how he wambled inside, was the captain who, given luck, would succeed. Hab had known intimately more than one captain, and the honest ones admitted that it was largely a matter of luck—of luck, that is, *and* of looking as though you believed in your own luck, whether you did or not!

Mr Riley there didn't believe in his luck. Mr Sanders, like the other mate, had a long record of uneventful sailing, but he didn't believe in his either. Si Wainwright, their junior by more than ten years, and additionally burdened by the realization that he owned most of this vessel and its cargo, *did* believe in his—or seemed to.

Even when he came up on deck this morning Si looked sure of himself. This is not to say that he looked well! For all the long sleep, his eyes were red, his legs rubbery; while his mouth jerked this way and that; his hands quivered; and his face was pale.

All the same, he didn't look discouraged or uncertain. The instant he stepped upon deck the ship was his again, and he knew it, and so did everybody else. Mr Riley exhaled in noisy relief. Si nodded to him.

"Good morning. All's well?"

"All's well, sir."

"Good morning, Swensen," to the man at the helm.

Then he saw Hab, and his face got if possible even more pale, and his eyes shifted. All the same, he went right to Hab and said in a low voice:

"I—I'm sorry."

"Well."

"Thanks for what you did, Hab."

Hab turned his head, embarrassed.

"You get me home," he muttered, "and that'll be thanks enough."

Si Wainwright touched his shoulder apologetically, and then, embarrassed, went to the wheel. His voice was clear if low, and it had dignity, as he asked the course. A thinking man again, straight and serious, as different from the boneless blubbering fool of the plantation house as black from white, he nodded approval.

"You did quite right, Mr Riley. Quite right. I'd take her out a mite further, though, and keep sharp watch on that shore."

"I'm keeping a watch there, sir."

"How sharp?"

Startled: "Eh?"

Si walked to the lee rail. On land he had swayed and teetered. Here, though the deck moved, he was solid. The lines around his mouth got long and tight.

Hab could see nothing but the shore itself, a hazy fuzzy light blue which strove to mix itself with the horizon. The peaks above the shoreline were faint and far, a filmy blue-purple, so that he couldn't rightly be sure that he even saw 'em: he could have been talked out of it. He saw no smoke, no boat, no sign of habitation.

"Will you fetch the glass, please, Hab?"

A moment later Si lifted his head sharply, his pumphandle chin upjutted.

"Ahoy the masthead! You, up there!"

"Aye, aye, sir!"

"Didn't Mr Riley tell you to watch the shore too?"

"Aye, aye, sir." Excitedly: "There a sloop putting out! Must've come from behind some point! Coming this way!"

"I know that" muttered Si.

"Coming almighty fast, sir!"

"I know that too" Si muttered.

He handed the glass to Hab, who had to do a heap of peering before he could make out anything but mountains, jungle, sea, and sky, though Hab's eyesight was always accounted better than tolerable. When he did see the sloop it startled him, it was so near. Jibs and mainsail were not white nor were they tanned in the usual tropical fashion, but as well as Hab could make out they were a sort of bluish-purple, as was the hull of the boat itself, a color which blended easily with the vague blur of the shore. This fact in itself made him uneasy. No city or village was in sight, even through the glass, and if such a sloop put out from a plantation invisible from the sea, like the Pontalis plantation, then why the attempt at concealment, why this chicken-hawklike swoop? Vessels of all sorts approached one another cautiously these days on the high seas. They were leery of decoys and even of distress signals, leery of anything they saw, and what with the multitude of prizes didn't trust any rig or hull, much less pennants. That is, they didn't unless they happened to be well armed and looking for something—unless, to put it another way, they happened to be war-ships or pirates.

There wasn't anything hesitant about this sloop. The wave at its bows as it sped through the water indeed was the first of it Hab had seen; and very soon he could see the sloop without the glass.

Before he had a chance to be scared Hab found himself studying this craft, and especially its hull. It was low and singularly slim for its length, and had sharp bows and a decided cutwater. As far as he could make out, the stern, which was low, was square: the stern was tossed a good bit by the speed, and shaken by the wake, but the sloop held her course easily. The rig did not interest him, except for its freakish-ness. The two headsails were conventional enough, if large; but the leg-o'-mutton main was upheld by the longest gaff Hab had ever seen—a crazy stick, three-four times as long as it had any right to be. A bad boat in a blow, Hab reckoned, though it'd certainly be sweet, if clumsy to the sight, when the wind was smart.

Si ordered a change of course two points to larboard, which would give them more leeway and probably more speed. At once the sloop too changed course. The lookout, alert enough now, called this down from the masthead. He might have saved himself the trouble. They all saw it. Everybody in the brig saw it; for everybody was on deck now—no alarm had been given, the off-watch hadn't been called, but they piled topside all the same, to line the rail, peering, calculating, their talk whispers.

The wind was from the east, wet and warm, a steady wind, a get-alonger. To run straight with it, the brig's best sailing point, would be to run for shore. Hab, who had descended to the waist, looked up at Si Wainwright. There was no longer anything shaky about Si. He was a statue.

There was little nervousness among the crew, for that matter, and never a hint of panic. As they watched the approach of the sloop mostly they were silent, and when they did talk it was to grumble, as sailors grumble at everything, or to remind one another of debts yet unpaid, making a considerable fuss about two shillings or perhaps a couple of carved shark's teeth quite as though soon the lot of them probably wouldn't be helpless in the water while the brig burned. When they moved it was to glance up at the quarterdeck, the sight of Si seeming to comfort them, or else to go below to collect debts or straighten bunks or pack bags or boxes: it was for all the world as though they were coming home, except that they showed no jubilation.

Home? How many of them had homes they could remember? Aside from Hab himself, only one of the sixteen men before the mast was from Connecticut—Jabez Fortman, a New Londoner, the bosun, the oldest there, a first-rate seaman but a drunk ashore. Jab had been brought aboard at Stonington penniless and unconscious, though previously signed on all proper enough; but he had prepared himself against the first port of call by selling his birth certificate to one of the Englishers for two eight-pieces—which would buy considerable rum anywhere. "I don't need a paper. Nobody'd ever take me for anything but a Yankee." Now when Jabez gazed at the skipper Hab thought he saw a glint of envy in his eyes, envying Si his hangover, his misery. Jabez had seen, they all had, how Captain Wainwright was brought aboard. This had not lowered Si in the estimation of most of the hands: Jabez Fortman incredibly thought the more of him because of it! But when Jabez turned back to watch the oncoming sloop, his eyes went narrow, and he cursed, while his knuckles white-skinned on the rail. He was truly, Hab believed, thinking about those eight-pieces in his pocket and reflecting that now he'd never have a chance to spend them, never get drunk again. Behold what he thought, this old sailor, in the very face of death!

For that death was close not a man doubted. Coasters did not spare:

they couldn't afford to. These were not pirates of the high seas, outlaws against whom the hand of every decent man was turned, who could consort only with their own kind but who because of their very boldness and strength need fear in open fight only warships. *Such* pirates—few enough now, what with the British Navy—might seize a ship and all its cargo; but they were out-and-out black-flaggers, hangable when taken, known and hated everywhere; and because of this they had no need to murder prisoners. If such men killed it was in battle or afterward from sheer deviltry, for amusement; it was never to cover up their crimes. The dead-men-tell-no-tales policy was not that of the Teaches, who had for the most part been exterminated anyway, but of these rats the coasters, these fierce small nibblers, who would dart out a few miles in fair weather, pounce, tear, gouge, and scurry away. These men were not hugely brigands, or leaders of buccaneer armies, as Morgan had been. They were jackals. They were wreckers. They struck when they were overwhelmingly sure of victory; and where they struck they left nothing. Not for them was the loot with which estates and baronial arms might be purchased. They sought only small things, things which could be carried away, readily hidden, disposed of. The rest they'd burn. They would not be pleased with the Horace T. Wainwright's flour, these grabbers who approached the brig. They'd fly into a rage when they learned that there was nothing else. They would strip officers and men, take every watch and small trinket, every coin too, of course—Jabez Fortman's eight-pieces would surely go—and then they'd be off after setting such fires as could not be doused.

There were a good many of them for that small sloop, as the men in the brig could see. They crowded it. For a little while Hab Jones, the only man forward who'd looked through the glass, was asked questions; but soon the figures of the coasters themselves were visible, and the sparkle of their weapons, and it was no longer necessary to ask what death would look like.

Only a miracle could save them now; and aside from God, Who didn't seem to be with them any longer, the only person who might conceivably commit a miracle was of course the skipper. This was why they glanced at Si Wainwright, not really hopefully but with the knowledge that if help came from anywhere it would come from the after-deck rather than from Heaven.

Habakkuk Jones watched them furtively, himself frightened now and at the same time hopeful that a sign of fright among them might settle him to courage. They were only a little clipped in their talk, somewhat grumpier than usual. The general attitude could have been that this was going too far after the food they'd consented to eat and the work they had graciously done: nobody had any right to come and slaughter them now: wasn't there any justice anywhere in this God-damned world, even at sea?

There were three other Americans, but two were Mainers, one was from New York, and Hab had never got rightly acquainted with them. There were sundry Swedes and Finns and Dutchmen and others of whose nationality Hab was uncertain, who professed, however, vehement loyalty to Connecticut. There were five Britishers, all deserters from the British Navy, who vowed that they had been innocent honest sailing men until impressed. *Their* fear was re-impressment in the event of a British warship overtaking the Horace T. Wainwright, and they didn't show more troubled than the others now at the prospect of ordinary elimination. These Britishers clung passionately to certificates of American birth. Four had owned such certificates before sailing; and the fifth, small Arty Walsh, once of the Royal Marines, had purchased his the second day out from the bosun, Jabez. Arty had been carried aboard, or else he would not have come. He sighed a happy sigh, and sang often, after he had bought proof of American birth. Hab studied Arty Walsh now. The short man was no more worried about the pirates—though no less worried either—than were the rest of them. The pirates at least weren't R.N.

Hab had been aquake, but he steadied, holding the rail hard. The others were quiet, if not easy; and so he was quiet. He was glad that they didn't jump around. With a sicky-scared feeling inside of him he had been all right with John Rellison, and now he was glad that the others were making it easy to be all right here.

A rain came, but they paid it no attention. It slapped and splattered them, but they did not move, only watching the place where the pirate sloop would emerge when the rain went.

Hab felt that too. He felt the fascination of watching the end come. He did not even turn, when the rain had bumbled off, to stare at the lovely bright sea behind him. Entoiled, he simply watched the sloop. Well, they were in God's hand now. Gripped hard in God's fist. For all this, not only did he take comfort in the presence of the others but he felt no impulse to pray. If past prayers hadn't counted, present ones hardly would, he reckoned. He did think of Deliverance, not wildly but with deliberation, warming in the thought, pleased all through that she loved him and would have married him had he survived. He took his time thinking about Deliverance, remembering not only how she looked in every particular but also how she spoke and smiled and held her head, how she hummed when she moved about the kitchen, the way she placed her feet while walking with him along the shore. There was no hurry. Nobody at that rail moved much. Even the coasters, coming fast though they were, stood motionless in the sloop, which could scarcely be expected to come alongside for at last half an hour yet.

There must have been sixty of the coasters crammed into that little boat, silent, expectant, lip-licking, leaning forward but not yelling or waving their cutlasses. They made no pretense of threatening with a small bow-chaser, no doubt seeing that such a threat after rain would be silly. No, this was to be a boarding party, with little gunpowder burned; and why crow when the fight was theirs already, before it had even started?

Hab looked aft again. The helmsman, the two mates, were motionless. Si Wainwright stood near the waist ladder staring out at sea.

What was he planning, if anything? To improvise a dummy wooden stern-gun and paint it black in the hope of frightening the boarders away? It was too late now, even supposing that such gentry could be fooled by any toy contrivance. To wet the sails, in the hope of getting more speed? But they were wet already from rain, had been wet for hours. To change course and run straight for shore, grounding the brig? The sloop, which could sail circles around the clumsy leaky old Horace T. Wainwright, could cut them off if they started for shore. To toss overboard the cargo, Si's own precious eight hundred barrels of flour? That would take several hours, and several hours would be too long. Even empty, the brig probably couldn't walk away from that sloop with the long gaff.

As Hab watched him, Si went to the head of the ladder and cupped his hands to his mouth.

"Hab! You there! Habakkuk Jones!"

He started aft on the run. The spell was broken. Time was in operation again.

"And you, Jabez Fortman! No," as his word started a stir in the waist, "I want the rest of you to stay right where you are—for now!"

Hab was before him, dripping, panting. Si, a gangling young man, raised a schoolteachery forefinger all knots.

"Under my bunk, two muskets, two pistols, plenty of lead and shot and wadding. Another pistol and musket under Mr Riley's bunk. Rack with four cutlasses in my cabin. I want you to load those guns— and prime them good. Real good! 'Twon't hurt if a few eyebrows are burned off! But don't bring anything up till I call. Now—wait! You, Fortman. When the next squall hits us, five-six minutes from now, I want the vessel put about so that it runs straight down the wind. I want it put about *while we're in the squall,* understand?"

Fortman nodded.

"Nobody's even to leave that forward rail until the rain comes. Then I want 'em to move smarter'n they ever moved before in their lives. You pass along the word."

"We go aground then, if we make it?"

"Aye, if we make it. And then it's every man for himself."

Fortman nodded again.

"Might do if the squall lasts a while, but most of 'em finish up pretty quick, Si."

158

"I know. But I've been timing 'em, and I figure every fourth one is a long one. Well, this one coming's a fourther. If it should only last a few minutes, like most, we'll have to fight with whatever we have. Knives and marlinspikes, of course, and what Hab'll fetch. Tell the cook to get out his cleavers. But not now! I want him to go aloft with the rest of you, when the rain starts. Riley and Sanders and I'll be there too. The only ones not topside'll be Swensen at the wheel and Hab down below." To Hab: "It'll feel as if the brig's doing a Morris dance. Be braced. I don't want a grain of powder spilled. All right, go to work, both of you—but not smartly! I want no running until that rain comes!"

Hab could hear it coming too, thudding closer, as he moved slowly to the companionway hatch. Moving slow was hard, where before it had been easy to be motionless. Now he wanted to run, or jump up and down, or shriek bloody murder. He descended the ladder carefully, facing aft; and all the while he heard the storm getting closer.

It was a great filling roar, louder and louder.

Si's cabin was small and so low that he had to stoop as he worked. It was good to be doing something. He placed the guns on Si's bunk, took the rods out, measured powder, tore up wadding, found the mold and had started to cut balls—when the squall hit.

There was a deafening clatter, and the spray from raindrops came drizzling down the companionway. Hab shielded the powder against this with his body, filling the narrow doorway in which he braced himself.

The lantern suspended from the ceiling had been rocking ever so gently. Now it rocked wider, at the same time turning a little and turning back.

The brig did not act like a dancer, as Si had warned; there was no dramatic shock. Only, the whole vessel strained as though twisted sideways by a gigantic squeezing force. He remembered what he'd reflected in the waist: we're gripped in God's fist now. It could have been that literally. It didn't seem possible that the leaky old structure could fail to come apart, so that, alone, Hab thought wildly of the deck where at least he'd be free to jump, to try to swim. Even through the thunder of rain—much louder here below than it had been up there—Hab could hear the agonized squeal of timbers. It was a pain in his own heart to hear them, he who had helped to build so many ships. It went into him again and again, wildly, like a knife in the hands of a maniac. He pushed against the sides of the doorway, lifting his head as high as he could, doubtless with a face contorted with pain.

The lamp was spinning crazily now, and rocking back and forth.

The terrible squealing didn't last long. Soon there was only the insistence of the rain, and the brig righted itself: it had never heeled far over.

Hastily Hab poured in powder, dropped in balls, crammed in wadding with the whippy rods. He knocked the butts against the wall, so that powder upspilled through the touchholes. He cocked the strikers. He got out the cutlasses and laid those too on the bunk. Then he began to cut more balls.

The rain went away. Through the sudden stillness, Si's voice: *"Hab! On deck!"*

No one up there ran to him for weapons, or even paid him any attention. Yet there would be a fight. He saw that instantly. He didn't know how long the covering rain had lasted, but not long enough anyway. They'd put about but they hadn't cut between the pirate sloop and the shore. They were in fact closer to the sloop than ever.

"Thank you, Hab." Swensen had left the wheel, but Riley and Sanders were back, and Si. Si took up a musket. "We'll just keep these here. They'll grapple at the waist, sure to, and this is a good place here for picking off as many as we can."

"Well, I guess I don't get back to the Point."

"I guess you don't, Hab. I guess we don't any of us. Too bad."

"Aye."

He picked a good place in the after chains, and squatted, a musket across his knees, powder and ball and wadding between his feet. He looked up at the coaster's sloop, meaning to estimate the time it would take—matter of minutes now, he supposed—and then he rose sharply, spilling some of the balls and causing his head to strike the lower ratlines so hard that he almost went overboard.

He didn't curse or say anything. He just stood there with his mouth open.

Nobody else said much.

It was so difficult to believe, though they all saw it, that the pirate boat had put about and was making for shallow water and the shore.

Si Wainwright slammed down his musket, raised his head.

"You, up there! You gone blind?"

Then he realized that no lookout was stationed above, not any longer. He snatched the glass from its case at the binnacle and himself clambered up the ratlines faster than Hab Jones had ever seen it done before. Hab joined Mr Riley and Mr Sanders at the rail.

Had they seen John Rellison's sea serpent then they would not have been amazed.

"Three masts anyway" Mr Riley reported. "Looks like a double row of ports."

"Can't tell the color of the masts, though" said Mr Sanders.

Si came down.

"It's a frigate all right. British, I think. Anyway, she's a-comin'."

Some of the hands laughed and some cried. A few, jubilant, jeered after the fast-retreating sloop and shook their fists. Some looked the

160

other way. Arty Walsh, for instance, little Arty the ex-Royal Marine, fingered in his pocket the precious birth certificate he'd bought from Jabez Fortman, and his eyes were dark as he picked out the rescue ship.

"Maybe the local blighters might've been better company at that" he muttered.

. 18 . . .

You'll wait a long spell for that spot to get bigger, Habakkuk, Hab told himself, and you need sleep; so he went below, first taking one long good breath of air. Another rain was coming.

The forecastle, steamy and wet, stank worse than ever; but Hab was so tired that he heard only the first of the off-watch tumble down, grumbling, to seek out bunks. The last thing he heard was Si's voice above, competently giving orders to heave to; the last thing he saw, in his mind's eye, was that dark speck on the horizon out there, the speck that had wrought a miracle.

The spot had indeed grown when an "All hands!" brought him to the deck again. It was only a few hundred yards away now, hove to as the Horace T. Wainwright was, and already an officer and a corporal's squad of marines had boarded the brig, together with various sailors. Hab, however, was less interested in the boarding party, at which at first he scarcely glanced, than in the frigate itself. This was the first time he had ever seen a large war vessel near at hand.

The Pactolus, a forty-four, a mountain of a ship, rested as easy in the water as Deliverance the cat-schooner did back in Stonington harbor—if Deliverance was still afloat. Everything about the Pactolus excited Hab Jones, but it was its hull in particular that he studied. The bluff bows, the amazing number of gun ports, the thickness of the sides as evidence at the ports, the weight of the ordnance, the bulging bellied tumble-down, all combined to give Pactolus when motionless an appearance of clumsiness. It looked, now, slow. Yet it was new; and Hab had heard that since they'd been taking the lines off captured French warships the English were turning out frigates slow only as compared with those of the United States. The Pactolus was bulky, but if heavily gunned it was also heavily sparred and must have carried a tremendous spread of canvas: the masts were tall. Hab found it notable, too, that Si Wainwright had not even thought of escape but had submissively waited for the frigate, though nobody knew better than Si the uncertainties of British Navy procedure in these waters, where, neutrality or no neutrality, the chances of his losing ship and cargo, or getting them so wound in long-time admiralty litigation that he might as well lose them, depended entirely upon the frigate's skipper.

Yes, the Pactolus wouldn't be slow. Hab thought he would like to see it under full sail. A sight that'd be, surely!

Even motionless, the Pactolus at least was showy. It rode high, so that the upper part of its copper-sheathing was visible. Above this was a broad stripe of yellow, a gay yellow, about the color of those lemons the Count de Pontalis had shown Hab. The rest of the sides was painted a very dark blue which was all but black, except that there was another broad lemon-yellow band to mark each gun deck. The gun ports, checkering these bands, were blue-black. The masts and most of the upper works were painted mustard-yellow, but a band of scarlet edged with gold ran around the forecastle and continued down the beak to the figurehead, a polychromatic rampageous lion, while the sternworks were brave with glazed windows, a walk, and elaborate carvings of lions, cherubs, drums, wreaths, cornucopias, stalactites, what-not, fairly aflame now in the sunset.

The frigate rode so much higher than the little brig that it was difficult for Hab to see its decks, but what was visible was, like the rigging, and like what could be seen through the open ports, immaculate.

What amazed him as much as anything, after the clumsiness of the frigate's lines, was the number of men it carried. Though there was nothing to suggest that the Pactolus was being used as a troop transport, all except the usual marines being obviously sailors, men peered from almost every port, lined every rail, even loafed in the crosstrees, staring with interest at the brig. There were scores of them, there must have been hundreds—enough just there in sight to man the whole Stonington fishing fleet—and this on a vessel which was not a sail of the line! Few were engaged in any work now, but Hab's eyes saw plenty of evidence that work was found the rest of the day. Hab was used to smaller vessels which sailed with as few men as possible. Being shipshape isn't so much a matter of pride-in-appearance as of common sense; and the vessels Hab knew were shipshape—excepting the whalers, of course, those floating slaughter-houses which in the nature of them were always filthy and on which nobody with any sense of decency would sign—but the skippers of them would have thought it childish to *make* work. Not in Stonington, and nowhere in the sound, would you have found a vessel of any description with such an array of over-painted surfaces, over-carefully coiled lines, over-polished guns and fittings. Too much had been done aboard the Pactolus. Every gun port was opened at a certain angle. Every hand was properly jacketed and pigtailed, every officer on the quarterdeck was resplendent in gilt buttons and epaulets. A squad of blue and scarlet marines, with pipeclayed belts, varnished boots, and polished bayonets, solemnly paraded in the waist. Though surely the Pactolus would be under sail again in an hour or less, every spar was canted at the proper angle, every sail fully furled.

All this, Hab knew, was "smart"; and he supposed that if you were a king and could look at such a vessel and say to yourself "That's mine," it would be excellent to have all those bright and useless trappings; but he couldn't help thinking that it must have been hard on the men.

They, the sailors, stared and stared at the Horace T. Wainwright. Here and there one shouted something or waved derisively, but most were motionless, just staring. What could be of such interest about this commonplace brig? Could it be the sight of the free men who manned it? The distance was too great, the failing light too weak, for Hab even to attempt to make out the expressions on individual faces; but he believed that he could *sense* the envy of those men who stared, those prisoners who gazed from the cage of the great glittering strong "smart" frigate to the world outside as concentrated in this small, helpless, leaky, and slow craft from Connecticut.

The water between the two, very quiet, was beginning to tingle with red.

Hab turned from the rail.

Lieutenant Bullan was a tall and fattish man of about thirty-five, a man with a worried expression, large serious blue eyes, a mouth that suggested a coin purse, a little round fat nose, a little round fat chin. A man with a grudge against the world, as you could see to look at him, he had, as clearly, decided that there was nothing he could do about it. He was pettish and precise. Though regulations pained him—almost everything pained him—he would know them all and would insist upon their observance.

Lucky we got an old one, reflected Hab. From what he had heard, midshipmen and the newly created lieutenants were the worst. This Lieutenant Bullan at least was bored: he would try to get the business over with as soon as possible.

He didn't look around him, and he addressed only Si Wainwright. His manners, to the amazement of everybody, were quiet. He had a low musical voice.

"Would you be kind enough to consent, Captain, that we examine your ship and papers?"

"I don't reckon it'd do me much good to object."

"You do consent, then? Good!"

He spoke to one of his own sailors, a bosun's mate, who promptly led a squad of five below and started a systematic search of the brig. The marines took no part in this, but only stood at the ladder, their arms at attention, as a sort of guard of honor.

"Marines couldn't find anything anyway," one visiting sailor gruffed from a corner of his mouth to Arty Walsh. "Marines couldn't find their own feet when they put boots on, they didn't have a sergeant to show 'em."

Arty flared.

164

"Now see here, you bloody damn deck-swabbin' galley-begotten child of a gun! There ain't a bloody lobster in this whole——"

Arty stopped, abashed, remembering himself, while his face went pale and his lips quivered. The sailor from the frigate, busy, straightened only long enough to give him one brief puzzled stare.

Slowly: "Sounds to me you might be one of us yourself, matey?"

Sweat sprang upon Arty's face; but the sailor only shrugged and moved on. Gasping a little, Arty leaned against a bulkhead. His hands trembled. He looked as if he was going to be sick.

Lieutenant Bullan had an old-fashioned air of pomposity. His head was lifted, his eyelids lowered; he rubbered out his lips. For a moment he looked as if he were going to draw and tap a snuffbox. He cleared his throat.

Si Wainwright spat thoughtfully over the rail and belched.

"Got the papers right here."

"Oh, I say! Another wetter coming. Shall we go below and examine them over the wine?"

Si winced, shivered involuntarily.

"Ain't got any wine aboard. Sorry."

"Oh, I say, damn it, that's quite all right! Matter of form's all. Didn't really fancy the stuff. But let's get under cover anyway, what?"

Si nodded, flicked his eyes at Hab, and led the way to the hatch. Hab, who understood that Si wanted him to stand by, nevertheless followed with reluctance; for he knew the story Si had prepared and rehearsed, knew that Si would lie through a nine-inch plank in order to save his flour, and didn't like to hear a man he knew lie, even for flour, and especially a man he knew as well as Silas Wainwright. Nor could Hab believe that even so patent a dimwit as Lieutenant Bullan would swallow the whopper Si Wainwright had concocted; and he wished to witness his friend's humiliation no more than he wished to witness his mendacity. Still and all, he went. He didn't enter the cabin, which could hardly have held three men when one of these was Lieutenant Bullan, but loitered at the foot of the ladder, ready to intervene if needed.

There was a considerable rustling of papers, and Lieutenant Bullan went "Hm-m . . . hm . . . hm . . ." any number of times, while Si emitted nothing more than an occasional thoughtful belch.

At last Lieutenant Bullan, his well-modulated voice tinted with wonderment, cried softly: "Why, everything seems to be in order!"

There was some silence. Then the Englishman spoke again, and for the first time there was a hint of sarcasm in his voice, as startling there as goose grease in a pie.

"In perfect order—except, Captain, that it does seem odd to find you fifteen hundred miles off your course, eh?"

Hab caught his breath. The Horace T. Wainwright was properly cleared from Stonington to New Orleans, no questioning that; and the most arrogant and presumptuous Royal Navy officer would hardly contend that he had any right to interfere with the passage of an un-armed vessel between two neutral ports of the same nationality. At the same time, and even though it did not occur to a questioner to wonder why anybody would take flour to a port from which that product was ordinarily shipped, the dullest and most unimaginative officer, without so much as a glance at the map, would know that Martinique was, to put it mildly, a bit to one side.

Everything depended upon Si Wainwright's answer, the attitude he took. Bluster? Argument? Or would he wheedle? In fact he laughed.

"Oh, say, now, Lieutenant, not fifteen hundred! I'm a long ways off, I admit it, but the way I make it is I'm a little less than a thousand miles from Florida. Well, say, that's a heap, but still——"

"But see here, my good man, I said fifteen hundred miles. And you are! At least that!"

"Oho! Don't you think I know how to navigate, Lieutenant?"

"Well, frankly, it doesn't look so."

Bullan was offended, stiff. He was sure he was right, but this Yankee was actually laughing at him. Not good at argufying, the Englishman instinctively ducked back into his dignity.

"Now say, I knew what I was doing when I came over this way, though it's true I never meant to come so far. I wasn't going down through the Florida Channel, the way you'd expect a ship to do on that run, because I'd heard from the skipper of a schooner I'd stopped for a gam with that the wreckers and coasters were busier'n ever along the Keys. Well, sir, I'm wide open for such as them. No speed, low in the water, no guns, no boarding nets, only a small crew . . . I reckoned I'd better be safe than sorry. So I made for the Windward instead."

"But see here——"

"Now wait a minute, Lieutenant! It wasn't the fear of pirates made me head for Mona Passage at last, and it wasn't bad navigating either. This time it was a blow. Two and a half days there, a humdinger it was, nigh onto being a hurricane, though I know as well as you do that this ain't the season. Well, sir, I got a mainmast I'm afeared about, and I figured the best thing for me to do was run right before it. And by the time the wind fetched off and gave us a chance to straighten out, I figured I was nearer Mona Passage than the Windward. Matter of fact," Si went on easily, "it took me some time to learn just where we *was*. I didn't get that figured out till this noon."

Though the big officer, a quiet man, in fact made no sound, Hab seemed to *feel* him leaning over the table and tapping the chart with a fat well-kept forefinger.

"Ah? Well, then, perhaps you could tell me where you *are*, Captain,

166

since your calculations put you only a thousand miles from Florida? I should like to know that, if you don't mind telling me?"

"Sure thing. See, right here. Where my thumb is. And that island you see through the port out there, that's Porto Rico."

"*Porto Rico!* Why, damn it, man, that's *Martinique* over there!"

Si laughed, stretching.

"Lieutenant, you're sure as snakes trying to play me for a fool, telling me things like that. Do you reckon that a Connecticut man don't know how to calculate his position?"

"Oh, indeed, I'm wrong, am I? Indeed, sir, I am vastly sorry for that. But just on the chance—— See here, why don't you tell me what your own infallible figures make our present position to be? I should like to tell Sir Henry Hatfield when I return to the frigate, so that he can make the necessary corrections on our own chartered course. Would you be good enough to do that, Captain? I'm certain that Sir Henry would be grateful."

"Why, sure thing. Always glad to oblige."

"I see. And this is where you think we are, here?"

"Where we were this noon. I ain't moved much since then."

"How thoughtful of you. Yes. And that's Porto Rico over there, eh?"

"That's Porto Rico. Only thing is, you seemed to think it was Martinique, which is five hundred miles further over——"

"Why, you blithering fool, it *is* Martinique!" Bullan's voice was no longer musical: it rose shrill and petulant. Screeching, angry in a spoiled-womanly way, he pounded the table. "Here's your position, here on this paper. Four of us took it this noon, and Sir Henry Hatfield himself checked it. Do you have the temerity to tell me that Sir Henry himself might be wrong?"

"Well, sir, I don't know. I ain't acquainted with this man."

Si sounded shaky, for the first time.

"Why, I tell you that four of us plotted our position at the same time, four officers of the Royal Navy, not to mention half a dozen midshipmen."

"And you still calculate that's Martinique over there?"

Si had lost his jeering Yankee manner. He sounded uncertain, even a little scared.

"Why, man, I *know* it's Martinique!"

"Four of you, you say?"

"Yes, and Sir Henry himself—— Oh, see here, what's the profit in talking to a bull-headed——"

"Now wait a minute, Lieutenant. I never had anybody to check my figures with, and it did seem to me we'd made a lot of easting in that gale. But I never thought we could have got as far as—— But if you think so——"

"My dear Captain, it isn't a matter of *thinking* so. It's a matter——"

"Excuse me, Lieutenant."

Si sprang to his feet, and in one stride, so small was the cabin, he stood in the corridor, his face a scant few inches from Hab's. Si's face was fixed in its part, solemn, apologetic, somewhat frightened, awed. He did not change expression, but he winked once, deliberately; and then he stepped back into the cabin.

"Nobody out there. I was afraid that maybe if anybody heard this—— Look, Lieutenant, you won't let on about it to anybody out there on deck, will you? If they thought——"

"Oh, see here, Captain. That's quite all right."

"What you say on your own ship, I can't help that. You can laugh at me all you want to, over there. But if my own men was to learn the way I calculated our position, why, I'd never be able to get any real work out of 'em and they'd desert the minute we reached New Orleans. Understand?"

"Perfectly, perfectly, Captain. That's quite all right. You may depend upon it I'll be discreet. After all, anybody could—— Well, of course it *is* a pretty big mistake, at that. But we'll forget it, eh?"

"Now say, that's mighty white of you, Lieutenant! I sure feel grateful for that!"

As Habakkuk Jones grinned and withdrew he overheard Si whisper that he did have some wine after all, which he'd produce right now. Si explained that he'd previously been afraid to admit to the presence of wine in his cabin, thinking that he might be overheard and the stuff stolen. It was so difficult to keep discipline with men like this, on a merchant vessel, he complained. Lieutenant Bullan, stroked just right, tut-tutted sympathetically. Lieutenant Bullan started to tell him how it was done on one of His Majesty's ships of war.

Well, the cargo was safe, Hab reckoned. It was wonderful what a man could do for eight hundred barrels of flour.

The two vessels, the big one and the little, floated motionless in a red-smeared sea. It was very quiet, all the world seeming to have ceased to move. The seamen and marines of the Pactolus continued to stare. The seamen of the Horace T. Wainwright, forward and in the waist, shapeless stumps, in the gathering darkness showed rather as fixed parts of the vessel they occupied than as men with lives of their own and the ability to move. It was grayish in the failing light of the deck, but the water was tinted with red and the sky in the west glowed in splendor.

When Lieutenant Bullan came topside, Si Wainwright at his elbow, Hab noticed that few of the men moved in anyway. The marines at the ladder stiffened slightly; and even in the poor light and from the afterdeck, Hab could pick out the British deserters by the way they instinctively started to pull themselves to attention: it was difficult for them to lounge in the presence of an officer.

Bullan felt good. His cheeks, previously pasty, held a tinge of color now. He laughed and said something to Si.

"Oh, they're all right" Hab heard Si say. "I signed 'em on myself."

"A formality, Captain, merely a formality. It's required of me. And then you never do know when you'll pick up a deserter or two or three. Your ships are crowded with them, Captain, positively crowded with 'em."

"Not this one" said Si.

Thereupon Lieutenant Bullan, if affably enough, took matters into his own hands. He addressed himself to the bosun's mate who had come up from below, and when he'd learned that everything was in order and that there were no suspicious circumstances, he asked if all the men were now on deck. They were, the bosun's mate reported.

"Good. Keep 'em here, and be sure every one files past me while I examine their birth papers. No doubling, or passing papers! I'll hold you responsible!"

"There aren't any Englishmen here" Si Wainwright said earnestly.

"Likely to find 'em anywhere, Captain. Absolutely anywhere."

"Can't you take my word for it?"

"Afraid not. Strictest kind of orders. Positively no exceptions."

Here was a duty Lieutenant Bullan did not like and so he was surly about performing it—surly and conscientious. He had been liberal in the matter of Si's whopper, but he'd be letter-of-the-law now. Traditionally, and especially when it had its guns trained on you, the British Navy, which had never been in greater need of men, considered everybody a deserter who couldn't prove that he wasn't. Complexion, accent, or the testimony of shipmates seldom counted. Many officers, Hab had heard, scornfully refused even to look at the birth certificates with which most American sailors provided themselves. They took what they needed, and that was all. Lieutenant Bullan was more conscientious than this; but he would surely like a few impressed men to take back to the frigate, having nothing else.

Hab saw Jabez Fortman go to the end of the line. Hab himself sidled into about the middle of the line. The sailors from the frigate watched them, and so did the Royal Marines. Some more marines came up from the gig.

Bullan examined each birth paper with care, holding it up to the fading sunlight. They were not long or complicated.

When it came his turn Hab said simply that he had no paper. Si Wainwright stepped forward quickly and explained. But the visiting officer was unexpectedly stubborn here, as though his good nature had given out. He shook his head, dewlaps flapping.

"You're English" he said in a flat voice. "If you was American you'd have a paper. No American goes to sea these days without a paper."

Hab explained, or tried to explain. Si tried again to explain.

"Nonsense" snapped Lieutenant Bullan. "You'd all cover one another up, any chance you got. You," to Hab, "can explain that to a board of inquiry."

"Now hold on a minute!"

Hab frowned, but he wasn't truly angry, only annoyed. He could not take this business seriously. He thought that he *should* laugh. But at the "Hold on a minute!" the officer stiffened, and so did the marines. "You can't do this!" cried Hab, approaching him. Hab raised an arm, meaning to tap the lieutenant's chest with his forefinger, to emphasize his point. It could be that the lieutenant had a bad case of nerves anyway. Perhaps he really *did* think that Hab Jones was about to strike him. In any event, he sprang backward, screaming.

"He's assaulting an officer! Assaulting an officer!"

Hab stopped, dumfounded. He started to waggle his hands at the wrists, to try to explain. Then something about Bullan's face frightened him. He whirled around—in time to face the first musket butt.

They were clubbing their muskets as they came, those Royal Marines. They jabbed with the butts, and jabbed and jabbed, being careful, however, to keep the bayonets high.

Hab backed away, ducked, stumbled, went to one knee. He raised his arms above his head. He saw Si, his mouth open in a shout, running toward him; and then a marine stepped in front of Si. There were four marines or five around Hab, jabbing in with the muskets, and as they got closer they began to kick him too. It only lasted about half a minute.

. 19 . . .

It would be by far the smallest as it would be the least lovely boat Habakkuk Jones had ever built, but it would be all his (though all stolen), exclusively his design and manufacture. It would be bobby and gawky and crank, a tiny triangular uncaulked thing without paint, a patchwork quilt of a craft made up of hackmatack, pencil cedar from Bermuda, red oak, and some wood even Hab himself didn't recognize. Certainly it would have no strength; but it was to be asked for but one short voyage.

It would consist of nine parts, not counting the treenails which he kept in his pocket; or eleven parts if he succeeded in rigging a mast—with his hammock for sail. With or without the mast he'd have a paddle, which would serve also as rudder. That paddle-rudder had already been carved and smoothed: it was in a locker near the forward cockpit, along with the bow-post, hidden beneath a pile of shot-plugs.

The other pieces were scattered about the frigate, though most of them were on the orlop somewhere near Hab's hammock, near also the gun port by which he meant to escape.

Deliverance II he had named the boat; but there would be no spirits or wine served when it was launched, no speeches made, no crowds a-cheering. Hab knew that the as-yet-not-assembled boat would slide through the port, for he had measured both with care. He knew the port well, and had greased its tackle, softened its oakum packing so that it could easily and quietly be opened even in rough weather, and oiled the riggle outside. All this had meant a power of work, most of it done in the dark. He had so fastened the hook to the bar that it could be slipped free without a sound, if you knew just where to put pressure, and yet would clip back into locking position when released. That port fastening wouldn't be very firm, in the circumstances, but it would hold for a little while anyway—and a little while, a little start, was all Hab asked.

Getting the various parts, fashioning them too, since he had become an unofficial carpenter's mate with the privilege of swinging his hammock on the orlop, had not been difficult. The difficulty had been in hiding them conveniently enough to enable him to gather them swiftly and without noise, at dead of night, and yet well enough so that nobody would be likely to find and take one of them. Unlike the Stonington Deliverances, Deliverance II would have straight sides. None of the

171

pieces had any curve, or any other suggestion except the auger holes that it was intended as part of a boat. It was not arrest that Hab feared, at least until he had assembled his craft. It was that a piece would be stolen from its hiding place at the last minute: he couldn't possibly do with fewer pieces, nor could he improvise anything late at night. A little while ago it would have seemed incredible to Hab Jones that anybody coming upon a mere slab of wood would think of appropriating it: a while ago he had not known what things were like belowdecks of a British warship, where men stole whatever they could get their hands on. A board's value even in barter might be little or nothing, but still they'd steal it, if only to keep in practice, if only for something to do. A large number of the men, Hab soon learned, had been hauled direct from jail to the Pactolus without ever having their own wishes in the matter consulted. Well, they practiced their art as they remembered it, these burglars, cutpurses, pickpockets, and thugs; and they taught it to others, too. Many members of the Pactolus crew were tradesmen or artisans who had been snatched from their homes by the press gangs. Never having put foot on ship before, some were resigned to the belief that they would never put foot on land again, precautions against desertion being what they were. Hab had met men, men who hated the sea, as almost everybody here did, who had not been ashore *anywhere* in eight years. Among criminals, they became criminals. Petty assault, theft, and a thousand small meannesses were the order of the day, the taken-for-granted procedure against which you best protected yourself by joining in. Not much more than half the sailors, Hab estimated, were English or Scottish or even American. There were dozens of other nationalities represented, and many races, Hindu, Negro, even a Chinese, a Lapp, and a couple of Polynesians. These too took whatever they could get in any way they could get it, for what did money mean to them? Sailors were traditionally cheated anyway, cheated of their grog allowance and their food allowance, cheated for slops by the purser, docked or fined by every officer, midshipman, and warrant officer who had a grudge against them or who just happened to feel nasty; and if they ever did get their money, and got ashore with it, the Jews cashed their tickets at a ruinous discount, after which the whores and pub keepers took the change. For English sailors this was bad enough; for the poor ignorant foreigners, who spoke the language haltingly or not at all, it was worse. So these, like the others, stole. Hardly a day went by but that one or two men were flogged for the offense and their blood and bloody bits of their skin splashed out on the grating while their screams filled the air; yet not one theft in a hundred was officially reported. The men had their own justice, their own punishments and acts of revenge, below. What happened there at the gangway every morning at eleven, after Captain Sir Henry Hatfield himself, his hat off out of respect for the King (and everybody else in the crew had to remove his hat or cap then out of respect for the captain: they made everybody be present every day), solemnly read the Articles of War; and one of the bosun's mates, stripped to the waist, flexed his great muscular arms, spread his feet wide, and drew the cat from a red baize bag; and the first of the poor devils, as drunk as his messmates could contrive to make him, though probably whimpering at that, and sure to scream, was triced to the grating—this was bad enough, and it always made Hab and many another sick to his stomach. But a flogging was clean open-handed justice, and even liberal and merciful, compared with what sometimes went on betweendecks.

Hab shifted a little in his hammock. Beneath him, but with some clothes stuffed beneath *it,* so that its outline shouldn't show against the bottom of the hammock, was the last piece for Deliverance II, the ninth piece, the stern, complete with auger holes. For it was tonight that Hab hoped to make his escape. Sometime during the middle watch, probably a little before dawn. This was a Saturday night, which meant generally heavier sleeping. True, there would be church service, but to make up for this there would be no floggings, for Sir Henry Hatfield was a devout man. Attendance at church service, like attendance at floggings, was compulsory, one being esteemed as morally improving as the other. The early watch was to be turned out at four o'clock as usual; but in fact, the men having been permitted to holystone the decks on Saturday afternoon, so that it was only necessary to sand and swab them, even the bosun's mates were inclined to be liberal about the piping, and would wait, some Sunday mornings, until fifteen or twenty minutes after four before they went below with their shouts and their thwacks. Thus the men of the middle watch, on deck, were made to serve a little extra time on Sunday morning; but they did not protest, being, for the most part, fast asleep. It was a hanging offense, sleeping on duty in time of war; but aboard the Pactolus it was ordinarily only punished by a caning at the hands of the bosun's mate or ship's corporal who came upon the culprit: this would cut a man about the arms he'd raise to protect his head, so that he would be sore for weeks afterward, and find it hard to sleep or even to wear a jacket, but it saved him from sick bay and kept him at work. They were short-handed aboard the Pactolus. This of course was why Hab Jones had not been hanged for assaulting an officer, the most serious of all offenses. However, on Sunday mornings, again, a dash of liberality was permitted and even encouraged, and a man on deck who snoozed between four and four-fifteen, unless one of the bosun's mates or the master-at-arms had something personal against him, was often left untouched. That one quarter-hour was the only time in the whole week when discipline was even slightly relaxed aboard the frigate, and even if unconsciously everybody took advantage of it with deeper slumber, heavier drowsiness, a watch less alert than usual.

Hab had long ago decided that a Sunday morning was the time for him to escape. Conditions this time were perfect. There was no moon and the air, which was chill, felt like rain. There was enough of a sea running so that all gun ports were battened, making it dark on the orlop, yet not so much of a one as to prevent him from slipping out through his doctored port on an up-roll: it was not a choppy sea. The wind was from off the unseen land to larboard, but though this would make the sailing of the Deliverance II that much trickier, it also meant that the navigators of the frigate were not forced to allow plenty of leeway: when he last glimpsed it, at sunset, that low sandy indeterminate shore had been no more than six or seven miles away, and probably it was no more than that now.

Yes, this was the time. Tonight.

Just before turning in he had tried again the port by which he meant to leave, and it worked perfectly. He held it open only a moment. When the larboard side swung down again he closed the port quickly, and saw the hook slip silently back over the bar. That was a heap of water out there. Launching a boat, one man alone, in the darkness, within a matter of seconds, wasn't going to be easy. But by God, he thought savagely, as he made for his hammock, if I can't get that boat out I'd rather try to swim it than stay here!

He raised his head, and looked about, and listened. The light, such as it was, came from horn lanterns and down through the main hatch from the deck: the orlop, however, would have appeared in pitchy darkness to anybody unaccustomed to such quarters. The orlop was a paradise compared with the hold below, where there were no ports to open, even in good weather, where no light penetrated from above, where the stink of bilge all but suffocated you and the planks were always wet and slippery with oakum-smelling drippings from above. Hab had known great luck in this matter of a place to swing his hammock. He'd spent the first two weeks down there in the hold, all of them, every minute of them, for he'd been too weak to move after his flogging; but then, after he was questioned and it came out that he was a shipbuilder, he'd been made a carpenter's mate, the carpenter's mates both being on sick-list with scurvy. He'd been a find, even his master, the saturnine rasp-voiced Mr Ellis, delighting in him—at the same time giving him the dirtiest jobs. The carpenter was an important personage, and Ellis the irascible shared what amounted almost to a cabin near the fore cockpit with the bosun, with whom he also shared the services of a boy—services, it was snickeringly said, of many kinds. A carpenter's mate was entitled to swing his hammock on the orlop. Hab probably wasn't getting the regular wages of a carpenter's mate, didn't even know what these were, but he didn't care: the opportunity to sleep on the orlop, not far from the air itself, a place which except in the heaviest weather was scarcely worse than an ordinary cesspool back home—

this was pure joy. Also, he could never have escaped from the hold, but he believed that he was going to escape from the orlop.

The ship swayed, creaking regularly and somewhat sadly, and the lanterns moved back and forth. The wind was steady. There was never a splatter of reef-points from above, and not even a thick slow "All's well!" Nobody around him moved. The snores were even and easy.

He slipped a leg out.

He had heard seven bells strike some time ago; soon the middle watch would be called, and he wanted to get rid of the stern of Deliverance II before this happened. For it was after the late watch had started to snooze, just after midnight, that the snatchers were thickest; for a little while then they would scurry about like rats, not as noisy, possibly not as clean either, but as active and fully as malicious. If one of them felt the outline of Deliverance II's stern on the under part of Hab's hammock he was as likely as not, once he thought Hab asleep, to try to cut the canvas with a knife and see what was there. They had started that more than once. The first time Hab, hearing, had reached suddenly under the hammock, where all was utterly dark, and grasped a head of hair, and tumbled out and to the floor, and then for a few glorious panting moments had pummeled a man he couldn't see and who soon broke sobbing and bleeding from his grip, to scurry away, still the rat. The second time, when he tried the same tactic, Hab had been badly cut about the hands before his fingers could even find a throat or a wrist. After that he found it advisable simply to grump and swing a little, showing that he was awake. As a buzzard avoids a living thing, so these creeping thieves avoided a man awake, who might raise a shout and summon the master-at-arms. However, tonight Hab didn't want to appear awake.

It was his misfortune to be favored often by the visits of these nocturnal sticky-fingers; and this was not because he had any extra clothing, or because he was not liked—on the contrary he was popular; it always touched him to see in what high regard he was held by his messmates and hammock neighbors—but because the report had it that he was accumulating a store of grog in preparation for a souse. You were served, each noon, one gill of pure navy rum mixed with three of water, to which a little lemon juice and sugar was sometimes added, and at supper each night the rum and water alone in the same proportion. If you were an abstainer—there were a few—you could waive this ration and have the wages you never saw be credited with a certain number of pence a week; or you could sell it or trade it.

Now Hab Jones liked rum; and though he did not ordinarily think of it as such, there had been times aboard the Pactolus when he would have found it a solace. However, he had taken but one small sip of grog, just to see what it tasted like, in the three months he'd been aboard. Before his flogging he would have admired to have had all he could hold; but he'd had no friend then, and had not yet been assigned to any regular mess, and so he'd had to take the punishment for being a deserter and officer-assaulter, and the terrible weeks-long pain afterward, alone and sober. Now he could do without. He liked rum, yes, but he liked other things more; and he'd had no kit. Grog was currency belowdecks. Put your allowance into your jack and save it, and you could trade it for many things and many favors. No stomach would hold the ship's drinking water straight, so that Hab was obliged to spend some of his hoarded grog on vinegar, tea, and cocoa; but there would be plenty left; and unless one of his messmates or acquaintances was to be flogged next day and Hab contributed, as he always did, to getting the man stupefied, he usually was in a position to bargain. Having been carried aboard with nothing but the clothes on his body, he needed some small personal articles. But he permitted himself no luxuries! Mostly when he bargained he bargained for favors rather than things. He would wait until his savings had a higher value, other grog having been consumed. Though the punishment for intoxication was the same as that for theft, there was never a night when at least a dozen men hammocked on the orlop weren't violently drunk: Hab had seen as many as fifty of them milling about, shouting obscenities at one another and up through the hatch, pushing, punching, kicking. More than once he had been threatened with a knife; but he'd consent to surrender his grog—when he had any—only after a bargain was struck.

This was the reason why the rats who moved crouching under the hammocks seldom failed to pay Stoney the Yank a visit.

He dropped with no sound, and fished out his shoes. He was otherwise fully dressed. You had to hit the deck after being piped on the Pactolus unless you wanted a rattan across your calves, and the men all slept in their clothes, keeping their shoes in with them lest these be stolen.

He stood still. No sound.

The allowance was the customary one, fourteen inches to each hammock. Enforced, this would have meant that the men could lie only on their sides, never on back or belly, a highly inconvenient arrangement for anybody but especially for those groaners who had recently been flogged and whose backs resembled nothing so much as masses of putrefied liver. In practice, the watches were mixed, half the larboard watch being hammocked on the starboard side and the other way round. Also the frigate was short-handed, and there were many men strapped to the bilboes each night for having offended some officer or warrant officer, many others in sick-bay. Hab Jones, for example, who these nights could lie on his back without wincing, even in that position could thrust his elbow out some distance before ramming a companion. He touched nobody now, when he got up.

He scooped his belongings from the hammock, even the blanket, and silently went forward. He was not afraid of being seen when he passed a lantern. He was simply, apparently, going up to the head. The fact that he had all his kit with him meant nothing. At this hour nobody would even go to the head and leave anything in his hammock. The hammock itself was safe because of the number stenciled on it—and because it was King's property.

His shadow sprang monstrous upon the bulkhead, black against gray, and swaying: the blanket about his shoulders, the things he held in his arms, gave to the shadow the semblance of a twisted hobbling hag who was at once pregnant and hunchbacked, and this grotesquerie was touched up by the mincingness of his walk, for he took careful prim steps, the deck being wet with drippings from above and sour slimy vomit very hard to see.

Nevertheless, and since underground creatures develop other senses in the absence of light, he was recognized here and there by still-awake men. "Hi, Stoney . . ." "Do some for me too, Stoney . . ." followed him in drowsed accents. The drunks had long since subsided.

They called him Stoney as naturally and casually as they called the French emperor Boney. All of Hab's messmates and most of his acquaintances were genuine Englishmen, and they had taken Hab into their circle with a spontaneity and cheery warmth which touched him: he was obliged to admit that in Connecticut a stranger would hardly be accepted so swiftly. These men looked with open admiration upon their Boney as one who, though of course he would be squashed in the end, all the same was proving himself a sporty opponent. Like Hab, they believed that Bonaparte was the epitome of all evil, a bloodthirsty, dangerous, dishonest, utterly selfish little upstart who must be crushed before a decent world could go decently on; but whereas Hab had been used to hearing the Emperor's name spoken only in tones of horror and high disgust, coupled with references to the "savage beastly republican mob" which "pelted, slavering for more blood, at this fiend's heels"—for on the Point the mere name of Napoleon stirred the plainest-spoken to oratory—these English tars of the Pactolus actually sounded rather proud of their Boney. Oh, he'd have to be whipped, right enough, and perhaps the time had come to do it; but meanwhile the little 'un had put up quite a fight, what? Good old Boney! Why, he'd even thrashed all the rest of Europe before he turned to take his beating from England. You might not want to play games with a man like that, who was an Eyetalian to boot, and who'd be sure to do you the dirty in close, but you couldn't help kind of applauding him. Why, after thrashing all the rest of Europe he had turned around and offered to take on the British Navy! The rest of Europe didn't matter, of course. He could do what he wanted with that, as far as Hab Jones's messmates were concerned. It was almost a pity, they sometimes thought, that he hadn't confined himself to it, instead of committing suicide, as you might say, by making faces across the Channel. Well, there was nothing else for it now, and they only hoped that it wouldn't last much longer, that he'd stand right up and give them a chance to knock him out of time, for in days of peace some of them might be discharged.

They were sorry, however, for the Frenchies. "Lot of talk they make about freedom and equality, the poor benighted frogs," Willie Lacewin spluttered once to Hab, near the cattle pen, "but the fact of the matter is, they're practically like slaves!" Mr Ellis the carpenter, like the sail-maker and the armorer, in good weather often set up shop in the waist near the cattle pen, the upkeep of which itself was a part of Mr Ellis's—and Hab's—duty. The cattle of course were for the officers, not for the tars, who rated a little salt pork twice a week, a little salt beef once a week. "Why, you put a Frenchy down among free Englishmen, and he wouldn't know what was going on!" This was five o'clock in the morning, and Willie Lacewin, who was forty and had been a fishmonger before a press gang kidnaped him, was on his bare knees, swabbing the deck with ice-cold seawater. In his excitement, looking up at Hab, he waved his swab too emphatically. A passing midshipman, the youngest son of a man who knew a man who knew a baronet, was violated; he was a peaked, pale, pallid lad, at once homesick and sea-sick; and he'd only finished scolding his servant for lack of diligence in the polishing of these very boots which now were splattered. He was of course furious. Shrilly: *"Start that man!"* A bosun's mate drew his starter, a stumpy stiff length of tarred rope. Willie didn't try to rise from his knees, and he barely had time to get his arms up over his head. The bosun's mate laid some of it on his back too, cutting his coat, but most of it fell on the arms. After a while the midshipman said pettishly "Oh, very well, very well! That will do." Nobody had looked around. Willie Lacewin, when he could move his arms, touched his cap and muttered "Thankee, sir," between chattering teeth; but the midshipman was walking away. Willie went on working, though the salt water, splashing all around him, must have blazed in his cuts. "Aye, they *talk* about fraternity and equality and all that, but what could a Frenchy know about such things? They wouldn't recognize it if they was to fall into it, ain't that right, Stoney?"

Hab did go to the head, and while there he withdrew from the bulk-head a board which had shown as a temporary repair but which in fact was carefully designed to serve as the bottom of the boat-to-be. He thus had two boards, well hidden under his blanket, when he en-countered the master-at-arms: they all but collided. The master-at-arms was a large man and he carried a rattan. "Visiting somebody, Yank?" "Visiting you-know-what." Hab was glib, stepping past the master-at-

178

arms, who glowered. "Walk as if you had a dose of clap, Yankee."
"Maybe I have" Hab returned, and got past.

A little further on, after making sure that the master-at-arms had
descended to the hold, Hab nipped into the space between larboard
guns 9 and 10. It was dark there, and Hab didn't go far but hunkered
down, elbows on knees, and called low. "Are you here, Marv?" Out of
the darkness a furry voice: "Aye." "Are you drunk?" anxiously. "And
on what should I be drunk, my Stoney?" Hab mentioned grog, and
added that he had a little with him; and at that two shaky skinny hands
came out of the darkness, and soon he could see the outlines of a pale
thin womanish face. The hands fumbled at Hab's hands, caressing
them, and fumbled at the blanket around Hab's shoulders. "For the
love of Jesus, Stoney, if you'll but let me have a pull or two——"

Marvin, though not an Irishman, had lived in Ireland most of his life
before a press gang lifted him from the street outside a tavern. At once
the village-idiot and the village-drunkard of the Pactolus orlop, he was
laughed at, kicked around, cursed, tolerated, by a few even pitied. His
passion for rum was absolute: he seemed literally to know nothing
else. In an earlier time he would have been called an innocent. Aboard
the Pactolus he was called all sorts of things, but never that. There was
very little of him, and even in the coldest weather very little on him.
He'd trade everything but his breeches for grog, and there were some
who avowed that he'd often offered the breeches themselves, but without takers, they being so greasy and sleazy and thick with fleas: he
hadn't had them off in four years. Marv was all the same a privileged
character. The pressers, it was generally agreed, must have been more
than customarily avid for their damn blood money, more even than
normally hard of conscience, to grab Marvin, who never should have
been at sea. The wonder was that he stayed alive. He was on a sort of
unofficial but permanent sick-call. The ship's surgeon had long ago
pronounced him too weak of heart to endure a flogging, even a mere
half-dozen; that surgeon had been replaced by another and then another, and his very name was forgotten, but his verdict remained un-
challenged by his successors, who never examined Marvin and perhaps
had never even heard of him. So Marvin, though batted around a good
bit, and the butt of over-many practical jokes, escaped the severer forms
of punishment. It was agreed even by the bosun and the master-at-arms
that he should never be forced to go up to the open deck. It was feared
that daylight, which he had not known in years, might strike him blind.
Never leaving the orlop, he was supposed to assist the captain of the
head, and indeed when sober he did all that functionary's work. He
was not good for anything else. Because his hands had no co-ordination
he couldn't sew or darn. He was useless as a messenger: he couldn't
remember a message long enough to deliver it.

Marvin had no regular mess but roamed like an unwanted dog, eating where he could. However, since Hab's emergence from the hold, since Hab, able to move about again, had been made an acting carpenter's mate, Marvin, doglike in this as well, had often followed him, and it was Hab's mess that Marvin now clearly preferred. Though his table manners were deplorable, Marvin was rather liked there. Most of the time he was quiet, and occasionally he made them laugh.

These messmates, to whom Hab had been arbitrarily assigned, made much of Yankee, as they called him at first. They had of course witnessed his punishment, two weeks before, and they were proud of him, the first one in months who had not screamed. He'd been given three dozen, too, a lot even on the Pactolus! Not a lot, to be sure, for a bloke who had tried to punch an officer. In peace times, at home, he would have been flogged through the fleet, which might take days, or be hanged, which would have been better, since nobody ever really survived a flogging through the fleet. Hab had replied mildly that he *thought* he had screamed: he'd known that his mouth was open, though he hadn't been able to feel anything in his throat. Where he had felt it most severely, oddly enough—though he didn't tell his messmates this —was in the chest and in the fingertips and toetips. The agony of waiting for each next stroke had been almost as bad as the immediate pain itself, but when the cat landed his back hardly felt it at all— though the back was to hurt hideously for weeks afterward. It had felt, at the time, as though white-hot needles were being jabbed into the ends of his fingers and toes. Even worse had been the heat in his chest, which didn't come with the strokes but went right through the whole business. He had truly thought that his lungs were about to explode. The pressure had been excruciating. He was sure that he couldn't have caught a breath all through the punishment, and if he hadn't screamed, he thought grimly now, that was only because he couldn't. However, he had said nothing of this to his messmates; for he didn't like to recall his flogging to memory, though he knew he would never forget it and would always be ashamed. It wasn't of the punishment itself that he was ashamed, but rather of the way he felt about it afterward. It wasn't the pain, or even the injustice. It was the fact that they'd made such a damned *show* of the business, such a formal parade, all of them lined up there, the flamboyant pipeclayed marines, the officers in their big silly hats and with their dress swords as if they were going to a ball, the solemn sailors, the wide-eyed boys, nippers of no more than eleven or twelve many of them. . . . Hab had hated the men who watched him flogged, and it wasn't right to hate them, for it wasn't their fault. You might hate the evil in men, you shouldn't hate the men themselves. But Hab had, and still did. In the same way he had hated his mother that time she came down to the barn, a blanket wrapped around her hunched-up shoulders, to sit and watch her husband tie their naked son to a sawhorse and, shouting prayers, beat him senseless. Hab had never been the same boy after that punishment. He would never be the same man, he knew, after what had been done to him at the Pactolus gangway.

It was wicked to hate, but he couldn't help it. He had probably always hated his mother anyway, though he never would have admitted it to himself had it not been for the way she sat there watching him be whupped. It was wrong to hate your fellow men, horrible to hate your mother, and Hab worried about it and when he prayed often asked forgiveness for this. But the feeling persisted.

Immediately, however, he was pleased with his company. He despised most of those around him, but he got to like his own messmates. They liked him from the beginning, and made no bones about it. They admired him. They wanted to know where he came from, and they had the devil of a time trying to pronounce Connecticut, which amazed Habakkuk Jones. Which one of the colonies was that? they wanted to know. They always called the States the colonies. Were there many men like him in this Conn-ect-i-cut, men who didn't drink rum? Not many, Hab said. What kind of place was this Conn-ect-i-cut, anyway? "Well, it's a state full of stones and Yankees and poison ivy, but mostly stones. I don't reckon it's the prettiest place in the world exactly, but it's a good place to live in." This amused them—this description and the fact that he came from a town named Stonington were the reasons for his nickname—and often afterward they would ask him about life in Conn-ect-i-cut, which word they learned to pronounce well, though they invariably pretended to stumble over it. Were all the men there as strong as him, Stoney? How'd he ever get such strong arms, anyway? Turning a grindstone, he replied. But, they cried, you don't have to turn a grindstone very long in order to sharpen a tool, and anyway hadn't he said that they didn't have many tools on that farm he was brought up on? " 'Tweren't the tools, it was the livestock. Four times a year we had to hold every cow's and horse's and sheep's snout against the stone, so's to keep 'em to a sharp enough point so's the critters could get them in between the rocks to where the grass was." "Sure, if it was as bad as all that," pop-eyed Marvin had exclaimed, "I should think you would all have starved to death!" "We all did."

Hab got out the jack of grog, but first, hand-diving into his blanket like a street peddler into his cloak, he got out the two boards. He told Marv that he wanted them guarded. The half-wit whined suspiciously that he was already guarding three such boards for Stoney. Was there anything up? "There's this up" whispered Hab, elevating the leather jack. Piteous hands reached for it, but Hab rose, holding it too high for the little man. "All right, Stoney. Let me have it, for the love of Jesus!" "These boards——" "I'll take care of them!"

Holding the jack in both hands, he emptied the two-day grog allowance in a couple of long gulps. Then he retired, coughing, to his lying-down place at the bulkhead. Marvin did not have a hammock, didn't want one. Years ago his hammock had been cut down so many times, whether by jokesters or by bosun's mates because Marv was not prompt about rising, and he had so often been punished for tardiness by being deprived of the use of a hammock, that he had forgotten how to climb into one. He'd get seasick if he ever got into one again, the sailors used to say. So Marvin slept just anywhere, usually between two of the guns. Recently he had favored the space between guns 9 and 10 on the larboard side. It was through the port for the No. 8 gun that Hab Jones planned to escape.

Hab hunkered, shaking his head, staring into the darkness from which came little whimpering animal-like sounds as Marvin fussed himself to rest.

Previously, with the pieces scattered, Hab had not often worried about them. If one were found it would scarcely be taken for part of a boat. Now, however, for the first time, five of them were together; and if *these* were found the finder could without too great a mental effort guess their purpose. The other parts were still scattered on the upper deck. He planned to get them later, just before he went.

"It won't be for long, Marv" he called gently.

There was no answer.

Still, nobody ever visited Marvin. The bosun's mates were disgusted with a man they couldn't flog; he had nothing to steal; and as for his messmates, well, it was all right to guy Marv at suppertime, but you'd never seek him out for his conversation. If the five pieces were to be safe anywhere, it was there; and the place was marvelously convenient.

Hab went back to his hammock. He had barely got into it when the middle watch was piped and the bosun's mates went bawling along the orlop, using their colts indiscriminately, with their sheath knives cutting down the hammocks of those who tarried a moment. *"Show a leg!" "Out and up!" "You—out and up!" "Hit the deck!"* The middle watch was a small one, but everybody on the orlop was awakened. There was a great deal of grumbling. A little later the late watch tumbled down, made their hammocks, climbed in. The little thieves began to prowl.

Hab lay for a long time, on his belly, as he had used to do when his back was still sore. He was going to wait until four bells. Everybody should be asleep by that time.

He felt weak and a little scared. He lacked his usual confidence in his own strength. Life at sea had done that to him, he told himself. It was an unnatural and unhealthy way to live, getting so little fresh air, so little food and that bad, so little sleep—what with the changes of watches, the brawls, fights, calls for all hands, emergency jobs, holding off of thieves, and hearing the screechings of the victims of 'tweendecks punishment, Hab did not believe he had slept two hours on a stretch in the three months he had been aboard this frigate. Deliverance II was going to be a ludicrously small boat, true, but he did not know how far he was going to have to paddle. He had noted no change in the movement of the ship, but still, despite the favorable wind, with the coming of night they might have moved a little further from the shore. Suppose he had to paddle fifteen-twenty miles? Well, he could do it, taking it easy after daylight had come: he'd want to paddle furiously in the hour or so of darkness left to him.

He wished that he did not have to hate people. His mother was dead, but his hate for her lived and tortured him. And he shouldn't hate these poor men around him, not any more than you should hate animals in cages. Perhaps the feeling would pass, he'd grow out of this when he was back with Deliverance and with Judge Watts, doing real work again, living a healthy life. He hoped so.

After a while he pushed these thoughts too away and did nothing with his mind except keep it awake.

Everything was quiet on the orlop when four bells struck. Hab said a little silent prayer and then got out of his hammock.

. 20 . . .

THE SEA WAS AS BIG AS FOREVER; AND THOUGH THE SKY was sprinkled with frosty stars there was no sign of the moon, so that you couldn't see far, the black of eternity edging right up to the rail. The frigate's movement was regular, easy, large, confident, full. The frigate must have looked very lovely, had there been anybody to see it. Hab, in the waist, thought that he would like to be on land, of a bright sunny day, and watch such a ship as this go by. That was about as near, he estimated, as he would ever want to come to a warship again.

The standing rigging spoke very little. The bows spoke a little, shushingly. The hull, the masts and spars, worked monotonously with a thin far squeal.

He had done several small repair jobs that very afternoon at the cattle pen, and he went to these now, touched them, looked them over, nodded, as though to satisfy himself that his workmanship of a few hours before had not been at fault. While he did this he loosened the two boards he had come for. He did not take these boards out. Somebody might be watching him from the break of a poop, or from the quarterdeck, or even from somewhere here in the waist. His manner was offhand; he didn't hurry; when the muzzle of a softly snoofing cow appeared between two of the close-set bars, he paused to rub it. Poor critter, he thought, not knowing why you're here in a meadow that keeps rocking back and forth. Nothing to do but stay in that narrow place until they come to slaughter you. Well, no! He reckoned that maybe the cows in there weren't so bad off at that. True, they would be killed, but they'd be killed quietly and quickly: they would have been slaughtered on land anyway. No doubt they missed the false freedom of the pasture, where they could roam in search of fresh-scented tufts of grass; but they were no less closely confined than those around them; and they were well fed—Hab reflected that they were not as badly fed as the men who fed them. They were not subject to regulations, and they got plenty of fresh air.

He drifted to the larboard rail, the weather rail, and leaned upon it, arms folded, hands cupping elbows. This move had been planned. If anyone *should* be watching him, Hab's behavior would seem natural. Unable to sleep, he had drifted up to the deck for a breath of air. He had absently but naturally enough examined the work he had done that afternoon; and absently he'd petted a cow. Afterward he had gone to the weather rail, to moon and dream. If such conduct was not customary aboard the Pactolus this was because the men generally were not given to dreams, and were much too tired from work to indulge them if they had been; nor did many of these men any longer find the air betweendecks obnoxious, as Stoney the Yank, a quiet one anyway, clearly did. A carpenter's mate did not stand regular watches, and he was likely to be up and around, testing things, in any part of the ship, aloft or alow, at any hour. Also, on Sunday mornings things were always a little different, a little easier. Hab's jacket was too small a thing under which to hide the wood he had come for, but the blanket, again draped squawlike about his shoulders, was ample. There was nothing unusual in this, either. When a man's blanket, along with his extra duds, had been rolled up in his hammock and stowed, properly labeled, in a netting guarded by marines—that was one thing. But only a fool would leave anything in his hammock at night. Besides, it was cold.

Hab reflected that he didn't even know the date. It was October, he was sure of that much, about the middle of the month, he thought, but he couldn't be certain. None of the men he met cared. Nor did any of them know where the ship was, which way it was going, what it was headed for. They were concerned with more immediate matters.

True, the frigate appeared to be taking a haphazard course, if it was actually taking any course at all and not just knocking around to see what would happen. For the first couple of weeks after he'd been impressed Hab, remaining in the hold, knew nothing of the vessel's movements, though he did know that it had *been* moving all the time. When at last he had come topside it was to find the Pactolus cruising lazily and rather lumbrously some eight or ten miles off a bright-blue-and-green little town he overheard an officer call Montego. There, just loafing back and forth, far enough away so that nobody would venture to swim for it through those shark-infested waters, they had remained for more than two weeks. The captain and certain of the officers had gone ashore repeatedly, sometimes for several days, but none of the men was allowed ashore and there was no fresh fruit. Then another frigate appeared, and Captain Sir Henry Hatfield had been rowed over to visit her commander and had spent two days there. Afterward the Pactolus had started north: this much Hab knew from his knowledge of the stars and of the prevailing winds in those parts. But its progress, as before, had been leisurely; it had yawed often, as if indifferently searching the seas, though its general course continued north. Three times they had overhauled small ships; and the names and nationalities of these at least were generally known because the men who rowed the officers over would gam with the crews: none was a Connecticut ship. Two had been released. On the third a prize crew had been placed and it had disappeared to the south, presumably headed back for Jamaica.

The previous day they had sighted land, the first since Montego two months before.

It occurred to Hab Jones as he leaned upon the rail that he didn't even know whether that land over there, the land he couldn't see but meant to reach, was one of the States. He thought it was and hoped it was, but again he couldn't be sure. Nobody showed charts to the men before the mast. The helmsmen merely kept the ship steady and steered as they were told: they could see the compass, to be sure, but except when they were on duty they were never told about any change of course.

Nor did anybody seem to care. The indifference of these men to everything that was not of the Pactolus, that was not a part of their own particular groups and cliques aboard the Pactolus, was astounding. Was that the Colonies we'd seen over there, yesterday afternoon? Might have been. Might have been Canada, though, or maybe Florida. Might even be they'd crossed the ocean again and were back somewhere off France or Spain. Who gave a hoot? Except that some had palm trees and some had mountains, while a few had both, one shoreline looked pretty much the same as another, especially when you knew you weren't going to be allowed liberty anyway, no matter where the blasted place was.

The Pactolus might have been a ghost ship plowing a sea unknown. Except for the creak of the timbers, and the slight whooshy sound of the water, there was silence. Hab had not known such a silence in three months. Nobody called all's-well. Nobody paced the deck, or even moved. The helmsman was a statue. On the quarterdeck the lieutenant, the midshipmen, the hands, stood motionless, apart. No orders were given, none being needed. No one sang or hummed, no one even snored.

That lieutenant up there, *he* knew, and those two midshipmen probably knew too, the bearings of the Pactolus, the course it was taking. As far as Hab had been able to make out, the gentlemen of the quarterdeck did little else besides navigate—but they sure did a power of that! The warrant officers really ran the ship. The quarterdeck men seldom spoke to a hand, or even looked at one. They remained aloof, glittering in a world of their own, where it could be that they had their peculiar duties and pleasures and pains. Very seldom did you see one come down off the quarterdeck. Hab had never seen one go below to the men's quarters. He believed that they were afraid to, and didn't blame them.

However, at any hour of the day that the sun shone you might see lieutenants and midshipmen tinkering with their sextants and astrolabes, squinting at the sky, moving things, computing things, conferring. At noon the lieutenants, still in their gay dress uniforms after attending the performance at the gangway, repaired once more to the quarterdeck, in full force this time, and gravely made calculations, gravely and very politely agreeing with one another. They were usually joined there by Captain Sir Henry Hatfield, the fatherly, who checked their figures. These sessions were devoted purely and simply to officer gibberish, so that as far as the overhearing watches and helmsmen were concerned they might have been conducted in Russian, and nobody less than an officer pretended to understand a word of it—or ever seemed to want to. Not even the bosun, not even Mr Ellis the carpenter, indeed not even the purser, though they rated high, higher in many respects than the midshipmen, ever touched or aspired to touch a sextant. It was perfectly understood that navigation was a rarefied language to be used exclusively by men who held King's commissions. No others need apply. A master-at-arms, though he might be a fine sailing man and a first-rate disciplinarian, would no more think of touching a navigating instrument than a foremast hand would think of flourishing a dueling sword.

So they gathered every noon, and fussed and fingered and chattered, pointing things, marking things down, these brassy officers; and sometimes, watching them, Hab would remember that Si had done all that alone aboard the Horace T. Wainwright—done it correctly too, as far as Hab knew, and in about one-quarter the time.

There was one other occasion which filled with bustle the ordinarily staid quarterdeck, and this was the only time when officers addressed the men direct—and they did it this time, as might be expected, by means of curses and threats. This was whenever Captain Sir Henry Hatfield elected to race mast against mast in order to keep the hands smart.

Smartness was the watchword aboard the Pactolus frigate. Not only was it an important part of discipline, but like gold lace it looked pretty. A smart crew flattered a captain, even when there was no admiral about. Pactolus didn't seem to be going anywhere and it certainly wasn't doing anything, all alone, but it must always be smart.

Smartness aboard this frigate was in large part a matter of running: it was haste. Warrant officers *ran* to commissioned officers when summoned, the hands *ran* to the warrant officers, and ship's boys ran to the hands. From the time he was piped up to the time he tumbled back in, everything the ordinary or the a.b. did was done at the double; and even Hab was obliged to conform with this routine. After you had fallen out in the morning, and put your shoes on, and lashed your hammock and tucked in your clues, you slung the hammock-bundle over your right shoulder and *ran* up to the nettings to stow it. And so it went, more or less all day. If any got it worse than the others, unless it was the much-kicked boys, it was the topmen. They were divided into three crews for the three masts, and were generally good men, men impressed from merchant ships rather than from jails, able sailors who looked with scorn at the afterguardsmen, the holdsmen, the waisters, and who esteemed a Royal Marine the lowest of the low. Smartness was demanded most violently of those who toiled aloft, where they could be seen. Whenever Sir Henry Hatfield elected to have a drill—which to him must have consisted almost entirely of the handling of sail, for he could have known little, if he knew anything, about what went on below—he would order that all hands be called to make or perhaps to shorten sail: it made no difference which, for this exhibition always took place in fair weather, and afterward the made sail was shortened again, or the shortened sail made. *Then* was when there was a great yelling and cursing on the quarterdeck, with all the lieutenants eager to show the captain how smart they too were and how authoritative. There were forty-odd men in the foremast crew, about the same number in the mainmast crew, but only about twenty took care of the mizzen, a shorter mast with fewer yards; and the result was that the mast-against-mast races, about which the lieutenants bawled so profanely and on which they laid so many bets, in reality were the mainmast topmen against the foremast topmen. No prize was given to the winners, but the entire crew of whichever one was last to be cleared had its grog cut off for three days; and what was worse, the last man down at *each* mast was flogged. This meant, invariably, a mad rush, a frantic scramble once the job was finished. Somebody was sure to be hurt. Twice Hab had seen men killed. It meant too that the best man usually was punished, the last one down having probably been the first one up, often the captain of the top, a fact which did not seem to have occurred to Sir Henry Hatfield. This could have been the reason, however—this together with the fact that the frigate was shorthanded—why the punishment for being the last man down in these contests was a mere dozen lashes. After a dozen at the gangway a young and tough topman—and they were all young and tough, they had to be—might be damned uncomfortable for a few days or weeks but he couldn't claim the refuge of sick-bay or even of his own hammock: he stayed at work.

These drills in smart handling occurred once or twice a week, depending upon the weather and how the captain felt.

No, it wasn't the lieutenants he feared, Hab thought as he glanced contemptuously toward the quarterdeck where the officer on watch, a portly fellow, stood in silhouette, his face all shadow. They were too filled with their own importance to notice anything strange about the behavior of a mere carpenter's mate. But the warrant officers—*they* knew almost everything that was going on. Sometimes too the midshipmen could be troublesome. They were scared lads who took their fear out in arrogance.

About thirty of the Pactolus crew were boys, most of them in their lower teens. Of these nine or ten were midshipmen, officially called, for reasons not always clear, "the young gentlemen." The other twenty-odd were just "boys," the lowest things on the ship, guttersnipes, bastards, or juvenile criminals, whose parents, when known, either wouldn't tolerate them or couldn't afford to keep them. They were as hard-bitten a lot as ever Hab had seen, vicious, treacherous, profane, and all but indestructible. Theoretically they were treated the same as ordinary sailors—though they got no wages and only rated half the usual rum ration, and when they were flogged it was with a rattan rather than a cat-of-nine-tails—but in fact they were treated even worse, the sailors themselves taking out all their accumulated spleen on these boys. Some, the smarter, were personal servants to officers; the others did the ship's dirtiest work. They all slept in one cabin, and a marine was stationed at the door of this cabin every night, but it was perfectly understood that he was there rather to keep sailors out than to keep the boys in, and it was known anyway that he had his price, not a high one. The boys of the Pactolus constituted an open scandal, though it scarcely seemed a scandal any longer, so generally was it taken for granted. There probably wasn't a one of them who had retained his sexual purity long after coming aboard the frigate, assuming that he'd had any at that time. Some joined in beastly practices in order to get more rum, for there were habitual drunkards among them, tipplers of thirteen and fourteen; others sought favors, or were forced.

Hab, leaning over, made a face. He watched the sea fall swiftly, exposing the gun ports; felt the frigate poised for an instant; then saw the sea rise swiftly again, coming almost up to the rail on which he leaned. It would be good to get into that water, on his own again, in the clean water, away from this floating garbage wagon. He felt elated. He felt like singing, for now his confidence was high. He didn't stir, and made no sound.

In a moment he would straighten, yawn, stretch, and saunter back to the cattle pen for a last look at his work, and then he would slip the boards under his blanket. He would take them down to the space between larboard guns 9 and 10, silencing Marvin with a promise of the morrow's rum. There remained after that only the pieces hidden in the carpenter's shop forward, the shop next to the cabin Mr Ellis shared with the bosun. Hab some time before had with rum hired a former professional burglar to make a key for the lock of this closet. He would have to move some shot-plugs in order to get at the pieces, and Mr Ellis, on the other side of the thin partition, was a mighty light sleeper; but Hab felt confidence now, he knew he was going to get away. He even smiled to himself, and reached a hand under the blanket and patted the treenails in his jacket pocket. He had a few extra treenails, in case he dropped some: he didn't want to waste time feeling for them in the dark.

Smiling still, he straightened, and turned aft. He did not stretch and yawn, however, for something about the quarterdeck caught his eye, though for half a minute, standing stock-still, he couldn't be sure what it was. At last he realized that the portly lieutenant no longer stood there.

Well, there was nothing unusual about this. The officers not infrequently left the deck while on watch. They weren't supposed to do so, even with two midshipmen there, as now; but the Pactolus discipline was lax—among the officers.

What *was* unusual, as Hab realized a moment later, was the fact that the lieutenant was coming down the ladder into the waist.

Hab felt no alarm; but he leaned against the rail again, deciding that it would be better to wait until this officer had gone.

There was a step behind him.

"Hoping to see your native land over there, if you peer hard enough?"

There was no mistaking the low, even, musical voice. Hab instantly came to attention—he had seen men started for being slow about this —though he was damned if he'd touch his cap. Lieutenant Bullan waved carelessly, and even smiled a little with his small weak rubbery lips.

"Stand at ease, Jones. There's the lad."

Lieutenant the Honorable Jordan Bullan, R.N., better known betweendecks and in the hold as Old Arsy-Mouth, was disposed to be gracious. The quiet of the night had affected him, or perhaps it was his conscience. Hab was amazed. Many times since that afternoon three months ago when Bullan had caused his impressment they'd passed on deck, and never once had the lieutenant's eyes shown a flicker of recognition.

Hab did not stand at ease—none of the men ever did on those rare occasions when they were permitted to do so; they found themselves unable to—but he did spread his feet a little and clasped his hands behind his back. Lieutenant Bullan nodded genially, as though at a polite salutation. Then Lieutenant Bullan nodded toward the darkness beyond the rail, as the sea hissed up and hissed away.

"Turns out that that really is your native land over there, that you really do come from the Colonies, as you said, eh, Jones?"

"No, sir."

"Eh? But the men all call you Yankee, don't they?"

"Yes, sir. Begging your pardon, sir, but what land *is* that over yonder?"

Lieutenant Bullan rolled and rubbered out his lips.

"Maryland, I believe. Or Del-a-ware. But that's all part of the Colonies, isn't it?"

"I come from the State of Connecticut, sir."

"Ah?"

The lieutenant astoundingly placed a hand on Hab's left shoulder and turned Hab a little so that again he faced the sea. It could be that he was embarrassed. It was probable that he was lonesome, a shy man who had unexpectedly obeyed an impulse: Lieutenant the Honorable Jordan Bullan, R.N., must always have been lonesome aboard this frigate, even among his fellow officers, with whom he had little in common. Now he kept the hand on Hab's shoulder, leaning a little on it, so that even through the blanket Hab felt the fingers, soft, fat, pale, and heavy.

"Well, it has come to my ears, Jones, that you really are a Yankee. You must understand, though, that I didn't know this when I examined you on the brig. I had orders to impress any seamen unequipped with birth papers, regardless. And then your attempt at resistance—most unfortunately, Jones, most rash—that precipitated matters, you understand?"

Hab said nothing. He knew that while the marines had been carrying him bleeding and unconscious to the gig, Arty Walsh and Jabez Fortman did not offer resistance, not even anything that the panicky Lieutenant the Honorable Jordan Bullan, R.N., could interpret as resistance; yet they'd been taken too. Jabez, after seeing what happened to Hab, had lost his nerve and started to shout that though he didn't have a birth paper this was only because Arty Walsh over there, who used to be an English marine, had stolen it. The lieutenant, flustered, still twittery about Hab's supposed attack, had thereupon talked a minute with Arty. A minute was enough. Arty's every word named his place of birth, and the lieutenant ordered him impressed. Then the lieutenant had ordered Jabez Fortman impressed as well, since Jabez had no paper. Thus he'd got three. Si Wainwright had tried hard to save his valuable bosun, as he had tried to save Hab, but the lieutenant was in no mood to believe anything told him by a man who less than ten minutes before had solemnly assured him that there were no R.N. deserters aboard the brig. The wine had soured in the lieutenant, who positively snarled— the snarl of a guinea-pig. Perhaps this was because he had been so badly frightened. He was a timid man.

Now, however, his voice was low and even, an intensely intimate sort of voice which would have been meant only for Hab and probably would have carried only to him even if they'd stood in a crowd. It was a caress, that voice.

"They appear to be doing well enough, Jones, those other two."

It was an apology, not a statement.

"Yes, sir" said Hab.

Arty Walsh the marine tramped here and there, did the manual of arms, stood guard duty doggedly, impassively; but though his mouth was set there was a beaten look in his eyes; he would never really hold up his head again. Jab Fortman was perhaps less miserable, for he had his liquor. A crack deck hand, "smart" in his work even by British Navy standards, though too old and unsteady to make a topman, he had become a sheet-anchor man. A real sailor, he had only scorn for most of those around him; and though he was acknowledged to be valuable his position was comparatively humble, and he had to endure the ignominy, particularly galling to one who had been a bosun, of taking orders from lubberly old codgers who wouldn't even have been allowed aboard a vessel from Connecticut. It hurt him. However, the rum ration helped. Jab Fortman, who was in a different mess, slept far forward, and what spare time he had he spent either in drinking or trying to get a drink; and so Hab Jones seldom saw him.

Two things at least were certain: Jabez Fortman would die in the Navy, as Arty Walsh would die in the Marines, unless Bonaparte was crushed. The cat-of-nine-tails had broken both; and neither would ever do more about desertion, now, than dream of it.

"From all I hear, you too have made a good showing, Jones."

"Thank you, sir."

That hand was still there. The lieutenant even stepped a little closer.

"Oh, I fancy that there'll come a day—if it hasn't already come, Jones, and you won't admit it—there'll come a time when you will realize that it was probably the best thing ever happened to you when I ordered you into the British Navy. Yes, I think that someday you'll thank me for it. After all," and he waved an orator's arm to indicate the unseen shore; but though his words flew high and fancy, the voice in which they were uttered, very close to Hab's ear, remained low, "you call them states, we call them colonies, but the situation remains the same, and a mother cannot help loving her children even when they're unruly, eh?"

Hab said nothing.

"After all, Jones, the Royal Navy will make a *man* of you! When you serve in the Navy you serve in a common cause, in a battle against tyranny. When you fight with us you fight for that which you yourselves profess to hold most dear in all the world—for freedom. Don't you understand?"

No, Hab did not understand how it could be fighting for freedom to be locked in jail; but he kept his mouth shut. Anyway he was much less concerned at that moment with battles against tyranny and struggles for freedom than he was with that hand on his shoulder, that breath almost against the back of his neck. Could Lieutenant the Honorable Jordan Bullan be planning, on this night of all nights, to get him below somewhere, even while he, the lieutenant, was on watch? It hardly seemed likely, and especially as half a dozen or more men might conceivably see them start away. All the same, a small cold ball of fear in Hab's chest grew larger when the lieutenant gave his shoulder an unofficerlike affectionate little shake. There were not many secrets aboard the Pactolus frigate, and Hab knew as well as everybody else Old Arsy-Mouth's reputation among the boys.

It could be that Hab stiffened at this thought, though he didn't intend to do so. Or it could be that his silence was answer enough. At any rate, Lieutenant Bullan suddenly took his hand away, hurt.

"Well . . ." He harrumphed loudly, seemed about to say something further, looked swiftly away, harrumphed again, and strode for the quarterdeck ladder.

Two minutes later, stiff with boards, Hab Jones tottered over to the main hatch.

The shop was long and narrow, more of a closet than a cabin, possibly forty feet by eight. Near the door—there was only the one door, which led into a companionway just off the orlop—there was a bench with racked tools, where Mr Ellis and Hab Jones worked when the waist was untenable. Beyond this the shot-plugs were stacked against the right-hand wall, leaving a clear floor space, a sort of alley, about two feet wide. At the far end was heaped, in a disorderly pile, oddments and remainders of lumber: it was from this pile that the nine pieces of Deliverance II had been one by one withdrawn for fashioning. Two of these pieces were hidden under the shot-plugs now. They were the last ones.

Hab didn't like this closet-shop, didn't like working there in close proximity with Mr Ellis, a cantankerous artisan whose greatest boast, endlessly iterated, was that he had been at sea twenty-six years, man and boy—as if that was anything to brag about! Mr Ellis used Hab Jones but never liked him. Mr Ellis was a tall man with broad shoulders and thick heavy arms, a head egg-bald, immense accurate hands, and the worst disposition in the world.

The shot-plugs were piled against the right-hand wall. The left wall, which was clear, was that which separated this closet from the cabin Mr Ellis shared with the bosun: it was no more than a jerry-built partition, the two cabins having once been one.

Hab got in easily enough: he had previously tried the key, and knew that he would not raise a squeak. Inside, he shut the door behind him and stood motionless for a while. This was not in order to accustom his eyes to the darkness, for the darkness was absolute, and even in the corridor outside there had been only the faintest drizzle of light. No, Hab knew every inch of this closet and had long ago fixed it in his mind, and he knew just how the plugs were stacked, just which ones must be moved and to where. He could work all right in the dark, here. What he was waiting for now was the slowing-down of his heart. He hadn't until this moment realized how excited and scared he was.

The shot-plugs, a specified number of which had always to be kept on hand in case of action, were of various sizes and made of several materials, oakum, lead, felt, rope, canvas, wood, or of sundry combinations of these. Here they were arranged, however, according to size rather than according to material, as Hab Jones well knew; and when at last Hab knelt beside them in the cleared space his hand found them and knew each infallibly, as a book-lover might go into his own library in complete darkness and without hesitation put his hand on any suggested volume. Hab began to shift the shot-plugs.

He shivered, his hands shivering, not from fear now but from cold. He no longer wore his blanket, which he'd left between guns 9 and 10, for he feared it might brush against something and knock it down, or in some other way, perhaps by making him clumsy in his movements, bring about a sound.

He *thought* he'd been a cat. Perhaps Mr Ellis's instinct rather than his ears had fetched him; for when the door suddenly was opened the figure framed in it was undoubtedly that of the carpenter: there was almost no light, so that the figure was faint to the point of filminess, but still there wasn't any mistaking the great stooped shoulders, the long arms.

Kneeling only a few feet away, Hab knew, however, that Mr Ellis was not able to see him.

Hab had one of his two boards out. He had just uncovered the second board and had been reaching for it when the door was opened.

He lifted his right knee from the deck, put his right foot there. He'd had nothing in his hands at the interruption. Now he began to take off his jacket.

Mr Ellis must have been possessed of an instinct surprising in one who had spent twenty-six years, man and boy, at sea—the instinct of a deer, of a Mohican. He took two steps forward, and then, though he could not possibly have seen or heard Hab, he stopped, *knowing* that somebody was there.

He whirled around and started for the door.

Hab jumped, whipping his jacket off.

He got Mr Ellis high, his arms around the neck, the jacket over the head, and hooked a leg in front of him, at the same time putting out an arm to break their fall. It did not knock the breath from the carpenter, who was full of fight, but it did stifle his first attempt to cry out.

Though Mr Ellis was a large and a strong man, in this combat Hab Jones had all the advantage by reason of his first attack. It was not doubt of his ability to beat Mr Ellis that troubled him but doubt of his ability to do so without making any noise. The bosun still lay on the other side of that paperlike partition, and bosuns are notoriously light sleepers.

He kept his grip on Mr Ellis, kept high on him, and behind him, and he forced him to roll a little away from that partition, which he might easily have kicked. However, Mr Ellis rolled further than Hab had intended, so that they were against the end of the stack of shot-plugs. If once this was disturbed—here was one reason why Hab had used such extraordinary care in shifting the plugs—it would come apart like a kicked pyramid of apples; and the plugs, most of them circular, would thump and bang across the alley with the insouciance of snowballs and bump against the partition.

Hab forced a roll back toward the workbench. Mr Ellis was breathing hard, gasping rather, there inside the jacket, the sleeves of which Hab had tied from behind. Hab never lost control of him. He thought of banging his head against the deck, but gave this up as too likely to be loud.

He got his legs around Mr Ellis's neck and reached up to the tool rack. He knew every tool in that rack as well as he had known the placement and size and make-up of every shot-plug in the pile. His selection was deliberate, a medium-sized caulker's maul, all wood.

Mr Ellis was not struggling so hard. Perhaps he was having difficulty breathing, or perhaps he was waiting, catching his breath, reserving his strength, for a chance to break free. Whatever the reason, he didn't move and uttered no groan when Hab hit him.

Hab hit him three times on the back of the head, low down. Then Mr Ellis was altogether still; and for a terrible instant Hab feared that he'd killed the man; but a hand told him that Mr Ellis's heart was going heavily and even violently.

Speed now. Still being careful to leave the heaped plugs undisturbed, he got his two boards, stepped over Mr Ellis, who didn't stir, and locked the door from the outside.

Marvin was asleep, but he too was a light sleeper and Hab played safe by moving all the pieces two gun-spaces away. He put his blanket there too, and cut down his hammock and put it there: he hoped to use the hammock as a sail. He put his shoes there. He had not worn the shoes to the carpenter's closet.

Seven bells were struck. In half an hour, or a little over that, since this was Sunday morning, the bosun's mates would be down here with their sticks and their shouts. In two hours' time it would be full daylight.

There was only the sound of snoring on the orlop, and the sound of dry rubbing timbers. It was chilly, but Hab's wrists and hands were beaded with sweat as he took up the first two pieces to fasten them together.

Then he stood stock-still. The treenails!

He stood stock-still, and the sweat which had been but a sheen now broke out vigorously all over him and rolled in large warm oily blobs down his chest and back and belly, down his legs and ankles; and his breath came hard.

He had made those treenails himself, shaped them, measured them carefully and surreptitiously, tried each where it was destined to go. He knew that they could be knocked in with very little noise, but yet would stay in place in the roughest sea for at least a few hours.

Well, there was no improvising now. No others would do, even if he could get others. Nothing else would do. Only the treenails in his jacket pocket would fit the auger holes of Deliverance II.

195

He was shaking, his hands shaking, and his knees, when he started back toward the carpenter's closet. He had to clench his teeth to keep them from chattering. Bent low, holding his breath, he went on tiptoes past the door of the cabin where the bosun slept.

His chief hope was that he might be able to get the treenails out of the pocket without fully removing the jacket from Mr Ellis's head. He wouldn't have minded leaving the jacket. It would make it easy for them to identify Mr Ellis's assailant, but on the other hand it would make them suppose, when that assailant couldn't be found, that he had jumped overboard. Good men before this had killed themselves rather than face the British Navy's punishment. For the assault of a warrant officer Hab could not expect less than two hundred lashes, none of which would be administered while he was unconscious. Any man who survived that would be a cripple for life.

However, what made Hab shake most of all was the fact that he knew that he would have to feel Mr Ellis's heart—he wouldn't be able to keep from doing this—and what if it wasn't beating? What if the wild irregular thumping he'd felt before, right after hitting Mr Ellis, had been no more than the final flutter of an organ about to stop? Hab didn't know much about hearts; but he did know that if he had in an attack from behind murdered a man, a man twice his age, in the darkness, then even escape in Deliverance II, even return to the Watts household, would not bring him real happiness ever again, for the memory of the shameful deed would sit on his chest night after night when he lay down, sit there unshakable like a great rock, and cloud and choke his thoughts when he tried to pray.

His hands outlined the lock. He reached into a breeches pocket—and found no key. Then he remembered. How could he have forgotten? In the excitement of leaving, and still flushed by the struggle, he had locked the door but dropped the key, which fell from sweat-slippery fingers. At the time that hadn't seemed to matter—though he remembered the "clunk" it made when it struck the floor, sounding heavy as a cannonball then, and how it had slithered back and forth once or twice with the movement of the ship, before Hab sped off.

He went to his knees. He would have to find the thing by feel, if he found it at all. It might have slid clear out of the corridor by this time. His fingertips patted the deck wildly; and always in his mind there was the fear that if he did get back into that closet it might be to learn that Mr Ellis was dead. He was very badly frightened, the worst he had ever been.

He found the key. As he rose, gripping it, the door and bulkhead were rattled so severely that for a fleet instant—such had been the silence of the corridor—Hab thought that the ship had struck. The door was thumped again, and a husky guttural voice, mouthing blasphemy, faltered but gained volume. The knob was shaken from the inside.

Such relief flooded Hab, hot and full, that he wanted to drop to his knees, right then and there, and thank God. But he didn't. There wasn't time.

Already the bosun was tumbling out of his bunk, calling questions, and Hab had scarcely darted back toward the orlop when the cabin door was opened. A moment later Hab heard the shop-closet door being smashed, while carpenter and bosun alike, the one almost as loud and immediate as the other, despite the door, were bellowing for the master-at-arms.

Along the dark deck, men were turning in their hammocks, mumbling, grumping, as Hab sped past. Earlier, or in port, some such disturbance would not have been noticed; but this was Sunday morning, and these voices were not the voices of drunken brawlers. Men began sitting up, asking questions. They had recognized the bosun's voice, perhaps the carpenter's too.

Hab ducked under some hammocks—and the master-at-arms thudded by on bare feet, in his underclothes, but gripping a rattan. The master-at-arms was swearing, if not loudly yet with much feeling, and his head was low, his jaw was out, as he ran.

Unnoticed in the hubbub, Hab reached the place where he'd left the unassembled Deliverance II. His shoes were there too, and his blanket, but he didn't touch those: somebody else might be able to use them. He snatched up the nine separate pieces, leaving the hammock, and he opened the port.

He opened the port as the larboard side of the frigate was on the rise and just after he'd heard the sucking water peel off. Even so, drops splayed in and slammed against his face. They were cold.

He slipped out, stockinged toes upon the slender welt of wood, the fingers of his right hand gripping the port-riggle, while he held the boards in his left arm. The port fell closed, locking him out.

He let the boards slip, one by one, though he held tight to the last and largest; and that was the end of Deliverance II.

The water far below hissed softly. The ship seemed to teeter on the brink of nothingness; and then it moved over into another long leisurely roll, and Hab went down and down while the water came steaming up.

He didn't jump. He just let the sea lift him off.

The board was wrenched out of his arm, and he went whirling and bumping along the side of the ship until with the abruptness of a pulled cork he found himself bounding in the wake and looking back at a mountainous mass of gilt window ledges, lions, cherubs, wreaths, drums, cornucopias, and what not, which soon vanished airily into the night like mist rubbed off a windowpane.

. 21 . . .

M$_R$ DIMPLEROSE TOOK GOOD CARE OF HIS WIFE. HE PER-
mitted her to go to town only at meeting hours, and then he marched by
her side, glaring right and left, touchy as a stallion in a far pasture. He
kept her indoors most of the time, and when anybody passed along the
road he would not permit the meek little woman even to show herself
at a window. If there was something almost Oriental in this jealous
guardianship, Mr Dimplerose suggested the Orient in no other way, being a long rawboned nut-brown dry man with large blue eyes, a pumphandle chin, and a mouth set by habit to harshness. It must have been
something deeply selfish inside of him, something inherently suspicious,
which made him behave in this fashion. It certainly wasn't his religion;
for Quakers, except in money matters a trusting lot, traditionally trust
their wives.

Hab never did remember Mr Dimplerose shouting to him, running
toward him, picking him up, but he remembered something of the
stumble along the beach to the Dimplerose house, a small one. Though
thin, Mr Dimplerose's arms were steel-strong: he all but carried Hab,
who talked without pause, gasped and coughed rather, weakly trying
to push Mr Dimplerose away, calling him John, and insisting that he,
Hab, wanted to let go, to give up.

It came back into Hab's memory later—that belief that he was swimming by the side of John Rellison. He had been only partly aware of Mr
Dimplerose. Most of the time he had supposed himself to be dead. He
had meant to be dead, he'd given up, stopped swimming, stopped all
struggle. There was no feeling in him or on him, not even any coldness
now, and as far as he was concerned he *was* dead.

"On First Day too" muttered Mr Dimplerose, and shook his head and
clucked his tongue. "Swimming on First Day!"

This was when he was putting Hab to bed, and he said it again and
again, fussing about First Day, which meant nothing at the time to
Habakkuk Jones, who was just becoming aware that he was alive after
all. This knowledge did not cheer Hab. If he wasn't dead, he would be
soon, he was as good as dead: he was convinced of this. He had no pain;
but then he had no feeling of any sort, and no strength; he was limp,
a corpse, in Mr Dimplerose's hands. He didn't care about living anyway.
This was the only time he had ever felt that way.

Yes, he remembered talking to a John Rellison who wasn't there. That had been a long while back, hours back, soon after the beginning of the dawn; and then he had known that of course there was no John, and had only spoken like that—not actually speaking most of the time, just making his mouth go—in order to give himself something to think about. He had kept urging John to stick to it and not give up, and now and then, at first, he had even reached out to give a playful push to an imaginary face. Later, for a time, he had truly thought that John Rellison *was* swimming somewhere near him, but he was past the play-fully-pushing stage then and didn't do much talking, even of the silent kind. Later still he didn't know and didn't care, having given up.

Mr Dimplerose paused a moment, after stripping Hab. Evidently Hab had asked him some question, though Hab couldn't remember this.

"Where did thee come from? I reckon the Lord sent thee. I reckon that makes it seemly that I should take thee in, even though thee was swimming on First Day—because the Lord sent thee."

"I reckon that's right" murmured Hab.

He had not been able to assist in the undressing, nor was he able to feel anything when Mr Dimplerose rubbed him vigorously with a rough towel: the only reason why he knew that this was happening was because he saw it. However, Mr Dimplerose threw a blanket over Hab's poor stunned numb body and Hab after a while began to feel the skin tingle and prickle pleasantly. This was only on the surface! He still felt dead inside.

Mr Dimplerose called something to the next room, a kitchen from the smells, and soon there was a step, and Mr Dimplerose went to the door. He did not permit his wife to enter, and of her Hab Jones saw only a pair of plump wrists in unornamented gray drugget sleeves of a seemly length, and a pair of plump white hands which held a bowl. Mr Dimplerose took the bowl and approached Hab with it.

"I'm going to die anyway" Hab mumbled.

"Thee will die when the Lord is prepared to take thee" Mr Dimplerose answered sternly. "Here, drink this."

He held Hab's head up, held the bowl to Hab's lips. It was warmed milk, and Hab realized after a few swallows that it had no rum or wine or brandy in it. At first Hab supposed that his interior numbness accounted for this, but he came to know that the drink contained in fact no alcohol. All the same, it tasted good. He drank every drop of it, and lay back panting a little. He looked at the glum Mr Dimplerose. He tried to say "Thank you." He did smile. Then he closed his eyes and slept for twenty-two hours. Mr Dimplerose awakened him. There was no alarm in the face of the Quaker, whose expression, or lack of expression, never varied, no matter what was going on; there was no haste in his dull disapproving voice; but his hands, as he pulled down the blanket, communicated to Hab a certain urgency. Hab tried to sit up, and couldn't. He was very hot now, flaming over every surface, and no longer numb but rather feeling one great ache; and he was too stiff to move. Mr. Dimplerose thrust his dried breeches and dried shirt at him.

"Thee is from off a ship of war?"

"Aye." Then he said it again, aloud this time, up through a throat that burned. "Aye."

"They come for thee. Thee would go back?"

"I'd kill myself first."

Hab started to dress. It was very difficult; and Mr Dimplerose helped him.

"It is wicked to kill thyself. Suicide is a sin."

"Not as bad a sin as serving on a British frigate. I'm from Connecticut, understand? They impressed me. I'm an American citizen, born in Connecticut."

Mr Dimplerose showed no interest in the injustice of this. He wished only to be reassured that the ship Hab had escaped from was a ship of war. "It sure was" Hab told him. Mr Dimplerose led him through a kitchen to a back door.

Not only was Hab's brain working: it was working at a pace he'd never known before, a feverish pace, humping along at a speed that scared him for fair. Yes, he could think. Moving was more difficult. It seemed to him as he went out through the back door that he creaked and squealed aloud, like a metal machine that lacks oil. All his joints hurt.

Here was no gnarled rocky hard-bitten Connecticut farm. Though this was October and nothing grew in the fields, those fields yet looked productive and even warm in the full morning sunshine: they were not rocky—to his amazement he saw no stone fences anywhere—but they were a fine deep firm red, and looked as though, disregarding the season, they would graciously produce more and more. They were flat: there were no hills. He saw some lanes, but no road. The nearest patch of woods, to which his eyes flew, was at least half a mile away. Hab didn't even know whether he could walk half a mile, much less run it, in his present condition. Indeed, he could hardly stand.

Directly around him was the sort of neatness with which he was more familiar, though he had not known it at his father's house or at Old Man Rellison's. Prim gray flagstones were set in the ground, and grass showed untrampled between them. A rambler rose bush, flowerless now, had been trained over the doorway. On an unpainted bench, which had been scrubbed so that it shone, a cat slept curled into itself; and there was a row of milking pails all so well scoured that they glittered in the sunlight. At one end of the bench stood a white churn, its plunger precisely centered. Somewhere a bird sang.

From the dimness of the kitchen a woman said: "Sayre Fleming just passed. He called that they're nigh the Atwater place now."

"Has he ridden on?"

"Aye."

They heard hoofbeats then, from the other side of the house, fading swiftly. Mr Dimplerose almost grimaced.

"Thee might have rid behind him. Too late now."

Hab nodded toward the woods. That's where he should be, he said. They'd never search far inland: sailors were always uneasy when they got away from the shore, and anyway the officers'd be afeared of desertions that far back. Mr Dimplerose shook his head.

"If they are nigh Brother Atwater's they'll be here afore thee could get to the woods." Disconsolate from his appearance, defeated, resigned, he nevertheless took Hab's elbow briskly enough and led him to a well. "Get in" he said simply.

The bucket, a thick broad one with a metal handle, was wound high, as high as it could go. The spool was a stout one—white oak, Hab noted —and the crank too was stout and was made of metal, with a metal clip-tongue to hold it in place.

Hab did not hesitate but he wasn't able to move fast. Mr Dimplerose helped him. Hab brought the bucket down a little, after Mr Dimplerose had unclipped the tongue, and while Mr Dimplerose held the crank Hab got his legs around the metal handle so that he was sitting half-on and half-in the bucket. Promptly Mr Dimplerose began to let it down.

"Hold thy head close to the rope" he called sadly.

The bucket turned one way, then turned the other, slowly. It swung from side to side, so that Hab's shoulders and knees and buttocks thudded against the stones, which were damp. Sometimes a bit of wet moss would be dislodged, to fall with a soft throaty plop into the water below.

Hab's lower legs hung down, and when the feet felt the water he called a halt. He heard the tongue click into place up there, and heard Mr Dimplerose walk away.

The water was bitterly cold, and Hab had not called a halt until his bare feet were submerged. At that instant he ceased to burn and began to shiver. He felt gooseflesh all over him. His fingers on the rope stiffened. He tried to lift his feet but there was no other place for them and the attempt caused him to swing back and forth, bumping the slimy walls: that movement of the rope might be seen from above. He put his feet back into the water, and shivers passed over him in quick-following waves.

That they had come after him did not astound him, for he knew what importance they attached to even a single desertion—not so much because of the loss of the services of the deserter, serious though this might be on a short-handed ship, as because of the effect of his act upon others. Everything possible, and a great deal more than was legal, would always be done to prove to the remaining prisoners—Hab always thought of them as prisoners, and indeed they thought of themselves as such—that escape was dangerous. The British Navy was famous for making examples.

There was the additional reason, in this case, to be sure, that Hab had feloniously assaulted a warrant officer.

No, Hab's astonishment concerned only their speed. He had calculated that it would take them at least four hours after the discovery of Mr Ellis to have the ship searched thoroughly by men they could trust, and to learn that he was not aboard; at least another hour to find the doctored gun port, to agree that he might have tried to swim it, and to calculate their position at the probable time of his jump; and finally as many more hours getting back to that place and putting search parties ashore. Yet here they were, in the morning light. (Hab did not know, at this time, that more than thirty hours had passed since he quit the Pactolus.)

The voices came suddenly to his consciousness. For some time he had heard, as though from the corners of his ears, a bumble of preparation or search from the direction of the house—voices mouthing indistinguishable words, tramping feet, grinding, shuffling, the opening and shutting of doors. But this, now, was nearer, clearer.

"D'ye think we'll nab 'im, 'Arry?"

A grunt of disgust; then: "I think it's Davy Jones's done that already."

"Hawr! Some relative, maybe?"

"Must've been eight-nine miles. In October? No man alive could've done it."

"But from what I 'ear, I 'ear there's a *wery* strong tide current in this bay, and it'd just turned, just after Stoney Jones took 'is leap, so's a *wery* strong swimmer might've been wooshed ashore along 'ere somewheres. 'E couldn't 'ave known that, on account of we didn't know it ourselves till we spoke that fishin' wessel last night. Still, you never can tell. Some of these Yanks know more'n they let on. But most likely it was luck."

Yes, it was luck, Habakkuk Jones thought, clinging to the rope. The voices came to him jumbled and hollow and deep, each trailing pesky bass echoes, so that they bumped into one another, fell over one another, stepped on one another's heels, and it was hard for Hab to disentangle the syllables. Just luck, he thought. He wondered if he spoke out loud would his voice go to those two men up there the way theirs came to him? He kept his mouth shut.

"What about a drink of this water? Ain't tasted well water in almost a year. How d'ye suppose this crank comes undone?"

"Y'know, 'Arry, right after 'e conked old Ellis there——"

"Ahr-r, that one!" 'Arry, from his voice, might well have forgotten about the crank. "I tell ye, Stoney was lucky if he made it, right enough, but even if he didn't get here he must've been happy when he went under, to remember that he'd had a chance to conk that dirty old bugger of an Ellis! He should ought to've killed him. That's the only thing I've got against Mister Stoney Jones the Yank, that he didn't kill the bugger when he had a chance."

At the expense of a terrible effort Hab lifted his head. The bucket swung to and fro, and he was afraid that the rope must have moved and they must have seen it up there. He couldn't see any part of either of them, couldn't see anything at all except a round slice of sky exactly defined. No, he couldn't see the stars. He had always been told that if you were at the bottom of a well you could look up and see the stars even in broad daylight, but he couldn't see any here. Maybe it wasn't the right kind of well. Not that it made any difference. Nobody was going to believe him anyway, assuming that he ever got out alive to tell the story. Everybody else, all those people who had never been down to the bottom of a well in their lives, would go right on saying and believing that you can look up and see the stars from the bottom of a well even in broad daylight.

Hab didn't look up any more. He clenched his teeth to keep them from chattering.

"Y'know, 'Arry, I'm 'alf 'opin' that we don't find that Yank, if 'e's still alive. And I think most of the others are 'oping the sime."

"Most of the others're wishing they could get lost, but there's too many sergeants watchin'!"

Marines, thought Hab Jones. Lobsters. Whiteys. The hated jaunties, policemen of the Navy, sent along to see that the tars didn't object with violence to their lot. Sailors wouldn't be trusted ashore. This was dirty work for the marines.

" 'E was sportin', that one. I almost wish 'e did mike it. 'E deserves it."

"He should have killed old Ellis. Should've bashed his head right in."

"Y'know, 'e *might* 'ave mide it, at that. 'E was powerful strong. So many of those Yankees are."

"It's a pretty country. I've been ashore at a couple of other parts of it, I forget the names. All pretty country. They just take things easy, and they don't fight Boney, and they ain't got any press gangs——"

"They ain't got any *nivy!*"

"They don't seem to miss it. No wonder they grow up strong. Keepin' out of war—that's good sense. How d'ye suppose this thing unfastens?"

"Why won't they fight Boney, like any decent country ought?"

"They just don't like fighting, I suppose. They're farmers, they're not soldiers."

Hab felt the rope quiver. He had eyed the reachable stones: they were all too smooth and slimy to give him a grip.

"Sometimes you 'ear blokes siy that if we don't watch out they might turn around someday an' fight *us*."

This made 'Arry roar with laughter, and he must have taken his hands off the crank. The bucket dropped a few inches—all it could—and spanked into the water, where it rocked precariously, submerged by the weight of Hab, who rocked with it, bumping the walls with shoulders and elbows, clinging still to the rope, which remained taut. Hab's legs and hips were wholly in water now. He shook violently.

"Fight *us*? With what? Awr no, Bertie me boy! They may look beefwitted, the most of 'em, but they ain't *lunatic*. If they're going to fight anybody it'd be Boney. Ain't he been playing duck-on-the-rock with their shipping?"

"Ain't we too, for that matter?"

"Oh, I know, but we got a right to. They're our colonies, practically. We're protectin' 'em. That's why we can land troops like this, any time we've a mind to. D'ye think if they was going to fight they'd let us come ashore anywhere we wanted, with muskets and bayonets and all, and march around? Not to mention blockading their harbors and stopping all their ships? Awr no, they won't fight. Not us, anyway. If they was to declare war on Boney, that would be different. They got us between him and them, so's they could just shake their fists and yammer about how fierce they are, knowing we're there all the time. But if they was to declare war on *us*—why, they'd be colonies again before you could see Jack Robinson."

"After we'd finished thrashing Boney."

"Oh, aye. After we'd finished thrashing Boney. Give me a hand with this, will you, Bertie? Must be a powerful big pail down there."

The line tightened. The bucket wobbled.

The voice of Mr Dimplerose came in accents, for him, almost genial.

"Tut, tut, my men. Drinking *water*? Now I never did hear that a British marine would drink water from a well if there was something stronger for him. Would thee fancy a sample of my wife's cherry brandy, eh?"

The line slacked. Hab braced himself against the wall on either side, to keep from splashing. He was seized by another spasm of shivering.

"Thankee kindly, sir, but if the sergeant——"

"He's in the kitchen right now, having a small glass himself, so he'll hardly chide thee for doing the same, eh? Come along."

"Well, sir, per'aps you're right. I never did care much for water anywie."

"And anyway, sir, me and Bertie here was just saying we really hopes the poor Yank gets away after all. That is, if he ain't drowned."

A long while afterward—half an hour, three hours, Hab didn't know —Mr Dimplerose returned and without a word proceeded to crank up the bucket. Hab held on: that was all he could do. Mr Dimplerose had to lift him over the lip of the well and carry him back into the house.

The last thing Hab saw, before, flat on the bed, he lost consciousness, was that same pair of plump gray-drugget-clad wrists and the plump white hands holding a bowl of broth out from the kitchen.

. 22 . . .

He was to see those wrists and hands often in the four days that followed. Almost every time he woke up—he slept a lot —he faced the long disapproving countenance of Mr Dimplerose, who never went into the kitchen for salve or food or drink but only called to his wife's hands and wrists: Hab thought of the woman that way, as hands and wrists. Mr Dimplerose was a farmer, and Hab wasn't used to farmers who could afford to spend all day and most of the night by the bedside of a sufferer, even in October. That sort of work was left to the womenfolk. Nevertheless Mr Dimplerose probably knew what he was doing. He looked as if he did anyway.

If uncheering, Mr Dimplerose at least was conscientious. He saw his duty clear. He never smiled, but he nursed well. He saw that Hab was kept covered, even when feverish and kicky; though it was evident that he found all physical contact disgusting, he bathed his patient regularly and well, and rubbed him down with a solution of (as nearly as Hab could figure) vinegar, mustard seed, and hot water; he fed Hab with a spoon until Hab was able to feed himself; he smoothed Hab's pillow, emptied Hab's chamberpot, kept Hab's water glass full. But he never introduced Hab to his wife. He never even mentioned the fact that he had a wife. Hab often heard her moving about in there, cleaning things, cooking or baking, but when Mr Dimplerose had need of her in the sickroom he'd go to the door and call her in a soft voice: Hab did not even know her name.

Mr Dimplerose had saved Hab's life; but as certainly, while Hab hoped that he was grateful, it was impossible to like the man. He brought nobody else into the house but guarded his patient with the same unflagging and humorless zeal with which he guarded his wife. He was not often in a chatty mood, and when he did talk it was usually to pray or to read the Bible. He often read the Bible to Hab, who admired to listen, waving a weak forefinger above the blanket to the rise and fall of the lines as though to music. Their tastes were not similar, though each preferred the Old to the New Testament. Mr Dimplerose liked the more recent, shriller prophets, Malachi, Zechariah, Habakkuk himself, whom Hab had always found turgid as compared with Daniel, Ezekiah, Jeremiah, and best of all Isaiah. He never touched upon Genesis, a great favorite of Judge Watts, as it had been of Hab's father, or on Job, Hab's own favorite. He liked to read the Psalms, and he liked to read and to quote from Proverbs, but when Hab asked for the Song of Solomon the Quaker pretended he hadn't heard. Mr Dimplerose read well. He had a fine deep resonant voice and a sense of the dramatic. Hab was less fond of his praying. His voice rose a little when he prayed, getting edgy, and it held an urgency, a note of something almost like fear, absent from it when he read. Anyway Hab had always thought of prayer as a personal business. In church—well, that was different, though even there you said your own prayers in silence and only the preacher thundered. Family prayers, yes. But when he prayed alone he didn't even like to have anybody see him, didn't like for anybody to know that he *was* praying, except, of course, God. He went to his knees when it was convenient; he was most comfortable in that position; but often too he had prayed while lying flat on his back in a bed or in his hammock on the Pactolus's orlop. When he prayed in bed, however, he always closed his eyes and clasped his hands under his chin, for he reckoned he owed at least that much show of humbleness to the Lord; and in no case did he ever speak aloud. What's more, Hab usually prayed at stated intervals or else at appropriate times—when in church, or before going to sleep, or when he'd been lucky or there was some other special reason. Mr Dimplerose, now, was likely to break into prayer at almost any time, and perhaps a little more than likely to. He didn't always go to his knees. He might be crossing the floor to get something, and he would stop suddenly, stiffen his arms a little away from his sides, drop anything he had happened to be holding, spread his palms outward, throw back his head, and in no uncertain tones begin to address the Deity. His words then would echo through the house and probably would travel for some distance outside as well, even though the windows were closed. The sounds in the kitchen would subside; and when the prayer was over the woman in there would speak a swift flurried birdlike "Amen," a somewhat frightened, somewhat breathless "Amen," as though eager to get it heard before the larger, louder, more reverberant "Amen" of the petitioner himself solemnly doused it. Mr. Dimplerose, as though in awe of his own eloquence, always allowed a considerable interval between the end of a prayer and his "Amen." Excepting the time when she warned them of the approach of the marines, these hurried "Amens" were for four days the only words Hab heard the woman in the kitchen speak.

Hab always spoke his own "Amen" aloud on these occasions, in order to show Mr Dimplerose that he'd been listening, and also because he wasn't sure whether Mr Dimplerose hadn't seen him peeking between his fingers. This had always been a habit of Hab's, a deplorable one which he indulged more than ever when Mr Dimplerose prayed. For the man fascinated him. When he prayed he often kept his eyes open, though they were not seeing anything. His favorite position was with legs wide-spread, arms a little out from the sides, palms spread forward, head back; and on these occasions the eyes would be strained open, bugging half out of his head. Sometimes he would start a prayer with chin on chest, the eyes closed; but most times, before it was finished, he would raise his head with a snap and the eyes would fly wildly open, and he'd finish the prayer staring at the ceiling. Whenever this happened, if Mr Dimplerose chanced to be facing the bed (he was likely to be facing in any direction, for his praying spells were seizures, fits as abrupt in arrival as an epileptic's), Hab would watch, fascinated, between his fingers.

Yet he *practiced* Christianity too, as Hab was forced to admit. He might have been unsociable about it, and even unpleasant, but he didn't tire. He tended Hab faithfully and well. He never asked Hab where he came from, how he had got aboard a British warship, how he'd escaped. He never reproached him by look or word, never showed a touch of impatience or weariness.

He was not remarkably communicative, and Hab, tired, didn't ask many questions anyway. Hab did learn that, as Lieutenant the Honorable Jordan (Old Arsy-Mouth) Bullan had said, this was Delaware. The town of Wilmington was not far away, and there were always ships at Wilmington. There were physicians in Wilmington too, of course, and Mr Dimplerose, Hab knew, would unhesitatingly have ridden there and fetched one out, had either he or Hab esteemed this necessary. They didn't. They were agreed from the beginning—or at least from as soon as Hab had got over the idea that he was going to die—that exhaustion and a thumping bad cold were all that was the matter with him. Though the cold proved the lesser of these maladies and the easier to cure, for both the treatment was the same: an occasional rubdown with the mustard-seed concoction, plenty of food, plenty of good thick warmed milk—he never did see or hear any more about that cherry brandy, which he assumed was kept for very special occasions—and, best of all, as much sleep as he could possibly get.

That Mr Dimplerose would have given him anything else he seemed to need Hab Jones never doubted. Still it was impossible to like Mr Dimplerose and very hard even to keep from disliking him. He did sweet things in such a sour way.

Hab tried. He thanked Mr Dimplerose with eyes as well as words after each of the Bible readings, which in fact Hab did thoroughly enjoy; he never mentioned the woman in the kitchen or tried to peer at her or cocked his head to listen to her; after each prayer he made his "Amen" loud with deep-feeling; an orphan and therefore an expert in the art of making himself agreeable, when he learned that Mr Dimplerose took a naïve if somber pleasure in swapping Scriptural quotations, Hab not only played this game with relish but succeeded in slanting his own quotations so that each of them appeared as praise of Mr Dimplerose's practical Christianity.

Thus, though Matthew was by no means his favorite book, even in the New Testament, Hab was fond of quoting "I was an hungred, and ye gave me meat: I was thirsty, and ye gave me drink: I was a stranger, and ye took me in."

Decidedly Mr Dimplerose liked that. He was a lonesome man, Hab came to see, lonesome and shy, a man who simply wouldn't permit himself to show in any ordinary way that he liked anything; but he did like that. He shrugged and answered mildly, though not without a touch of self-congratulation: "Though I speak with the tongues of men and of angels, and have not charity, I am become as sounding brass, or a tinkling cymbal."

Well, he had charity all right, though it wasn't the sort St Paul had meant. He was more specific and a mite less pompous when he quoted from Luke: "He that hath two coats, let him impart to him that hath none; and he that hath meat, let him do likewise."

Hab sighed, remarking that Mr Dimplerose could certainly say with Job: "I was eyes to the blind, and feet was I to the lame."

Could he have done so, Mr Dimplerose would have cooed. As it was, he only rolled his eyes and drew upon his memory of Proverbs: "He that hath pity upon the poor lendeth unto the Lord; and that which he hath given will he pay him again."

"Amen" said Hab Jones. "Blessed is he that considereth the poor."

Yet he was miffed at being classified as poor. Undeniably he had needed help for a little while there, and he was never going to forget that he owed his very life to Mr Dimplerose and his liberty to Mr Dimplerose's wit; but all the same he didn't like to be esteemed poor. When he stopped to think of it, excepting a cold and a desire to get home, he had nothing but a pair of well-worn breeches, an old shirt, two stockings, an undershirt, and a pair of underdrawers. Well, that was true. But still he wasn't poor.

Another thing about this game of matching quotations, though Hab played it sedulously and well, was the inconvenience of not being sure whether Mr Dimplerose *was* quoting or was talking naturally. Hab had never before met a Quaker. He had heard of them and had heard that they talked in this queer thee-thy fashion, but he'd never quite believed it. Now it sounded a shade sacrilegious to him, when it didn't sound plumb foolish. If they were going to talk like Holy Writ, or try to, then why didn't they go the whole hog and say "Thou hast" and "Thou art" instead of "Thee have" and "Thee are," which just don't make sense? Startled and embarrassed at first, amused for a little while, presently Hab came to find it difficult to keep himself from feeling disgust. He had to remind himself persistently what he owed to Mr Dimplerose, and to tell himself again and again that Mr Dimplerose after all was a very lonesome and ordinarily taciturn man unaccustomed to the sound of his own voice, and that the thee-thy way of talking might not sound so bad in the mouth of a more sympathetic person.

He was to verify this thought four nights after his rescue, when Mrs Dimplerose came to visit him.

He did not see or hear her enter: he just opened his eyes and found her there. She was seated at the side of the bed, and looking at him.

It had been both Hab's custom and policy in the Dimplerose house to snooze a great deal, to let sleep have him whenever it pleased. Previously, with the exception of those two memorable nights in Martinique, when he hadn't wanted to sleep, and the fourteen horrible days and nights of recovery in the Pactolus hold, when his pain had kept him awake most of the time, Habakkuk Jones had always thought of bed as a place for sleep—and for nothing else. Drowsiness was something he had not known, never having had time for it. When he had thrown himself into a bed or bunk or hammock it was with wearied limbs and a tired brain, and then he would lapse almost instantly into dreamless unconsciousness; and when he'd wake up, or be awakened, he would spring to prompt life: the bosun's mates of the Pactolus had never been called upon to cut down the hammock of this farmer's son, who didn't know what couch-dalliance was like. True, there had been times in the old days, the old nights rather, when he had *tried* to stay awake in order to talk with John Rellison, who was at the same time trying to stay awake in order to talk with him; and there had also been times when for a little while they fought off sleep with success, though feigning it outwardly, because they were going to sneak out of the house for a piloting job. But such occasions had been few and their duration brief, and Hab had enjoyed them only because of John's presence, not because they happened to take place in bed: he would have enjoyed them as much had he and John been sitting on a stone bench. You are born in bed, the doggedly philosophical aver, and you die in bed, and between those two events you have most of your good times in bed. Well, Hab couldn't remember having been born; he couldn't conceive, now, of dying—certainly not in bed anyway; and those two nights with Suzanne were already unreal in memory, enveloped in a fuzzy golden haze.

At the Dimpleroses' it had been different. There, to lie still was so obviously the way of common sense, in the circumstances, that he never questioned or discussed it. At first he had no choice; but even when he felt himself growing stronger he did not twist and turn but lay quiet, not squirming after his one-time strength but instead allowing it to flow without sound or fret back into his limbs. There were times, there were hours-long stretches, when he didn't honestly know whether he was awake or asleep, and what's more didn't care. He never did fall asleep while Mr Dimplerose read the Bible, for he enjoyed that too much to be willing to miss any of it, but often he dozed off immediately after the Book had been closed. Often too Mr Dimplerose's praying would awaken Hab—for though he was thoughtful and hushed about everything else, the impeccable sickroom attendant, Mr Dimplerose never lowered his voice when he prayed—but this in turn left Hab smilingly prepared to slip back into slumber. Hab would hold out till the end, from politeness, but when he had attested his attention with a firm-spoken "Amen" he would lapse into unknowingness, sometimes even without having heard Mr Dimplerose's own "Amen."

Not infrequently when he woke up, whether it was day or night, he would less than half open his eyes, and if he saw Mr Dimplerose there, and especially if Mr Dimplerose didn't have the Book on his knees, Hab would close his eyes again and pretend to be asleep. In the daytime there was always light from a window—too high, though, for Hab to look out of—and at night, all night, there burned a long tallow candle in a sort of lamp chimney, what Si Wainwright and others who'd visited the sugar islands would call a hurricane lamp, on a table by the side of the bed. This night light was so set that it would not shine into Hab's eyes, though it did illuminate the face of Mr Dimplerose when he sat in the chair at the bedside looking down at Hab.

Now, this fourth night, it shone upon the face of Mrs Dimplerose. Hab was crashingly wide-awake, and his eyes fairly popped out.

She was a small woman, plump, as the hands and wrists had promised, and extremely pretty. She was all roundness—round head, round eyes, round breasts only faintly indicated under her heavy cotton nightgown, which came right up to her chin, and he supposed round arms. She wore no nightmob and her hair, a dark even brown with hints of red, straight but not heavy, not lank, was only half done up behind her head: it framed artlessly her demure round face. The eyes too were brown, and they too held flecks of red, Hab believed, though he couldn't be sure of this since the woman, immediately he looked at her, dropped those eyes. She blushed a bit; but she didn't stir. Despite the informality of her garb, she sat straight in the chair, her hands folded on her lap, like a schoolgirl about to recite a lesson. Nor could any schoolgirl have blushed more entrancingly.

Hab said nothing and did not move, he simply lay there staring at her. It was some time before she spoke. Maybe she had expected him to speak first.

"Thee is abashed to see me so brazen?" she asked in a grave, even, but very low voice, not looking up.

Hab said nothing.

"I—I wished to meet thee. I felt sorry for thee. Thee was hurt so bad, there on the back. Sometimes I have seen it when my husband treats it. So cruel, the stripes!" She shuddered, still looking down at her hands. "It was wrong of me to peek," she admitted, "but I was so sorry for thee."

It was Hab's turn to blush. He felt the blood bang right up to his eyes, but he kept those eyes open and he kept his mouth shut.

Her own blush had gone, but soon it returned, mounting very slowly: she must have sensed his gaze on her. She moved her hands a shadow, twining the plump round fingers. Her cheeks took on a deeper and deeper red. Her eyelids fluttered.

"Thee—thee is horrified?"

She whispered it. The whisper went all around the room.

"I didn't say so" muttered Hab.

She rose swiftly, and put out a hand to touch his cheek. The fingers just grazed the cheek, just the tips of them, and then they were withdrawn. She lifted her gaze for a moment, and smiled straight down at him. Yes, there *were* bits of red in the eyes. The smile was a fine bright thing, even while timorous, which involved all her face and not merely her mouth alone. She dropped her gaze again.

"Good night" she whispered. "The Lord rest thee."

Then she was gone.

He stared at the doorway through which she had passed, the kitchen doorway at which until this time he had seen only her wrists and hands. He heard no sound of her. He stared at the chair she'd just quitted; and after a while he sat up and reached out and touched the seat of the chair; and though the room was chilly, or had been, the chair was warm.

It was a long while before Hab Jones got to sleep. When he woke it was dawn, and Mr Dimplerose sat there, the Book on his knees.

"Good morning" said Hab. "I reckon I'd better start for Wilmington today."

"No" said Mr Dimplerose.

Further than this Mr Dimplerose refused to go, confining himself to the monosyllable and scorning to give any explanation, though Hab two or three times in the course of the day brought up the matter. Hab was restless now, at last. He stirred and twisted. His cold had lowered itself to a mere sniffling, and he knew that he was strong enough to get out of bed and get dressed and simply walk away. But that would be to offend Mr Dimplerose. He could wait another night, Hab decided. Just one more night.

He knew that she was coming, had known that all along, and indeed he was waiting for her, his skin tingling. After Mr Dimplerose had tiptoed out, in the belief that Hab was asleep, Hab fully opened his eyes again and lay on his side, watching and watching the kitchen doorway.

He was sure he hadn't slept, for he'd been too tense to sleep; and even if she had been the way fanciful people used to say that the fairies were who would appear and likewise disappear completely inside the twinkling of an eye, still he didn't understand how she could have done it, for he hadn't blinked once. Yet there she was, trig in the chair, her hands folded in her lap, eyes downcast, the unfrilled nightgown buttoned right up to her chin, which was round. There she sat, blushing a little and seeming not to breathe.

Oh, he knew! She was listening to sounds not yet made; for she was lonesome, and hungry for other people's words, not for conversation, just for talk, words. After a while she looked up, but only with her eyes, not lifting her head. It was a movement of fear: she had become afraid that he was asleep again and that there'd be no talk. When she saw him looking at her she smiled swiftly and frightenedly, a wonderful warm smile, and then looked down again and began to blush. The blush deepened and spread as she felt his eyes on her, and colored her forehead, her neck, even her ears. She did not move and she probably couldn't have managed to speak in that moment.

Odd, thought Hab Jones, that I feel more guilty simply lying here and looking at a married woman who must be almost thirty years old than I ever felt after what I did with Suzanne. For he had not known the onset of conscience he'd expected after lying with the sangmêlé. That business must have been shameful, abhorrent, vile, by everything he had ever been taught a venial sin; the fact that he had enjoyed it so much at the time no doubt made it even worse; and yet he was hanged if he didn't still love it in memory, so that no matter how hard he tried he couldn't feel ashamed of himself. Here, now, doing nothing but looking at a woman, he was covered with shame. Like her, he was blushing: he felt his face hot. Like her, he could find no words to coax past the lump in his throat. For some time the two were silent, while the wind soughed softly outside and rain beat an unsteady tattoo against the window.

When talk did come to Hab it came with a rush, burstingly. He was willing enough to talk! He had not told anybody at all about Deliverance; and now he spoke to Mrs Dimplerose in eager spurts, his voice low but excited. She sat more at ease, relieved when the words came, relaxing as though ropes had been cut away from her torso and straps unfastened. The blush all but went, and for the first time her breast moved. Now and then she'd lift her eyes and smile at him, but she'd close her eyes again promptly when the smile stopped the flow of talk, chopped it off in mid-word, for Hab couldn't go on speaking when he saw those eyes.

He did not tell her about John Rellison but he did tell her a little about Judge and Mrs Watts, but most of all he talked about Deliverance. He told Mrs Dimplerose that he had always loved Deliverance, ever since he first saw her, but that he had accepted this condition rather coolly for a while, rather casually, not in fact thinking much about it one way or the other. Then, he told Mrs Dimplerose, he had suddenly become very conscious of Deliverance, of her body and the way she moved about, of the way she looked when she bent over, and he'd found himself wanting her with a terrible pushing passion which frightened him—as suddenly as he had become excited he became also afraid. Then he despaired. This too had come quickly, confusing him, who was unaccustomed to such forceful feeling. He had asked Deliverance to marry him; and he told Mrs Dimplerose about how she had accepted him and how they'd kissed and how they had decided not to tell anybody until Judge Watts her father came back from Hartford next day, and how hard it was to hold the news in. He even told her about the magnolia blossoms. "That was June. It's October now, getting on for November. I wonder if she'll wait for me." He told Mrs Dimplerose how he had been obliged to stay aboard a vessel he'd piloted out to Montauk, and how he had been impressed into the British Navy because he didn't have a paper proving he was a Yank. Then he was silent, talked out, but feeling cleaner.

The woman opened her eyes. She leaned toward him. "She—she'll wait for thee, all right! She'll wait! Oh, I know she will!" Her eyes were bright, her lips were parted, and she leaned close to Hab. She was sobbing a little inside, very quietly. She reached out both hands and took his face in them, so that he trembled and burned like a man in high fever. "A woman would always wait for such as thee! She'll wait, don't fear!" Tears gleamed in her eyes.

Hab drew his hands out from under the blanket. They were very hot, and they trembled. He put them over her hands. He too was beginning to weep: he felt the hot tears forming in his eyes, and the near dear face of Mrs Dimplerose was blurred to his vision, though still lovely.

"It is late, Jane. Thee had best be abed."

They fair jumped, shied away from each other, for neither had seen or heard him come in; yet there he was by their sides, tall and gaunt and ghostly in his long rumpled nightrail. He tipped back his head and started to pray. Mrs Dimplerose got out of the room before the prayer began.

It was a long prayer but not an angry one. It didn't particularize. There was in it no mention of woman or adultery or the sins of the flesh or anything like that.

When it was finished, when even the "Amen" had been uttered, Hab put his hands back under the blanket and turned on his side and said in a quiet voice: "Thank you, sir. That was edifying. I—I think I should be strong enough to go away from here tomorrow."

"Yes" said Mr Dimplerose; and that was all he did say.

Hab never saw Mrs Dimplerose again. There was no mention of her at breakfast, which Mr Dimplerose watched him eat. Several times

Hab was on the point of bringing up the subject, but he crammed this impulse back down into his chest. If he spoke of it at all it would inevitably be on a defensive note; it would smack of confession—and he had nothing to confess. What Mr Dimplerose would say to his wife when he, Hab, was gone, Hab didn't know and couldn't guess; but he was tolerably sure that Mr Dimplerose's charity, that terrible relentless charity, would encompass the situation. Certainly there would be no violence. There would probably be no conversation even; but then Mrs Dimplerose by this time surely knew how to endure silence.

How Mr Dimplerose felt about Hab, Hab couldn't guess that either. There was, as always, no change in the man's expression or in the tone of his voice. After breakfast, wearing his own field boots, he fetched his meeting shoes.

"It is a long way to Wilmington. Thee'll need these" he said.

Hab thanked him but declined. Hab pointed out that, for one thing, the shoes were much too large for him; and he also pointed out that his own feet were tough. He did not put on his stockings, for fear of wearing them out below, but wrapped them around his neck as a scarf. He declined, again with careful thanks, to accept Mr Dimplerose's proffer of a wide-brimmed hat, only implying, not saying, that his head too was tough.

Mr Dimplerose went into the kitchen and came out with a bundle containing an apple, two hard-boiled eggs, a tiny packet of salt, half a loaf of bread, and a slab of cheese. Yet Mrs Dimplerose was not in the kitchen when they passed through that room on their way out (the front door of the house was never used, Hab gathered), nor did she appear on the terrace by the milking pails.

Hab faced the man squarely, thanked him, thrust out a hand. Mr Dimplerose seemed somewhat surprised, not by the thanks but by the hand, which, however, he shook.

"I but did my duty to the Lord" he said apologetically. "God be with thee."

"Amen" said Hab.

He looked back once, from a short distance down the road. Mr Dimplerose stood on the flagged terrace, exactly where Hab had left him, but now his head was thrown back, his arms were a little out from his sides, and his lips were moving. Hab could not glimpse Mrs Dimplerose at any of the windows, as he had hoped to do. He waved anyway, just on the chance that she might be peeking.

. 23 . . .

THERE WAS A BROOK SLITHERING ACROSS THE TRACK, AND he walked up a ways and found a pool and knelt by this and drank. Afterward he washed, which made the ripples rock every-which-way. Then he stood, blowing and grinning.

It was a glowery day—it had rained earlier and probably would rain again—but to Hab, the way he felt, the low glum sky looked cheery. This was a clear space, seemingly not used as a meadow, for he saw no evidence of livestock having recently visited it, and it was chock-full of rocks. There were no trees immediately about, but there were many stumps. The Newport people'd taken the trees for making boats, he reckoned.

He looked back toward Newport, which he couldn't see now—he couldn't even see the bay—and wished he'd had time to visit it right. But there was a long trip ahead of him, and it would be after dark when he got home, unless somebody gave him a ride behind, which wasn't likely; so he had scarcely glanced around but started to find out how he might get across the bay without paying any sort of fare: he hadn't a penny. That scrawny surly chaw-chewing skipper accosted in Wilmington, the only one who was making for these parts soon, had lost almost half his crew, as Hab later learned, when he was forced to put in at the Delaware port after being demasted. He didn't feed well, and he worked the men to the bone; and sailors after all these days could be, to some extent, the Embargo being ended, choosers; so a goodly number of them had failed to return to the ship. That skipper should have been delighted to get an unexpected hand, after having combed the pubs in vain; but he was a mean man, who must have seen the glint of desperation in Hab's eyes, and he gruffed at last that he'd take Hab along and permit him to handle sail as far as Newport—but he wouldn't pay anything. He even hinted that it ought to be up to *Hab* to pay *him,* though he didn't press this point. He was a Rhode Islander, and that, Hab reckoned, was the reason. Hab had accepted with alacrity, nor had he been flustered by the scorn the other hands heaped upon him.

Wilmington he had seen something of. Still fresh and full of twang, not yet hungry, he had permitted himself a few hours of roaming the streets before he went to the waterfront. What had impressed him

216

deepest were the brick houses. There were some wooden houses too, but most of the houses, even the littlest and humblest ones, were made of trim red brick. They shone bright, as though it had just rained—it was still early morning when Hab had entered Wilmington—and their white woodwork shone too, and their brass bootwipers and brass knockers and brass doorknobs all shone, while their windows glittered. Yet even as Hab strolled along, up one street and down another, the daughters and the blond buxom bound-girls came out with buckets and rags and brushes, and they began to scrub and polish. They polished the brass as vigorously as though it had been specked. They scrubbed the little low doorsteps. Down on hands and knees, their skirts kilted high, they scrubbed the very flagstones before the houses, which had previously been as clean, in Hab's eyes, as the doorsteps themselves. Hab liked that, for he always liked cleanliness. He saw much that was interesting in Wilmington—the only foreign city he had ever visited—and he would have liked to spend more time there; but he had to eat. Besides being a clean place, it seemed very prosperous. It was rather like what he had always pictured New York to be, only grander. It had seemed a pity, too, to be so near Philadelphia, that greatest of all American cities, and not visit it; but he really did have to eat, which meant he had to work. So he'd signed on. And now, here less than two weeks after leaving Mr Dimplerose's house, he was practically home.

He had only about thirty-five or forty miles to walk.

The wind blew a dry leaf against his face and firmly pressed it there. He peeled it off, held it at arm's distance, and beamed on it as on an old friend. He released it, and it skittered away.

When they came alongside in Newport early this morning Hab had made no pretense of waiting to be discharged. *He* didn't care what the sour skipper shouted, now! He had made friends with the cook, and he was stuffed with lobscouse, which, though it was the sort of mess landsmen would throw to their hogs, was far superior to the burgoo of H.M.S. Pactolus; nor did he, like the others, have to work until all unloading was finished before he got his pay. So Hab had vaulted the rail promptly, with only a good-by wave to his fellow hands, and ignored the command to help in the unloading, the threats of imprisonment.

It was a pity that he didn't get a chance to look at Newport as he would have liked; for Newport was one of the places he and John often used to talk about, and John never had been there, though he'd been to New London. John of course by this time had been to so many places, really foreign cities, in foreign countries, that is, that it didn't matter; but Hab guessed he'd never been to Newport and Hab wished he could gloat a little before John and tell about the wonders of the place, if there were any. However, he didn't look around much. He reckoned he didn't have time. For one thing, that skipper might conceivably cause some trouble at that, Hab being without a coin in his pocket and no friend nearby. More important, every minute wasted now was a minute away from home.

He had of course thought to pick up some sort of craft rounding Judy, but he learned that the weather down that way was dirty and that he would have to wait. They none of them liked rounding Judy, nor did Hab blame them. Hab himself had never done it, never having been paid to, but he knew seamen who swore they'd rather round Hatteras than round Cape Judith, that melee where the sound and the sea and Narragansett Bay all bang into one another, pushing in half a dozen directions. It had been different when the Embargo Act was in force and Tom Jefferson's pestiferous little heel-tappers had been set to pounce upon honest coasters making an honest living, or trying to: *then* they'd used to round Judy, as Hab had used to guide vessels out to Montauk, in the worst possible weather for preference, waiting patiently for a good chance to risk their lives in order to safeguard the cargo. *Now* they weren't going to do any such thing. Judy was bad enough at the best of times. If he had any hope of getting aboard a boat scudding around to Stonington, Hab had been told, well, sir, he'd better make himself to home right now, for he was going to be around here three-four days at least. So he walked. He did manage to get a free sail across the bay, and from the western shore he walked to Kingston.

There wasn't any stage. A horse was out of the question, involving money. So he walked through Kingston and now he was fairly on the track for Westerly and the Point.

Well, anyway, he had been *in* Newport. He could say that. He'd sure tell John Rellison that when they met again. Not that he reckoned there was much chance of meeting John when he got to the Point. It might be months or even years before he and John came together again.

However, he was going to see Deliverance soon, and old Judge Watts. Yes, and Mrs Watts too: even the disapproving face of Mrs Watts, with its shifty eyes downcast whenever you glanced her way, would be a welcome sight. And the food! And a real bed!

Fists on hips, he looked around and saw the stumps and rocks, and he grinned. Leaning over a little, he looked down. The ripples had run themselves to rest, so he could see his own head and shoulders in the water. He had no hat, and his tousled brown-red hair, which hadn't known a comb in a long while, still hurled itself this way and that, looking in fact about the way it had looked even when he bear-greased it just before starting out for the meetinghouse. There wasn't anything to be done about that hair. Wet or dry, short or long, it was perpetually rebellious.

There seemed to be fewer freckles, he thought, across the bridge of his nose. There never had been many, a mere brush-splash of them, but Hab always had been conscious of his freckles, and now, critically viewing himself, he believed that they were fading. That made him feel glad. He looked peaked enough, he reckoned, without having those freckles to flame out like smallpox spots. Still, this might have been because the surface of the pool was not altogether still—a few leaves had landed on it and were floating listlessly and ineffectively here and there—so that the reflection wasn't the clearest, the light too being poor. Or it might be because his face was darker now. The face certainly was darker, no matter how wavy the reflection.

Never one to spend much time before a mirror, now he was pleasantly astonished by what he saw. He had remembered what he looked like, oh sure, and he could recognize this reflection of a man; but—right there was the point—it *was* a man. The blue eyes, even through the grin, and in spite of it, no longer held the moist wonderment of boyhood; they shone hard now, shrewd, cautious. The chin too was harder and more nearly square, and its down was stiffening. It might have been that the way he was leaning over created a sort of optical illusion, but anyway he was downright flubbered by the sight of his shoulders, so much wider and thicker than he had remembered them. Yes, by gum, he was getting pretty big. Coming to think of it, month after next he would be eighteen.

He knelt swiftly for another drink. He followed the stream back to the trail and started west again, singing a little song, a capstan song.

> *Then it's haul, haul,*
> *Tarry-breeks all!*
> *The captain's a cripple,*
> *Got only one ball.*

It was getting dark when he reached Westerly, not getting dark abruptly and indecently like a whuffed-out candle, the way it had done each night in the islands, but with decorum, reasonably; and it was chilling up; and he felt tired. There was no stir around the inn, where he didn't loiter to ask questions. People in Westerly were none too fond of the Pointers; and indeed the only other time Hab had visited this town was in the company of John Rellison and a dozen others, when they'd come looking for trouble with the Buckies—which trouble they'd got. Hab smiled a trifle, but shamefacedly, and as he trudged along, or sometimes trotted, he felt his nose with a rueful hand. You could still feel that bump on the bridge where it had been broken, and it had hurt like thunderation at the time—though it hadn't hurt as much as Háb's bottom when Judge Watts was finished with punishing him. They'd been worried about John's right eye too, for days, almost a week—afraid he'd lose the sight of it. Judge Watts in fact had waited exactly a week before he whupped John for his participation in the raid, saying that he didn't want to whup a half-blind boy. He would have waited another week or two or three, if necessary, but the whupping would have been given sooner or later, eye or no eye.

It had been silly, Hab reasoned now, feeling the wind on his left cheek as he crossed the bridge, sniffing the salt of the sound, hearing that capstan song in his mind—silly to fight like that, for no reason or cause, just for the love of it or because some harum-scarums talked you into it. Well, he reckoned he wouldn't ever do that again. You might do a lot of foolish things once, if only out of curiosity, but they got really foolish if you did 'em twice.

He entered a woods, which he remembered. That is, he remembered it as of the second time he passed through it, retreating, sobbing, his nose hurting something frightful, John sobbing too and crying out that he was going to be blind, while the Buckies followed them, outnumbering them now three or four to one but contented to throw stones and to jeer. He didn't remember having gone through it on the way *to* Westerly. They'd all been too worked up then.

> So it's haul, haul,
> Tarry-breeks——

He couldn't see much: there was no moon, and if there was starlight the trees barred it. He felt the track with his feet, which were bare, but he kept his arms outstretched; and even then he sometimes caught a whiplike branch fair across the face. The wind raved softly, and leaves he couldn't see touched him and tumbled on or slapped against him and stuck. When he heard a horseman coming, fearing to be run down, he got off behind a tree, which he found with his hands.

Nevertheless the horseman stopped, sensing something. Even now Hab could not see him, though he did see the sheen of the horse's flank and he caught a fugitive fleer from a pistol. Leaves whooshed by.

"Who's there? Who is it?"

The voice was high, though a man's voice, and very nervous. Hab, frowning, decided to stay behind his tree. He heard the pistol striker click back. He didn't fancy the thought of that pistol.

"Speak up or I'll shoot!"

Then the thing went off with a terrific crash. There was a flare of light, too sudden and disappearing too swiftly for Hab to see which way the shot was aimed. Hab had an idea that it wasn't aimed at all— that the pistol had gone off by mistake, nervousness having made the horseman's finger twitchy. He never knew where the ball went, if there was a ball. The sound of the shot itself precluded everything else. It roused few echoes, and those were wee muffled sounds soon

220

gulped by the wet air of the woods, but it left the ears singing, the heart beating a wild tattoo. Hab indeed had almost fainted.

There was the prickly smell of gunpowder. The horse was galloping away—panic-filled, it sounded as if—in the direction of Westerly. Shaking his head, Hab stepped out from behind the tree and with his feet found the track again. Sure were a lot of damn fools in this world, he reflected.

It started to rain again. The wind rose, moaning, and when he came out of the woods he did as he had often done before on this trip —he broke into a dog-trot, to keep some feeling in his feet. It hadn't been bad, having no shoes, while walking from Mr Dimplerose's house to Wilmington. It hadn't been so bad on this walk now, most of the way, so far, though it was getting bad. It had been very bad coming up from Wilmington to Newport short-handed, with the weather squally. Hab had sometimes been obliged to lie aloft for hours on end, in an icy rain. He hadn't enjoyed it. He was afraid that his feet might have been a bit frostbitten: he couldn't otherwise account for them being so numb, though he'd kept walking. The dog-trot helped.

He was still trotting, and it was about ten o'clock, when he reached Stonington.

It was too dark to see what was lying in the harbor, the place to which his eyes went instantly. It was dark in the village itself too, and as he trotted along Main Street the square white houses which looked so friendlylike in daytime behind their white fences were wan and ghostly on either side.

He could not yet see Judge Watts's house, but he did see one light, over on Water Street and far out near the end of the Point. Though out of his way a little, it beckoned. It would be Oliver York's public house, he knew, and he wanted to go there just long enough to peek through the window at the sailing men drinking inside. There would be a fire on a night like this, and the pewter mugs would glow fine, and the jacks and glasses would glitter. Just a small look, that was all. Just a glimpse. He had come this far, and a few feet further wouldn't hurt anybody.

All the same, his conscience tugged inside his breast when he peered through the window. He knew as well as anybody that he *should* have gone straight home. He was painfully hungry, having had nothing to eat since breakfast; and he was so cold, his teeth chattering, that what with his weakened condition he was afraid he might be freezing. He would go home, let himself into the dark house by means of that same window he and John had used so many times, find something to eat in the kitchen, and go up to his room, to the bed he'd used to share with John, and climb in and fall asleep. There would be covers on the bed, he was sure.

He thought maybe he ought to wake up Judge and Mrs Watts and Deliverance, but that would scare them and maybe it wouldn't be polite. But he certainly should have gone straight home and not turned aside to look through the window of Oliver York's entertainment.

Oliver himself was seated at the biggest table, along with four or five sailing men. They all had jacks of flip or some other drink, and they were listening to one who faced Hab—though he couldn't have seen Hab—and who waved his arms while he talked. This was John Rellison.

Hab's heart leapt. He had all he could do to keep from running around to the door and bursting in. He wouldn't throw his arms around John Rellison, but he might just stand there, up close to John, arms folded, and grin and grin at his friend. He forgot about how John had treated Mrs Watts, and he even forgot for a little while how John had treated Deliverance. That was past. You couldn't unscramble scrambled eggs. John was John, after all, and his smile was still the warmingest in the world. John was smiling in there right now, as he waved his arms, making a point. Whatever it was he was talking about, it had all the attention of the others.

Hab didn't go in. It wouldn't have been right. He would have been obliged in common decency—common sense too, in his condition—to have a drink with them. He would have had to tell them at least something of what had happened to him, and to learn something of what had happened to John, who was, Hab saw now, a little drunk and for that reason likely to be more talkative than usual. No, it was best to go on his way. It was a wrench. It seemed to hammer something inside his chest, and he even wept a little; but he did turn away. He trotted again, forcing himself to do so.

John would be coming home in a little while, he told himself again and again, and would find him, Hab, in the bed. Then they'd stay awake as long as they could, talking in whispers, talking about old times. Hab only hoped that John didn't get really drunk. He hadn't looked very drunk, just mellow, his dark eyes shining, his head thrown back as he told his tale.

From the dog-trot he broke into a real run when he saw that there were lights in the Watts house. He panted heavily, his heart going lickety-click. He was a little dizzy. He couldn't feel his feet, could hardly feel any leg at all below the knees.

Even the front hallway was lighted. Special guests? It could be. Judge Watts had been known to permit guests to stay as late as this when there was a particularly big contract in sight, an especially large order to fill. Just the same, Hab was scared.

The back door was locked, and he knocked on it, and in a little while Mrs Watts opened it. She leaned toward him, squinting.

"John—John!" Her voice quavered. "Is that you?"

He stepped into the light.

"It's me, ma'am. Habakkuk. I've got back."

"Oh . . . I thought it was John. We sent for John."

"Aren't you glad to see me, ma'am?"

"Well, I—— Well, yes, I reckon I am. Come in. Truth is, I'm so flubbered, I'm so—I hardly know what to do!"

She sat down with a bump, and put her face into her hands, and began to weep.

But Deliverance had heard his voice, and there was a rush of steps, and she came running across the kitchen, arms outstretched. There was not the slightest shame in her joy at the sight of him.

"Hab, Hab! You're all right? Oh, the Lord be praised, you're all right!"

When they left off kissing, a few minutes later, and looked at one another, still holding on tight to one another though, Mrs Watts raised her head to stare balefully at them. The tears shone in her eyes but on her sagging cheeks they'd dried, and she was cold with her stare, even hating them.

"Mother is so worried she hardly knows what she's doing" Deliverance whispered. "She's been taking on for hours."

Was there, he asked, still almost breathless, some special guest? Deliverance looked up at him strangely. She nodded, still looking at him.

"I mean, besides me" he smiled.

She was a straightforward girl ordinarily—not simple, for it was never easy to guess what she was thinking—but without subterfuge. Hab had never before known her to wax dramatic like this.

"Yes, there is a special guest, Hab. He—— Well, I reckon his name is Death."

. 24 . .

The judge lay in the middle of bed, on his back, his head sunk into the pillow, and so pale was his face, almost like the very pillow itself, and so firmly closed his eyes, that Hab thought him dead then and there, when he first looked at him. But the judge was breathing a mite. You had to get close and peer very hard to see it; but he was breathing.

Hab went up to a member-of-the-family place only a few feet from the bed. He had noticed others back against the walls, silent men and women, neighbors, some of whom nodded to him: he'd nodded back briefly, with his eyes rather than his head, thereafter giving all his attention to the judge, a man who'd been kind and clever to him, who had always been good, a good man.

Deliverance came and stood beside him, and Mrs Watts came in and stood beside her daughter. Mrs Watts was better now, quiet, not even sniffling, with eyes for nobody but her husband.

That's the way they stood, just doing nothing. They were doing nothing, Hab knew, because there was nothing that they could do, everything having already been done; for when a man that old dies his close people are ready for him to die, and have made arrangements. Later on Mrs Watts and Deliverance would get out something to eat and some cider or even wine, and then there would be a certain amount of hushed talk, most of it about Judge Watts but some little about Hab and his return. But that would be later, after the judge—well, after that special guest had arrived. Right now there wasn't anything to do but just stand and wait.

When the judge did open his eyes it was so slightly that those back by the walls probably didn't notice it. Deliverance and her mother and Hab leaned forward. The judge looked at Hab, though at first they didn't think he saw him; but then, quavering and very low: "You're back?"

"Yes, sir" whispered Hab.

"John, John's not coming?"

Mrs Watts started to say something, but Hab cut in: "He's on his way, sir. He was held up. But he'll be here soon."

"Um. Should be. I—I reckon I'm going to die."

The judge lifted a forefinger so thin as to seem transparent. He closed his eyes; but then he opened them abruptly, and there was more light in them than there had been before.

"But Aaron's not here?"

He said it loud enough for the folks back against the wall to hear, and they stirred, shaking their heads, feeling choky; for everyone knew that it was more than eleven years since Aaron Watts had gone to sea.

"No" the judge muttered, answering his own question. "No, he's not here. He won't come."

He closed his eyes again, and again you had to stare hard to be sure that he breathed.

The unabashed wind outside and the tentative, sibilant, very low breathing of the watchers were the only regular sounds. Now and then a leaf would scrape a window. Now and then somebody'd shift his position, and an ankle-joint or a knuckle would crack with explosive suddenness, jarring the air.

After a while, when it had become tolerably certain that the judge slept or else lay in a coma, Hab nudged Deliverance and they backed to the kitchen like devout worshipers backing away from a shrine, on tiptoe. Mrs Watts did not follow them, and didn't even appear to notice them.

"Say, he's here, right here on the Point" Hab whispered fiercely, in the kitchen.

He was so excited that his nose began to bleed.

"You should wear shoes, Habakkuk" she said as she got a towel and staunched the flow. "Yes, we know he's here. Mother knows it too. I don't know whether Father does. You ought to get shoes. Maybe I can get you a pair of Father's, without anybody's wiser?"

"But see here, first John! Didn't you tell him?"

"Oh yes. His ship came in yesterday, and he was here himself this morning, but Father was still asleep then. He said he'd come back this afternoon, and when he didn't I sent Eph Tooker to tell him that Father was much worse. I sent Eph again, only about an hour ago."

"I'll get him!"

He broke away, and the blood started to flow again, fairly coursing out. His nose didn't hurt him—it never did on these occasions—but it annoyed him, and sometimes, as now, infuriated him.

"I'll fetch him back! I'll get him here if I have to——"

Blood filled his mouth then, swarming over his upper lip, so that his words came all blubberish and he was obliged to let Deliverance swab his mouth with the dish towel again, and to hold it there a while. They looked into each other's eyes, standing close, while she did this. Her eyes, only a little below his, were opened very wide, and she had her chin tilted high as she so often did. Her eyes were hazel. She regarded him gravely and tenderly, wishing, as he was wishing, that she could weep, yet knowing that joy was a feeling you shouldn't express in a

225

house in which death was about to appear. As for Hab, as he looked down at her, and yearned for her, he thought of all the times he had dreamed about this hour—this time of his return—and certainly among his mental pictures there had not been one in which they stood not even touching one another except that Deliverance held a wetted dish towel to his nose.

When she lowered that towel he said gently: "You know I didn't go away on purpose?"

"Of course I know that, Habakkuk."

"You know I didn't *run* away?"

"Yes, I know that. You wouldn't run away."

He swayed a shade toward her, meaning to kiss her, and she, not moving, would have permitted him to do so; but he drew back, fearing to start the bleeding anew, recalling to mind too his errand. He touched her forearm.

"I'll fetch him!"

"You be careful now. John has a sharp temper." She went to the door with him. "And you really ought to be wearing shoes, a night like this."

Several additional neighbors had been about to knock. They stood aside, looking curiously at Hab Jones.

It was still raining. Hab indeed carried a goodly portion of that rain with him when he flung himself panting into Oliver York's common room. They all turned, but he didn't glance at the others, didn't know or even care who they were. He wasn't cold any more, his teeth were not chattering: in fact he was damned hot.

John Rellison had been in the act of lifting a large leather jack to his lips but when he saw Hab over the top of it his eyes grew enormous and he lowered it. He was absurdly happy to see Hab, and began smiling. He looked a shade darker in the face than he'd used to, Hab thought, but this might have been the drinks he'd had, or the light. His eyes were clear and warm. His slick dark hair was as smooth as ever, the queue impeccably sacked. He still wore those rings in his ears. Yet at the same time he looked a boy, this lad of almost eighteen, this world-traveler and drinker with men in taverns. When he smiled he was the old John Rellison of upstate, the boy who always babbled about the sea.

He clacked the jack upon the table, and rose.

"Hab! Oh, Hab, you're back safe!"

Hab wasted no time in greetings. He was good and sore. He stabbed a forefinger at his friend.

"You! Don't you know the judge is dying? Don't you know that?"

"Well, I did hear he was pretty dauncy but I didn't suppose——"

"Didn't Deliverance send Eph Tooker twice to tell you, while you stayed here tossing gum?" He grabbed John's jacket. "Come on."

It wasn't just the drinks. John Rellison had always had an expressive face. Emotions came and went swallowlike within him, and they showed in his eyes as clearly as that many posters held up to the gaze. He had been astounded at first sight of Hab Jones, and then he'd been very glad, deliciously happy to see his friend; in another instant he'd become mystified; now, the hand on his jacket, he was angry. The eyes got hard, and somewhat smaller, and they wrinkled a little at the corners. The mouth stretched thorny and thin.

"Now wait a minute, Hab. I'll go with you all right, but you don't have to act that way."

"Well, come along then!"

Hab released him, and turned abruptly and went outside. He was afraid that if he remained here he would start to curse. He was trembling all over—from rage, not from the cold. Even the rain hitting his face didn't soothe him.

John came out, buttoning his fearnaught, slamming the door. He faced Habakkuk.

"Look here, and I don't care if you did just come back: Next time you have occasion to call me out of a public place before friends of mine you'd better do it like a gentleman—or else by God you'll soon wish you had!"

"Never mind all that cow droppings about gentlemen. You wouldn't know a gentleman if you saw one anyway. Come on."

He was turning away, for he knew that in argufying John Rellison was his better, John being glib and ingenious of thought; so Hab was turning away, when he caught in his ears the last words of what John Rellison said: ". . . and you can tell Deliverance that I'm not to be ordered around like a bound-boy and that just because I rolled her once don't mean she has any right——"

Hab turned back and punched him in the mouth.

Then Hab stood appalled at what he had done. Many a time, both up at the farm and here down to the shore, he and John had scuffled it rough, wrestling and batting one another like bear cubs; but that had been pure play, with never a hint of hard feeling: Hab could not even remember having got sore at John before, with that one exception of the time when John told Mrs Watts about the sea serpent, when the feeling he'd felt had been watery compared with this.

John too was amazed; but he recovered quickly. Blood came to his lips, and even as he slid his tongue out to lick it he was peeling his fearnaught, which he dropped to the ground. He hit Hab over the left cheekbone, and he hit him on the point of the chin, shuddering Hab's feet hard into the ground. To a third blow, Hab, recovering, rolled his head. He stepped back. He didn't raise his own hands; and when John, chin down, eyes dark jets of hatred, came on in, Hab shook his head.

"No, no! We can't do this!"

John swung another blow, which was a wild one Hab caught on his neck. Hab kept shaking his head, backing away.

"Not us, John! No! We can't!"

John was breathing heavily, his breath being rummy. He looked down.

"S-sorry I acted up, John. Just got too excited."

"Well, I guess I'm sorry too." He was, you could tell from his voice. "You made me mad. You oughtn't to have done that, Hab."

"No, you're right. I oughtn't to have."

They did not look at one another. Hab's head was singing, and he was so dizzy he could hardly stand. Part of this was due to exhaustion, no doubt, and part of it to the punches, which had been mighty hard, especially that one on the chin; but chiefly it was due to the emotions which had been teeming in him, crowding and cramming him, almost to suffocation. He wasn't used to so many emotions all at once. He felt as if his head would bust. He expected his nose to start bleeding again at any moment, even after all it had bled back there to the kitchen.

"Reckon I didn't mean that, what I said about Deliverance. She's a fine girl."

"Let's go get washed up" Hab mumbled.

It was principally John's mouth, which would soon be puffed if it wasn't cold-watered. The kitchen was not the place: all sorts of folks would be swarming in that kitchen. Instead, with the same old understanding they'd always had, that same no-need-for-talk, they walked without conference to the shipyard, and they climbed the fence the way they'd always used to do when they went to sneak a ship out to Montauk. Down by the little dock John knelt to splash water on his face, but Hab Jones stopped short, blinking in amazement.

"What's the matter?" John looked up. "Oh, that? Heard about it yesterday, right after my ship came in. Seems they found it next morning in the harbor. Must be it never got out near the Race. Must've slipped the painter right after you got under way."

Hab climbed down into the little cat-schooner, ran his hands along the gunnels, stroked the tiller as he might have stroked a pet. He smiled with shy affection, for it was good to see this Deliverance again—Deliverance I, he supposed he'd think of her as, now.

"Here's a good boat, John."

"Sure is. Smart too. Knew when to come home, which is more'n you did."

"Well, anyway, I got home at last."

"You aim to stay here, then, Hab?"

"I reckon."

"You didn't like the sea?"

"Not much."

So they talked on, once they'd started, talking quickly and jerkily, in a monotone, trying to be light about it, not looking at one another. Each knew that he was never going to forget those blows, not as long as he lived. They welcomed Deliverance I as a topic of conversation.

"We ought to get a pretty good price for it."

"Why, you wouldn't *sell* it, would you?"

John shrugged.

"Why not? I've got no more use for it now. Me, I'm a high seas man."

"Why don't you be shut of the sea? You're grown up now, practically."

Kneeling, washing, tenderly touching his mouth, John Rellison shook his head. Presently he looked sideways at Hab: it was no more than a fleet stolen glance from under his arm, and there was something slightly sneaky about it, so that Hab was shocked, and John quickly went on with his washing.

"*You* could still use it, of course. You, uh, you might want to buy out my half?"

Hab frowned a little.

"We'll talk about that later, eh?"

John had a little comb he carried in a jacket pocket, but it wasn't much use: his own hair hadn't been mussed, looked as if it never would be mussed, no matter what, while a comb wasn't much good in Hab's hair, even wet the way it was. But the washing had helped their faces, and they brushed their clothes with their hands, so that when they appeared, two quiet lads, at the kitchen door of the Watts house, and knocked humbly for admittance, they guessed they looked all right. Mrs. Watts made a subdued sort of fuss about John. Deliverance, suspicious, tried to catch Hab's eye, but he wouldn't grant this. There was a power of folks in the bedroom and upstairs hallways now, with more coming all the time. Sometimes Deliverance let them in, sometimes her mother, and sometimes it was John or Hab. Whichever greeted, the other three stood by the bedside gazing into the face of the old judge. After a while, near dawn, when Mrs Tooker, who knew all about such things, said that he was going to die, they knelt. He died about ten minutes after that, a man who had been honest and kind.

They didn't get much sleep that night, any of them.

. 25 . . .

The widow watts was a problem, though not at first, for at first she appeared to take it well, with courage holding the tears back, sometimes even essaying a smile; indeed, she seemed less teched than she had seemed before. But this slid off almost imperceptibly, this politeness air, like a cloak of filmy silk, unveiling what was hard, sour. She seldom spoke and never smiled. Head down, she would work without a sound for hours, but glancing up now and then, even when nobody else was in the kitchen, with a sharp suspicious glance, as though she expected to surprise somebody in the act of stealing something. Her hands were steady with their old-time skill; but there smoldered in her eyes a fire she seldom showed, for she kept those eyes lowered most of the time, so that it shivered you when you looked straight at her and caught her looking at you; and her mouth would twitch as though in sympathy with violent if muffled thoughts.

Her infatuation with John Rellison was more marked than ever; yet John was seldom at the house, preferring to drink and gam in one of the local entertainments, when he was ashore at all. John had a might to do, he said. He was second mate now of the same schooner, Northern Constellation. Deliverance asked him to live at the house while his ship rode. Hab, half hoping that they would get to know one another again as they'd known one another before, offered to share the same old room with him, the same bed. The Widow Watts implored him to linger. But John shook his head, smiling. "I'm a sailorman." Yet John saw more of Oliver York's flip, Hab reckoned, than of salt water.

Nevertheless when John was in the house he made himself to home, going where he wished, picking up whatever he felt like eating or drinking, occasionally though not regularly helping with the work. His manner with the Widow Watts was offhand, for her attentions, which once had flattered and later had amused him, he now found a bore: she kept staring at him so intensely, so adoringly, and it may be that he was even a bit frightened of her, as Hab himself sometimes was. John's manner toward Deliverance was one of easy cordiality and intimacy. He would lean across the table to touch her forearm while he talked with her, or lay a hand briefly upon her shoulder as he passed; and once a darkening Habakkuk saw him spank, gently and playfully to be sure, but unmistakably, her backside. John had a possessive air when he talked with her. We two, he implied, share a secret. Deliverance never gave a sign that these touches annoyed her, or even that she noticed them.

Toward Hab, curiously, the widow's attitude showed little change. She had never concealed her distrust of him, and only the stern insistence of the judge had kept her from shrilling more often. With the judge dead, however, she treated Hab much the same. She didn't rail at him, but still regarded him with distrust. Though the house was hers by the terms of the will, she never challenged his right to live in it, and did not seem offended when he took over such of the late judge's household duties as seemed proper—the carving, the locking-up, the reading of prayers. She did watch him more acutely than ever, appearing reluctant to turn her back on him, stepping sideways when she went through the doorway of a room he was in. When he'd look at her she would drop her eyes; and for this reason, since it embarrassed both of them, he seldom studied her appearance, as he wished to do, wondering why she disliked him so much. He didn't dislike her. At times he was frighted of her, frighted of what she might do if ever her mind broke loose altogether; but mostly he just felt sorry for her.

Deliverance too felt sorry for the widow, her mother, who took to watching her with eyes that were lit with suspicion. Previously Deliverance, too placid to join in any dispute, but a stubborn girl, when her mother would reprove her for the way she was doing something, would, if Deliverance herself thought that she was doing it right, simply go right ahead without saying a word or showing any sign that she'd heard. Previously she had refused to be flustered, as she refused to be a slavey. Now, though not quieter (she couldn't have been quieter), she was more considerate. Scolded unjustly, she would lower her head and murmur "Yes, Mother," and do what she had been doing another way. It was not likely that she loved her mother—who could love so wild and eccentric a woman?—but she was sweet and sympathetic, she was unresistant.

The neighbors were like that too. Not in years had the Watts house been a notably warmy one, though folks were always welcome there. The judge, since his son's failure to return, had scarcely been an affable companion. Still, he had been liked and respected, and, more important, consulted. Hab remembered when almost always, day or evening, there had been somebody waiting to see the judge—waiting in the yard or the woodshed if he were very humble, more likely in the kitchen, or if he were a ship's captain or owner, in the parlor itself, unshuttered for the visit. Well, the law practice was finished: Hab himself knew he would never learn the law now. The various involved bits of business, shares of establishments, lays in one vessel or another, in one voyage or another, promissory notes, partnership agreements, mortgages, all the like of that, were in the hands of Judge Palmer, who would presumably take a long while getting them straightened out.

Judge Watts had been a secretive man, and most of his papers, though in order, were meant only for his own eyes. The shipyard affairs were more profitable than ever before, but Hab, as he had done some time before sailing for the islands, conducted these in the office shack. The house itself, then, always a solemn place, in which visitors instinctively dropped their voices to a whisper, now became a house of downright gloom, a dim eerie mansion, where even the three residents, who should have known better, were twitchy or tense.

It was remarked that the judge apparently had been unaware of his wife's queerness, or else had sought to draw attention from it by ignoring it. There were a few who suggested obliquely that maybe the old judge himself hadn't been too sane toward the end, what with his unsmilingness, his elaborate caution, and the way he managed to make the simplest business deal complicated; but this thought was generally pooh-poohed. The fact that Mrs Watts was teched had been accepted on the Point. No mention of this fact was in Judge Watts's will, an extraordinarily long document over which he must have spent much time and thought, for it had been rewritten, rewitnessed, revised, amended, and plastered with codicils right up until a few months before the judge's death. This will was read in the parlor five days after the funeral, and nobody, not even Judge Palmer, who had helped to write and change it, who had witnessed it, and who now formally read it, was certain what it conveyed.

Understand: the will didn't *leave* anything, but *conveyed* or *bequeathed* sundry *bequests* and *conveyances*. Why, its language flubbered even old Judge Palmer, no novice. There were so many beneficiaries, most of them friends or employees who should get small shares of something: for example, there was even mentioned a scrimshaw knickknack, a carved whale's tooth worth not more than a few pennies, which the executors were directed to hand over to Mrs Joseph Wallace, a directive which stumped the auditors until somebody remembered that Mrs Wallace, now the wife of a fisherman, when a girl years ago had twice been taken sailing by Aaron Watts, though they'd never been trothed. John Rellison came in for a sixty-fourth share each in two coasting sloops and one schooner, all small vessels. Hab Jones got the same, in addition to a sum the judge as his guardian had held for him, what was left after the farm he'd inherited upstate had been sold for taxes, a matter of $22.45, all of which had recently been lent out at eight per cent to Eb Baxter, a fisherman. Besides these bequests, Hab and John each got fifty Spanish dollars, notable as almost the only cash distributed. The chief beneficiaries, of course, were the Widow Watts and her daughter, neither of whom, though both were numerously mentioned, ever was mentioned by name. Thus Mrs Watts was always "my lawful wife and helpmeet," while Deliverance was "the lawful issue of my body in marriage." This latter phrase, repeated outside, caused some tittering over the possibility that the judge had had a bastard or two; but the serious ones, those who had known him best, if they ever even heard it discarded with scorn this libel.

Well, "my lawful wife and helpmeet" got, in addition to many paper items, the house and the land it stood on. "The lawful issue of my body in marriage" got the farmland back of the Point, which didn't amount to much, and the shipyard, which did.

"I reckon if I own it you'd better go on running it, Habakkuk."

"I reckon I had."

What the estate amounted to nobody knew. It would take some months, if not years, to find that out.

There were sincere well-wishers who, viewing Mrs Watts askance, advised Deliverance to petition for the appointment of a conservator. Otherwise, they pointed out, she might, when it came time to inherit from her mother, find that there was nothing left. Deliverance refused to do this.

"She might be teched," to Hab, "but I see no profit in our telling everybody so."

He nodded, gravely fingering his chin.

"Of course, if we should have any—if there should be——"

All one blush, she turned back to her skillet.

"Time enough to fuss about that," she reproved, "when they come."

True, he thought with bitterness. Time enough to fuss after there was a marriage; but oh, the weeks seemed so long! It was sure (and they'd required no talk on this point) that they couldn't be married until a decent interval had passed after the judge's death. But what was a decent interval? Nobody knew. It was longer, presumably, for Deliverance the daughter than for Habakkuk Jones the ex-apprentice, but it might be, by the reasoning of some, longer still for the both of them together! The widow at least was not ready to compromise. Soon after Hab went south, soon after the cat-schooner was found and towed ashore, Deliverance had told her father and mother that she intended to marry Habakkuk Jones when he returned. Her mother then had opened her mouth to object, but the judge had looked at her. The judge had accepted the information gravely and without show of astonishment. He'd said that he would think it over. Four or five nights later, at supper, he had announced that he was willing to give his blessing to the match, provided of course that Hab came back, and also provided that he and Hab had a satisfactory talk about Hab's future.

"He only said that to make it large. He was dreadful happy, really. But Mother wasn't. She was all over cratchy."

Now Mrs Watts insisted that the judge's consent had never been given, even informally, and that what's more it never would have been given had he lived. She had become very excited, screeching (Deliverance told Hab) that Deliverance was philidaddlin' with a bound-boy while her father was still warm in his coffin. This accusation was made more than two months after the judge's death, and Hab would have been free for almost that time even if the judge hadn't died; but the widow was immune to reasoning, and she had screeched and carried on something frightful, Deliverance told Hab.

"I reckon we better soothe her a mite and not bring it up again, because if we don't prod her she may not grow any worse."

"I reckon she won't grow any better either" Hab muttered, holding Deliverance, squeezing her shoulders, while the blood pounded in his heart and face. "I've heard of daft people getting worse but never getting better."

Deliverance tightened up a little, and he loosed his grip and kissed her face and apologized.

"I'm sorry. Reckon that ain't a proper word, really."

"Well, I reckon it's the truth. But I don't like to hear it spoke."

"I'm sorry."

It was hard, living like this, seeing one another three times a day, sleeping in separate beds, in separate rooms not more than ten feet apart, all the while feeling the way they did. He could not even spark her, court her, as he might have done if they lived in two different houses and he'd appeared calling. The parlor of course was never opened except on special occasions—they'd hardly have been comfortable there anyway—and the kitchen, the natural place for them to sit and talk and love, they never had alone: the Widow Watts, watching them with jealous eyes, alert and spiteful, would have waited up all night. They could sit on the bench out front, but the magnolia was bare now, admitting moonlight, and so was the shrubbery, and with winter coming, a harsh winter too, it was powerful cold sitting out on that (for the Point) high place: the wind sometimes seemed like to go right through you, scraping your bones with knives. They could walk, and they sometimes did walk at night after supper, but walking too was cold, and the Widow Watts would wait up for them no matter how they loitered; and not infrequently, even as late as nine o'clock, they would pass others, on which occasions they were certainly recognized. Hab stewed about scandal. He would take his arm away from Deliverance whenever a step sounded, before or behind, but how could he be sure that they weren't seen from the windows?

"Folks might talk."

"Folks are talking" she assured him tranquilly. "Have been. For some time."

He looked down at her, startled, but she only smiled straight ahead and put her cheek closer to his shoulder as they walked, pressing it.

"You mean, they know how we feel, you reckon?"

"Of course. They're guessing, but it ain't hard to guess. They're likely guessing too much though" she added darkly. "They think we

234

do a lot more than just take a walk and you put your arm around my middle."

He was shocked, but she wasn't.

"Why, you're not *ashamed* of me, are you, Hab? You're not *ashamed* of loving me?"

"No, no, no, no!" He held her, kissing her face again and again. "No, no! It isn't that! It's just that I don't like the thought of—well——"

"If I don't mind, you shouldn't."

"Well, I do." He scowled, not looking into her eyes, looking past her to the ground. This was about in front of the Palmers' house. The Zeph Palmers, that is. "D'ye suppose they—well——" Remembering, he resolutely closed his mouth.

"Me and John?" A little earlier she had given him one of her sweet rare smiles, but she was grave now. "No, I don't think so. I don't think anybody ever guessed that. It ain't what you *do* they guess, it's the way you *feel*. They can't see through walls. When you kiss, you can hide that, but you can't hide it when you're in love, I reckon. Leastways *you* can't, Hab."

"Why, I thought I was very careful!"

Looking up at him, she tipped on the verge of a smile. It made the corners of her mouth twirk.

"You have such wonderful eyebrows, Habakkuk," she whispered. "I always want to take them between my fingers and twist them back and forth."

A moment later, hearing a step he didn't hear, frantically she pressed his back. They broke away, gasping. It was only a drunken hiccoughing sailor who wouldn't have seen them anyway; but they hadn't known that. They resumed their walk, a discreet distance separate, their heads averted, their hearts pounding, and his hands were in the pockets of his fearnaught while hers were hidden in her muff.

This was the way it was with all their kisses, stolen but not the sweeter for that. Some men spice their love with sneakiness, and enjoy it so; but Hab Jones wasn't one of those. No, he was no more ashamed of loving Deliverance Watts than she was of loving him, though they were obliged to act that way. They discussed a private marriage, but agreed that it was impossible. For them both to be away from the house for a few hours, much less all day, would whip Mrs Watts maybe clear to hysterics. The pastor (they knew him well) would never consent to perform a hidden ceremony. And of course marriage by a justice-of-the-peace wasn't truly a marriage at all.

"It might kill Mother. You can see that, Hab? It would be worse than killing her if it drove her right out of her mind. That would be worse than murder. We couldn't do that, could we?"

"No," miserably.

It was harder on the girl, for she perforce was in her mother's dour presence all the day and must keep a maidenly mien. Deliverance's work was not so great as it once had been, what with two fewer mouths to fill and the back-country fields readied for winter; but it was drudgery all the same, and it gave her too much time to think. Though of a friendly disposition, she had few friends, never having had time for friends, which do take time; and so it was that she had nobody to babble Hab to. She might have developed some acquaintance—of these she had a dozen or more—but she was a shy girl, and considerate, and she feared that an intimateness might kick back viciously and unfairly at the confidante in the event of Deliverance herself being entoiled in a scandal—an event she was cool enough to know was chancing.

Hab, on the other hand, could and did work with a consuming passion. His labors were not drudgery, though once they had been. He was now, astoundingly, master of the Watts shipyard. No notice was published, no proclamation made, and Deliverance the new owner didn't issue any order; yet it was understood that the Jones boy was in charge. Him! A full journeyman, he was not a master builder; it would be some years before he rated that title; but except in technical matters, and sometimes even in those, the master builder himself, Nathaniel Tooker, a glum one, deferred to Hab. Hab alone handled contracts, collected bills, ordered supplies. His was the final say as to when the seasoning timber was ready for use, also when new timber should be felled back-country and brought down for seasoning, a process the Watts yard had never glossed. He was immensely interested in this work, as he'd always been, and even more interested in design, in the laying down of lines for new vessels, the taking off of lines of visiting vessels which fancied him. He sought greater speed, and always, in his way, he was making experiments. He talked whenever possible with the mates and skippers of vessels he had had a hand in building, questioning them in detail. He wished that he had the time to make a voyage or two in one of the new topsail schooners, just to see how it handled; for though he had no love of the open sea itself, or of shipboard and that life, he did enjoy sailing. He studied canvas, talked with sailmakers, and in his mind at least, and sometimes in actuality, changed and changed again the rig of this sloop or that schooner, never being satisfied.

Now that it was edging on toward winter he was up every morning before dawn, and it was well after sunset when he returned, dog-tired and glad of it.

Judge Watts had had little to do with the physical work at the yard, about which he hadn't known much, but he had conducted all the business affairs himself. Straightening those affairs was not easy. Hab learned early what old Palmer already knew: that the dead man had been neat and orderly and yet at the same time, and paradoxically, confusing. Judge Watts had had a passion for putting things on paper, inconsequential things most of them, mere notes of his own, personal reminders, and he had been reluctant to throw anything away, no matter how trivial. Some slight facts were recorded five or six times, in as many places. All the timber and planking, the sticks and spars as well, were fashioned right there in the yard, as were of course the treenails; but it was necessary to purchase, sometimes in Stonington itself, sometimes as far afield as New London, the metal for fittings and for sheathing, and some of the cordage and canvas. In this labor the old judge had indulged a passion for dispersal. He had never bought ten articles in one place when it was possible to buy one article in each of ten places, regardless of cost. He seemed even to have resented giving out a canvas contract, and in at least one case, the papers showed, he had caused the jibs to be sewed in one loft, the main and fore in another. All this had cut down the profit and contributed to the delays— the Watts yard had been notoriously slow in the construction of fast vessels. The old judge, it seemed, hadn't minded. Hab did.

"Hear your skipper's fixing to rerig" he said to John one night when John was to supper. "Why not bring it over? We'll make room for it."

"Want to sail before Christmas" John said lightly.

Hab frowned. He'd thought he was doing John a favor. The captain of the Northern Constellation had been eager enough to get some work done at the Watts yard last time he visited the Point.

"We'd get you out afore Christmas, long while afore. We could rip that tub apart and put it together again in that time."

John laughed.

"Something like what he's got in mind, from all I hear."

Hab raised eyebrows.

"Decks too?"

"Decks too."

"He ain't going to go to Willison with a job like *that?*"

"Oh no. Back to Newport, where he came from. Got some friend there."

"Oh." Hab was looking at him carefully, while John ate, his head averted, chuckling. "Just, uh, just now what is this job, John?"

"Don't rightly know. Heap of work though. You wouldn't want to have to handle it. You've got more'n you can do now."

"Sure. All the same, I'd give him an estimate."

"I'll ask him" said John. "But I reckon his mind's made up and we'll go to Newport."

They did. They sailed a week later, sailed quietly and without fanfare, in daytime, an empty schooner with a skeleton crew, just enough to take it around Judy. There were indeed as many officers as hands, and they didn't look too pleased, the officers, when Deliverance and Hab and the Widow Watts came aboard to go good-by to John. Sure, the vessel was only making for Newport, but it was not likely that they'd see John again before he went south or wherever.

Hab buttered the skipper, Northrup, by complimenting him upon the looks of his vessel, and then he commented on its rig, going aloft several times, testing sheets and falls, asking questions about speed. Captain Northrup, who was inordinately interested in speed—"Aiming to privateer, come a war" Hab reckoned—asked many questions in return. Hab made some suggestions, sound ones.

"Tell you what, bring it over to the yard and let me do that redecking job for you and I'll show you what I mean about sky canvas. Won't charge you anything extra either, mister."

Northrup seemed tempted, opening his mouth as though about to dicker. Then his eyes shifted. He surveyed the Point warily, as though fearful that it would creep up on him and pounce. He shook his head.

"Can't do it. Agreement. Well, we'll sail now, sir."

This bidding good-by to John Rellison was not like the previous time. This was a bleak day, without sun. There was no piping, no scampering of hands, no brave display of colors this time on the schooner, which indeed could have been sneaking out of the harbor as though in fear of a writ. John himself played a good part, laughing easily. He kissed Mrs Watts. He meant to kiss Deliverance on the mouth, but to Hab's delight she moved in such a way that his lips only grazed her forehead: he showed a whit astonished at this, but not resentful. He shook Hab's hand, grinning into Hab's face.

Rowing the women back to shore, Hab watched his friend, who stood at the weather rail waving. John's varnished hat was aglitter, for all the lack of sunlight; and the ribbons stood straight out in the breeze. His smile too, Hab knew, though it was visible no longer, would be broad and fine, a clean thing. Hab only wished that John Rellison would take those danged rings out of his ears and stay home.

It was some weeks after this, it was in December, the night of the first snow, a wet nasty inconsequential fall, that Deliverance came into Hab's room late and without a candle. This was long after they had all gone to bed, Hab having almost ceased to hope. It was not unusual for her to visit him for a little while, to kiss him good night; but other times, never as late as this, she had brought a candle. Now she was merely a wisp of whiteness, a body-smell. He heard her close the door. She stood stock-still, listening at the door for a while, and the wet slushy raindrops splap-splapped against Hab's window in soft futility, the wind moaning low. Then she came over to his bed, where he was now sitting up. She took his hands. Even before she said anything, and though he could scarcely see her face, he knew that she was looking hard at him. She had looked at him that way at supper and afterward at prayers: he would glance up from reading and see her looking at him that way, and he'd lose the place.

"Habakkuk."

"Yes?"

"We're practically the same as married, don't you reckon?"

He was scared.

"How do you mean?"

"They say marriages are made in Heaven, and if we both asked God if we can't be married that would be almost the same as *being* married, wouldn't it? I mean, to us? Especially since we really are going to get married as soon as we can. Don't you reckon, Hab?"

He trembled all over, but he drew her down to him.

"I—I hope you know what you're saying" he whispered.

"I reckon I do. I reckon we've waited long enough, Habakkuk."

She disengaged her hand, and he heard her wriggle out of her night-rail, and when she got into bed next to him he knew that they ought to have prayed first, they both ought to have prayed, but the touch of her skin drove him wild.

Afterward they lay lazy and talked of what they would do if there was going to be a baby. They decided that maybe the Widow Watts would be all right, in that event. She wouldn't like it; she'd rave; but if there was really going to be a baby she would probably settle down and prepare for it. Certainly in that case she'd consent to a marriage. She'd have to.

"I hope we have one, even though we're not married. People will count the months, but we don't care. They're sure saying that about us anyway."

She stretched, and Hab suspicioned that she was smiling there in the darkness by his side. He trailed fingers over her breasts, down her belly. But a thought came. He took his hand away.

"We should ought to have prayed first" he reminded her. "We want to be at least as married as we can, don't we?"

"That's right."

Filled with a sense of urgency, they hurried out of bed. Hab had some trouble finding his nightrail, which was under the covers, but the search gave him an excuse to turn his back to Deliverance, who then put on her nightrail. They couldn't have seen much of each other anyway.

Side by side they knelt, the raindrops splapping against the window behind them, their elbows and shoulders just touching, and they prayed separately and silently, asking God to esteem them married and to forgive them anything they did. Though it was very cold, they prayed for quite a while.

Afterward, feeling better, they got back into bed.

. 26 . . .

DAYS DANCED. A SULLEN WINTER TOOK HOLD OF STONING-
ton, stiffening all things, and the winds were harsh and cold; but
Habakkuk Jones was unaware of this, what with having spring already
in his heart. They didn't get much snow ordinarily in Stonington, not
the way it was further back from the coast, but they got plenty of wind,
a nasty wet penetrating wind; and this winter just arriving had all
signs of being the worst in memory. Folks looked mighty serious as
they went about tightening things, repacking things, blading in
weather stripping, putting up storm windows, and they'd stop now and
then and gaze at the sky, a dirty low gray cold sky, and shake their
heads. But Hab went around with a wide and no doubt foolish grin,
and he was likely to break into song at almost any time. He wasn't a
good singer.

> *A Yankee ship in the Rio River,*
> *Her masts they bend and her sails they shiver.*

At first he was afraid that he was too obvious, and that others, the
men he came in touch with, would guess what had happened. Then he
decided that they had guessed anyway, or their womenfolk had, as
Deliverance said, and that he didn't mind really—as long as she didn't,
and she didn't.

> *Her sails were old, her timbers rotten,*
> *Her charts the skipper had forgotten.*

Indeed he seemed to sense a new air of brotherliness among his
seniors, the married men, as though they half unconsciously had taken
him in. This might have been sheer imagination on his part; but it
made him happy. He certainly *felt* a man! When he was at the yard
he always took a tot when the grog ration was passed out at eleven and
at four. Sometimes too when in the town he would stop at one of the
public houses for a mug of flip. His opinion was asked, and listened to.
There were some as didn't take to him at first, for though good-
natured enough he wasn't as easygoing in business matters as the old
judge had been, and drove a hard bargain. But they got used to this.
After all, he wasn't doing it for himself. If he was over-conscientious
about money, well, that was a good fault. She was a proper young lady

too, that daughter of the judge. You never saw her but what she looked right.

When he squired the women to church each Sunday morning and afternoon Hab without ostentation would take the seat at the end of the pew, as Judge Watts always had done. They were side-looked at a lot in church, he and Deliverance, Hab reckoned, and thought about even more than they were looked at; but he didn't care. He used to have a hard time keeping quiet. He wished they'd sing hymns, or sing anything. He felt like singing.

> *She sailed away for London city;*
> *Never got there, what a pity!*

To try to keep from thinking of Deliverance, or from bursting into a chantey, he would stare hard at the preacher, without truly listening to him, and he'd wonder what that preacher would think and say—and do, for that matter—if he knew what Hab and Deliverance were up to. Maybe nothing. Maybe the preacher did know but preferred to forget. That wasn't likely. More likely anybody who knew—after all, they were only guessing—would not say anything about it to the preacher. Hab didn't believe that on the whole they disapproved. They were understanding folks, here on the Point. They had to look stern for fear that somebody from outside would take advantage of them; but when you got to know them, and they'd got to know you, they were very kind, deep down inside. Hab decided that he loved the people of Stonington. But then he loved just about everybody now anyway.

The men at the yard never minded taking orders from an eighteen-year-old. Many had made a sea voyage or two and been ruled by a youthful skipper or a mate in his teens. Hab was discreet, never pushy. He had for some time before his departure been thought of as the shipyard's heir anyway, as the owner's representative, so that the transference to him of full real power was a natural one. Old Karl, from New York, who must have been three times Hab's age, habitually and playfully called him Boss, which he said was Dutch, as he'd learned it, for uncle. When Hab protested, Old Karl added that it really meant more than uncle, it meant master, giver of commands. "So that's what you are, the Boss." The others picked it up, a convenient word—Boss Jones, or sometimes just Boss.

There would come to him suddenly, from time to time, the realization of how happy he was and how very lucky, and then he'd stop short, even stagger a bit, like a man who's been pushed; and he would blink, as though faced by a blinding light. Now and then, alone, especially in bed after Deliverance had gone back to her own room, he would weep a little—just a little, just a few contented tears, grinning through them all the while in the darkness there.

Only once did he break down. It was at dinner. The yard was always quiet at noon, for an hour or more, when the workers went home to dinner. They all lived nearby, and Hab, like the judge before him, was liberal about the dinner hour, liking a good full meal in the middle of the day himself and maybe a brief lie-down as well. This was not a notably big spread, this time he broke down; that wasn't the reason. There was no more than black bean soup, chicken oyster shortcake, some leftover broiled duck, a beefsteak and kidney pie with great gobs of gravy for the boiled potatoes, three or four green vegetables, a halibut soufflé, gingercake with stewed apples, and of course bread and butter and jam, and frycakes and cheese, and fruit and pie and some puddings, and milk and cider and tea and wine. Nothing special. Nor had there been anything in the conversation to cause him to weep. Deliverance, who seldom said anything at meals anyway—though she could be chatty enough in bed, a different girl!—ate in silence, her gaze on her plate. Mrs Watts was less chill than usual, was almost chirk, her watery blue eyes wandering, her loose lips slapping as she talked. She was asking Hab, as she so often did, about his experiences at sea and in the sugar islands. She could never get enough of this, though as Hab told it it was a dull story, for he left out the violent parts and of course made no mention of Suzanne, any more than he did of Si Wainwright's bottling. What remained he had gone over many times, but Mrs Watts was insatiable. Hab, then, was telling her about life aboard a British frigate.

It was no image raised in his mind, no nugget of memory unearthed. It was nothing—and yet everything. Like a flash of light it came to him, the misery he'd endured in those days, the beastliness and brutality, the stink, the dirt, the shame of it, and now, here in contrast, this immaculate table, this food, this good home, and the lovely girl he bedded with. It was like a revelation, a dazzling vision such as felled Saul on the road to Damascus. It caught at his throat, fisted his windpipe, and stung his eyes with a rush of sudden hot biting blinding tears. He dropped his head onto his arms. His sobs shook the kitchen.

The Widow Watts awkwardly tried to console him. Then she examined the wine bottle, but it was full. At last, tut-tutting, she fussed around the kitchen until she had concocted a horrid hot sassafras mixture, which all but choked him. It was good for his stomach, she said. She believed that all ailments started and often remained in the stomach.

Deliverance her daughter was wiser. She just reached a hand to squeeze Hab's forearm lightly and reassuringly, and when he looked up, blubbering apologies, she gave him a large long warm smile.

He drank deep at the pump out back, to get shut of that sassafras taste. He washed his face. The water was bitter cold, and it felt good. Twenty minutes later he was down to the yard again, on the deck of the newest job they were readying for a launch, weaving his way among the rope coils and tool chests and rail caps and thimbles and dead-eyes and heart-eyes and such, singing loudly and far off key:

> Pull, m'hearties, pull that hawse!
> Yo, ho, yo-ho!
> Captain's wife got dirty drawers,
> Yo-YO-ho!

There were men who shook their heads over this new vessel, a topsail schooner; but Hab Jones was accustomed to that. There were men who said that narrow as it was, with the greatest beam just abaft the main, and with its knifelike bows, so different from the usual puffed-cheek bows, and with all the live oak it contained, launched prow-on, as Hab proposed to launch it, the danged vessel would go straight into the water and never come up again! They said that even if it was launched stern-on, like any sensible builder would do, it would sink in the first heavy weather it met. It would simply go under. Bows like that were never intended to support the weight of a ship and cargo. To all this Hab Jones paid no attention.

It's true that live oak was mighty heavy, but it would float all the same; and though it was expensive and hard to work with, it was stronger by far than the hackmatack and larch and fir and local red cedar most of the Connecticut builders were using. White oak from backstate for the spars and yards and masts, when you couldn't get live oak, yes; but today you *could* get live oak again, though you had to pay through the nose for it. He used locust for the treenails, but for most of the timber he sent away. He got good light pitch pine from Georgia, and light red cedar from the Chesapeake country, which helped to offset the weight of the live oak.

Vessels from the Watts yard were not only fast, they were also strong. They were not big vessels: the channel was only twelve feet deep at low tide. Not often did one of them have occasion to cross an ocean. However, this was the more reason, in Hab's eyes, for building them firm. A ship far out to sea could run with buffetings a ship close-in might have to meet. True, your coaster could sometimes scurry for cover, but there wasn't always cover within reach, and the scurrying process itself could be dangerous. You can drown in ten feet of water just as easily as in two miles of it, and with two miles under your keel you don't have to worry about getting your bottom chewed off. There was an old woman over to Water Street who declared repeatedly that she had never been out of sight of land and didn't ever intend to be, for she considered it tempting God's mercy. She was a mite teched, of course, and folks used to egg her on, snickering. " 'Tain't *safe,* I tell you!" Hab grinned when he remembered her. He didn't know about the birds, but he rather reckoned that the higher they went the safer they were. It was certainly that way with sailing men. When they saw the last of Lantern Hill, the last of the Montauk and Block Island cliffs, then they stopped worrying for a while. They didn't feel truly safe until they *were* out of sight of land.

So the Watts vessels, while they might have been somewhat short of cargo space, could step with the fleetest, could sail close into the wind, could claw along a lee shore, skirt a cape with inches to spare, and stand out again unscraped. The Watts vessels were easy to handle but hard to catch. They were lightly manned, too. The forecastles were none too comfortable, what with those sharply steeved bows, and like all fast vessels the ones from the Watts yard tended to get and to remain wet forward in any kind of blow: they didn't dip themselves under the surface for good, as gloomily predicted, but they did seem to try to. What did this matter to sailing men, used to any sort of quarters? Matter of fact, though space was skimpy up forward, there were fewer to share it. This was important. The men who worked the ships these days, now that the removal of the Embargo had set them free, and now that the British Navy was winnowing them out to its heart's content, were demanding and getting unprecedented wages—sixteen dollars, seventeen dollars, eighteen dollars a month for American able-bodieds, and even the boys got eight-nine! The Watts yard turned out no ships, only fore-and-afters, sloops and schooners mostly, requiring very few men to handle. Partly this was because of the shallow channel, partly it was because the ways were too small; but the chief reason was this high cost of labor.

So Hab built coasters, as the judge had done before him, though more daringly. The growing fashion for speed didn't catch him off-guard. He had been studying speed and sailing qualities long before he aspired to be more than a master builder, much less the supreme ruler of the shipyard. He was all the time asking questions about fast boats and ships, and their rig, and how they handled. He pondered lines of vessels building. More than once he had rerigged Deliverance I—his own boat now: he'd bought John's share—in an attempt to get a whit more of speed out of it. Sailing Deliverance I, sailing it back with John after having piloted some ship out to the open sea, Hab, at the tiller while John slept, sometimes had dreamed of making a boat entirely for speed and nothing else—Deliverance I, after all, with its high pinked stern, had been designed for fishing—and sailing it for no other purpose than to see how fast it would go. He reckoned that this was improper, to dream of putting to a frivolous use that which God had given us to work with; but all the same, when he was tired, and his defenses were down, he sometimes used to fondle the idea. He was, then, prepared for the rush. Nor had he any illusions as to the use these vessels might be put to. They were to be fast not merely in order to deliver the goods ahead of rival vessels—though the coasting competition, it's true, was increasing, and speed did count in getting carrying contracts—but also and chiefly in order to run away from revenue cutters or to overtake unarmed foreign merchantmen.

Everybody was talking about the war-to-be as if there wasn't any doubt that it would come tomorrow or the day after. Well, Hab reckoned, it probably *would* come, since they were so bound and determined to have it. Everybody said that he didn't want war but went right ahead getting ready for it. The idea was that as long as the hotheads of the West and South were clamoring so loudly for it, it would be sure to come, and there was no reason why in that case it shouldn't be turned to good account. Privateering might prove to be very profitable. Hab Jones knew that, and didn't care. It was none of his concern what they did with the vessels he built. He thought all the war talk downright silly, when it wasn't vicious, and especially the talk of going to war with England in the hope of grabbing Canada, rather than with France, a more natural enemy with Boney in command; but he didn't see what he could do about it—except to work hard and make all the money possible for Deliverance.

He was never tempted to build bigger vessels. He didn't want a big shipyard, though he did want a good one. This way, he could be working on three-four vessels at once, and the money came in small spurts. With a full ship on the ways, even supposing that the channel were deepened (there was talk of this) to accommodate it, he wouldn't have the time or room to take care of anything else. He couldn't afford to experiment then. The greatest part of the money would come in one unwieldy lump at the end, when the job was finished. And if the ship itself was not an immediate success, his own prestige would suffer. No matter who designed a given ship, the owners were sure to blame the builder for any shortcomings.

Once a master builder from New York had come in his own sloop, knocking along the Connecticut shore to examine yards; he was a tall man who chewed tobacco, though he never seemed to spit it, and he talked through his nose; he had liked Hab, and had been interested in Hab's ideas about deadrise and the best rake for your stem. "See here, whyn't you come back with me? Or later—look me up in South Street. I think we could do business. Big business, son, not this penny razzle. Don't you know ships are getting larger all the time? You'll be left behind, here. New York's the real market."

Hab had shaken his head. He didn't even trouble to tell Deliverance about it that night when she came to him. He reckoned he knew where he belonged.

"When the war's come and gone," the New Yorker had warned, "you'll be sorry."

Hab shrugged. He was sick of war talk. He couldn't believe that the

Virginians would be that loony, but even if they did try to push the country into war Connecticut folks wouldn't have anything to do with it.

What was of much more immediate concern to him was the welter of work in which he found himself. Now Hab Jones had been used to work all his life, good hard work too, some of which he'd liked, most of which he hadn't, but all of which he took for granted, deeming it an ordinary bodily function like eating, breathing, moving the bowels. Work these days was different. It was hard enough, in all conscience! but it was intermittent, broken up. He would just settle down to one thing when two or three other things would come along to demand his attention. They were pinpricking him into a bad state of nerves.

His own affairs and John Rellison's he had taken care of since the death of the judge, or very soon thereafter, when John turned over all his affairs to Hab. As far as the shipyard was concerned, he had taken over a great mass of Deliverance's affairs, and was getting more all the time; he also had to see to it that the land back of the village was tended and the taxes paid. Gradually too, as old Judge Palmer, glad to be quit of them, handed them over, Hab took care of the Widow Watts's affairs as well, with no objection from her: evidently her suspicions of Hab at least were not financial.

These matters were unbelievably complicated. As the judge had purchased over a scattered area, so did he invest. A few dollars here, a few there. It seemed for a little while, to Hab, that in his capacity of agent or representative he was owed money by almost everybody on the Point and in the country immediately back of it. One man might owe four or five sums, each odd, each covered by a note with a different date. These items were usually small, but in the aggregate they must have been large. The judge too had held a part in many businesses. You would not have supposed, indeed, looking at the Point, that there would *be* so many businesses there. It was no more, at a glance, than four north-and-south streets crossed by nine smaller ones, a couple of stores, a tannery, four grain mills, the shipyard, a rigging dock, the meetinghouse. In truth there were many more mercantile establishments than these; but they weren't visible. Scarcely a one of those neat square white houses but harbored at least two or three minor, half-hidden businesses, most or all of which probably had been in part financed by Judge Watts. There were two rope walks, three sail lofts, but from the outside these were conventional houses surrounded by conventional gardens. There were two ships' chandlers, who were so well known that they didn't either of them reckon they needed signs: these had no painted windows, no counters or tills, but displayed their goods on demand in their own kitchens and backyards. The fishermen were seldom that exclusively. Most were amphibious, operating farms as well as fishing boats, or helping on both in different seasons. The judge had shares of or notes against any number of small boats and nets and traps, not to mention plows, harrows, and suchlike apparatus. He had been part-owner, as the Widow Watts and Deliverance were part-owners now, of the Point's principal salting business, all privately carried on, and he had owned a quarter of the backyard coopery Ab Orphington ran. He had been, and Hab was now, the "husband" or agent for seven or eight coasting vessels which put into Stonington at irregular intervals. He had probably been cheated many times—some of the notes were signed by men now dead; on others no interest had ever been paid, though Hab happened to know that the debtors could afford it—but there remained a pile of papers which Hab Jones was making it his aim to reduce to good sound metal money, preferably gold. It was not a task calculated to endear him to his fellow townsmen, among whom he had once been popular; but he didn't stew about this; and indeed his principal interest, his chief commercial love, was the shipyard itself, Deliverance's shipyard, which he estimated to be worth more than all the rest of the assets put together—and which had greater possibilities.

He watched the men there, and worked with them, and fussed about them: he paid them high wages and expected good labor. When John Rellison's brother Abner, Abner Rellison, Jr., appeared unexpectedly at the office one morning, having walked from the farm, and asked for a job on some ship, Hab was reluctant to talk him out of this and into taking work at the yard. The massive silent stocky man, the lumpish man, would be of no help unless there were rocks to be moved. Stubbornly he wanted to go to sea; but Hab, thinking of John, and for John's sake—they'd had no word of him since he sailed in November, though they'd heard indirectly that the Northern Constellation had long since left Newport—tried to keep him at the yard. He placed Abner Junior in a sawyer's gang, as a helper, but Abner was no good at this job, which required an ability to learn. Expressionless, he only nodded when Hab assigned him to the timber pile, where his duties were in effect those of an ox. But you don't have to pay oxen, and the wages came from Deliverance's money, and Hab took his responsibilities very seriously. He would watch the plodding Abner, whose over-sinewy assistance in fact did very little to assist, who was so like John in appearance, though thicker, so unlike him in everything else; and Hab would shake his head. Abner drank, as all the Rellisons did; but he'd go about his work stolidly and without pause, if without any enthusiasm either, every day, no matter how he felt—if he did feel. He was a loss, and Hab worried about him, wondering whether he ought to discharge him, wondering whether he ought to take up the matter with Deliverance—she'd leave it up to him anyway—and what he would say to John if he discharged John's brother while John was away. Abner Junior, one night in January, when he was drunk, ended this worry by signing on—making his mark, really—aboard an islands-bound brig. Hab didn't even hear about it until the brig was gone. Well, he thought, I did my best to keep him from being a sailor, but I reckon that's all he was ever good for anyway. At least, by gum, he thought, it wasn't a whaler!

They kept on not having a baby. Each month they hoped, each month they were disappointed. The Widow Watts was less vinegarish these days, less ridiculously suspicious of Hab, but she still was bad enough to worry them. She would talk queer sometimes. She would go off into muttering, a glazed yet rapt look in her eyes, as though she were listening to her own voice. They kept hoping that she would get calmer and more rational, just as they kept hoping that her daughter would get with child, but neither of these things happened; and when unexpectedly they did get a chance to be married, they knew they'd have to keep it from her, which of course meant keeping it a secret from everybody else.

There was a passing-through preacher, a Mr Lubbock, and his stubby tubby wife, who had not intended to put in at Stonington at all. Heading from Providence toward Mystic, their sloop had been badly banged off Judy, and that was the reason for the visit. Emergency repairs were being done at Willison's, the Watts yard being too busy, and the voyage would be resumed tomorrow. Meanwhile the Reverend Mr Lubbock might have slept aboard, though there were no accommodations for sleeping, but it hardly was seemly that his wife should be expected to do so. There were always folks on the Point, as elsewhere, ready to put up a preacher and his wife for the night, and Judge and Mrs Watts had been well known for this type of hospitality, their house moreover being famous among traveling preachers for its fare. Mr Lubbock at least had heard of it. He asked promptly if the Watts house would be convenient. And here they were.

It was a scanty meal, there having been so little time in which to prepare—only supper, not dinner—a chowder, baked eggs in sour cream, clam fritters, some stewed rabbit with rice, and of course pie and some puddings and things like that—but they did open a bottle of madeira in honor of the visit, in addition to the cider and the usual wine; and Mr Lubbock found the madeira good. This is not to say he got drunk! He was a small round man, given to beaming most of the time except when actually in the pulpit. He kept his dignity; but he did enjoy the madeira. It was the first madeira he'd had in almost a year, he told them. He sat back, looking as though he were about to start to purr. His wife watched him anxiously. She didn't drink.

The room they were to occupy, the guest room, had once been Aaron Watts's bedroom. Mrs Watts had cleaned it for the occasion, in a considerable flutter. Ordinarily Deliverance would have done this work, in order to spare her mother the pain, but Deliverance, as it happened, had been calling on a sick neighbor at the time the news arrived that the Lubbocks had invited themselves. This was perhaps the reason, at any rate the principal reason, why the Widow Watts showed so dauncy and acted so strangely during the supper. The Reverend Mr Lubbock, eyeing the wine bottle, and Mrs Lubbock, eyeing him, noticed nothing unusual: they had been warned anyway that the widow was teched and it may be that they purposely avoided her gaze. Nor was she in any way curious of behavior in the ordinary eye. If anything, she was more quiet than usual: she seemed to be holding herself in. Hab and Deliverance, however, knew that there was something wrong; and when, right after dessert, and before anybody had even mentioned the dishes, the Widow Watts complained of a sick headache, Deliverance was up and at her side instantly. The Lubbocks cried out that they wished to help, but she shushed them gently and led her apologizing mother upstairs. She'd be all right, Deliverance called, when she got her sleeping potion.

It was too good an opportunity to miss, yet Hab waited until Deliverance had returned. Then, having got permission from her eyes, he told the Lubbocks that they wanted to get married—and told them why they hadn't. Stammering a little, looking down, hot in the face, he gave them the whole story. At the end he asked Mr Lubbock bluntly whether he'd hitch them.

Mr Lubbock, leaning back, considered. He took his hand away from the wineglass, and probably took his mind away from the bottle. For all his rolypoly appledumpling look, he had dignity now as he pondered a question of professional decorum. He tilted his head a little. He m-m-m-m-ed.

Mrs Lubbock, Deliverance and Hab suspicioned, would have made objections—but she knew her husband. She looked at him. The only thing she said, however, and it was hesitatingly said, was to remind him that this was the Lord's Day. He shook his head impatiently, not even glancing at her.

"It's after sundown."

She subsided then, knowing as well as anybody else that the Lord's Day starts at sundown Saturday and ends at sundown Sunday.

After a while Mr Lubbock thoughtfully rolled his eyes toward the ceiling.

"She would not like it?" he asked softly.

They admitted that she wouldn't.

"Why?"

They didn't know.

He looked first at Hab, then at Deliverance, and very seriously asked each if there was any reason in the eyes of God why they should not be married. It was almost like the ceremony itself, then and there, and they trembled, and stumbled over their words; but each answered that he knew of no such reason.

The Reverend Mr Lubbock nodded. Again he rolled his eyes toward the ceiling.

"This is her house, this house?"

They said it was.

"I think that I might consent to bring you two young folks together into the bonds of lawful matrimony," said Mr Lubbock, drumming the table with soft pudgy fingers, while Deliverance began to weep, "*only* I do not think it would be Christianlike, in view of Mrs Watts's attitude in the matter—howsoever illogical that attitude might be—to do this here on her own property. Is there another place?"

Deliverance looked up, her eyes running with tears. She and Hab knew that there was no neighbor they could trust to keep such a secret, there was no friend, nobody at all here on the Point. The drumming of Mr Lubbock's fingers continued. Hab turned to him and said:

"Would *Miss* Watts's property—would that be all right?"

"It's near here?"

"Just down the hill!"

It had been sleeting but it was clear now, clear and very cold. It was slippery underfoot. The moon rose, big and bland and tired, and Habakkuk found that in his excitement he'd forgotten the key of the yard gate, so he was obliged to shinny over the fence as he'd done so many times with John Rellison and unlatch the gate from the inside.

Deliverance took off her tyer and patted back her hair, looking, as she always did, perfect. Mrs Lubbock thrummed pleasantly around her. Mrs Lubbock was a pale woman who'd had a hard life, and no doubt she disapproved of a secret wedding; but she was a woman, and it was a wedding.

Hab straightened his stock. He ran his hands through his hair, but it remained as bad as ever and maybe a little worse. He had found but two candles, and they were of unequal length, but this latter fact he thought fortunate: candles of equal length would have looked somewhat Romish. One of the candles spluttered fretfully.

So there they were married, there in the office of the Watts shipyard, surrounded by molds and forms and prints and charts, by compasses and calipers, by coils of tarred rope, suspended blocks and hooks, and the stacks of business papers on Hab's untidy shoved-aside desk. The office was very cold, so that they could see the steam of their breath. The wind gusted, tearing a row of rotten icicles off the eaves, and these tinkled as they fell. The ceiling was low, the light dim and flickering.

". . . pronounce you man and wife."

Hab gave him two shillings as a fee, and found a pail of rum, the same that was rationed out to the workers, and a mug, and they each swallowed a drink to the bride, even Mrs Lubbock swallowing one, though a short one. Then they all went up to the house and did the dishes and went to bed.

250

Deliverance had to look in on her mother, who was peevish though half-asleep, and it was late when she got to Hab's room. She stayed a long while, it was almost dawn when she went. She had been very gay. He kissed her.

"Like it any better, now that it's legal?" he asked.

She giggled, snuggling close to him for a final squeeze, running her hands over him. Then she slid on top of him, pressing her body against his, and so out of bed, where, silhouetted against the window and all unashamed, she pulled her nightrail on. She leaned low and kissed him again.

"I couldn't like it any *better,* darling. I couldn't nohow. Good night."

That was in March; and in May, when the front yard was dazzling white with magnolia blossoms, they had a caller at the Watts house who threw all their plans out of kilter. Until then Deliverance and Hab had been hoping more than they had ever previously permitted themselves to hope that the Widow Watts would recover her sanity—or at least that she might become reconciled to the presence of Hab and that they might soon perhaps tell her about the wedding. True, she didn't fawn on Hab; but she scowled less often at him, and surely several times she had noticed tender glances or even touches of the hand between these two lovers, and given only a disgusted sniff. She didn't mutter to herself so much these days, and seldom looked up swiftly to glance around the kitchen as though in search of a thief.

Then came the caller, and spoiled everything.

It was a dewy clear morning with a touch of frolic in the air, and Hab had lingered inconscionably over breakfast, so that it was full light, indeed almost half-past five, when he rose to go. The women, busy with dishes, paid him little attention. As he passed behind Deliverance on the way to the kitchen door he brushed his fingers lightly across Deliverance's buttocks, which she twitched in acknowledgment, though she made no other movement unless she threw a glance at her mother beside her in order to be sure that the caress hadn't been seen. These were demure and properly ladylike women, these two. They addressed themselves severally to the task at hand.

Hab had reached the back door when there was a knocking at the front. This brought them all up, the women stiffening, lifting their heads like startled sheep. Who in the world could be knocking at the *front* door?

Amazed, Hab faced the front of the house, as though expecting the door itself through its own thickness to shout him the answer.

This was opened only on the occasion of important visits, somebody who served in the Legislature or the captain or owner of a really large vessel; and for these, arrangements would be made well in advance, so that the whamming of the knocker, a heavy brass one, came as no shock. Such visits had ceased now, for Hab conducted all his business at the office. The last time the front door had been opened was the day Judge Watts was buried. The body had been carried out that way.

To be sure, Hab, as the judge had done before him, solemnly threw back the heavy latch each morning before breakfast, and drew it shut again last thing at night after prayers; but this was no more than a sort of unaccountable household tradition, and it didn't mean that anybody who felt like it could lift that knocker.

The knocker sounded again, firm and loud, passing through the house until the echoes were no more than a pattering of small soft padded leathery sounds, which presently died.

Like a somnambulist Hab walked to the front door. He opened it.

The man who stood there was a sailor, with a sailor's roundabout jacket, a sailor's bright kerchief, his hair in a queue, earrings. He was about Hab's height, though because he was standing on the step he was obliged to look up at Hab, who stood in the threshold. He was maybe thirty, a good-looking man with dark brown hair, dark brown eyes, a full and brightly red mouth. He was strong and clean, and had strong white teeth. There was a sea chest at his feet.

"Hello" he said pleasantly. "Who are you?"

Hab said nothing, but he felt his heart contract.

The man laughed.

"Better if I told you who I was first, eh? You must be one of the bound-boys they told me about. They told me, too," and he sobered, "that my father was dead. But Mother's all right, I hope?"

He moved as though to enter the house, but Hab just stood there.

"Oh, I'm sorry" said the man. "You see, I'm Aaron Watts." He wiped a corner of one eye, and then studied the fingertip with which he'd wiped it. "You see," he said softly, "I've been away for a long time. I've been in China."

. 27 . . .

AN ISLANDER WHO SPIES A STRANGER LOOKS THEN TO THE bay, the roads, or anchorage. Sure, a stranger in Stonington could have come by land; but few did. Hab's glance, over the head of the new-comer, was instinctive and swift, and it showed him that truly a new vessel was in harbor, a schooner with worn and dirty canvas which even then was being sheeted home, but otherwise wondrously ship-shape, shiny, bright, having, he reckoned, completed a long voyage. How slovenly they were when they sailed, he reflected sometimes, with the men drunk, the captain in a rage, the mates overworked, nothing clean, nothing in its right place, the cargo not yet properly stowed, hatches still open; but how neat when they returned! This schooner had come up from the islands or anyway had recently been in the tropics: he could tell as much from the condition of her paint, even at this distance.

"Came ashore quick" said Hab.

The man ascended the steps, and Hab stood aside to let him pass.

"Bring up my chest" the man said, and went into the hall. Hab stood watching him from the doorway. He first went right, then turned at the sound of a gasp from the kitchen and headed in that direction. The door was open. The man held wide his arms to Mrs Watts.

"*Mother!* It took a long time, but I finally got back! Aren't you glad to see me?"

She didn't move. Deliverance too was still, staring.

"Don't you know me, Mother? It's Aaron! Don't you remember your little Ronny-Boy, you used to call me?"

She started to weep, in short jerky small sobs deep in her chest, though there were no tears in her eyes, and he went to her and flung his arms around her and patted her back. He talked softly to her, all but cooed, reminding her of old times when he'd played about this house, men-tioning little loving intimate events. He had a clear fine soothing voice, and his hands were gentle on her back, so that after a bit she loosened, though still sobbing, and sat down. The man turned to Mrs Jones, and his smile was a grand toothy show, as Hab watched from the doorway.

"And you're Deliverance! Say, nobody told me you'd turned out such a beauty! Why, you're worth coming back from halfway around the world for just to see, just you alone!" He went to her, his arms out, and she stood staring, staring. "Why, I used to remember you, out there in

China—and I thought of you a lot, I can tell you!—why, then you were always the way I'd seen you just before I went, just a slip of a girl with dresses to her knees and her hair down her back. And now look at you! *My!*"

He put his arms around her easily, and kissed her. He would have kissed her mouth, but at the last instant, as though panicky, she ducked her face and he kissed her forehead instead; but he gave the forehead a good loud buss.

Hab, in the doorway, pushed his toes down hard and set his teeth, and though it was a coolish morning he felt rivulets of sweat on his shoulder-blades. He looked sideways at the sea chest, there on the bright wet grass. After a minute he went down to it. He paid no mind now to the glib cool contained musical voice of the newcomer as it recited old-time intimacies. He opened the chest, rummaged it. It contained about the usual. There were some shirts, well worn but good, one of them real cambric, and some extra stockings, two or three cotton kerchiefs, a stub of candle, flint-and-steel. There were several pieces of scrimshaw, yellowish-white, though whether they were whalebone or ivory he didn't trouble to learn. There were three lengths of fine rich brocaded silk with a dragon design.

He closed the chest, hoisted it to his shoulder, and marched back into the house and into the kitchen. The man smiled affably. Hab put the chest down.

"I'll be going to work" he announced.

"Oh yes. You'll be going to the shipyard, eh?"

"Aye."

He did go to the yard, for there was work which had to be done, there was always work, but he didn't stay there long. He went into the village and talked with several men. When he returned to the house it was still much before dinnertime, and indeed the newcomer had only a little earlier finished breakfast. He was talking, while Deliverance worked at the basin. His voice went on, clear and easy, friendly. Hab heard it even before he opened the door. The three pieces of brocade were on the table. They were beautiful things, though heathenish.

"Hello, Hab."

"You knew my name pretty early."

"Oh, I'd heard of you. You and John Rellison. *He* went away to sea, the way I did years ago. No more! I'm home to stay now."

"Oh" said Hab.

"I'd catch a gam now and again. Stonington men go to all sorts of places, you know. Met four at the Whampoa Anchorage, at different times. Met one in the Societies. And another just a few months ago, on the way up from Stiff. On a sealer we spoke, off the Brazil coast.'"

He saw that Hab was looking at the brocades. Deliverance was looking at Hab.

"I was a fool," candidly. "I did write two or three times, but I guess none of the letters got here, from what Dill tells me. I used to call her Dill, you know. Well, I came back with nothing, the way I guess most sailors come back. But I'm shut of the sea now. I'm home to stay." He smiled. "I see you're looking at those brocades, Hab? Pretty, ain't they? I put all the little I had left over into them. You see," and he swallowed, "I planned to give one each to Father and Mother and Dill. That was before I'd learned about Father." There were true tears in his eyes, but he stood up, trying to smile them dry. With an impulsive gesture he picked up one of the brocades and handed it to Hab. "Won't you take it instead, Hab? I mean, as a gift on account of how kind you've been to my mother and sister?"

It was giddy iridescent stuff, which rose and fell under his moving fingers, and glittered in the morning light. The dragons, then, heaved and lapsed in a shower of colors. Around the edges was a formal bat design in gilt.

Hab looked at his wife. She had been watching him all this while. His look was a question, which she answered aloud.

"Went upstairs. She—she's upset."

"Readily understood" said the newcomer, and his voice held sympathy that hummed. "It isn't every day, after all, that a son comes home who's been away eleven years, two months, and four days."

"That's right" said Hab.

To Deliverance he said "Shouldn't wonder but what you better go up to her."

She put down the dish she'd been wiping and took off her tyer. She passed very close to her husband as she went to the stairs.

"You be careful" she whispered. "He looks strong."

Hab didn't answer. Neither did he touch the brocade held out for him. Instead, but not until he had heard Deliverance go into her mother's room upstairs and shut the door behind her, he walked to a window. He couldn't see the harbor from there, but he could see most of the village.

"Yes, it looks expensive" he said. "It'd ought to pay your passage somewhere."

"O-ho *no,* Hab! I'm shut of the sea, like I told you."

"Not quite yet you ain't. The schooner you came on hauls out in a few hours, and you'll be there. But that ain't what I'm getting at. What I'm getting at is this: *who put you up to it?*"

There was some silence, Hab not budging, and after a while the man said in a wondering voice: "I—I don't understand you."

Two men were coming up from the yard, Nathaniel Tooker the master builder himself, and a sawyer's helper, probably to get Hab to straighten out some dispute: they looked angry, and weren't talking. Zaccheus Wheeler the cooper was coming along the road, would be passing the gate in another few minutes. They all seemed to be moving slowly, maybe because it was such a lovely morning.

"Heap of coaching, but it could have been better" Hab said. "Didn't stop to look, came right here, knocked on the *front door*. Couldn't remember my name at first, but you remembered all that Ronny-Boy and Dill talk. Said you'd been *in* China, *shut* of the sea. Man from Connecticut would say *to* China and *shet* of the sea. Told me to tote your chest, which no son of Jonathan Watts would do. Shirts got initials 'A.W.' sewed in 'em only a little while ago. Afore that what looks pricked out looks like 'T.L.,' which I take it stands for your real name. Started for the parlor, of all places——"

"See here, I don't know what the devil you're talking about!"

"Would have worked sure enough if you'd had time to palaver the widow" Hab admitted, still looking at the men climbing the hill. "Stay close to the house a few days, and you could've talked her into believing anything, shape she's in. *Then* nothing anybody said would have mattered."

"Are you trying to imply——"

"I could fetch a dozen knew Aaron Watts." Hab waved at the window. "More'n that. But that ain't what I want."

He turned. He'd had several hours of it, and he was good and sore, his heart beating fast, his fists sweaty and tight. He must have looked awful. Anyway, the stranger took a backward step.

"What I want" said Hab "is to know *who put you up to it?*"

He started toward the man.

"Now tell me!"

The man began to say something, but it wouldn't have been what Hab wanted to hear, so Hab punched him in the mouth.

"Tell me!"

The man's teeth showed red, like the rest of his mouth, and his eyes went loud with rage, and he started to punch, and Hab saw right off that this was going to be a real fight, and he started to punch too. Hab didn't rightly remember any of the details afterward, he was too sore— and also he got hit too hard. He found himself on his hands and knees without knowing how he'd got there, and he shook his head, bewildered, and then he realized that the man was kicking him, trying to kick his averted face, and he grabbed one of the feet and yanked, and the man went down with a crash that sent two dishes off the table—though only one broke, they found out later—and upstairs the Widow Watts began to scream.

Hab crawled up the man's body, keeping close, keeping his head in, for he was still dizzy. The fists clacked against the top of his head and his ears, but they didn't hurt much. Hab got one arm, and then he got the other.

Oh, the man was strong, but Hab was strong too, and sore, and this

256

was just the kind of fighting he was best at. They rocked back and forth a moment. Hab got his knees planted, then his feet. He heaved up, so mad that he pulled the man up along with him.

The kitchen door was open, as he'd left it. He pushed toward it, walking with his feet wide apart as though wading through hip-deep water. He spun completely around, and shoved the man off, and the man went backward through the doorway, tripping his heels on the threshold, down the three steps without touching them, to fall hard. It was just dirt there, no rocks. Nevertheless the man lay still.

Hab seized the brocades. He couldn't see well, and maybe he couldn't think at all. He never remembered much about it afterward.

He threw the brocades out of the door, and they rested gaudy and fantastically foreign, giving out little glitters.

"I'll get your chest for you!"

Mrs Watts had stopped screaming, but when he went upstairs Hab saw Deliverance standing before the door of her mother's room, looking deadly pale. He did not see her clearly, but he could hear her as he made for the guest room.

"Hab, is it——"

"It's all right. He's leaving."

This skunk had made himself very much to home in such a short time. Well, half a shipyard would be worth some haste. His chest was already partly unpacked, the shirts and things laid out on the bed. Hab swept them back, slammed the lid, lifted the thing. He did not see Deliverance on his way back across the upstairs hall. Mrs Watts was screaming again.

When he rounded the foot of the stairs he saw the man coming toward him from the kitchen door, walking unsteadily but with his chin forward and his arms out. This wasn't any coward! Hab dropped the chest.

"Good" he said. "I reckon I'd admire to have a little more of it, at that."

Nathaniel Tooker and the sawyer's helper, young Witten, and also Zaccheus Wheeler the cooper, who were the first to get there, gave the Point the juiciest part of the story the Point talked about for so long afterward. *They* couldn't hold Hab, though they tried. They tried clear out of the house and for a start down the hill toward the harbor, but it wasn't until some distance below the gate that the stranger managed to break loose and run for it. By that time a few others, neighbors, had come. By that time too Hab had been kicked with a knee in a mighty painful place, so that he couldn't chase the stranger very fast, though he kept trying. He'd fall down, and get up, run a little, twisting them off, and fall again, sobbing. They said afterward that his face was practically green, where it wasn't bloody, and especially under the eyes; but he kept trying to chase the man. Well, they carried him back to the house. There were seven or eight of them by that time.

"I want to ask him a question" Hab would rave. "Let me go! I want to ask him something!"

"I don't reckon" Nathaniel Tooker puffed "that he's just in the right mood to answer."

Nathaniel Tooker made it clear later that it was a violation of his principles to interfere in a fight, but that murder, after all, was against the law.

Deliverance met them, pale but perfectly quiet, with water and swabs. She worked on Hab's face as they half-led, half-carried him upstairs. When they passed the parlor door Hab glimpsed the best fireplace, so cool and clean and dim in there, and at the sight of the musket and horn hung above it, the musket with which the judge had hunted as a boy, the one of his eyes which was still open opened wider in dismay.

"I ought to've thought of that" he muttered.

He wasn't normal, and they weren't paying much mind to his words, but Nathaniel Tooker did make a comment here.

"You thought of enough."

Hab was always to regret this explosion, which amazed him, when it was over, as much as it amazed everybody else. He'd ought to have held himself in, pretending gullibility until he gathered witnesses. It might have been done all in that one day, if only he'd stayed calm. Hab was always a little scared when he remembered how he had acted that morning, how he'd felt. He knew that the Pointers were scared of him too, though not perhaps as much as he was of himself; for until then he'd had the reputation of a quiet speaker, a firm and stubborn but by no means argumentative man, who smiled easily and meant it, and who never raised his voice. But when once a thing like that had happened it couldn't be taken back. You couldn't just say: forget it. Why, he couldn't forget it himself! He saw that the rest of them eyed him a mite frightenedly, being a shade too respectful when they addressed him; and this didn't pride him, only made him feel ashamed, for he knew he had done wrong.

The stranger was never seen again at the Point, never identified, and seldom mentioned, certainly not in front of Hab.

Hab was in bed three days. He looked like hell for near a month, though Deliverance loyally said that she didn't care.

With all this, of course, the most important thing was the effect on the widow. Well, she was worse from then on. She didn't perfectly know what had happened, and it was fortunate that she never did believe that her son had returned. The name of Aaron was not mentioned in her presence, nor did she herself speak it. She'd been stunned by the entrance of the stranger, and even more by his talk of the old happy days before Aaron went away; but the shock of this, with the excitement of the tussle that followed, mixed her mind, the way a stick stirring the mud of a pool bottom causes clouds of dullness to rise, so that nothing is clear. You might hope for mud to settle, and for roiled water gradually to regain its clarity; but the widow's mind, it seemed, was not like that, not sensible like natural objects. She wept more often than before, and would not tell them why she was weeping, maybe didn't know herself. She didn't, as they had feared that she would, accuse Habakkuk of driving her dearly beloved son out of her own house. In a way, however, what she finally got to supposing was all but as bad. She knew that there had been a visitor who caressed her and talked gently to her, and she knew that this visitor after a dreadful fuss had disappeared. She assumed—nobody ever told her this—that Hab Jones had thrown him out. In some way, not immediately, but fairly soon, she began to identify that man with John Rellison, her favorite John. She had always accused Hab of driving John to sea. Now she accused him of driving him *back* to sea. She did this obliquely for a while, then directly.

"John, John!" she screeched suddenly one night at the end of supper. "He's a better man than you are any time, Habakkuk Jones, and yet you chastised him out of here! You chastised him forth into the wilderness, to wander alone!"

"Now, Mother——"

Deliverance put a hand on the widow's arm, but it was shaken off.

"No now-Mothering me! Don't you think I know what you two are doing night after night, sinful, sinful in the eyes of the Lord? You think I'm blind, but do you think I'm deaf? You—you *fornicators!*"

Deliverance got her up to bed, and Hab sat listening for a while. The widow's voice grew more shrill as her words grew incomprehensible. Hab sighed, and after a while he rose and cleared the table. He had started to do the dishes when all was quiet and Deliverance his wife came downstairs. She went right to him, and looked up at him.

"It will be a long time, I reckon."

"Aye" he said.

They kissed somberly enough, and turned to the dishes, and they were all but finished with them when the widow upstairs started again, crying twice.

"*John . . . John!*"

That was all.

Hab wiped his hands, and looked at them. This was more than three weeks after the visit, but the hands were still puffed and showed small scars.

"Aye, John."

She touched his arm. She said for the first and last time what both of them had been thinking.

"It *couldn't* have been him did it, Hab! It just *couldn't!*"

Hab looked at his hands, and opened and closed them, looking at them.

"Well, I hope it wasn't" he said.

. 28 . . .

The war at first made little difference in everyday
life on the Point. Even at the yard things went on about the same. True,
no orders for building came in, but Hab went ahead and finished what
he had; and the refitting work was about trebled, though the yard had
been doing a great deal of this anyway. Hab still opened rum—one
quart for every ton to leave the ways—but launchings were not the
gay events they had previously been. Folks didn't think England would
do much about the declaration of war, not with Boney to handle, but all
the same the biggest mercantile fleet in the world had the biggest navy
to protect it and the privateers were mosquitoes for stinging, so that
pretty soon things were likely to be closed. Just at first, though, you
would never have thought that there was a war. No drums were struck,
no trumpets blown, or fifes. Nobody hung out flags. Of warships there
was no sign. There was a trifle of recruiting for the federal army, but
not much: a man had to be pretty low to volunteer to go out of his
own state and fight for the Virginians and the westerners. The Washington government tried to sell bonds, but nobody on the Point was interested. Indeed the only martial touch was at Willison's and the Watts
yard, where lay the cannons brought from New York and New
Haven. However, there were not even many of these at one time, partly
because the merchants were reluctant to send them, having such a good
market at home, partly because they were fitted into vessels so promptly,
which vessels put to sea with the haste and exuberance of boys going to
a fair, but chiefly because privateers didn't use many guns anyway, not
being meant for fighting.

Folks at the Point, as at New London, where Hab often went these
days, having business at the courthouse, were agog about privateering,
which to them *was* the war, the military operations being far away
both geographically and in spirit. The talk everywhere was of prizes.
Whoever had any kind of schooner or sloop, or even as much as a
pinkie, was surer than apples getting it cut for a few guns, or at least
fixing to. They'd be sallying forth in rowboats soon, Hab thought. They
would pledge almost anything to raise the money for a bond; and there
was a heap of pressure brought against Hab.

He was skeptical. Though all his best friends were either privateers
or investors in privateering, Hab held the practice in scorn, esteeming
it little better than piracy with a printed license. You pounced upon a

lumbering merchantman—unless the merchantman happened to show teeth, in which case you ran like blazes—and sacked it and sent it home with a prize crew in the hope that the admiralty court would award you the full booty; and wasn't that valiant and bold? There were times too when the courts weren't trusted, and the vessel, after being stripped, was burned, and maybe its crew murdered, that being considered a safer procedure than trusting to the law: at least, there came to be whispered talk to this effect, though how true it might have been Hab never knew.

He had contempt for the crews too. The officers were good sailing men, and a gunner here and there had served in the Navy, but most of the rest were green raw youngsters from upstate, the Abner Rellisons pouring to the shore in greater numbers than ever. Privateers carried huge crews, not for fighting but for the manning of prizes; and when he watched some of them sail, crammed with eager awkward country boys who didn't know one end of a ship from the other, each starry-eyed about how rich his lay, his one-hundred-and-twenty-eighth or whatever it was, was going to make him, Hab wondered how it happened that some of those prizes ever made port—and maybe some didn't, at that.

Aside from the moral aspect of it—and he guessed that morals didn't really apply anyway in a war which itself was an act of appalling im-morality—he had his doubts about the financial stability of privateering. It was too risky. The profits, there in the beginning, were too big: that sort of thing couldn't last. Also, it was a business without a future, and its end was almost certain to be disaster; for Boney and the British, as the whole world knew, were locked in such a combat as couldn't pos-sibly be slackened, they had to fight to the finish, and whichever won would shortly afterward swat the privateers. Oh, it was a gamble all right, if you liked gambling! As in so many other things, all you needed to do was pull out in time. All you required was divine inspiration or a whale of a lot of luck. Hab stayed apart from privateering as much as possible. He might have ventured some of his own money, just for the devil of it, if he'd had enough to spare; but he was hanged if he'd venture any of Deliverance's or the widow's or John's.

This is not to say that he didn't profit by privateering, or that his womenfolk didn't, which comes to the same thing. Orders for piercing gunwales, building recoil platform, enlarging forecastles, sheathing magazines, fairly poured in; and these were easy jobs, quickly disposed of, and lucrative. Hab indeed could charge almost anything he'd a mind to, tut-tutting explosions of indignation, since few of these applicants were regular customers and many of them he'd never see again anyway. There was, too, as a result of prizes, a great deal of loose money in the village. The misers brought it out, avid to multiply it; and Habakkuk Jones was not slow to take advantage of this and to collect right and left, with full interest, on notes long due. The late judge's estate had never been in so good a condition. No, it was the direct investment that Hab shied away from. He took no shares, however small, in any of the adventures. The most he would do, and he did this only for fear of offending an old customer, was here and there make or contribute toward a man's bond. He never did lose in such a loan, for he watched them with care and collected as soon as a prize was taken, so that the man could make his own bond; but though Hab's profits were only eight and nine per cent he didn't care, he was satisfied. Indeed, in a few cases, where the bonded vessel was captured or burned or sunk, Hab had to wait a long while to establish his claim, and then the government granted him only six per cent interest, which probably was no more than you could expect from Virginians; but even then he didn't mind, being glad enough to get the money back.

It set him to grinning sometimes, the way men deferred to him. He wasn't fooled; *he* hadn't changed, only his position had. He had very little money of his own, but he controlled money, which meant every-thing. He suspicioned that he wasn't too popular, being maybe too urgent in collecting on old notes, over-reluctant to sign new ones. They didn't look at him fondly, as once they had when, running fingers through his leaping red hair, he would start the story about Ferguson and the barrel of bad fish; but again and again before strangers they would call on him for this and similar stories, which he was sick of, and they'd laugh loudly at the end. He didn't mind. He went his way. His "no" was a practiced one, firm and final.

Making money in these circumstances was almost too easy. Saving it wouldn't be hard, for the Watts house was well built. The difficulty lay in using it. Hab didn't want a filling chest of coins. He wanted the wealth to be working the way the men at the yards worked, the way he worked himself. But what could you trust, these days?

The old judge had scattered his; but Hab, even if he had cared for this method, knew that it wouldn't suffice now. Not only was there much more money but there were fewer small businesses, and what businesses there were weren't struggling. Indeed he was engaged in taking money *out* of those enterprises, rather than putting it in. Men weren't concerned these days with patching nets or sewing sails or making harrows, nor even with grinding grain, when privateering dangled such promises before their infatuated eyes. There was a heap of farm-land backstate to be bought for practically nothing; but practically nothing, if that much, was all he estimated it was worth; and besides, and even if you did invest in such land, where was your profit going to come from if you couldn't get men to work it? Hab had a hard enough time getting men for the shipyard, though he paid some of them as much as a dollar and a half a day for no more than ten hours' work. He couldn't even get men to go back country with him and cut timber

—had to draw on the store he was seasoning. They were probably afeared to get that far from the beach, afeared somebody might drop a dollar and they wouldn't be there to jump on it.

Before the war, and especially during the hard times of the Embargo, there had been a power of talk about the West, and there had been men mooning around with vague plans and trying to raise money to get themselves out of debt so that they could go to the other side of the mountains. These were always men, Hab noted, who did have debts to settle. They weren't the prosperous, they weren't the diligent, they were the restless ones, the misfits, with grandiose plans in their heads, yes, but with holes in their pants. Hab had been tired of hearing about the West and the great scads of money to be made there, where presumably there were fewer rocks and you could just shoot your supper—if you saw it first. He sometimes wondered what kind of land it was, filled with men like that.

Well, there wasn't much such talk now, the loose-enders, the bigmouths being all full of privateering. Hab wouldn't have dreamed of investing in western lands anyway. He didn't believe in putting money, especially other people's money, into something he'd never seen.

As to the war itself, it did not even occur to him to invest in that, not only because he believed it doomed to failure but also because he believed it wrong in the first place. He was never to forget how shocked he was when they heard that war had been declared against Great Britain, and how that feeling stayed with him, making him a little sick even after he'd got used to it. He was ready to grant, sometimes, not always, that perhaps sooner or later we would have had to pick sides in a fight which virtually involved the whole world. In that case, and assuming that it *was* the case, the thing to do was declare war on France, for there wasn't any French army in Canada, and the French Navy had been pretty thoroughly squashed. However, there *would* be a real French Navy, as there would be a French army in Canada, if France won. God knew Habakkuk Jones had no fondness for the English, and especially for the British Navy, while he knew next to nothing personally about France or the French; but it seemed to him obvious, all the same, what with Boney in power, a man nobody could do business with, that if England won this finish-fight we might still have some chance of keeping our independence, whereas if France won we wouldn't have any. Hab never even considered enlistment in either the Navy or the federal Army. He did think of the militia, but decided that he was too busy and that in the case of an invasion of Connecticut, the only event that would cause him to fight, he could take down the judge's musket and do just as good a job without any uniform on. True, he did thrill at the early frigate duels, and he was proud of the Yankee sailors, and particularly of Isaac Hull of the Constitution, a Connecticut man; but his interest here was partly professional and mostly sporting, the way a raiser of blooded cocks might watch a main, a horse breeder a race. As far as the outcome of the war was concerned, what did a few frigates mean to England, which had hundreds of them, besides more than a hundred ships of the line? Hab Jones never doubted that David had killed Goliath; but in the first place, that had been a long time ago, when things were different, and in the second place, God certainly had intervened in that fight, whereas Hab just couldn't believe that God meant to have anything to do with this one. As did everyone else he knew, Hab heartily approved of Governor Trumbull's refusal to send the militia out of the state; and when federal officials came around peddling war bonds he simply sniffed: he did not believe, as some did, that these salesmen ought to be run out of the Point on a rail, for he thought they had a perfect right to try to sell their bonds, this being a free country, but he himself wouldn't have bought any if they were a penny apiece.

In peace, to be sure, he'd know what to do with this cash which kept accumulating; and indeed he had plans carefully drawn on paper. He would enlarge the yard, he'd do more building and less refitting, and except in certain cases of good customers or old friends he would build only for himself—or rather for Deliverance and the Widow Watts. In other words, he'd invest in ships and boats, coasters, made in his own yard from his own timber, and operate them with skippers of his own choosing. However, this was impossible in war times.

Later in the war, and about the time that privateering profits began to fall off, Hab succeeded in arranging through a former friend of the judge in Hartford to send cash to Canada. Those further north generally sent cattle and grain over the border to feed the British Army, accepting payment in British Treasury notes at a liberal discount. Hab, however, and the Hartford lawyer—he was a member of the Legislature —and hundreds and perhaps thousands of others, sent cash, hard gold, regularly; and received the treasury notes later. These notes, they reckoned, were at least as safe as anything else; and they never had to pay full price for them. There was a certain amount of mutter against this traffic, but Hab couldn't see why. Money was money, no matter what you did with it; Connecticut wasn't threatened by the English; and as for the federal government at Washington, which he considered to have acted in an unconstitutional manner and thereby to have forfeited all allegiance from the separate states, well, sir, he didn't think that there would be any such government after this war was over. So why not protect his womenfolks' funds as best he could?

That left, in the first months of the war, privateering or the root cellar, and of the two Hab usually preferred the root cellar. However, he did not always have the choice. Either he or John Rellison, or else the Widow Watts or Deliverance, sometimes had a piece of a given vessel whether they liked it or not—not a big enough share to keep that vessel out of privateering but a big enough share to be worth protecting. Sometimes too, increasingly often as after the first flush of spending the Point's cash got tighter, he was obliged to accept such a share or lay in a vessel or venture in payment for a refitting job—either that or accept a note of doubtful value.

After the first few noisy months the reaction set in. The British Navy, startled, irritated, forbade all British merchantmen to travel except in convoys protected by warships, while other warships scoured the seas for privateers.

With the patent purpose of encouraging disunion among the states, the British at first blockaded only the southern and middle ports; but that left too many breeding pots for mosquitoes, so when the war was scarcely half a year old they corked up Philadelphia and New York as well. They let Boston go, but they couldn't let the sound go: that would be to leave New York's back door ajar. Soon Pointers saw the large and ominous shapes of war vessels cruising in a little way, then out a little way, stopping all boats, even small fishermen, and patrolling with stodgy thoroughness the gateway formed by the line Montauk–Watch Hill. The British didn't touch the Massachusetts men until later; they didn't seem worried about what the Rhode Islanders did; and probably they didn't care, either, about the Connecticut Yankees, except that they had to block Connecticut's vessels in order to keep in those of New York. The New York port was too busy to ignore; and besides, they had the greater part of the U.S. Navy bottled up there—all three vessels.

This slowed privateering, though it didn't stop it, for a few fast boats could slip through; and it all but smothered coasting. Prices went wild. Coffee sold at nineteen cents a pound at the beginning of the war, and had moved up only to twenty-one cents; but now abruptly it was thirty-six cents. In a matter of two-three months tea went from one dollar seventy cents a pound to four dollars. Rice cost, for rice, a small fortune; but on the other hand, you couldn't get rid of your smoked fish and flour—except by selling it to British warships, as many did.

Hab for one stayed away from those warships, and this was not because he lacked curiosity—he had never seen a liner close-up—but because the name of one struck a chill to his heart. The fleet off the end of the sound varied a bit from week to week, from month to month, though it was always two or three times bigger than Decatur's in New York. The larger ships, the liners, stayed far out, and for folks on the Point were vague though terrible blurs, enormous even at that distance. The Ramillies was the most constant of these, commanded by Thomas Masterman Hardy, the same in whose arms Lord Nelson had died. The Superb came along sometimes too, and sometimes the Valiant, a 74. There were the brigs Despatch and Nimrod, and the Orpheus, a bastard rig. The bombship Terror usually was there, occasionally with a sister. The Acasta and sometimes another frigate or two would join the watch now and then. But the steadiest of all, even including the Ramillies, was the Pactolus.

Hab stuck mighty close to Stonington.

What he was most afraid of was a landing party, not a battle party, just a friendly group coming ashore to purchase food. This was often done. Folks in Connecticut had nothing against the English sailors provided they were well behaved and in small groups, and provided they paid. *They* of course were delighted, stretching their legs, drinking real milk, eating real bread.

To Hab's knowledge such a group had never entered or even approached the village itself—after all, there was a war going on—nor would any be likely to do so, since the countryside and its food and drink were what the sailors were interested in. Nevertheless it was conceivable. And if such a group ever did come it would be sure to be in charge of a bosun's mate, and if it was from off the Pactolus the bosun's mate was sure to recognize Hab. Then what? The man in charge of the party could scarcely fail to take some action—he'd be savagely flogged otherwise for failing to do his duty—unless indeed they all decided to desert. Mass desertions had not been uncommon before the war; but the British temper was shorter now, and if such a thing happened the village would almost certainly be bombarded. Similarly, if his townsmen protected Hab—he wondered whether they would, whether they cared that much for him—and drove the sailors back, why, the village would be bombarded then too.

Those ships out there were big ones. They could tear every house on the Point into splinters if they'd a mind to. No fort defended Stonington, no army encampment was nearby. There were two Long Toms, ancient eighteen-pounders, behind a four-foot earthwork in Water Street: that was all.

Hab glanced often at those ships, and his lips would stretch tight.

He never told Deliverance that one of those ships was the frigate he'd served on, and she never asked him, though he suspicioned that she had guessed. Deliverance knew a lot more than she let on she did. She had never asked him much about his experiences in the British Navy, having seen that he didn't want to talk about them. Even the Widow Watts, these days, was fairly taciturn on that subject; but the widow was getting quieter and glummer all the time anyway, and queerer. She seldom raised her voice, but she went around mumbling pauselessly, now and then waxing hysterical; and she had some fantastic ideas about the way the house should be run. For instance, the declaration of war might have been expected to make no difference in her everyday life; yet she became markedly cautious right off. Though Hab and Deliverance would explain time and again that the possibility was so remote as to be absurd, she was sure that the

British were going to come and burn the house any day. She remembered—she'd been a girl—when Benedict Arnold and his Britishers had burned New London: she had watched the flames from a hill behind Fort Trumbull, and they made a deep impression on her. Now she insisted upon keeping the house locked tight as a drum day and night, even sneaking into Hab's room (he never saw or heard her do this) late at night to close and lock his window. She had always been a locker of doors and windows, a seer of nonexistent intruders; but Judge Watts for many years had demanded that the great bolt of the front door be drawn back all day every day, and the judge had been master. Not that anybody ever *used* the front door! The open bolt was rather a symbol of hospitality and lack of fear, and it became a household custom. Hab believed that the shutting of it had been lumpier in the judge's mind than the leaving of it open daytimes. That pushing shut of the heavy bar—it was the last thing he did before starting upstairs every night—had more than once been a signal to John and Hab, lying fully dressed and tense under the blankets, that very soon they could expect footsteps on the stairs, and the good-night visit, after which they might begin to count five hundred by ones before slipping out of bed. When John had gone to sea, and the judge was away attending the Legislature, it was Hab who slid shut that ponderous bolt every night, a mite pleased that he was privileged to do so, and trying to get into the act all the deliberate solemnity of the judge himself. When he came back, too, and the judge had died, Hab resumed this traditional chore—until war was declared and the Widow Watts wanted the front door locked all the time the way the back one was. Attached as always to the memory of Jonathan Watts, Hab had opposed this for a while, not openly, for you didn't fight the widow that way, but silently and stubbornly; but of course she won. He would wake up with a headache, his window locked, and he'd unlock the front door before breakfast, but that door would be locked again when he left for the yard—or else he knew that it would be locked immediately *after* he had left. The same thing would happen at noon, and again at suppertime. He seldom saw the widow push the bolt, a heavy one for her, and he never heard it; but he'd turn his back—and the job was done. He gave up at last, though it always did seem like being unfaithful to the judge's memory.

Hab himself, now that she was undeniably crazy, was in favor of having a conservator appointed to handle the Widow Watts's affairs, though indeed the widow never disputed the way *he* was handling them. Deliverance forbade. She wasn't going to confess to everybody that her mother was that way, she'd say; and besides, Mother might yet recover. So Hab lost out there too.

With all this, he was not permitted to stay away from the blockading fleet. There were vessels, smallish schooners most of them, which simply had to be cleared if the cargoes they carried were not to be total losses. Not infrequently Deliverance or the widow, or Hab, or John through Hab, or even all four at once, owned sizable portions of those cargoes. Often one of the women owned a large share of the schooner as well.

He didn't like it. It was a dangerous occupation; and he was getting too old (he'd vote soon) to be scudding through the night at the risk of his life. Gum, it was a risk worse than any of them knew! Hab had not forgotten the squosh of flesh, the splash of blood, and the screams, at the Pactolus gangway.

He didn't like it, for another reason, because it stood for a boyhood that had gone, a boyhood he wasn't ashamed of but which now looked a little silly on him, as though he were wearing a shirt and breeches many sizes too small.

He didn't like it, too, because it kept reminding him of John Rellison. It was different from the old days, though it was the same. It was different because John no longer was with him to keep him company and to hold his courage up, and also because instead of Lieutenant Ferguson in a small government sloop he now had to creep through an entire fleet—though in truth Red Ferguson had known more about the islands and waters of the eastern sound than all the Englishmen in that fleet put together. It was, still and all, the same thing that he was doing. Only it wouldn't be the same if he got caught.

Fatuously perhaps, though he had always been a stickler for form and tradition, as witness the case of the door bolt, he would leave the house each night when he had a job of pilotage to do by way of that same back window he and John had always used. And each night Deliverance would be waiting there in her nightrail to kiss him and to beg him to be careful. He always came back the same way too, unless it happened to be after breakfast.

They were bragging about him again in the village, but he felt scant pride. It had been a glittery thing for the boy: it was only a well-paid risk for the man of twenty-one—he was getting fees fourteen-fifteen times as big as those he'd once received. He still felt a bit ashamed of it, as though he had been caught in church with a sling-shot.

He couldn't help remembering how John used to grumble "We take 'em right out to the gates of romance and excitement—and then we turn back!" Well, there was no romance in it now, though it is true there were flashes of excitement, like the time when the Ramillies hailed him.

"You'll be safe, Habakkuk? Reckon you can find your way back in?"

Hab stared at the skipper.

"Found my way out all right, didn't I?"

He threw a leg over the taffrail.

"But after all, this fog looks as if——"

"It'll last long enough to take another, I reckon."

"You ain't aiming to take *another* one out tonight, Hab?"

"I reckon." He started down the ladder. "Obe Griswold's been waiting near a week. Wanted me to take him afore you, but I said I'd promised."

He dropped lightly into the cat-schooner, and cast off. He waved; and in another moment, heedless of the turbulence of the wake, he had put it about and was heading landward. He hadn't said so, but in fact he was uneasy, troubled about an early lifting of the fog, which reeled in bafflement. There shouldn't have been any fog at all. The breeze should have had the water to itself, as no doubt it did further out. The fog was formed of tremulous ribbons which twisted and turned as they hurried shoreward in an effort to hold back against the breeze, and tried sometimes to curl under and sometimes tried too to curl over, like so many vaporous white snakes being driven inshore with a stick by Neptune-turned-St Patrick. All the same, it made a good screen. Here and there it showed a blank space; but for the most part, despite the breeze, it was thick; it was low upon the water, crowded, bunched; and Deliverance I could hide in such a fog the way a rabbit would hide, crouching, in grass too low for a deer.

The breeze held astern, and the sails stood out winglike, one on each side, as though the cat-schooner was trying to pretend it was a gull that skims low in search of fish.

When Hab heard the ship working behind him he sat higher, catching his breath. It might have been the whole fleet. It made a medley of thin dry squealy wooden sounds, hushed sounds, sopped up by the wetness of the air, gulped by the fog almost before they could be heard. Though they were close to hand Hab couldn't determine their exact direction. Sometimes he thought they were dead astern, sometimes a little to one side or the other. One thing at least was sure: they approached.

They grew louder.

Badly scared, Hab brought both sails to the same side and put the dogbody a bit to starboard. The sounds appeared to follow, swelling a little, though he could see never a thing in the fog.

Chin on shoulder, his heart beating fast, he put the boat several points to larboard. Still the sounds got closer. That monster back there, never showing, stayed right behind him. The sounds no longer were blended, for he could distinguish them now, one from the others, and there were many. He could hear a half-sprung timber complaining, complaining . . . Another complaint was higher and less regular, but as persistent, somewhere aloft: a throat block maybe. There was the thunk-thunk of a jib that struggled. Two bells struck. A cabin

hatch slammed. Hab could even hear the tread of a sailor on watch—
no, not a sailor, it must have been a marine: no sailor would walk like
that.

All this stayed close behind him.

It was as though he was being chased by the fog itself, which
presently would swoop upon him and wrap him in wet arms to kill.
It was as though the monster played with him, chuckling, *it* being
able to see *him,* though *he* couldn't see *it.*

He could hear the shush at the bows, and the sibilant sirr-ee-ee as
water pranced along the sides. It wasn't loud, but it was mighty, it
was multitudinous.

Habakkuk Jones took his hand off the tiller and almost screamed
when the Ramillies burst into sight.

"Ahoy the deck!"

"Aye, aye, masthead?"

"Small boat right under starboard bow! Dory, looks like! Two
sails! We're almost rammin' it!"

"Bow ho!"

"Aye, aye, sir! Saw 'er too! Just about——"

"Damn your eyes, bow! Why didn't you sing out, you afterbirth?"

Hab was fascinated by the sheer immensity of the thing which bore
down upon him. Somebody had once told him that to build a ship-of-
the-line two thousand oak trees were needed, and to handle her almost
a thousand men. Hab had laughed. He didn't laugh now. It was hard
for him even to swallow.

"Damn you, *answer* when I hail!" This came down at him through
a trumpet: Hab could tell as much by the hollowness. "What the
devil are you doing? *Grab that line!* Have you got it?"

"Yes" replied Hab, who was hanged if he'd say sir.

"By God, you God-damn blue-bellied Yankee, bring that butter-tub
in closer and be quick about it! And see here—if you don't want to be
scuttled, right now, you say 'sir' when you address a British gentleman,
God-damn your God-damn stinking sweating balls! You understand?"

Hab drew himself upright. He cupped a hand to his lips.

"What ship is this?"

He thought he heard a snicker. He thought he could see the man
with the trumpet go red—though in fact he couldn't see him at all.
The answer was prompt.

"You know bloody God-damn well what ship this is, you drooling
Yankee smuggler! Hold onto that line till I get a look at ye! And say
'sir' when you speak to an officer!"

Hab held the line, trying to think fast. If they got him aboard they'd
keep him; and soon enough he would be recognized by some officer
from the Pactolus—they were always visiting back and forth.

"You, Welsh! Bear a swivel on him. And if he lets go—*shoot!"*

Welsh, whom Hab couldn't see, evidently replied in a low voice that a swivel, sir, could not be brought to bear on a craft so close, sir.

"Well, damn you then, get a grenade! And fetch that match!"

Hab, looking up, saw over the quarterdeck rail the hands of the sailor called Welsh, and in one was a glowing red spitting match, while the other held a round black bomb about the size of a man's fist.

"Now then, Yankee, what've ye been doin'? You've been smuggling something, eh? *Answer* me! Damn you, you've been smuggling?"

"No."

"Why, you——"

The officer was vituperative, first through the trumpet, and then, when this appeared to impede his blasphemy and obscenity, with his, as it were, naked mouth. He fairly shrieked.

Hab looked along the side of the ship, at the three firm rows of cannons. The Ramillies, all right. He felt some less fear now, though his heart was still going lickety-click. He sensed that they had an audience, he and the officer. Hidden men, sniggering, not daring to move, strained to keep the thunder packed back in their lungs. The watch forward, the lookout at the masthead, the helmsmen, a marine or two here and there, a ship's corporal doing his rounds, Welsh himself who held the grenade . . . they all listened.

The officer knew this too. When the officer called again his voice was slower and lower, though it wasn't more even. He used the trumpet not because of the distance, which was piffling, but because the trumpet was a symbol of quarterdeck authority.

"Yankee, I'm giving you one more chance. I asked you a question. Answer it. Are you smuggling?"

"No."

"Damn him, drop it, Welsh! Drop it on the bastard!"

Welsh touched the short fuse to the match, and dropped the grenade.

Hab had not stirred, not at first believing the order. He hadn't even let go the line. They were moving slowly. There was not much pull on the line.

The grenade flumped horribly, and rolled, its lighted wick pinwheeling, almost to Hab's left foot. He screamed—but he reached out with his foot and kicked the thing.

For an instant that was all he could do.

The grenade struck the cowling not four feet from where he stood. There it paused, hesitated like a living thing, as though uncertain whether to drop over into the water or to blow up this cockleshell. It teetered. The fuse gave off a keen penetrating sulphurous odor.

The grenade was round and black. It could do nothing mentionable to the side of a British ship-of-the-line, but it could tear the cat-schooner to bits. It rolled a little this way, the spitting light of the fuse rolling with it. It rolled, uncertain, a little that way. It hung.

Hab let go the line and threw himself at the tiller, at the sheets. The dogbody fell back as though pushed. Hab put the tiller over. With a hiss the grenade toppled into the sea.

Hab would have broached the boat if it hadn't been so high-sided. But he knew it well. When it heeled he was ready for it. And by that time he was bobbing under a stupendous stern-castle, all gilt ginger-bread and balconies and windows. He put Deliverance I clear around. Handled as he could handle it, it would spin almost on a coin. In a moment it was running almost straight up into the wind, and then he threw himself flat, holding the tiller from below.

There were several musket shots. The lieutenant must have called the marines. There were some hard harsh *bapps,* like the slap of two boards slammed together. Hab lay grinning a tight grin.

At Oliver York's there was a to-do about his scrape, and he was twitchy when he told the tale, and all covered with greasy sweat, though the night was cold. Obadiah Griswold, who knew a lifting fog when he saw one, was troubled.

"Don't you fear" Hab said angrily when after a single drink he started outside. "I'll get you there."

The fog held, hurling itself impotently at them, streamers of it breaking in soundless rage against them, as they prepared to shove off.

"Thought I was scared, eh?" Hab's voice was a whisper, but a mean one. "Sure I was! But—*you know what they did?*"

"You mean when they——"

"They called this boat a *butter-tub!* That's what he said! I'll get you out there! You watch! The sons of bitches! A butter-tub, eh?"

. 29 . . .

THEY DIDN'T AND THEY DIDN'T HAVE A BABY; AND THE Widow Watts glowered and growled at them, knowing perfectly well that Deliverance was often in Hab's bed, and indeed even mentioning that fact sometimes; but on the few occasions when they suggested that they get married, hoping to tell her that they *were,* she squawked so loudly and fell to talking and bumbling such foolishness that, scared, they dropped the subject. They'd just have to wait for her to die. This was not a reverent thought nor a very clean one, but doubtless, Hab reckoned, it was a thought many other young folks had about many other old folks elsewhere, and hated themselves for it, as he and Deliverance did. The widow's attitude, as far as they could gather it, or as far as she could be said to have an attitude, appeared to be that it was bad enough that there were such goings-on here under her own roof—and she used to get mighty detailed about it, and shrill, and dirty-mouthed sometimes when she was in bad condition—but at least they could keep other folks from knowing, the way other folks would if Hab and Deliverance got married. Just as though others didn't know, probably everybody on the Point by this time; but the widow was not aware of this, or perhaps never conceded it, as Deliverance herself refused to concede that everybody knew that her mother was insane.

When the widow was in one of these rages—it was always at mealtimes, as far as Hab Jones knew, and usually at supper when she was tired—the daughter would sit erect and humble, head down, as always at table, ever since Hab had come to this house, but with both hands instead of only one hand in her lap, for she wouldn't be eating, only sitting there listening to the tirade, and color would flame in her face. That pose, so exact, no longer calculated but habitual, so prim and at the same time apologetic, fascinated Deliverance's husband. She seldom spoke, and then it was in a hushed bashful voice, head still down. She'd been brought up that way, of course, as a lady. She wasn't that way in bed! The contrast between his wife in bed and his wife demure and reticent at table thrilled Hab, but it embarrassed him too, and when he thought of it he'd hang *his* head and do a little blushing of his own.

The scene usually ended with Deliverance helping her mother upstairs. Hab never heard Deliverance answer the Widow Watts, never even saw her give the widow a reproachful glance—and this in spite of

273

the fact that some of the things screeched made Hab himself shift his feet on the floor, his buttocks on the bench, and study intently food which it had become very hard to swallow. For the widow waxed increasingly outspoken when she spoke at all, and sometimes as her voice rose and her eyes blazed she was even obscene—obscene, that is, without being Biblical. Hab supposed that this was a privilege of old age and madness; but he didn't like it and certainly poor Deliverance didn't either.

When the widow was helped upstairs like that, sometimes even before the dishes were cleared away, Hab and Deliverance used to have prayers and the reading of the Book alone together.

His summons to war came in the form of an oblique suggestion from somebody that he call on a certain Mr Martin, an acquaintance, a shipbuilder in New London; and so Hab went there, knowing just what it was about, as did virtually everybody else on the Point. He smiled a little to himself, not on his face, as he went up the steps of Mr Martin's house, when he was remembering how he had once envied John Rellison a trip to New London, that glittering distant city. Well, things were a lot different now. Then he had been a wistful youngster, a bound-boy, an orphan apprentice; now he was a money-man, looked up to, deferred to. Then he had been engaged in off-hours in slipping vessels past a government sloop at three dollars the slip; now he was calling by request at one of the finest mansions in New London in order to have a conference with a distinguished personality—not meaning Martin—about a matter on which you didn't need to stretch imagination too far to say that the fate of the nation hung.

Mr Martin was most affable and gave him a cup of tea and talked about shipbuilding and what it might be expected to amount to after the war, and Hab judiciously agreed without paying much attention. Pretty soon a certain friend just happened to drop in, and this was another Jones, Captain Jacob Jones, U.S.N. Hab was startled—at the rank, that is. He had expected that they'd look him over first with mere lieutenants.

He liked Captain Jones, a youngish jovial man with beautiful manners. They talked about any-old-thing, wasting a pile of time.

Looking at Captain Jones, not much listening to him, Hab reflected what a contrast here to Captain Sir Henry Hatfield as Hab remembered him—the only way he'd ever seen him—with his hat off in respect to the King pompously reading the Articles of War before the assembled crew previous to another flogging at the gangway. The comparison was fair enough, too, for Captain Jones commanded the captured and refitted Macedonian, a British frigate only slightly smaller than the Pactolus. The Macedonian, together with the flagship frigate United States, a 48, and the sloop Wasp, a 20, some time ago had tried to sneak out of New York port by the back door, by the sound. They'd struck a terrific storm, a freak electric storm, and had been spotted and chased by the British, and they had taken refuge up the Thames at New London. Why the British didn't sail up after them, knocking out Fort Griswold and Fort Trumbull on the way, and destroy them, was a question only God Almighty and the British themselves could answer. They might yet decide to do so, any day; but it was not only this possibility but an inherent love of action and a desire to fight his vessels which caused the commodore to chafe in his cabin. He wanted to get out, and everybody knew it. If that pitifully small fleet, which happened to be almost the whole U. S. Navy, could get past the blockade and out into the open, or if even one or two of the vessels could do so, it would be to play most wonderful smash with British shipping, greater than all the privateers put together. It would hasten the peace, which everybody on both sides of the ocean so ardently desired, now that Boney had been whipped, and would give our own negotiators something they had hitherto lacked, a war record that wasn't one of unmitigated defeat.

Sometimes the blockading force, or one or two vessels of it, would come right up to the mouth of the Thames, as though to sneer at the helpless American warships. A couple of times the commodore had started out of his hole, rabbitlike, but rabbitlike he'd ducked right back again, lucky to get there, when the big fellows closed in.

After the third cup of tea Captain Jones very casually asked Hab, apropos of nothing whatever, whether he would like to meet the commodore.

Would he, that is, like to meet the hero of Tripoli, the darling of all American women, the envy of all American boys and girls, beloved in North and South alike, by everybody's admission the handsomest, dashingest, daringest, fightingest officer ever the Navy had produced?

Captain Jones was waiting for an answer.

Hab said he guessed so.

It turned out that the meeting could not be arranged until the following day, which disconcerted Hab Jones, who never liked to be away from home overnight. Captain Jones took his departure, smiling, bowing, saying pleasant things; and Mr Martin, who never mentioned the whole purpose of this visit, any more than Captain Jones had done, put Hab up the night.

Next day they kept him waiting four hours in a large anteroom with a street door at one end and a door guarded by two marines with fixed bayonets at the other. Somebody was all the time coming or going, most of them navy officers, and they all stared curiously at Hab. The marines examined passes, though not carefully. Four or five times Captain Jones came out to apologize for the delay, and he introduced Hab to various lieutenants and to Captain Biddle of the Wasp, who examined him pretty sharply.

At long last Hab was ushered into the presence.

His first disappointment, as he was to realize later, really wasn't fair. Irrationally, if naturally enough, in view of the stories of his exploits, Hab had expected the commodore to be physically vast, a giant. Well, he wasn't. He had a good carriage, without being a ramrod, but he was of no more than medium height and he was very thin, in the face even gaunt, so that his cheekbones showed high almost like those of an Indian; and his chest was puny, his arms were sticks. Nor was he notably handsome, as everybody said. His face was dark, not dark like an Indian's but more like that of some Latin European. It was not a weatherbeaten face. Hab didn't know about the teeth, for the commodore never even pretended to smile, but the mouth was loose and ugly, the nose long and none too straight. The commodore did have fine eyes, hazel eyes so dark that they showed almost black: when he looked at you the first time you seemed to feel the impact of a blow.

He was sloppy, and this was a more easily explicable disappointment. His lank dark hair hung down over his brow, and he needed a shave. His coat was unbuttoned at the top, his stock was smudgy, his boots not shined. One of his epaulets was askew.

He was very high-strung, at least at this time, very nervous; and he talked in jerky bursts in a rather high voice, and walked back and forth a great deal, sometimes gesticulating with his hands, sometimes clasping and unclasping them behind him. For several minutes he paid no attention to Hab Jones but continued to address somebody else, maybe everybody, on a business Hab knew nothing about. There were perhaps twenty officers in the large room, and they all appeared to be listening to what the commodore said. They were all standing. There wasn't much furniture.

Abruptly, extending his hand, the commodore wheeled upon Hab. He introduced himself informally enough, though Hab caught no glint of the celebrated charm, which it may be was saved for more distinguished visitors.

At least he didn't waste any time, but dove right into the matter at hand, which until this moment nobody had even touched upon.

Did Mr Jones believe that, given a reasonably dark night, he could pilot a ship out through the eastern end of the sound and so to sea without being spotted?

Hab allowed that he did.

"Why?"

"Reckon it's because I've done it so many times already."

"How many times?"

Hab shrugged.

"Never did count. But there was God's plenty."

This seemed silly to Hab. They must know his reputation; they must have made inquiries about him, or they wouldn't have asked him to come. He had expected to be questioned, but not as to his knowledge of the sound. He had expected to be questioned about his feelings about the war, perhaps asked whether he had bought any British Treasury notes. Well, if they asked him he'd tell the truth—though he saw no use in blurting it unless they *did* ask him—and that would, he assumed, end the conference, the commodore being what he was. The commodore, touchy because he was idle, fretful, fearing that folks might think him a coward (*him!*), and uneasy among these Yankees who talked so freely with one another but clammed so emphatically when a stranger appeared, had been, as everybody in that part of the state knew, waxing twitchy as the blockade held. It began to look as though he'd be stuck there for the rest of the only war in which he might hope to play an adult and high-glorious part, and that the Navy wouldn't ever get a chance to fight. The commodore believed that the Navy might even be betrayed, right where it was, and he considered plans for tiptoeing out to sea. He had no trust in the people by whom he was surrounded—the townspeople, that is, the civilians. He'd been busy afloat during the first part of the war, and it had never occurred to him until now, now here in New London, that there might be those who were not wholeheartedly in favor of this conflict. He'd been shocked to overhear men speak in favor of Connecticut breaking away from the Union.

He was walking back and forth now, clasping and unclasping his hands. The other officers obsequiously watched him, nobody saying anything.

He stopped, threw out his arms.

"You must forgive me if I appear to interrogate you closely, Mr Jones. We are hemmed in by spies here. We can't be too cautious."

Hab said nothing. He was thinking and he reckoned that the commodore was thinking of the blue-lights episode a little earlier. The commodore had made all plans, then, to drop down the river with the two frigates and the sloop, and to try to reach the end of the sound, to try to reach the sea, where he belonged. At the last moment, in panic, he'd called the whole venture off. The Navy had been sold out, he declared in his violent official report as well as in his talk. British sympathizers, traitors, noting the preparations and deducing what it was all about—they wouldn't have had much trouble there!—had summoned the British fleet by burning bright blue fires at the mouth of the river. The commodore had a lot to write and to say about those blue fires, which he was one of the very few to see.

He stopped pacing. His mouth jerked, his eyebrows went up and down. He was eye-fixing Hab.

"Now tell me, Mr Jones—tell all of us here—you can trust everybody here—just how would you go about getting a fleet beyond Montauk?"

"Well——" Hab frowned. This interview was not going at all as he had expected. "I'd get 'em out of the river first. I mean, somebody else would have to. *I* don't know anything about the Thames. Never said I did."

"We understand that, Mr Jones. We all of us here understand that, I'm sure. But from there?"

Hab was frowning, and knew it, and tried to straighten his face. This was pretty stupid stuff. Sometimes in the old Embargo days when a skipper hired him and John there would be questioning first, if the skipper was a stranger and could hardly believe that such youngsters could do the job. They would be asked exactly how they were going to go about it. That had always rattled Hab, though John Rellison had been glib enough of answer, making it all up as he went along. The truth of the matter, of course, was that neither of them had known which way they were going until they got out there, not any more than Hab knew nowadays until he got out there. It depended on so many things, things he couldn't go into here in this office with all those men standing around. It depended on tides, currents, the wind, the fog, the moon if any, rain, the size and speed of the vessel he was piloting, and his own opinion of the rightness of its officers and hands. It depended on a lot more than that, too. He would calculate distances, listen and listen and listen, and sometimes have soundings taken so that he could examine the cup for bottom. In the old days he and John would try to read Lieutenant Ferguson's mind, and outguess him. That had been a game. Today, with four or five large ships patrolling the place one tiny cutter had formerly patrolled, he had to depend a great deal on just plain common ordinary luck. Red Ferguson, though alone, had been thoroughly acquainted with the waters, and himself was a shrewd and conscientious public servant. The thousands of British out there now were not that. They were bound by routine, hating their masters, hating the life they led. Blockading was the dullest and most exasperating of all navy duties, and even the officers would be lax. Alert watches wouldn't be kept. Even so, even taking all that into consideration, the fact remained that whenever you got through, these days, you were lucky.

But Hab couldn't tell the commodore all this. He only shrugged.

"Don't have any plan. Never do."

"But you can't go out there without knowing where you're going."

"Why not?"

"Is that the way you would do it, Mr Jones?"

"Way I always have."

The commodore's manner changed. He was regarding Hab with bleak suspicion, but furtively, as though he thought to surprise some telltale expression of guilt on Hab's face. He was still thinking of those blue lights, Hab surmised. He leaned back a little, and without turning his head, though partly covering his mouth with a hand, whispered to one of the officers behind him. Then he nodded like a man who reaches a resolution. He took something from his pocket. He strode toward Hab, holding up a coin.

"May I ask you what is this, Mr Jones?"

"Sure. Two shillings."

The commodore turned in triumph to the others and spread his arms. "You see?"

They nodded portentously.

"They're so enamored of everything English that they even speak of the currency that way." He faced Hab again, still holding the coin high. "This, Mr Jones, for your edification, is an American half-dollar, so designated by the Congress. It says right on it there: 'Half Dollar.'"

"Sure" said Hab. "I can read."

"Then why——"

"Everybody around here calls it two shillings. Always have."

"Everybody around here was once subject to the whims of the British king, Mr Jones. Would you like to have it that way again?"

"Well," Hab was getting annoyed, "we fit 'em all right when the time came, didn't we?"

"But you don't believe that the time has come to do that again, eh?"

Hab didn't answer.

The commodore pocketed the coin, turning away.

Coldly, "I'm afraid it would be better if we went no further in this deal, Mr Jones. I think the nation needs a more trustworthy agent."

He no longer looked at Hab, so none of the other officers looked at Hab either: they all looked at the commodore.

"Suit yourself" muttered Hab, who could not see why this decision hadn't been reached the previous afternoon, so that he could have been with Deliverance at this moment. "Well, good-by now."

He made a little half-bow, which nobody acknowledged, and went out.

"Why, then, they everything but accused you of treason!" Deliverance cried that night when he told her about it.

She didn't cry this very loudly, for she was in bed with him, lying on the side next the wall.

"I reckon it does sort of come to that. Hadn't thought of it that way."

"The man must be crazy!"

"Maybe. But I expect it's mostly just nerves."

She started to say something else, but he reached out and put a hand on top of her head and shoved her firmly under the covers. At the same time he let his arm drop half over her, and hitched up a knee, making the mass that the two of them composed mighty bumpy and uncertain of outline in that dark room. She knew what was up, and didn't stir.

Mrs Watts came in an inch at a time. Motionless, breathing regularly, Hab could see her from under one outflung arm, and she was like nothing so much as a wraith compounded of moonlight and fancy: she made so little sound, she moved with such a gliding motion in her white nightrail, that you half expected to see objects through her.

She went to a point about halfway across the room, from where she was able to see that the window was closed and even locked. She only glanced at the bed, of which she couldn't have seen much. She glided out, shutting the door without a click.

Hab reached down for Deliverance's chin, and she put her head forth.

"Don't reckon she'd see you anyway, but it's better to be safe."

"'Bout time I went back to my own room anyway."

"There's no hurry."

"Were you aiming to tell me some more about Stephen Decatur?"

"Well, no, that ain't exactly what I had in mind."

Half an hour later, just before she left, she opened the window for him.

On an April morning at once restful and tangy in the nostrils, at once promising and accomplishing, with the sun bright as could be, and the breeze, still a shade nippy, out of the north, Hab was in the yard shack piling some patterns and singing, singing partly because it *was* such a beautiful day, partly because he was convinced that the war would end soon, never having touched the Point, but chiefly just because he felt good: he felt as fat and sassy as a squirrel in October.

> *Oh, the boys and the girls went a-huckleberry hunting,*
> *To me way-aye-aye-aye-aye-i-yah!*
> *Oh, the boys and the girls went a-huckleberry hunting,*
> *And sing high-low, my Ranzo Ray!*

There was a discreet cough behind him, a cough spaced to fall into that pause between verses, that air-chink birthed by the renewal of breath, but he supposed that it was just one of the men and didn't immediately turn.

> *Then a girl she ran off and a boy he ran after,*
> *To me way-aye-aye-aye-aye-i-yah!*
> *And the girl fell down and he saw her little garter,*
> *And sing high-low, my Ranzo Ray!*

The cough again, and there sounded an unfamiliar voice begging forgiveness for the intrusion, and this time Hab did turn.

"Oh, hello. Come in. Still carting whitefish?"

Mr Macgregor did not recognize Hab. This might have been due to the fact that he had quit an almost tropically brilliant sunlight for the

280

dim shack, where Hab's features could scarcely have been clear; but more likely it was because that walk in the woods had made a deeper impression on the boy than on the man, who must have struck up many such off-hand acquaintances while traveling. That had been some years ago—five? six?—well, anyway, a long while ago. Mr Macgregor could have been failing, too. He looked much smaller than Hab had remembered him, and weaker, bonier. The wee goat's whisker under his chin was colored as before (and it still waggled when he spoke), but there were streaks of gray now in the orange of his hair just above the ears. His watery-blue eyes didn't have their one-time twinkle. He lacked leap, and his manner was humble here, where he was a petitioner.

"This is Habakkuk Jones?"

"That's right."

"I wonder if you would take it amiss, Mr Jones, sir, if a simple man of peace asked permission to exhort the workers in your yard?"

Hab smiled.

"Not going to try to make democrats out of 'em, are you?"

"No. Oh no. I'm no longer stirred by politics. I lecture only on higher matters now."

"Didn't know there was anything higher than politics—provided they happen to be Tom Jefferson's kind."

Mr Macgregor squinted at him, but shook his head.

"No doubt we've encountered, sir. I travel a goodly bit."

"It was some time ago."

"Before the war, I'll warrant? The war, sir, has been a great shock to me."

"That's an easy idea to catch onto."

Sunlight struck the water and was reflected in bright wriggling lines on the ceiling. With a smile, Hab glanced out the door, past the yard, along the stone-littered shore, to the end of the Point where on the public flakes the fishermen's wives were cleaning and drying a catch: there was talk of constructing a lighthouse there someday, after the war. The sunlight felt very good, though it made him blink. The gulls were tiny above, their cries unhearable over the tap of mauls from the yard. The rocks and stones were a bright gray, almost a *gay* gray, in the sunshine. Far out, the blockaders stood, it seemed, fixed, not sailing; but that was very far out.

"Sure, go ahead." The request was in no way unusual. "Long's it's not politics, and long's the men keep working, does 'em good to be preached at." Impulsively, "Come in. Have a drink."

Mr Macgregor assented with alacrity, looking tired as he sank upon a stool. He sipped rum-and-water, savoring it. It was pretty good rum, better than the stuff Hab dished out in the yard, though that was good rum too.

Mr Macgregor sat forward, elbows on knees, holding the jack with both hands and staring at it thoughtfully, reluctant, it was clear, to swallow its last few drops. He sighed. But he said nothing.

"Yes, it's easy to see" said Hab, who felt chatty, "how a man of peace like you, sir, and specially a man who's worshiped Tom Jefferson, wouldn't like this war much. Don't like it myself, comes to that."

Mr Macgregor nodded. He murmured without looking up that he felt like a trust betrayed. He was pathetically pleased to find someone who'd seem to take him seriously—or who at least was kind and refrained from poking fun at him. He made no mention of Jefferson, whose name had been constantly on his tongue that afternoon behind the oxen.

"I've fought evil wherever I've found it" he said, and shook his whisker. "But ah, Mr Jones, I've found it in so many places!"

"I guess that's right."

"I used to think that all evil was negative, not a thing in itself but just a vacancy which goodness would naturally try to get into if it had a chance, the way air rushes into one of these vacuums that the scientists can make. But I don't know, Mr Jones. I don't know. I used to think that spreading goodness was only a matter of explaining evil away and that when you'd done that everything would fit in and get along with everything else, like where it says in Isaiah that the wolf also shall dwell with the lamb, and the leopard shall lie down with the kid, and the calf and the young lion and the fatling together, and a little child shall lead them. But now I don't know."

"Speaking of leopards, you remember what Jeremiah asked, 'Can the Ethiopian change his skin, or the leopard his spots?'"

"Yes . . . it's confusing. My *faith* is as firm as ever, believe me, Mr Jones, but it's confusing nowadays. Nemo sua sorte contentus. I have a harder time talking to men and trying to lead them into the way of light. I wish it could be like where it says in the Gospels: 'I am the Lord, I change not.'"

"That's Malachi, I think" Hab corrected gently. He smiled a little, for all this quoting reminded him of Mr Dimplerose the Quaker on that immaculate little farm down in Delaware. Now he looked at Mr Macgregor, feeling sorry for him, the tired man. "Never mind" he said. "You preach to the men all you want. They're pretty pure men, but I don't reckon it ever does any harm to be preached at. They might even like it."

Mr Macgregor sighed, looking at the almost-empty jack.

"Depends on what you preach. You just give them the Word of the Lord without applying it to things around you, and they don't mind that. They like that. It makes 'em feel holy. But if you begin to ask them to *act* on what you've been saying . . . I don't know, Mr Jones. It started in Newport, some years ago, and they wouldn't let me stay there any more, and then I walked to Westerly. I hale from Westerly originally. I'm a Buckie."

"Yes, I know" said Hab.

Mr Macgregor glanced up, then glanced down again, discouraged. He shook his head.

"Now I'm here, but I won't stay here, Mr Jones. I think I'll wander over all the face of the earth, like that Jew I forget his name. Whenever I try to translate the Word of God into action I'm thrown out. I'm just not strong enough. I'm too old, maybe."

There was some silence, and then, since his guest seemed disinclined to talk without prodding, Hab asked politely what it was that had started in Newport.

"My persecution, when I tried action the first time" the preacher replied. "That was some years ago, just before the war. It was in Newport, where I'd been preaching the Word to some carpenters and riggers at the Brown yard, and they brought this schooner up, handsome thing she was, and tied her alongside and began to work on her. It must have been quite a job, because everybody at the yard was taken away from everything else and put onto this. So of course I went to this schooner too, to be with the men, and there I got to know the mate, a fine strong dark-eyed lad with a fine laugh and lots of teeth in it. Came from here too, he did. Here on the Point. He was a Fishtail, I could tell the way he talked. But very good-natured. He let me preach all I'd a mind to—until the second week, when I noticed that they were putting in four extra-large water tanks."

"Uh?"

"Then I looked around and really saw what they were doing. I guess I'd been too busy spreading the Word to notice it before, and nobody in Newport would pay much attention to such a thing anyway. Mr Jones, they were building a 'tweendecks into that schooner. I ran below to make sure, and before God there were the staples and everything all lined up."

The day was not so lovely, the air was not so balmy as it had been. Hab's jaw came out below. His eyebrows went down.

"I see what you mean" he said quietly. "Mr Macgregor, I saw a Guineaman once, was right up close to it, at sea. Stank to high heaven, the worst stink I ever have known. Well, sir, there wasn't what-all we could do excepting let them have the water they'd asked for, but I swore to myself then and there, just before I had to vomit, that if I ever met any slaver face to face I'd go right at him without even warning him to put up his fists. I will, too. I still mean that."

The scarecrow nodded approval. He finished his drink, and he was a mite afraid of the look on Hab's face.

"That becomes you, Mr Jones. But you are a man of action and would know what to do. I wasn't—and ain't—and didn't. That such abomina-

283

tions in the sight of the Lord existed I knew, of course, but I'd never dreamed that they could be born in a Christian community, among our own kind, like you and me, Mr Jones, and be winked at."

"What did you do?"

"Ran up to the mate—the skipper was a local man, a Newport man, and he was ashore most of the time then—and I went up to this fine-looking youngster and took him by the jacket. *'See here, you can't do this!'* I yelled. *'Don't you know what they're making?' 'Sure I know what they're making, Grandpa'* he said. *'Well, you've got to stop them!'* At first he only pushed me aside, laughing, but when I kept after him, clawing him and yelling at him, he got sore. He knocked me down, and when I got up he knocked me down again, and after a while he threw me off the schooner. He did that himself because there wasn't any sailors around."

Hab nodded. He knew why that mate had been unassisted. Hab had little enough respect for sailors, but at least very few of them were low enough to sign aboard a slaver. The officers, yes, because of the money they were paid, though they'd always deny it afterward; but the hands would be picked up in another port, drunk, not knowing what they were doing.

"I came back again and again, but he hired bullies to keep me away. I went to the owner of the shipyard, and he laughed at me. I went to the mayor. I said, 'Remember: Longa patientia trahitar ad consensum, which is to say that long-sufferance is the same as consent.' But he said it was none of his business. I went to the other Spreaders of the Word, but they evaded it—said how could they know what trade a ship was intended for, and anyway where could I point out anything in Holy Writ that condemned slavery? Well, sir, that schooner sailed, but I kept on. Every new one that was fitted out, at that yard or any of the other yards, I was there to raise a clamor. Like that young mate, they laughed me off at first, but after a while they drove me away with blows and curses, until finally I was told in so many words that if I didn't want to be killed I'd better get out of that Gomorrah and stay out. That was the beginning. Then I went to——"

"Excuse me, Mr Macgregor. That mate on the first one, the schooner, you remember his name?"

"No, I don't—if I ever heard it."

"But he came from the Point here?"

"Oh, sure. He was a Fishtail. Tell the way he talked."

"And the schooner itself, you remember the name of it?"

A forefinger twisted the small orange goatee, and even Mr Macgregor's face was goatlike when he nodded in answer.

"Sure, remember it well. Never forget it. The Northern Constellation."

Boss Jones rose and went to the doorway, where he stood for a time in sunlight he didn't feel, and with his thumbs hooked into the top of his breeches. On the ceiling behind him the wave-reflections wriggled sportively. Mauls thudded in the yard.

"Thank you, Mr Macgregor. Yes, you can preach to them all you want. Excuse me, I'm going to take a little walk. Help yourself to some more rum."

He truly did take a walk, but back-country, not along the shore. He didn't go near the house, not only because of the Widow Watts but because he knew he'd never tell Deliverance such a thing about John Rellison.

His throat felt tight, and he kept his head down, kicking small stones as he walked.

It had been a long while to be away from work, when he returned. The shack was empty; and Mr Macgregor's high earnest voice came from the yard, announcing that his text would be from Job, Hab's own favorite book: "What is man, that he should be clean?" Hab went into the shack, into the room where he'd been married, where the lines of reflected water shimmered and shook on the ceiling. He flumped down into his chair, and began again to sort patterns.

. 30 . . .

THAT MONTH, THAT SAME APRIL, THE BRITISH FLEET closed in on Stonington and several times tried to land parties, which were smashed, and at last backed out of range of the two gallant Long Toms, the village's only artillery, and went on with the bombardment for two more days, using not only balls and bombs but also rockets, which nobody on the Point had ever before seen. This attack was unprovoked, barbarous, stupid, and expensive—for the British. Nobody ashore could understand it. The British had many friends in Stonington—or *had* had, before this savagery—and the fleet had often got fresh supplies from there, indirectly. Perhaps the commanding officer had gone balmy as a result of too many months in that dreary blockade work? Nobody could find any other explanation.

A southwest wind to start switched to the north, and that was bad for the British gunners, who thereafter had their own smoke blown back into their eyes. Maybe the gunners were balmy too? Their aim was good but their range was absurd. When a bomb or rocket did hit the village it was because the thing was defective and fell short. Though they'd been out there a year and a half, off a village, off a whole series of villages which according to Commodore Decatur swarmed with spies, the British didn't seem to know Stonington. They must have supposed that the two easiest aiming points, the two highest buildings, the meetinghouse and the Watts house, were in the very center of the village, and they shot just over these, north of them, where assumedly they hoped to start fires which would be carried by the north wind into the houses of the Point proper. Heaven only knows what that mistake cost the British taxpayers. In fact the meetinghouse and the Watts house, neither of which was touched except for a few broken windows, were on the extreme northern edge of the village. The shells and bombs and rockets day after day fell into empty fields among disinterested rocks.

The whole business was unbelievable. Everybody in Stonington—every man was out with a musket, of course, and before it was finished so were most of the men from the countryside in back and from up and down the shore, in addition to some regularly trained militiamen—fully expected to be overwhelmed. Yet they won! The flag stayed up on that flagpole all through the fuss: it'd been nailed there. Some windows were broken, a few roofs knocked in, a few chimneys damaged, and a

286

great many small fires were started and promptly put out. The muskets were hardly used at all, except to pick off swimmers after the Long Toms had shattered some landing barges near shore. Most of the time the volunteers were fighting fires rather than invaders, or else standing by prepared to fight them. They could scarcely believe their own luck. The British losses must have been great—over a hundred. A few villagers were cut or burned, nothing serious; and the only fatality was a poor little old crazed woman who literally died of fear when the shells shrieked over her house, a heart attack interrupting her screams.

The Widow Watts had always known that she was right, no matter what the others said. The British *had* come again, and it was too much for her. She never learned that no Britisher managed to get a foot on the beach.

Seen this way, the Battle of Stonington, a trifling affair in history, loomed big as a landmark in Hab Jones's life.

The Britishers didn't bother the Point after that; and the following February a messenger riding post from New York to Boston—the sound was closed by blockaders—passed near enough to the village to shout his news to some farmers. It was important news to justify riding like that—the messenger made it in thirty-two hours, a record. It was the news that peace had been signed two months before, in Europe.

And a few months after *that,* in April, John Rellison returned.

How many times in the sizzling hissing heat of emotion have how many of us vowed wild things, altogether meaning them, only to wonder afterward what had (so long ago) brought about such feeling? Rage or love in its immediacy, as everyone knows, smothers common-sense; but the man who is entoiled in such a passion *thinks,* if he could be said to think, that he has common-sense by the tail. "I adore you!" —and it is perfectly plain to the man or woman that this was an accurate statement, and that the adoration would of course continue, love containing in the very essence of it a belief in its own immortality. You know you'll die, your body will die, and they'll bury it; but stay certain that your love never will die; since there couldn't be an ordinary fleshly death for such love, or otherwise how could you have felt a thing so strongly? You feel it with more force than you feel your own very self and skin, and that makes it, doesn't it, an existence mightier than yours, a push from outside, something like what the preachers mean when they prate about your soul? As to the common-sense, there is no easier way to justify madness. The woman, or man, who has just cried "I adore you!" somewhat later, alone, explains it in terms of logic, arguing, even *knowing,* that the beloved is not only desirable but inevitable, and, what's more, the best possible choice anyway. This becomes diamond-clear after a little while. The life-partner is not only going to be delicious to possess but it can be elucidated by terms of reason that the choice is the only correct one. There might be chasmic differences of income, background, education, age, even creed or color; but the miraculous heaven-sent clearness of mind granted to that person who has recently exclaimed "I adore you!" is capable of sweeping these away—not hastily but well, coolly, one by one, each sweep a masterstroke of ratiocination. Afterward this clearness appears muddied, and you wonder how in hell you ever could have thought that you *were* thinking then. Afterward, mixed inside you with the dullness and sourness, with the heavy ache of emptiness, is a feeling of embarrassed wonder at yourself. It becomes incredible that you'd ever been so blind.

Well, with hatred it is much the same. If few men can love thoroughly, few can hate thoroughly either. The proportion, it's probable, will never be determined. Genius is needed for the full job; and genius is something nobody should count upon.

When they came to Hab and told him that John Rellison was on this ship which had a little earlier, at dawn, dropped the hook outside, he turned quickly away and began walking back and forth, trying to promise himself again what he had once promised himself, trying to assure himself that he'd meant what he said. He did not succeed. John might be a seducer, a coward, a quitter, dishonest, selfish, John might even be a slaver—but he was John. There had been times when Hab truly felt like killing him, and indeed Hab could feel that even now, at this moment, if he permitted himself to; but the truth was that Hab was too eager to see John again, to warm in his smile, and to shake his hand, after these years, even to worry about anger for deeds past.

Be sure that he had an excuse! He called old common-sense to his side, and was able to point out to himself, quite lucidly and without passion, that business considerations, a sense of his duty as guardian of the Rellison property here, required him to meet John as soon as John arrived. Not only was there the money and the shares left to John by the judge, and which John had left in the care of Hab, who'd almost doubled them, and the money John himself had saved, plus the money Hab had given him for his half of the cat-schooner Deliverance I, all of which had likewise been very nearly doubled; but in addition, the Widow Watts, leaving Hab nothing, leaving Deliverance the house and property—the widow had never owned any share of the shipyard—had left to John Rellison the greater part of her paper estate, temporarily and unofficially in Hab's hands, and it wasn't inconsiderable. The will, written only a few months before her death, was unwitnessed and almost certainly, in view of her known mental condition then, could have been broken—that is, in Deliverance's favor. Deliverance, however, thought, and Hab agreed with her, that it would be fairer to do what the widow obviously had wanted. This was going to give John Rellison a sizable estate, and it was something he could not have expected and would scarcely have heard about. It was a complicated matter, but Hab had it well in hand and was ready to give a full accounting, and moreover anxious to do so, to get rid of the responsibility.

So this was the reason, and the only reason, Hab told himself, why he was on the shore when the moses boat containing the passengers pushed away from the brig out there.

For it had come out that John Rellison was a passenger. John and a woman, two passengers. This information and more like it had been brought in by fishermen who spoke the ship further out while she was sounding. The ship wasn't stopping here, only discharging those two passengers. It had come up from the sugar islands, the fishers reported. It had not dropped the hook, as at first believed, but was simply standing on and off and would depart for its destination, New York, as soon as the moses boat returned.

John was, of all things, a passenger. This seemed as curious to the others around him as it seemed to Hab himself, all of them remembering how John Rellison had many times asserted his fondness for the sea and his determination to stay afloat until he'd made his fortune. It could be of course that he *had* made his fortune? They strained their eyes.

The morning was muggy, the sun not yet up, and the wavelets spat on the stones of the shore. The water was the color of lead, copying the sky so close to it. In such a setting the sprightly little moses boat, brave and white, danced like a living thing. Nor were its occupants, especially the two in the passengers' seat, remarkably drab. John turned several times to wave, and though his features weren't visible it was John all right, from that carefree gesture, that high-held head. There was the black varnished hat worn jauntily far back on the head, its ribbons snap-snapping in the breeze. There was the roundabout blue jacket. Hab even imagined that he could see the flash of teeth when John smiled, as he was undoubtedly smiling now, and the twinkle of the rings in his ears.

The other passenger, the woman, though Hab paid her scant attention at first in his excitement about John Rellison, was even more spectacular. Matter of fact, she was out-and-out giddy, even at this distance. She wore yellow and blue, the most eye-hitting yellow anybody there had ever seen, and she hoisted a ridiculous tiny oval saucy parasol made mostly of lace.

Gray was the color of fashion at that time, of female fashion. There were rich grays and dull ones, deep grays and light grays, but there wasn't much else besides white and black. It was the rule, nobody knew why. It was what the ladies were wearing in Paris, so it was what the ladies in London were wearing too, and those in Philadelphia and New York, *and* those in Stonington, Connecticut. A muddy purple might be flaunted now and then by some daring dame, or a swart and turgid blue; but by and large it was just gray, and there was apparently nothing that anybody could do about this. The ladies themselves, bless them, didn't like it and wished with all their hearts that Paris would return to bright colors. Their husbands, putting on coats of bottle green, mulberry, claret, cerulean blue, would grumble at the sight of that same flat unswerving undeviating gray. "Why can't you wear something *lively?*" And the wives would sigh, poor slaves, and reply that they only wished they could. You couldn't buy bright colored materials if you wanted 'em, the wives would say.

A woman at the Point, though not if she valued her reputation, might occasionally get hold of and even wear a pelisse of some subdued bombazine the color of bad mustard mixed with mud; but nothing in yellow so dazzling as this newcomer had ever been seen there, or dreamt of.

She, prim in her seat, wore lemon-colored sarsenet with insets of valenciennes, which lace was on the parasol too. She wore a lavinia, an unbleached chip hat waggishly acock, which was fastened under her chin with broad white sarsenet ribbons. She wore blue silk stockings, by Jesus, and white nankeen slippers. She wore short blue gloves. There was a gold chain around her neck, rings on most of her fingers, and jonquil clips in her ears, so that when she moved ever so slightly, even in that dull morning light, she quivered and glittered and sparkled and shone.

Fact of it is, the Pointers there on the shore were so taken in by her habiliments that for a minute or two after she'd landed they barely even thought to look at her face—though that was something to see too.

But Habakkuk Jones had eyes only for his friend. They were waving to one another, and John was grinning, flashing those teeth. Old impulsive John! Before the prow of the boat could scrape the stones he had leapt over the side, laughing at the damage the water did to his fine varnished pumps and his stockinet breeches, and he waded to Hab, both arms outstretched. They shook and shook hands, and they pummeled one another on the shoulders and slapped one another's forearms, laughing and asking questions.

How was he? Good! How was Deliverance? Good! What? Married, eh? His heartiest congratulations! Put it here again! They shook hands some more, Hab, who had been married more than four years, finding his face hot, his hands wet. And how was the widow? When Hab said that the widow was gone John was sober for a moment, only a moment, for form's sake. Then he was laughing again, and slapping Hab's arm, and telling Hab how good it was to be back.

He even did a brief jig, John did, there on the shore, the beginnings of a sort of hornpipe, stamping the stones as though they felt good under his feet.

"It's grand to be here, I tell you, Hab! And here's where I stay now.

I'll build a house. I'm shut of the sea, Hab. I've made my pile and I'm shut of the sea, you can count on that."

"I'm glad to hear it."

"Come along, we'll have a drink, eh? A mug of flip. Oliver makes the best flip up and down the coast anywhere. But first," turning, "I want you to meet my wife. Habakkuk Jones, darling. Hab, this is Mrs Rellison. But we'll let you call her Suzanne."

Hab bowed low. The movement was prompted only in part by manners. To a large extent it was instinctive, a defensive reflex, like ducking the head when a missile in the air is suddenly seen and before its distance or speed can be estimated, its direction noted. He bowed to cover himself, and stayed down a long while, gazing at the tiny nankeen slippers. He knew that his face was scarlet, darker even than it had been when John congratulated him on his marriage, and he could only hope that the back of his neck, which would show, wasn't that same color.

For it was a naked woman he saw. The others standing there on the flakes were agasp at the flamboyancy of the woman's dress, but to Hab Jones she wasn't dressed at all, not even the feet he gazed upon. She was golden. The color of honey, yes, but honey though sweet is sticky stuff; and this woman was golden; and the sunlight crashing in bars between the slats of the jalousies landed with joy upon her firm unbobbing breasts, her flat belly, her sateen hips, and her round outstretched arms as she walked on bare perfect feet across the enormous room toward Hab, walked slowly and with the unbelievable grace of a cat.

"Welcome to the stony state" he murmured.

Straight again, he saw that she was smiling at him. There was a hint of rouge high on her cheeks, the faintest daub of paint on her lips. Her teeth were exquisite. The eyes held him, as they had done before. They were green delicately flecked with gold, and lynxlike in shape, being somewhat pointed at the outside ends. There was not the slightest hint of recognition in them as she smiled up at Hab Jones. Either she had forgotten him completely—which seemed unlikely when you thought of the uproar his departure from the Pontalis plantation must have caused—or else she was an actress of very great natural talent.

"Enchantée."

She extended a hand, palm down, and on impulse Habakkuk Jones bowed again, kissing it.

There was another sucking-in of breath among the onlookers, who might have been thought to be breathless. Hab was to hear a great deal about that kiss later. He was to hear some of it from Deliverance herself, who of course was given the news early. Deliverance ordinarily was a compliant wife, and a complacent one, who if she did want to wheedle something out of him or to reprimand him for something she waited until she got him in bed; but on the subject of that kiss-of-the-hand, a subject brought up in conversation by her, she was to wax uncommonly tart. "I only did it because she's French and that's the custom in France." "You're not in France." "Well, she's a foreigner, and I thought it was only manners to make her feel to home." "*She* may be a foreigner, but *you* came from right here in Connecticut, Habakkuk, and I wish you'd recollect it once in a while."

At the moment, however, aside from the gasp, the kiss produced only a laugh, John's.

"Easy there, H. Jones! Easy! I didn't fetch this beautiful bashful blushing bride all the way up from the islands so that you could steal her heart away with funny tricks!"

Hab smiled. Suzanne smiled; and by God, she was lovely! The crowd watched.

John Rellison hooked a chin toward the pile of boxes and bags the sailors had left on the flakes. The moses boat already was halfway back to the brig.

"We can leave those. This is an honest town. No niggers here, darling. Hab, let's get over to that entertainment."

He slipped arms into their arms, one on each side, and he was laughing like a boy, and eager and worked-up.

"Let's get that flip first and study about the baggage afterward. Hab, you've got to tell me everything that's happened. We're going to live here now, we're going to settle down, build a house, and I want you to start us right. I want to know everything! I'm shut of the sea now, Hab, you can count on that. I'm here."

. 31 . . .

SUMMER CAME EARLY THAT YEAR, AND IT CAME WITH A
rush. There was a mere flicker of spring. The cold winds died, the sun
was turned on full as though by somebody in Heaven turning a wick-
turner, and leaves and flowers began popping forth almost before you
had a chance to see the buds. The daffodils, for instance, notoriously
short-lived, were downright rude this year and like the forsythia had
scarcely shown themselves when they were scattered and gone; and
this was a shame, Hab thought, because he had always known a par-
tiality to yellow, the most discussed color on the Point just then. But
that's the way it was that year. The last soggy clumps and corners of
snow had no more than disappeared when the carrot weed (which the
mincing Mrs Eb Tooker always called Queen Anne's Lace) was standing all dusty along the edges of the fields and over-flushed sumac
drooped in the sun.

Summer usually didn't do that to Stonington, and indeed not in the
memory of the oldest inhabitant (Zechariah Harvey's father, close on to
a hundred) had it ever done so before. It usually crept up, only to creep
away again, playing coy, cat-and-mousing it with the Point, coquetting,
reluctant to yield all its charms finally and irretrievably; so that by the
time you'd really got yourself settled down to enjoy the warmth, the
winds began to tingle with chill again and the leaves got their first dark
fallish edges.

This year, however, there was no hesitancy, for summer came early
and came hot, all but announcing in a human voice that it meant to
stay for a long time; and more than a few folks said, not altogether
playfully, that this was because of the presence of Suzanne.

Everybody called her that, from the beginning. Nobody ever thought
of calling her Mrs Rellison.

What to do about her, how to treat her, was a subject which en-
grossed the village. The Pointers were a homogeneous pack and by
ordinary not inclined toward heated important arguments. This isn't to
say that they were not disputatious, for assuredly they were, starting
lawsuits at the drop of a hat, carrying on feuds for years. But they quarreled, if often, and violently, along agreed-upon lines. They fought with
vigor; but they knew their weapons and used them according to well-
remembered rules, rules they had inherited along with the weapons
themselves.

Suzanne was something else again. Nothing like Suzanne had ever before happened to Stonington.

The Pointers were not accustomed to talk much about one another, because they didn't need to: they knew one another mighty well. Religion, then, together with politics and taxes-and-prices, were the favored subjects of conversation. But virtually all the Pointers were members of the same church, and even the few Baptists as Baptists went were not wild. Disputes about religion on the Point were disputes about dogma, that's all. Likewise in politics: the Point was almost unanimously Federalist, never mind that the Union as a whole was overwhelmingly anti-Federalist. The only jiggling by-subject of politics upon which men seriously disagreed was the advisability of breaking away from the other states, whether in company with Massachusetts and Rhode Island and New York or alone; but even this, after the failure of the Hartford Conference, and after the news of the peace, had become a dead issue. As to prices and taxes, everybody agreed that they were too high, and that the fault lay in the Washington administration. You could haggle over figures, but figures weren't likely to break up old friendships and even threaten to break up families—like Suzanne.

On the whole, the men liked her and the women didn't; or, to put it more accurately, the men, blunter in such matters, liked her right-off, the women only after a considerable amount of suspicious smelling-around like that many dogs around a bitch new in the neighborhood. Well, most of the men had been to places far away, but the women hadn't. In time, though, almost everybody, even those she jolted, and they were many, came to like Suzanne, who was in fact a highly likable person.

There was at no time the whisper of a hint that she had any touch of negro blood or had once been a slave. Clearly this wasn't known. Hab thought it probable that even John didn't know it; for John often in her presence referred to niggers as such—"You must miss all those niggers waiting on you," "You've got to fry your own eggs here, you know, sweetheart: we don't have niggers to do that"—and always without a touch of self-consciousness. In Martinique the exact proportion of her negro to white blood would be known (one thirty-second, wasn't it?), but this was not Martinique.

Hab had a bad half-hour when Si Wainwright, who had been stuck in Lisbon throughout most of the war, involved in lawsuits, returned with the Horace T. Wainwright. But Hab recollected after a while that Si, coming to think of it, had never even seen Suzanne—or much of anything else at the plantation, for that matter. Anyway, Si showed early and with considerable force that he was not eager to talk about those days, being, of course, thoroughly ashamed of himself; and this was all right with Hab Jones.

There were many embarrassing moments, not all of which it may be that Suzanne was aware of, though she caused them all; but for Habakkuk Jones the worst of the embarrassment was reached in the very beginning, that first morning, when he had a drink with the new-comers at Oliver York's and invited them to dinner but didn't say anything about them moving into the Watts house. He was hanged if he'd have them; and he had already made up his mind to this effect before they reached the inn. It would be much commented upon, he was sure of that, for everybody knew that they had plenty of room now, just the two of them and a dog in that big house; but anyway he was hanged if he would. Fortunately John said nothing about this, so that Hab was not obliged to refuse him point-blank. John must have wondered about it, but he acted as though he'd intended all along to stay at the inn while he built a house, and he engaged rooms from Oliver York as soon as they arrived, and even before he had his first drink. He gave a silver coin to the Jamaican boy who brought the bags and boxes from the shore. It was more money, probably, than the Jamaican had ever gripped before in his life. Oliver York took it away from him, to keep it safe.

They sat there. Folks were looking in at the windows from all around, looking at Suzanne; but in the entertainment, in the room itself, they were alone. Hab didn't ask anything about their marriage, and John didn't offer anything. John anyway was bubbling with questions. He really did seem interested in the Point and the folks there, and really did seem to mean to settle down, and he asked Hab questions about what pieces of property might be for sale. Hab looked at the ceiling and mentioned some bargains. "Too near the shore! I want to be back. I told you I'm shut of the sea." Hab, afraid to mention the false Aaron, which was what he was thinking of, and wondering to himself why he was afraid, observed that John could buy acres and acres and acres backstate a bit for almost nothing, if that was what he wanted. But no, John wanted to be fairly in close. He wanted good food, and wanted to be able to buy pretty things for Suzanne, at whom he now beamed. Hab finished his flip, refused another, and said offhandedly that what John wanted it would look like was a plot of ground just back of the village, all torn up by the British bombardment, and there were a few there, not many, but one of the best was the Watts property; and Hab said that for all he knew Deliverance might be willing to sell some of that. "If you don't mind living over a place where you used to hoe potatoes," added Hab. John laughed, glancing at his wife. Suzanne had been following the talk with a smile, but Hab saw her eyebrows tupp down at the word "potatoes." She had never heard that word before. Hab didn't dare look at her much, only enough for politeness. She was very beautiful. She looked older than the girl he had known; she didn't have that immediate flower-freshness; but she still was an angel for beauty, and dazzled.

John did take a second flip, despite Hab's refusal, and he laughed. He insisted upon paying for all of them, which Hab didn't argufy about. John said that there was a thought—to live over a place where you'd once worked. "I used to work a little, sometimes" he told his wife. He felt good about his money, though he'd yet to learn of the inheritance. He said that they must talk about that land sometime soon, because he did want to build on a good piece of property. Hab nodded. After John had finished his second flip, which he somewhat hurried, gulping it, they went to call on Deliverance.

She showed not a mite of astonishment, for she had known for some time that they were coming, and also she'd heard about how Hab had saluted the foreign woman. She was a lady. She probably would even have let John kiss her cheek, had he moved to; but he didn't, and didn't even hold her hand very long when he greeted her. She must have had a hard time keeping her eyes from bugging out at the sight of Suzanne's finery; but she was a lady, and she smiled in just the right way, and said, when she said anything, just the right words.

Dinner was a pick-up, this being the worst time of year, before the vegetables or any fruit came and with the muggs all but empty. They had enough, sure, but not much variety, and both Deliverance and Hab apologized, while Suzanne smiled and John assured them with brisk-ness that after having been to sea *any* meal was a good meal. All they had was bean soup and some clams and a herb omelette and baked sea bass and mashed potatoes and carrots and a turkey stuffed with walnut dressing and some milk and tea and cider and pudding and pie. The cider was tolerable hard, as it's likely to be by April, and John drank a good bit of it. When Suzanne sipped the cider her eyes filled with tears and she had to cough, but she smiled very pleasantly. Later, still correct, she more cautiously finished her glass; but she refused, with a smile, a refill.

"By God, it's good to be back!" John cried, stretching his legs, wiping his mouth.

Hab had been worried about grace, because of that crucifix around Suzanne's neck; but he said it all the same, just as he would have done anyway; and nobody seemed to mind.

They had hired a room at York's. That part of it was all right. Would they go to church on Sunday? This was Tuesday.

John said things like "By God" fairly often, and when he'd say one Hab would glance at Deliverance, but Deliverance remained the lady, her head down a little, her eyes down, one hand in her lap, as she al-ways was at table.

At least there was nobody looking in at the windows, as there had been at York's.

It was a strange meal and uncomfortable, with only John, always a mixer, showing easy. *He* gushed questions, perhaps in order to stave off other questions. He was delighted when Hab formally told him of his inheritance and even read a short statement accounting for every penny of it. "Good old Aunt Watts! Her heart was in the right place after all!" Straightening, he asked for details of her death, but they glossed over this, Deliverance and Hab alike; for it wouldn't have made either of them happy to tell about how the widow had passed away in stark madness, after fighting them, and spitting at them, screaming even above the whine of bombs and the vicious slee-ee of rockets that this was the judgment of the Creator come in the form of the British in order to strike down a house in which shameless fornication had been practiced. So they mumbled past that scene; and John was alert to change the subject. Hab never brought up the business of the false Aaron, though certainly John would hear about it later. Deliverance understood this. Hab was afraid that John would betray himself.

They ate in the parlor, this being such a special occasion. Suzanne said very little, though she followed each speech with interest, sometimes moving her lips to repeat silently a word new to her. She smiled constantly, an attentive, slight, sympathetic smile. She was not condescending, not aloof; but Hab sensed that she was startled by the crudity of this place. After all, she'd been brought up much better. Her English, when she did speak, was flawless: indeed it was so good that they had difficulty understanding it. She had more confidence in the tongue than when Hab had slept with her; and if she still spoke slowly it was not with halts and great spaces, as it had been then.

Hab was uneasy. The room itself oppressed him, as it always had. He tried so hard to keep from looking at John's wife that it fairly hurt his head. He knew that Deliverance was having the same trouble, but it was easier for her because she'd been trained to sit demure. He couldn't do that; in him it would have been churlish; so he did the opposite, keeping his chin so high that the back of his neck began to ache. When he'd turn to Suzanne he would find himself looking over her head, and he tried not to do this because after all it wasn't good manners. On the wall beyond her was a sampler Deliverance had made many years ago, and though Hab had often seen this he had never before stared at it so hard. It was large and in many colors, and the lettering was intricate. It said:

XERXES THE GREAT DID DIE,

AND SO MUST YOU AND I.

At the end of the meal Suzanne didn't do a thing about helping to clear the table or wash the dishes; didn't even offer to. She just sat there, smiling politely, now and then bashfully asking the meaning of a word. Deliverance was very sweet with her; and indeed, Deliverance was to tell Hab afterward, in bed, that she'd liked her right-off.

They left the cider jug on the table, with the glasses. Hab suggested wine, but John declared that good old Connecticut cider was good enough for *him*. John averred that you could go all the way round the world and not find anything better to drink than good old Connecticut cider. Deliverance asked him whether he had been all the way around the world, and he said no but he'd been a long ways. Suzanne was watching him, but covertly and always smiling, concealing her anxiety pretty well. John was sure-enough drunk. It turned out to be a little hard to get rid of him, despite Suzanne's amiable help. He insisted that they ought to celebrate his good luck. A lot of money, then a beautiful and loving and obedient wife (and he smirked at Suzanne), and then unexpectedly a lot more money. Good old Aunt Watts! How 'bout another one, there?

When they rose at last, "Why, we're *rich,* sweetheart!" and he slapped his wife's rump. She did not stiffen outside, only smiled; but Deliverance knew, and even Hab knew, that she didn't like it.

Again because this was a special occasion, they were shown out by the front door. Since the widow's death this door was always kept unlocked until bedtime.

The Joneses stood in the doorway watching them, and John turned twice to wave and they waved back. John wasn't walking well, but he was all right: he'd get as far as the inn. Scarcely fifty feet from the house he slipped his arm around Suzanne's waist and drew her close to him. She didn't like that either, but she was yielding, compliant, probably knowing that they were seen. John, oblivious now to host and hostess, put his cheek against the top of her head and made blubbering fatuous animal sounds. "Mm-m-m . . . m-m-m . . ." That was the way they were when they passed out of sight.

The sky was crammed with stars that night.

"He sure loves that woman, Habakkuk."

"Well, he ain't the only man around here loves his wife."

He had taken her hand. She smiled sideways and poked her head against his chest, but immediately withdrew it, and when he stooped to kiss her she slid away.

"I've got some things I want to talk to you about when we get up there."

They were sleeping in the big room now, in the big bed.

"Is that what I'm supposed to do, then? Just answer questions?"

"Habakkuk!"

She never did approve of mentioning matters like that before evening prayers. *After* prayers it was different, and she wasn't a bit standoffish then; but she didn't think it was right even to make a reference to such things while the candles were still lit and God's forgiveness had not yet been asked.

So Hab read the usual number of verses, reading them low and solemn, as he always did. It was their custom to go through the Book regularly, as the judge had always done, and when they finished it they started again; and for this reason there were times when the readings, as distinguished from the prayers themselves, were undeniably dull: the mind of the most devout can wander when begats are being intoned. This night, however, it happened that they were in a book they both liked, Joshua.

"'And ye, in any wise keep yourselves from the accursed thing, lest ye make yourselves accursed, when ye take of the accursed thing, and make the camp of Israel a curse, and trouble it.

"'But all the silver, and gold, and vessels of brass and iron, are consecrated unto the Lord: they shall come into the treasury of the Lord.

"'So the people shouted when the priests blew with the trumpets: and it came to pass, when the people heard the sound of the trumpet, and the people shouted with a great shout, that the wall fell down flat, so that the people went up into the city, every man straight before him, and they took the city.'"

Deliverance whispered that it had been very lovely, and then Hab closed the Book and they knelt and prayed. Deliverance straightened her dress after she'd risen, and she marched for the stairs. Everything was ready now. They were very happy, these two. People aren't often that happy. Hab Jones put the Book away, and put away the jug and the glasses, and then he blew out all the candles but one, which he held, and he very seriously slid shut the bolt of the front door. It sounded a large low hollow "clunk." When he was sure it was in place he went upstairs, smiling in his eyes.

. 32 . . .

The question that absorbed the point all those first five days—the Rellisons had landed on a Tuesday—was whether John would take her to church.

They remained at the inn most of the time, John hail-fellow-well-metting in the ordinary, while the bride languished in the seclusion of her bedroom upstairs, where she spent hours, it was whispered, with cosmetics. They seldom even went for a walk. It was particularly remarked that they did not call on Mr Smith and that Mr Smith did not call on them. No doubt he was playing safe. A fiery man in the pulpit, an arm-waver and passionate scold—the Pointers wouldn't have had him if he were otherwise—he was mild and conciliatory when down on a level with his parishioners. In this case no doubt he too was waiting to see what Sunday would bring. There were those who averred that the sermon he was working on would contain some stinging references to painted women; but nobody found the courage to ask him this to his face.

Amiable enough when they met anybody on their walks, when they'd stop and John would introduce his wife, who would smile and shake hands not a whit standoffishly, the Rellisons nevertheless didn't go calling, and since they did not have a home, really, they were not called upon. Just what would happen when they *did* have a home nobody knew. The more immediate question was Sunday and church.

The one exception to the Rellisons' aloofness was the Watts house, for everybody still spoke and thought of it as the Watts house, and even this was because of business, though it was something of a company occasion too, the Joneses having invited them to dinner. Then it was that Hab sold John, for a good stiff price, about two-thirds of Deliverance's property north of the village—the Watts "farm," which in fact had never been anything more than a large kitchen garden inconveniently far from the house itself. John, familiar with every foot of this land, and who had that very morning revisited it, wanted to buy it all; but Hab wouldn't sell it all, insisting that Deliverance ought to keep and to work, either herself or through some bound girl or boy, at least a nominal cabbage patch or some rows of beans: the judge wouldn't have liked the complete abandonment of the "farm," Hab said. True, it was in bad shape at the moment, having been ruthlessly pitted by the

British, and would need replowing, and a good part of the wall would have to be rebuilt; nevertheless some of it should be kept and worked, and Hab wouldn't budge from that position. John assented suddenly but at the same time contended that in that case something ought to be taken off the price. Hab said no, the price stood.

John was vexed. Though his hand was shaky and his eyes somewhat red from drinking the previous night, he had gone easy with the cider on the table before dinner, and such self-denial, he must have thought, should be rewarded. He acted almost as if he didn't think Hab was being fair. Hab and he in the old days had always shared and shared alike, with never a dispute over a penny. John Rellison esteemed himself a right slick dealer, and in his only real dicker with Hab, when he'd sold Hab his half of the cat-schooner, Hab had meekly accepted his high price and paid it. What John didn't take into consideration was the fact that while Hab had been doing that for himself, he was doing this for Deliverance, which made all the difference in the world. At any rate, Hab was firm.

John appealed directly to Deliverance, who was setting the table, clumsily assisted by Suzanne: John must have spoken to Suzanne after that first meal out. Deliverance was all household, all kitchen, and indeed showed not a sign that she had even overheard anything the men said, or had wanted to, as she moved from place to place. John appealed to her jokingly, yet half earnestly too, in the name of old memories, old days. He didn't leer or gloat, he was much too smart for that, but all the same, and even in the presence of his wife, there was an edge of you-and-me in his voice, a glint of possessiveness in his eyes. Once you have tumbled a woman, Hab had heard men say, you can always tumble her again. Well, he didn't know how true this might be. It God-damn well wasn't going to be true in *this* case at least, he thought savagely; and then reproved himself for the word, even though it was unvoiced.

Deliverance only replied that Hab could speak for her. She didn't even seem interested. John stared across the table at her, frowning a little, but she didn't look up from setting out the spoons.

Suddenly again, John gave up. Laughing, and with a flourish, he signed the purchase agreement. After all, he said, he had plenty of money anyway, so why haggle about a few miserable dollars? This dismayed Hab, who realized too late that he could successfully have asked for a little more; but he too signed. John reached for the cider.

This was not a fancy meal like the other one, not served in the parlor, and when it was finished, which was still early afternoon, Hab had to go back to the yard. He would do this without lingering to help Deliverance with the dishes when, as usual, there were only the two of them. Today, however, the admonished Suzanne tried so hard and with such marvelous maladroitness to help, and got things so badly mixed, that Hab stayed around long enough to set them straight for Deliverance.

It was pitiful the way Suzanne tried to help. They could see that John, though laughing, was angry. It had just occurred to him that his wife had probably never washed a dish in her life; and while in one way he was proud of this, in another, and especially in these circumstances, he was irritated and apologetic. Any woman ought to know how to wash dishes, just naturally, even if she'd never done it before, John all but said. Hab smiled sideways, recalling to mind that packed hot fascinating kiosk behind the Pontalis mansion into and out of which the slaves moved with the unpausing persistence of ants at an anthill, each bearing a platter heaped high. Why, they must have dirtied two hundred dishes a day there, five hundred, for all he knew! But he'd bet Suzanne never even saw that kitchen. Deliverance now was very sweet with her, and a flushed Suzanne was grateful, her voice low.

Before bowing his head for the grace Hab had experienced again that soaking qualm about the propriety of praying in the presence of the crucifix around Suzanne's neck, but he made up his mind more briskly than the previous time, and went right ahead.

This, in small, was the same problem the villagers grappled with. There were those who contended that the crucifix was a heathenish emblem and should not be admitted into a House of God, assuming that John Rellison was going to try to bring her, and assuming too that she kept that thing on. Others answered scornfully that the crucifix was a symbol of Christianity, and what kind of House of God would it be that wouldn't admit a symbol of Christianity? The first came back hotly that like thunder it was, it was a symbol of the Roman Catholic Church, which was a totally different thing.

Mr Smith refused to comment.

On the whole, at least in the beginning, the sides were roughly divided, here as well, according to sex. Most of the men having been in other countries, Portugal, France, the Canaries, the sugar islands, had seen more than one unblushing Catholic, had seen Catholic churches, and indeed a few rash ones (though they kept quiet about this on the Point) had even out of curiosity attended mass! These were able to assure the women, who for the most part had never seen a Catholic in the flesh knowing that he *was* a Catholic, much less a female one with the badge of her heresy around her neck, that while they themselves of course did not approve of the Roman religion, nevertheless as far as they'd been able to observe abroad it was not true that Catholics habitually roasted Protestant babies alive, dancing naked around the fire. Some but only some of this sarcasm had an effect upon the wives and mothers and sisters. Forcing the attack, the traveled ones pointed out that in many foreign countries, in all the French and Spanish islands, for instance, everybody was a Catholic, that being the only thing to be, the Catholic church the only one to go to; they just took that for granted there, and it didn't mean anything to most of 'em; and, matter of fact, *they* considered *Protestants* heretics. To which the rejoinder was made that this wasn't a foreign country, this was Connecticut.

Back of all this, behind the technical arguments as to whether it would be proper for John Rellison to do such a thing, was the immense pulsating question of whether he was going to try; and the additional following question of what each individual should do about it if John *did*—whether to consent to meet the woman, or, having previously met her, consent to speak to her.

Only a few die-hards kept ranting about the wickedness of admitting ungodly objects into the presence of those who wish to worship, at the same time keeping that crucifix in mind. Most of them, though they too talked of the crucifix one way or another, all the while were thinking not about sacrilege but about impropriety.

Mr Smith would take care of the technical question, they guessed, always, however, reserving the right to veto his decision; but would it be proper to bow to her, *if* John brought her?

Stonington seethed with this question. A stranger wouldn't have known it, even a non-Point Yank from some nearby place never would have supposed that any mentionable discussion was afoot. There were no demonstrations, no groups of any kind except such as normally formed each noon and evening at the several pubs and which were not now in any way over-animated or unnaturally hushed. Men who talked to one another didn't waggle their elbows or even raise their voices. Mr Smith went earnestly about his rounds, as everybody else went about his own. When John Rellison did walk out with his bride they were not openly stared at.

Among themselves the villagers were passionately discussing the point from every angle, and feeling ran high, and enmities were being made; but a sailor lately off, or a commercial visitor from say Sag Harbor or even Westerly, wouldn't have caught a hint of this.

What made it so exasperating, and notably among those not her defenders, was that Suzanne seldom appeared in public that week, nor were they able to learn what she did with herself all day long in the rooms at the inn. Men who knew the islands and had known some women in the islands explained when they dared that what she was doing was probably nothing at all: women from down around there sometimes spent whole days just lying in bed looking at the ceiling, or sitting down looking at the things they made their hair up with, or leaning against something without any imaginable dream to nudge them. But this was too simple. It would never be believed by the agin-hers.

Each night John Rellison, after having had supper upstairs with his wife, descended to the ordinary, where he lingered, instead of going to bed early as a bridegroom should, sometimes even until closing. John drank a heap, and talked a heap, but he didn't let anything significant about his wife slip his lips, no matter what his condition. There wouldn't be any women there—the fact that Suzanne had sat with her husband and Habakkuk Jones in that room when first she landed, even though that was only for a little while in the middle of the morning, had been and still was being discussed vigorously—but the husbands and brothers were catechized later. They could only report that John Rellison seemed happy, though he sure was drinking too much, and as anybody knew it wasn't the thing for a man who was happy with his wife to drink too much. What would happen after he went upstairs? Well, they could hear scrapings and almost stampings, but that might only have been caused by her having some trouble getting him undressed and to bed. Didn't anybody ever go up and listen at the door? Well, yes, some of the boys had done that one night, to tell the truth, sure; but they hadn't heard much. There was another door, y'see, atween the room that hall door led into and the bedroom, and that second door must have been shut too. They'd heard voices which sounded right angry, but they couldn't make out a single word.

John himself, accessible and always affable, was still uncommunicative. He talked a lot, but he didn't say anything about what they wanted to know. He talked a lot about himself; but even there, and even drunk, he spoke cautious; and anyway, they weren't interested in him; they knew him.

Oliver York couldn't contribute. He wasn't playing the discreet boniface either. He knew he could sell more drinks if he gave out to divulge some secrets about Mrs Rellison; but he didn't know any more about her than anybody else, and he was too honest to assert that he did.

The servant? Now as it happened the servant responsible for keeping those rooms clean and taking up the meals was that quiet small negro boy from Jamaica, a boy of uncertain status and uncertain age, low-spoken and respectful, efficient, melancholy, and with curious grown-up courtly manners. This Jamaican couldn't be bribed. He knew that Oliver York would take the money anyway; but he probably wouldn't have talked about Suzanne even if this had not been the case. Always a mum one, despite his pompous polysyllabic speech, he had formed an immediate attachment for Suzanne. He wasn't demonstrative; and at no time was there a whisper of scandal: not even the most vinegarish prude, not even the owner of the loveliest and most lecherous imagination, ever suggested that Suzanne would have relations with a negro. All the same, the two seemed to have something in common. When Oliver York sent another waiter up one time, Sammy Bludge, Joey Bludge's son, he was returned with a note asking if they couldn't have the Jamaican back. That boy even followed her when she went out for a walk, and walked a little ways behind, looking up at her for all the world like a fond dog. He had little enough attention paid him when John was along, though John obviously liked the show as much as Suzanne herself did; but twice Suzanne walked out alone to the tip of the Point, out to the common flakes where the women were cleaning fish, and almost continuously then chatted with her follower, she never looking around at him, he never taking his eyes off her. Not even their speech was the same, though they both spoke English slowly. Her voice was high and light, his low. She had a gay quality in her; he was all seriousness. They listened to one another carefully, and seemed to understand one another, though passers could make out few words and some of them even believed that what they had overheard was in a foreign language.

The first time Suzanne walked out to the flakes she wore a long blue bombazine pelisse trimmed with fur and caught in front by huge yellow silk brandenburgs, and a white lace mob, and black satin slippers. Her clothes were always warmer than anybody else's, and far brighter. The second time she went out there, half the population watching her, she was largely covered by a cashmere shawl, and it was hard to see her face inside the long and narrow oldenburg bonnet, which was trimmed with feathers in dark green and black zebra stripes and tied with apple-green ribbons.

The Jamaican boy, each time, wore his customary drab.

She would stand watching the women for a little while, amusement and much interest in her eyes, on her lips the small smile she seemed always to wear, while they went about their work trying to act as if they didn't know she was there. Then she'd speak, somewhat timidly, but pleasantly, asking them questions about their labor. She had a disarming way of asking questions, as though she asked them not because she really wanted to know the answers but because she wanted to make friends; there was something touching about her eagerness to get along with these women; and several of them replied to her, gruffly but readily enough—they were usually gruff anyway, those fishermen's wives. Suzanne would thank them, and a little later go back, walking slowly, smiling at everybody she passed, and twirling her parasol, while the Jamaican boy trailed along.

As it happened, Hab Jones saw her that second time, on a Saturday, through the window of a sail loft in Water Street, and promptly forgot what he had gone there to get, and fell to wondering again about her.

He was sure by this time that she remembered him. But after all she was probably as fearful that *he* would betray *her* as a little while ago he'd been fearful that *she* would betray *him*. She had a wealthy husband—or so she thought, so she'd been led to believe—who knew nothing or next to nothing about her past. The less said about those days in Martinique the better, she must have reasoned. And Hab, as in the case of Si Wainwright too, reckoned that this was just about right.

She sure knew how to walk, he thought, watching her.

She'd thought she got a very rich man. Hab knew that by the way she looked about and by the way she answered things John said. She had expected a grand mansion, she who had been born in one and brought up in one, she whose thirty-one thirty-seconds or sixty-three sixty-fourths, whichever it was, were aristocratic as all-get-out. Well, John Rellison could talk smooth all right, making some folks believe what wasn't anywhere near the truth; but even though John had found himself with more fortune than he'd a right to expect, it still wasn't what this woman had settled herself in for. Had John bought her as a slave? No. If that had happened, then John would have used her as a slave, and not married her, or at least he wouldn't have come home telling everybody that he was married to her—if he was. No, John probably thought he had a princess, before whom, not being of notably good breeding himself, he figured he'd better show off big with his money. He was ridiculous with her, a child, adoring her even when she irritated him. And she, regarding him, was astonished. Whatever she'd thought she was coming to, it wasn't Stonington. She hadn't got what she guessed she'd get; and Hab wondered whether John had. Hab sort of felt that this marriage was a bad thing. Now a bad marriage could be all right in some families; Stonington folks took such things as they ought to be taken, and made the best of 'em; but Hab had a notion that there was a great deal of trouble coming from this one.

But she certainly knew how to walk.

"Now this canvas, Habakkuk——"

"I told you. Wasn't what I ordered."

"Habakkuk, if I could only get——"

"Sorry. You show me the right thing and I'll buy it, cash."

Sunday was clear. Hab and Deliverance went to the first service, the morning one, the most important one, somewhat early, neither having said why. Even so, John and his bride were ahead of them—just ahead. They had paused at the meetinghouse doors, confronted there by Mr and Mrs Eph Tooker, and it looked like neither side knew what it was going to do: they stared back and forth like strange animals suddenly met.

Deliverance pushed ahead and went up to the Rellisons, and smiled, and spoke to them. Hab followed immediately. Suzanne smiled. The men lifted their beavers clear off their heads and made small correct bows.

Deliverance was wearing a beehive with white ribbons, and a Regency mantle with long sleeves and epaulets over gray jaconet muslin; she looked mighty fine, and for her mighty frisky too.

Suzanne wore a light gray Duchesse d'Angoulême tippet edged with Vandyke lace, a plain poke with plain white ribbons, white gloves, *and* no crucifix. Fact is, she wore no jewelry of any sort, even rings. The tippet was open at the top, as though casually, so that everybody could see that she wasn't wearing the crucifix.

The Tookers spoke to her then, and the Taylors came up right afterward and they spoke to her too, and inside the church the Rellisons took a back pew and not once did anybody deliberately turn around to stare at her. She sat silent, her head a little averted, her hands in her lap. Mr Smith didn't mention painted women in his sermon. Afterward everybody spoke to the Rellisons. Nor did the heavens fall.

Again that afternoon Suzanne took a walk out to the end of the Point, deserted on the Sabbath of course, so that just she and the high screeching gulls were there. Not so many people saw her that time, but those who did reported that she was wearing the crucifix again. But it was all right then. She'd been accepted.

All the same she was a lonesome figure, standing out there in the sun and wind while the birds wheeled far overhead, scree-ee-screeing. The birds kept turning, stretching their necks, looking for something; but Suzanne stood there silent, faced south.

. 33 . . .

THEIR HOUSE BEING OUT OF AND AWAY FROM THE VIL-
lage, north, the only direction it could be away without getting wet,
though they didn't farm any land—this too contributed to the singularity
and apartness of the Rellisons; but it was only one contribution; there
were many others.

When summer finally ended, trailing itself deep into September, in
a blaze of sunlight, and the air waxed nippy, just before they were hit
with that hurricane, Suzanne it seemed turned sour. Fact is, she had
been turning for a long time, but with the fall, for some reason, it became more apparent. She had triumphed, she'd been accepted by the
community, but her victory meant nothing to her and ever afterward
she scorned to put herself out in order to make herself liked. This isn't
to say that she spurned the villagers! She still smiled right and left
when she walked out, and she was always ready to stop and talk, appearing to have plenty of time. It was chiefly against her husband that
her disgust rose. That they were quarreling frequently and perhaps with
violence was common knowledge; and even though nothing could be
got out of the Jamaican boy, and later out of the dimwitted bound-girl
they had in the kitchen, still folks knew well enough that Suzanne had
been disappointed in her bargain, while John, as much in love as ever,
was a flame of jealousy.

While the house was building, John, who did a good deal of the work
himself, kept away from the bottle most of the time; but when the
house was finished, more or less along with the summer, and he had
Suzanne off there to himself when he could keep her there, and the cold
weather began to set in, then he fell to drinking more than ever, and
night after night he'd leave York's barely able to walk. He had further
to go than just upstairs now, too.

Mr Smith the preacher, from whom an occasional classical allu-
sion was expected, was heard to remark darkly that Bacchus had
drowned more men than Neptune had; and even the sots in the ordinary
sometimes wondered aloud, after he'd gone, why John Rellison didn't
act like folks any more.

He rose a mite in their estimation, however, the time he hauled his
wife out of the Liberty Tree.

There was a French schooner in from New Orleans, and Suzanne,
on one of her rare walks, overheard French being spoken, and an in-

stant later she was in the midst of them, showing more animation than anybody on the Point had ever seen in her before, waggling her fingers, spreading her palms, jabbering, and even jumping up and down on her toes in excitement. She forgot her walk, she forgot about her pretty new house, she went with the sailors right into the Liberty Tree, into the entertainment, and sat down with them, jab-jab-jabbering all the while. She sat there with them, seven or eight of them, all afternoon and well into the evening, eating a little, sometimes drinking a little, talking a very great deal. When John Rellison came to fetch her, just as it was getting dark, he walked mighty heavy, as those crowding the windows could see. He didn't even go right up to the table at which she sat surrounded by garrulous gesticulating Frenchies. Surly, he stopped halfway across the floor and commanded her to come back with him. She looked up a moment, to tell him to his face that she was talking with friends and didn't wish to be bothered. Even John, even a man as infatuated as he was, couldn't take that, which fair gave him a conniption fit. He went to the table then, and simply grabbed her and pulled her away. She made no resistance. Her bluff had failed and she was departing, angry though she must have been; but she realized that her husband here was absolutely right, and that in such a matter she would not have a single supporter, man or woman, in the whole village—indeed even the Frenchies, though they regretted the loss of her company, wouldn't have interfered. So she did not resist. But she didn't do any repenting either, any forgiveness-asking, as far as anybody could see. The single glance she gave her husband was filled with venom, but she smiled gaily at the Frenchmen, who had all stood up, impeccable in their manners, and were bowing, and she called out all sorts of good-bys in French, good-bys cut short when John yanked her through the doorway.

She wasn't seen outside the house for five days after that, though in ordinary times this would not be thought alarming, for the bound-girl did the marketing and Suzanne's own walks, always for pleasure, were irregular. This time it was asserted that she was staying home because her eyes had been blacked or some of her teeth knocked out. John, it had already been noted, had three deep angry dark scratches along the left side of his jaw; he said he'd cut himself on some bushes, but nobody believed this, and he was letting his beard grow in order to hide the scratches. However, when Suzanne did appear again, walking slowly but lightly, as was her habit, smiling to right and left, twirling her parasol, she was, as far as could be seen, unmarked. John glowered at her from the doorway of York's as she strolled down the street, and then he turned away and went back to the dimness of the bar, the blood throbbing in those scratches on his jaw. It wasn't more than three o'clock, but he was somewhat tipsy already. He'll kill that woman someday, folks said to one another.

This was the first time they said that; it was when they started saying it.

The house that John built was a handsome enough house but not a sound one, for he was in such a hurry to get it up (as though he had the notion that once his wife was enclosed within her own walls she'd prove more tractable) that he consented to use green timber. Seasoned timber was difficult to get. Now that the war was over Hab was able again to hire men to go upstate with oxen to the white-oak stand and haul logs back, but this stuff was seasoning now in salt water: he had no seasoned timber for sale, even to John. Hab himself never permitted an inch of unseasoned wood to go into any boat built or repaired at the Watts yard. He was an exception in this. Plenty of other Connecticut builders used green wood for hurry-up jobs. Their boats were cheaper, but of course they weren't as good as the boats made in New York, Philadelphia, or Baltimore—or in Stonington.

But John couldn't wait for seasoned timber. He had to get that house up right away, regardless of cost. Always handy with tools, he did a good bit of the work himself, but he spent plenty on labor too. Hab went into a rage one morning when two of his best carpenters failed to show up and he learned that they'd gone to the Rellison house. Hab went back there himself.

He found John with coat off and sleeves rolled up, a saw in his hand, working almost feverishly like a man trying to complete some chore before a thunderstorm broke. He hardly looked at Hab. He'd been having a quarrel with Suzanne, Hab deduced.

She was in a comfortable chair she'd recently had made, at an exorbitant price, by old Jethro Wheeler, which was planted now in the middle of what had been the potato patch and soon would be a lawn. She waved gaily at Hab, and paid no attention to her husband's churlishness. She was carrying on a lively conversation with some stonemasons, who were all grins as they worked. She spent almost every day in this fashion while the house was building, except when she was ordering furniture, when she was invariably cheated; and she could not understand why her husband, that rich man, worked like any commoner. Just now she was smoking a segar, and the stones in her ears glittered and the stones in her rings flashed as she waved to Hab.

John wasn't at all amicable about the carpenters. He kept right on sawing when Hab spluttered that it'd been hard enough during the war but now just when the men were beginning to get a little reasonable again was certainly no time for John to come along and offer carpenters a dollar seventy-five a day and three tots of rum instead of two! Couldn't he at least have conferred with Hab before he did that?

"I want to get this place finished" John growled.

"Why? Couple of years, and half your clapboards'll begin curling off."

John shook his head stubbornly, though at the same time showing worry. "Not if I fasten 'em on right." But he knew better. He'd worked under old Nathaniel Tooker, and he knew green timber when he saw it. He shook his head again. "You'd been less busy with those court injunctions there might *be* seasoned wood by now" he grumbled.

Hab flared. He was the angrier because John Rellison had not once since his return made any move to go back-country and visit his father and sister and aunt: hadn't even mentioned them. This would be partly because he didn't care much for them or the farmhouse where he'd been born, for which Hab didn't blame him, but chiefly, Hab inferred, because he was ashamed of his people and didn't want Suzanne to meet them. The attitude was understandable, if hardly commendable, but it didn't give John any right to pose as the aggrieved son of a persecuted father.

"Look at here, I didn't have that notice of injunction served till I'd warned him three times not to cut that stand any more. If he'd listen to me there wouldn't have been any delay. He's the one's to blame—your father!"

"It's his land."

"It ain't his land while it's leased to Deliverance!"

John had gone back to work.

"You and your Deliverance" he muttered.

For a terrific moment Hab thought of hitting him, John never looking up this while. Hab got hold of himself, shuddering. He had more than once marveled at the way he was accepting John Rellison, a cheat, a slaver. He reckoned it was because John, with all his deceit and his past at sea, with all his way of looking at Deliverance, sometimes, always unexpectedly, showed his old self again in a flash. Through a smile, just when you were getting most impatient, more often through one of those great laughs, the boy John peered right past the mask of the man, right out through those liquor-reddened eyes, and the voice abruptly was the glad ingratiating voice of the boy Hab had lived with for so many years. Then Hab himself would laugh, and forget for a little while what he really thought of John Rellison.

Just here now it wasn't that way. So far from laughing, John was leaning dourly over his work, meaning to dismiss his friend with a jeer. But Hab's rush of rage scuppered itself away in natural channels and without flood. He even began to grin, feeling a little sorry for John Rellison. Hab and his Deliverance indeed! Nobody knew better than John, wrapped up even though he was in his giddy wife, that Deliverance had fooled everybody, including Habakkuk himself, by turning into the finest figure of a woman in town. She had always been good-looking, far as that went, and had carried herself well; but now she was by everybody's admittance a real beauty. Maybe that was marriage, or maybe it would have happened anyway. Immaculate, poised, her eyes so sweetly clear and large, and with a slow smile that came seldom but lingered lovingly whenever it did come, she could by just looking at them stop men in their tracks. Hab knew this, and knew others knew it, and he was happy about it. He would have loved Deliverance anyway; but it was gratifying to hear men gasp when they first met her, and to watch her covertly as she moved around the kitchen. And just now, grinning down at John of the doggedly averted head, Hab wondered whether it wasn't possible that John was sorry he'd run away.

So Hab said nothing sharp, only nodded and strolled off. Ignoring Suzanne, who, lolling in her cushioned chair, beckoned him, he went upstairs to where his two carpenters were working. They had seen him coming, and their ears were red. In a low voice, and briefly, but competently, he told them what he thought of them. They were so embarrassed that they offered to go back to the yard with him right then and there. In a gentler tone he said no, to finish what they'd started; but he added that he hoped they wouldn't be too long about it. Then he went out to Suzanne.

He had got used to the artificial red on the lips and cheeks, but the segar disconcerted him, and he tried not to look at it. This was the first time he had ever seen Suzanne smoke a segar, and indeed the first time anybody on the Point ever had, unless perhaps John had.

He bowed over her hand. He was always courtly with Suzanne. He wished he could ask her about the Countess de Pontalis and how she was; but he calculated he'd better not mention that.

"It is a very long time that I no' see you, monsieur."

The stonemasons, excluded, tittering, listened.

He said, reproachfully, "You do not come Sundays any more."

She shrugged, and looked away, taking a pull at the segar: it was a very small and very dark segar, and smelled strong.

"It is maybe more hones'" she murmured.

The first five Sundays in Stonington Suzanne and her husband had gone to the morning service at the meetinghouse. The sixth Sunday and all subsequent ones they had not been there. The assumption, and it was nothing more than that, was that Suzanne had thought the effort not worth it, that she'd decided that the opinion of the villagers wasn't as important as her husband believed. Few blamed her in this, and there were many who applauded her sincerity. John, however, was looked upon with somewhat more contempt than before, a man who couldn't control his wife.

Hab and Deliverance had invited the Rellisons to dinner after each morning service, neither of them liking it much but doing it because they thought it only right to be polite to folks who seemed to have so few real friends. When on the sixth Sunday the Rellisons didn't go to church—well, they didn't show up at the Watts house either. There weren't any more invitations. Deliverance and Hab found it rather a relief; but they didn't say anything about it, even between themselves.

Suzanne wore the crucifix all the time now.

She rose, smiling at him.

"You go back to the village?"

"Well, I was."

"You will take me back there, 'Ab, yes?"

Her green eyes swam with those wee gold specks, and the skin of her face was smooth and warm. He swallowed, not smiling; but he bowed.

"Soon's I speak to one of the workmen. Shouldn't take me long."

The stonemasons were watching, leering. He ignored them. He went indoors to John's master carpenter, Redeemed Johnson, a sulky discontented sharp-tongued efficient man who had more than once worked at the yard.

"What about coming back to me after you've finished with this house?"

Johnson grunted.

"Couldn't be for long, if I did. I'll be called back to rebuild it pretty soon."

"He must be paying you a heap?"

"Aye."

"Well, you think it over, eh? You know what I pay, but there's a power of work, and you won't have to worry about something collapsing on you."

Hab had been watching Suzanne through the opening for a window. Now he saw her toss the butt of the segar away, and that was all he was waiting for. He'd certainly never meant to walk back to the village with her smoking that thing. He gave Johnson a curt nod and went out.

She took his arm, which all but made him jump, and started away, chatting with spirit about trifles, never once addressing or even glancing toward her husband, who sawed wood. Though she had so many other catlike qualities, and though she could well have thought that she was, Suzanne was not subtle. Hab knew almost immediately why it was she was walking back to the village with him. She wanted to find out more about her husband's financial affairs. She couldn't understand why a man who had as much money as she'd been led to believe that John had would work like an ordinary slave—no doubt she thought of it that way, since the only persons she had ever known to labor were slaves—and she believed, accurately, that nobody would be so well informed on this subject as Habakkuk Jones.

Oh, sure, Hab knew almost to a penny how much money John Rellison had left now; and it wasn't much. But naturally he wasn't going to tell Suzanne that. He pretended to miss her hints. Also he was very conscious of that arm linked in his, and perhaps he wasn't thinking too clearly.

Now John Rellison was a Connecticut boy, and ordinarily he wasn't throwing any cash-money into the bay. He could haggle with the best of them, and hold off, start walking away, all that. In a public house, granted, John was reckless, breathlessly so, buying drinks for men who were virtual strangers, in addition to the very many drinks he himself drank. Even this, however, as Hab saw it, was tied up with his love for his wife. He was lonesome. He wanted to be well thought of, as once he had been. He must have known that it was no secret that he'd once mated aboard a Guineaman and that for this reason decent men found it hard to be pleasant with him; and there were also ugly rumors about his eagerness to keep back from the shore, his reluctance to appear in the public houses just after a new ship had put in from some foreign place, which made men whisper that he was sure afraid of something and that they wouldn't be flummoxed to learn that young John Rellison hadn't at one time been mixed up with something even worse and more serious than slaving, if there was anything worse. But John desperately wanted them to like him, both for his own sake and for that of his wife; and there were times, from what Hab had heard, when he was even a mite frantic about trying to achieve this by means of laughter and a lot of rum.

In no other way was John Rellison, for all his big talk, spending much money on himself. The house was for her; and it was only his eagerness to have it finished, so that he could share it with her, away from the others, which had caused him to buy green wood and to pay a dollar seventy-five for a carpenter he could have got for a dollar and a half after enough back-and-forthing. That John was doing a heap of the work himself, even the dirtiest work, didn't amaze Hab any more than it amazed anybody else who knew anything about the condition of John's failing fortune, as many did. He could fuss enough about prices if it meant no delay! However, he was permitting Suzanne to order made the furniture she wanted; and that was a mistake, both because her ideas were extravagant and because she was so easy to skin. The folks generally liked Suzanne, were amused by her, and sympathized with her; but if she wanted to pay prices like that, why turn away?

"La, la, your manners, monsieur! You 'ave said nothing about my dress. It came off that ship from Le Havre only last week."

It was a phantasmagoria of greens and some yellow, over which cascaded ribbons and valenciennes lace. It made you blink. Hab bowed his head gravely.

"It's very pretty."

That was of course the deepest drain, her clothes, her trinkets. There wasn't so much to buy her, even with more ships coming from foreign ports now that the war was over, but whatever there was, if she wanted it John would get it. Sometimes it looked like she never wore the same dress or the same bonnet twice; while her boredom—for she was obviously bored—only increased her passion for gauds.

John couldn't keep that up, and Hab knew it. Prices were absurdly high. The small businesses in which a great deal of John's money was fixed were showing no profit, and every now and then one of them would fail. It was a time not to spend but to hold back. It was a time for waiting. John knew that, of course, not ordinarily being a fool. Trouble is, John was so deep in love.

If for no other reason, Hab Jones would have felt the down-slipping of all credit just in the men who came to him for loans to go West. They were always to be loans, usually with just about nothing to back 'em. Four years now, almost five, nobody talked about the West; but the craze had returned, sudden and startling as the splash of a frog jumping into water. You were forever hearing about the West—the great possibilities out there—the rich land and a heap of it for everybody—the opportunities. Only, as before, the men who prattled about these things were the men who would have to use somebody else's money to get to them.

She moved a little closer, squeezing his arm, reproving him with a shake, to repeat a question he hadn't heard, his mind having been elsewhere. He didn't even hear the question this time, though she walked with eager uplifted face while waiting for his answer.

"That depends" he said.

At the top of the rise next to the meetinghouse, really the northern edge of the village, he looked back. At the almost-finished Rellison house the hired workers were working on, but John had paused. John was upright, staring after these two; and even at that distance Hab thought he could detect the black hate and suspicion on John's face.

When he saw that Hab was looking, John went back to his work.

"That depends" Hab repeated judicially, though he still didn't know what it was Suzanne had asked.

. 34 . . .

The summer hung on, heavy with heat, three-quarters of the way through September; and then there was a hurricane.

It started as a stiff wind on Wednesday afternoon, but by night it was a gale or worse, coming from right off the sea. By Thursday's dawn some of the waves were smashing clear across Stonington Point, raking it from southeast to northwest like seas crashing across the deck of a floundering ship or chainshot raking a frigate helpless to maneuver. To be sure, these were small creamy ones at first, and quick to disappear, but they sucked at the foundations of houses and lapped insidiously under doors, and they were coming higher and faster all the time; so that from Thursday afternoon on, the greater part of the village was awash with swift currents that would knock the legs right out from under a man if he wasn't careful, and yellowish foam-specked whirlpools, and sand and bits of driftwood, and dead fishes that floated belly-up.

Still the wind rose.

Friday it began to seem to the toilers that there had never been anything but storm, never any other condition. It was backbreaking work, and dangerous too, for houses were collapsing all the time and many of the combers were likely to carry the unwary right out into the bay. It reminded some of the bombardment a year and a half before, for both were noisy and both lasted three days and involved everybody in town; but the bombardment had struck only the village and the land immediately to the north, whereas this blow undoubtedly covered a large area, and so far from expecting help to come in when it was all over the Pointers probably would feel obliged to go out into the country and see if there was anything to be done at the lone farmhouses. The bombardment had been largely a matter of smothering fires, the storm was largely one of fishing things out of water. The bombardment, for all its bluster, had hardly touched the village; the hurricane almost removed it. Anyway, there wasn't much time to draw comparisons.

Hab's first thought, now as before, was for the Watts house and the safety of Deliverance, and later he thought about the yard and did what he could there, and later still about the rest of the Point, where in fact he was occupied most of the time. His losses at the yard were

316

going to prove considerable, he knew. A lot couldn't be fastened down, hauled away, or even blocked from the wind, and this was flattened. He did save his patterns and his best tools, together with his office records; and he and five or six others carried the cat-schooner Deliverance I right out of the water and up the hill to the front yard of the Watts house, where soon it was joined by some lesser craft carried not by men but by the wind; for rowboats and dories were rolled up on land and tumbled and tossed a mile or more in some cases; and the trees afterward, those few still standing, were littered with bits of rope like Spanish moss.

The Watts house, being well built and as things on the Point went very high, stood firm—a circumstance for which there was certainly an appropriate quotation somewhere in the Book, only Hab didn't have time to remember it out. Indeed the Watts house and the meetinghouse were from the beginning the obvious places of refuge. To go further back-country would be to get away from the floods perhaps, but there weren't many farmhouses back there and the way would be made dangerous by falling trees. So as the waves grew worse, family after stubborn family at last agreed to leave their homes, to climb naturally to the meetinghouse and to a lesser extent, since it was smaller, to the Watts house.

Deliverance was never flustered, and she couldn't have got much sleep. She and Hab gave up their bed to Mrs Azariah Woods and Mrs John Wheeler, who were about to have babies. Deliverance before the crowd started to come had seen to the shutters and doors and all blow-awayable articles in the yard, and then, expecting visitors soon, had made tea and started to bake. She baked some mighty fine pies in those crowded days of the hurricane. It had been a good fruit summer, and she baked a lot of different kinds, which were much appreciated by the refugees. As it happened, neither Mrs Wheeler nor Mrs Woods birthed until later, but there were plenty of babies in the house anyway, and plenty of small children. There must have been sixty persons altogether. It was uncomfortable.

Hab fell to wondering about the Rellisons and whether they were hanging on out there, where, as a matter of fact, they ought to be tolerably safe, provided the new house held. He sought out a farmer over to the meetinghouse, a man who had come in to the village when his house up north was squashed by a falling oak.

"Aye. Passed there. Thought of asking for shelter, even though I didn't fancy Ettie getting a peep at all that foreign woman's dresses, but when I got nigh on to it there was such a ruckus I decided to keep moving."

"Ruckus?"

"Screaming so's you could hardly hear the wind. Her, not him. Though I could sometimes hear his voice too. Don't know what they was doing but it certainly warn't huggin' and kissin', and whatever it was I didn't want to get mixed up in it. So I kept along."

The farmer shook his head, clucked his tongue.

"He'll kill that woman someday."

Hab had never been in a hurricane, but many Pointers had weathered them in West Indian bays and ports and he had heard enough about them to expect in the middle of the blow a period of calm, when the static center of the storm passed. Then if you didn't know better you might think the hurricane was over, and you might step gladly outside —and be hit by the other half of the whirl, the wind coming from the opposite direction. This never happened in the hurricane on the Point. The wind kept coming from the southeast, and increasing all the time, shrieking hysterically, until Saturday morning around nine o'clock when it fell to nothingness. There wasn't any more wind after that, but before anybody had ventured far from shelter, for they were all expecting more, it started to rain. As though things weren't wet enough, the heavens opened in a regular cloudburst. Even the higher back roads and the upper end of the north-south streets of Stonington were almost impassable, what with mud and sand and slimy stones; but for all this, John Rellison, not chatty and jovial now, but glum, managed to make his way to Oliver York's, where he got drunk. He didn't talk to anybody, just sat there drinking. After a few hours, night having fallen, he sprang suddenly to his feet and rushed out of the pub. It was still raining but he slid and ran all the way to his own new house. In a little while he was back, less snappish now but still not his old self.

This jumping up and running home for a little while at night, and returning defiant for more to drink, was getting to be a habitual trick of his. Sometimes he even did it in the afternoon. Apparently nothing set him off, at least nothing anybody else could see, so that he must have been thinking all the while about his wife, and worrying about her, doubting her. He would break right into the middle of a conversation, even into the middle of a word, with a muttered apology as he sprang to his feet and hurried outside. He always said that he just had to relieve himself, but that didn't fool anyone, for they'd watched him more than once and he'd always head north. His eyes didn't used to look pleasant at those times, as he'd dash out, and they wondered, back at York's, if he would ever catch her. There were rumors that there might be some ground for this suspicion, though even on this point most of the villagers were inclined to be lenient with her, rather blaming John. "Way I figure it," Zeke Wheeler said, "Suzanne's not the kind of woman would stand for her husband thinking things like that. Way I figure is, if he don't stop all this surprise-visit ructions she's just as likely to give him some reason for it, if she ain't already. And I can't say's I'd blame her, either."

She was seen more often in the village these days, even though it was turning cold. She walked with that same jaunty step, turning her head right and left, always smiling, stopping to talk with the different workers. She made a regular round, cheering folks up, men and women both. She was a sight in Stonington all right, pointed out to visitors. She might be a painted woman, but she was friendly and no hag. Pointers for the most part were fond of her and rather proud of her. She smoked her segars openly now, right out in the streets, and when she felt like a glass of wine she'd not hesitate to step into one of the public houses and order it, and talk cheerily to the waiter while she sipped it. Her clothes were wearing a bit at the edges, and she seldom showed up in anything new these days, but they were still the most dazzling clothes most Pointers had ever seen, and she carried them with an air. She was the first woman in Stonington to wear brandenburgs on her pelisse, the first to wear a Duchess d'Angoulême tippet, and she introduced the Devonshire mob, pointed in front, jauntily cocked, and smothered in fine Brussels.

Hab Jones knew why Suzanne wasn't getting many new dresses and bonnets, and as discreetly as he could he offered John a job at the yard: in a very little while, with his past experience, John ought to qualify as a journeyman builder. John, however, indignantly rejected the offer; and when he wanted to raise a mortgage on his new house he went not to Hab, as almost anybody else on the Point would have done, but to a lawyer in New London—though if he thought this was going to result in secrecy he was mistaken, for the sum and interest and terms were pretty generally known even before he got back, though he hurried back, fearful that his wife might take advantage of his absence.

The village had been badly mauled, and it was weeks before things were straightened out again, weeks of work for everybody. Without joy, but without hesitation either, Hab Jones released most of the workers at the yard, postponing his rebuilding plans, for it seemed only fair that they, and especially the carpenters, should get a chance to repair their own and other folks' houses. Everybody helped everybody else, and no bills were rendered afterward. Even John Rellison chipped in, maybe glad of something to do with himself, though his hand was shaky and he didn't have the even eye he'd had when after working all day in the yard he and Hab would spend most of the night taking some ship out to Montauk. Even Suzanne did her part, the part of a brightener, a cheerer-up. She'd walk among the workers, so sunny a spot in that dull scene, twirling her parasol, speaking to everybody, swapping japes, laughing, occasionally singing in a husky contralto some quaint and perhaps mildly salacious French song. She always had a good audience; and if, as often happened, there was one face filled with sour disapproval, that of her husband—well, Suzanne didn't care, she didn't pay the slightest mind to him. John had once tried to keep her from smoking in public. She smoked more than ever now, probably more than she really wanted to. Folks said that that walking-around of hers must have had one good point for John Rellison: it showed him that she was at least out in the open. There were many reports that she wasn't always that way.

Their own house, the Rellison house, had survived the storm. Few Pointers had ever seen the inside of that house, and there were tales of dark goings-on there, of drunken orgies in the course of which John tortured her horribly. Hab and Deliverance had been there once only, on invitation to dinner, and that had been a ghastly mistake, everybody being stiff and uneasy, even the ebullient Suzanne, who was nevertheless very lovely in a blue and yellow Regency ball dress. The food, after Deliverance's, after the Widow Watts's, was insipid; and there wasn't even enough of it. The house too was dirty. Deliverance, who had been sincerely shocked, deeply shocked, couldn't get over it, and talked about it again and again, though only to Hab. That bound-girl, stupid almost to the point of imbecility, was no cook, granted, and no housekeeper either; but she wasn't lazy, and with a little help from Suzanne, and a little careful supervision, she could at least have made the place decent to live in. Why, it was a pigsty! Hab would protest that, well, it wasn't maybe as bad as all that, though he'd admit that it wasn't as trim as—— A pigsty! she'd repeat vehemently, breaking in on him. There were some things Deliverance was very strong-minded about. She and Hab had been wont to joke about the way certain neighbors attributed the hurricane to the wrath of God—Who must in that case, Hab remarked, have been powerful riled-up against the sugar islands. The usual explanation was that the storm had been visited on Stonington, on all Connecticut and Rhode Island more or less, as a punishment for having stayed in the vile federal union and endured without any breaking-away the despotism of the Virginians. Still others, though they were fewer, ignored the rest of the world outside of Stonington, of which they probably didn't know much anyway, and flatly blamed the hurricane on Suzanne Rellison. Though she had laughed previously, and though she was a woman of sound good sense most times, Deliverance after that visit to the Rellisons, Hab believed, was inclined a little to side with the second group. Anybody who would sit in a house like that and just lounge back in a chair as though nothing was the matter—— Yes, that's right, I guess, Hab would hastily say.

One thing the storm did stimulate, besides work, and that was talk about going West. Those who worked hard, and they were the majority, didn't have time for such chatter, but there were others, of course, as there always are. Hab told Deliverance he guessed it must be that there weren't any hurricanes in Ohio—no, nor any rainstorms either.

The yard had been badly damaged, and his building schedule had been put far back, what with the need for cleaning-up and the flood of emergency jobs, but Hab didn't too much mind; he was busy with plans for a new schooner, which would be Deliverance's own, and the delays gave him a chance to tinker further with its lines. In rig it wouldn't be anything special, though it would have taller sticks than was customary for its length, and carry a powerful pile of canvas; but the hull was something quite different and would cause a lot of headshaking. Hab hoped that it would be about the fastest boat ever built.

He was working on its lines, still only paper, one night in the shack, when Suzanne came in.

Unaccountably the shack had survived the storm the end of the previous summer—this was April now, early on a bitter cold night, with the wind from the north. Hab was glad of this, for the shack was a sort of shrine, the place where he'd got married. It was his office and designing loft combined, a smallish room crammed with tools and patterns, and containing also a small charcoal brazier and a pallet on which Hab sometimes lay down for a little while. The brazier was lighted now. The pallet was empty. Hab was on hands and knees on the floor, but he scrambled to his feet when she entered. He supposed that she'd seen the open gate and just strolled in, idly. She always did seem to have so much time. In a world that hurried, she always moved slowly.

This nightwalking was a new thing. Her appearances in Stonington streets until recently had all been in daylight, and preferably sunlight, for she loved the sun. Formerly too she had spent a good deal of time alone, standing on the flakes at the end of the Point, gazing to the south, maybe thinking of her home country, maybe not thinking anything at all, just dreaming. She seldom did this any more. The tip of the Point was a pretty bleak and cold place these days, and she kept to the friendlier village. Not glanced around at as often as before, she'd become less the strutter, more the prowler. Bored, she was dangerously restless; and there was in her walk more than a hint of the pacing of a tiger behind bars.

She was definitely feline anyway when she slipped into the shack. She smiled right at him, holding her head a little high, and for the first time Hab caught a flicker of real recognition in her eyes. She was very lovely in the candlelight, which softened the slight hardness her face had lately taken on, making her girlish again as Hab had first seen her.

She went over to the pallet and sat down, taking her hands out of a pert velvet muff in order to hold them over the brazier. The muff swung from her wrist. She patted the pallet at her side, indicating that he should sit down; but he didn't stir.

After a while, all the time looking at him, and smiling, she said slowly: "You remember me right-away, yes, 'Ab?"

"I reckon."

"But you say nothing because of my 'usban'—and your wife, eh?"

"Aye."

She shrugged.

"I do not care for my 'usban' now, 'Ab."

"Well, I still care for my wife."

Again she patted the place beside her, and again he was motionless. He knew what she was leading up to, of course, and he began to tremble all over, and sweat stood clammy on his body.

"You liked me when I was good to you, yes, my 'Ab? I gave you good time, yes?"

"Well."

Her laughter was sudden, explosive, yet not loud.

"I am just as much good time now, 'Ab. Look—you see I am just as much. Look——"

She had already opened her pelisse, and now with hands like small swift brown birds she unfastened her dress on the left side, unfastened and peeled down some underwear, and scooped out her left breast. She held it there in her two hands, and it was round and shiny, the nipple a perfect red.

"You see?"

He didn't turn away in time, but he did turn away. He even walked away, all drenched in sweat as he was. He went to the window, to stare out at nothing. He was scarcely able to breathe.

He often wondered afterward what he would have done if this hadn't occurred in the very room in which he'd been married. It didn't do him any good to wonder about that, but he often did.

"Put that thing away" he snapped. "Put it back where it belongs!"

She laughed again, but he heard her dress rustle and soon she rose and went to the door.

"I feel like 'aving love tonight, 'Ab. I would more soon it was you, but it will be somebody. You sure?"

"Yes, I'm sure. See here, you'd better let me escort you back, after dark like this."

"Oh no. Nobody hurt Suzanne."

You can hope not, Hab thought.

She lit a segar at the candle, and very slowly she went out, leaving an odor of strong tobacco and a floating ribbon of smoke.

A few minutes later, when he'd recovered his normal breathing, Hab put out the fire, blew out the candle, and he too left the shack. He did not feel like working any longer. And besides, she might come back.

Just outside the gate, in the street, he saw her again. She was speaking

322

to a sailor, a loutish fellow she'd evidently accosted and who now was agasp at his own luck. As Hab came out, however, the sailor put his arm around Suzanne's slim waist and they started down toward the center of the village.

That was the last time Hab Jones ever saw her alive.

. 35 . . .

IT WAS ABOUT A WEEK AFTER THIS, AS WELL AS HAB could remember, when the mutterings about Suzanne started, the rumor that she had been killed.

For three or four days nobody had seen her. During the first months on the Point this wouldn't have been thought odd, but lately she had been in the habit of making her rounds every day, regardless of what she might have been up to the night before; and folks missed her, and talked about her. Several of them accosted John Rellison, asking whether Suzanne was ill. John, always irked by the fact that everybody called his wife by her first name, curtly answered no. This was further than ever from the old John, who even when drunk had a smile for everybody who'd smile at him. He had changed greatly, even in his personal habits, his manners. He didn't talk so much, and he seldom laughed at all, or even smiled. His mien was one of suspicion. He would eye newcomers from some corner of an entertainment, when a new ship was in; and indeed, if he didn't know ship and crew pretty well, he would not even come to the village. It was clear that he was afraid of being seen by somebody. It was equally clear that he had very little money to spend. He didn't buy drinks right and left, as once he had done. He didn't buy them at all nowadays, except for himself. Add to this the fact that the villagers liked Suzanne, their institution, and it is easy to see why they took her side in the unhidable combat between these two, and why when Suzanne was missing they watched John with slitted eyes and with mouths tightly pursed, shaking their heads.

Gam Wallace, who had not liked John since John's return, and who never minded speaking out about the way he felt, said now that John had murdered her. Gam admitted that it said in the Book as to how we should forgive our enemies—but it didn't say anything about *trusting* them.

A party of women who hadn't heard of John's curt negative or did not believe it, impelled it could be as much by curiosity as by kindness, but undeniably kind for all that, descended upon the Rellison house with soups and jellies and medicine; but they got no answer to their knocking. Even when they went around to the front door they got no answer. That bound-girl too must have disappeared. The women hoisted one another up and peered through windows, but they didn't

324

see much except that the house was in a disgraceful condition and would take at least a week to set it straight; but they didn't see any blood or anything.

Whether because of this or despite it, the talk in town swelled. It wasn't only Gamaliel Wallace: plenty of others began to say that it sure looked as if he'd killed her. They were sore.

"You reckon they mean it?" Deliverance asked one night.

Hab shook his head, not too convincingly.

"My opinion, they've talked so much 'bout that he would kill her sometime that now they've got themselves all stewed up that he *has*."

"What do you reckon's happened to her then? Would she be on one of the boats out there?"

No, he told her. The boats had all been searched by volunteers, friends of the various skippers.

"Course she might be right in the house all the time, with a sick headache maybe, and just not feeling like answering the knocks of a lot of nosy gossips. Or she could have gone to New London, do a little shopping."

Though Deliverance didn't smile, she might as well have.

"Well, do you reckon there'll be trouble?"

"Shouldn't wonder but what there might."

"You keep out of it now," sharply, "if there is!"

"I'll keep out of it long as I can."

Well, he failed that very afternoon. He was obliged to go to Oliver York's, after he'd closed the yard, to consult with a certain skipper on a repair job the skipper might otherwise take elsewhere. This was new for Hab, drumming up trade, making bids for contracts. Until recently, until the slump after the war, they had come to him; now he went to them. The place to look for a sailing man when he's ashore, unless it happens to be his home town, is of course his favorite pub. This particular skipper-owner, a gaunt sharp New Yorker named Sheepshead who made the Boston run and often put in at Stonington, preferred York's. It was a part of Hab's job to know these things. And because he got in and out of the public houses so much these days Hab saw more than usual of John—more than he liked—but he'd never seen John look as bad as he did this afternoon.

It was not only that John was drunk, it was that he'd been drunk for several days, and he was angry, almost mad, a light almost of insanity in his eyes. His voice was unnaturally loud. Hab heard him some distance from the inn, and hastened his step.

John stood alone, no friends, all enemies, and his face was red and his fists were clenched. He swayed a little, though his feet were wide apart: he swayed forward and backward. Gam Wallace and some others were poking him up with taunts, but they weren't doing this the way they might do it to some ordinary everyday drunkard: they were in earnest, and mean. Three or four of them were doing this, standing before John Rellison very close, as though daring him to attack them. The others were back a bit, but they all watched John. If there was a fight, they were none of them going to take John's side.

And there was going to be a fight, too. Hab saw that the moment he opened the door. Indeed he got there barely in time.

"And I told you she's in New Haven, visiting some friends!"

"What friends?"

"Some French folks. I don't know who they are. And anyway, what business is it of yours?"

Gam said something else then, something low that Hab couldn't catch, but whatever it was it infuriated John, who lunged toward him.

Now John Rellison had been a fine fighter not so long ago. Hab remembered him as he'd been in that memorable raid on Westerly, before he'd got the blow that almost put his eye out and took the courage from him. Hab remembered too, and would never forget, the speed and snap of the boy John Rellison's punches right outside the door of this place five-six years ago.

Well, John wasn't that boy now. He swung lumpishly. His very rage was added to his drunkenness to make him miss. Gam Wallace didn't even step back, only swayed a little from the hips and let the blow pass his face. Then Gam jumped in, and he managed to hit John three times before John went down. They were hard punches to the face and each of them sounded loud.

Hab Jones got there then, and shoved Gam aside, reaching John just as John recovered his feet. He threw both arms around John's arms, so that you couldn't hear what John was saying, which perhaps was just as well. John's nose began to bleed. Hab's own nose was bleeding by this time, from excitement, and they made a gory pair as they swayed and struggled, with the crowd jeering them. John was heavy and very sore, but he didn't have much strength left and his balance was poor. Hab jockeyed him to the door, which somebody opened for them.

"And tell him I'd just as soon he didn't come back" Oliver York called. "He owes me for some drinks, but we'll forget that."

John Rellison was no longer the inn's best customer, hadn't been in some time.

Outside they didn't grapple long. John quit abruptly and began to sob and slobber, and Hab wiped his face and wiped his own bloody face, and then half-carried him up Water Street. This had been a great deal more than a mere tavern brawl, as both of them knew. It was late enough in the afternoon to be darkening, virtually suppertime, and Water Street was almost deserted; but even those few persons they did pass didn't make any offer to help Hab or even ask what had happened. Something strange had come over the Pointers these past few weeks,

326

something sure terrible that said disaster was near. Hab could feel eyes on him and John from all the windows, all along the line. There was a great deal of hatred packed into those eyes. Hab couldn't see the eyes, but he could feel the hatred.

It was a long walk—that is, it took a long time. Again and again John stumbled and almost fell, and he walked slowly, dragging his feet, bumping his knees together, and with his head down, slobbering and blubbering. He must have been conscious of Hab, but he never looked at him and may not even have known who he was. He was, however, talking to Hab.

". . . got to get away from here . . . going west, out to Ohio . . ."

Hab said nothing.

At the door of his house John pulled up sharp, fumbled for a key, found it. When he had opened the door he half-closed it, so that Hab couldn't see anything inside, and for the first time he turned and faced Hab. There were four steps up to this door, and they stood on the top one.

"Why didn't you let me hit him?"

"You're drunk, that's why."

"I'd have killed him! I'd have—— And you listen here, Hab Jones, you keep out of my quarrels after this!"

"Better get some sleep."

"You keep out of it or I'll show you what I'll do——"

Not expecting it, and not wanting to look John in the face, he was so sorry for him, Hab never saw the blow, though probably it was clumsy enough. Anyway there was a lot of weight behind it. If it had hit Hab in the belly it would have knocked his wind out. It did hit him in the chest, and he staggered under its force, and stumbled backward down the steps, and sat on the ground.

It didn't hurt him, only jarred him, but it made him as angry as he'd ever been in his life, so angry that he didn't dare move for a moment but only sat there. John had gone. The door was slammed.

Hab just sat there, battling himself. He forced himself to remember his rage at the time of the visit of the false Aaron—a rage directed not at this impostor so much as at the person who'd sent him—and how scared he had felt about it afterward, how breathlessly near he had come to murder. He was angrier now, even, than he'd been then; and he fairly shook all over, like a man with a chill, as he sat on the ground looking blankly up at the door. He did not rise to his feet until he knew that he was not going to smash his way into John Rellison's house. He walked away without looking back.

Though it was suppertime he didn't go home. He was too trembly: he didn't want Deliverance to see him in that condition. Wiping the blood and sweat off his face, he walked instead to the burial grounds near the Watts "farm," a burial grounds the judge had bought into along with five other local families, and where, Hab supposed, he himself and his Deliverance eventually would be laid.

It was a rustic ragged plot, square, surrounded by a stone fence over which poison ivy, just beginning to leaf, rioted. It was mostly weeds and headstones, no trees. The mounds were not conspicuous, did not stand out much: it was as though the bodies, once buried, themselves preferred to sink further into the earth, making as little hump on the surface as possible. Some places marked by headstones indeed were almost flat. There were of course a great many rocks.

Hab quieted, his hands quieted, and he ran fingers through his hair when he came to the Watts markers. These were simple redstone with cherub-face caps, and stood by themselves, with room on either side for more. They were well cared for, the ground carefully weeded, though this was still only April. On each grave was a small bunch of wild violets; and Hab reflected that Deliverance must have searched hard and long for them, this early.

JONATHAN WATTS

B. FEB 6, 1757   D. NOV 4, 1809
MOMENTO MORI

FRIENDSHIP WATTS
WIFE OF JONATHAN WATTS
B. DEC 4, 1761   D. APRIL 10, 1814
WIDE IS THE GATE
AND BROAD IS THE WAY
THAT LEADETH TO DESTRUCTION

The verse was from Matthew, Hab knew, though he wasn't sure which chapter. He wondered now as he had often wondered before why the judge had picked a Latin quotation for his own gravestone instead of something from the Book he loved so well. Hab wasn't sure what the Latin meant, except that it had something to do with death and remembrance.

These thoughts, however, occupied only a small corner of his mind as he stood there in the fast-gathering darkness. He heard the clock in the steeple behind him strike six. He prayed a little.

Returning, cooler, when he passed John Rellison's house he noticed no glimmer of light, nor did any sound come from the house.

It occurred to him that Deliverance must have passed this place much more often than he, Hab, had ever done, coming and going to tend the graves.

328

He washed the blood from his jacket at the well in the backyard by the light that came out through the kitchen windows. Perhaps he didn't do too thorough a job? At any rate Deliverance knew as soon as she looked at him that something had gone wrong—though how she knew this or how he knew that she knew it Hab couldn't have told you—but she said nothing. He mumbled an apology for being late, and added that he would have to go out after supper to see Captain Sheepshead at York's about a contract. He disliked this chasing after work; but he had been reproving himself of late for spending too much time on the plans for that fast new schooner. After all, it was Deliverance's time he spent, since it was Deliverance's money, her yard. Hab had great confidence in the schooner-to-be, refusing to be unsettled by the head-shakers; but after all, taking everything together, he had to admit that it *was* a gamble. On the other hand, vessels like Captain Sheepshead's, repair jobs like that, were and always had been the financial backbone of the yard.

While they were doing the dishes Deliverance said rather suddenly, offhandedly, and without looking at him: "John all right?"

"Well" said Hab.

No further mention was made of this subject.

The atmosphere in Oliver York's was a shade too offhandish. Everybody was conscious of Hab Jones, and everybody, catching his eye, nodded and smiled or bowed gravely as he always had done. Nothing was said about John Rellison, not even by Oliver York, who personally brought Hab and Captain Sheepshead their mugs; but Hab would have bet that a great deal had been said before his own entrance, as a great deal would be said after he'd left.

Dealing with New Yorkers usually was easy, but Sheepshead was another matter. He must have come of Yankee ancestry. He was good-natured enough and predisposed in favor of the Watts yard, which he knew well; but he was careful, and he rehearsed every detail of the job, argued every penny of the price. At last, however, and without ever being hotted up, they reached full agreement. They shook hands and finished their flip, and Hab went out into the night, giving the assemblage a chance to talk again about what it wanted to talk about.

Fact is, Hab himself was thinking about the same things, about what might have happened to Suzanne, about what might happen to John. Destinationless, for he didn't feel like going home just yet, he wandered down to the flakes, to the southern tip of the Point, and stood there a long while, listening to the wavelets, watching the stars, and breathing the air.

The tide was in, the wind was from out of the southeast, and the air was chilly and salty, otherwise without odor. No birds scree-ed overhead. There were plenty of lights besides those of the moon and stars. Lights blinked helpfully at Little Gull, over to Watch Hill, on Block

Island out there, and far off on Montauk. That was good, that was civilized, so that vessels could come and go honestly.

Hab liked the smell of the yard right enough, and knew he'd never get sick of it—the heavy pungent smell of sawdust and freshly peeled logs—and he liked the smell of the sea too, when the tide was out—the tangy odor of mud and marsh. But it was good every now and then to get away from those and come out here and breathe straight air.

This was instinctive. In consciousness he went on thinking about Suzanne and worrying about what might be done to John. The very fact that he stood where Suzanne so often used to stand, staring south as she did, filled him with memories of her.

It was a terrific shock then, the worst he ever had in his life, when in answer to some unnamed tug of his mind he looked down and saw Suzanne at his feet.

My God! he thought, John Rellison of all persons ought to know too much about the tides and currents around here to let this happen!

That was the only thought he did have for a long while, if it could be called a thought, and he stood staring down, very badly scared, at the thing rocking in the water. He didn't stoop, or move in any way; for though Suzanne wasn't notably bloated or puffed, so that there was no way to tell at a glance whether she had been in the water a long time, still it was easy to see that she was dead.

She was dead, she was broken, like a broken doll. Yes, she suggested a doll as she floated there on her back, rolling a little with the motion of the wavelets. Only—the mechanism had been removed, the cords cut. She was still pretty, not disfigured; but she wouldn't ever again squeak "Mama" when pressed or gently if mechanically close her eyes when put into her toy crib. Those eyes were wide-open now, and fixed that way, not only open but bugging out a bit as though in strain. There was absolutely no expression in them, and this made them the more horrible to see. They remained green, but the warm golden flecks no longer were there. They were lusterless. The eyes of dead or dying fishes, how many thousands of these had Hab seen? yet they always did give him a queer feeling of uneasiness, he never had got used to them. These eyes were the same, but much worse, being so much larger, and being so beautiful. The mouth was a little open, the lips red and full but not swollen, and the visible teeth were perfect. Though there was a red bandanna handkerchief tied around her neck very tight, from behind, and everything suggested that she had been garroted by this, her face was not mottled and dark as might have been expected: it was only a touch darker than usual, and even that might have been the moon.

She was wearing jaconet muslin, yellow slashed with green, her favorite color combination; and neat little white velvet slippers; and all her rings, and around her neck a couple of gold chains and the crucifix, which still showed below the bandanna and slid back and forth on her

330

breast as she was rocked; and on her head a bonnet she had recently introduced into Stonington, a bonnet called the Rutland poke, very elegant and stylish. This bonnet was made of white satin edged with swansdown and wadded and lined with white sarsenet. The front was cut in points, and the sides were tied under the chin (just above the encircling bandanna) with soft white ribbons, all soggy now as they floated on either side. It was placed far off to the right side of Suzanne's head, not accidentally or as the result of any struggle, but because this was the fashion. It was most rakish. Out of the top of it, literally its crowning glory, was a fine once-fluffy ostrich feather dyed lemon-yellow. The feather had survived immersion rather less bravely than the rest of the bonnet. It was utterly slack and sad, with all curl gone from it as it joggled back and forth. Even the dye was washing out, leaving the feather a mottled sickish gray.

The little waves slapped softly in, and then they shushed back, tumbling pebbles with a rattly sound, and then they slapped in again; and Suzanne rocked a little this way, a little that way, the crucifix sliding, one shoulder, one hip, and one knee feebly nudging the shore as if she were pleading to be permitted to stop floating and rest a while.

She ought to have her little lace parasol, Hab thought foolishly.

That was when he did begin to think again, and breathe again, after what must have been a very long while. He recognized the handkerchief, as everybody else would. It was John's. But Hab knew that he had not seen and recognized that handkerchief when, the first instant after seeing the body, he had exclaimed to himself that John ought to have known these waters better than to permit this. No, he'd had that thought instantly and instinctively. Everybody else would have the same thought. The familiar red bandanna, a favorite of John's, wouldn't be needed as proof.

Well, the giddy gaudy painted beribboned body of this lovely woman from the south in mute reproach nudged the stones, moving slowly to the west as though in search of a more hospitable place to land. The water must have been very cold. The rocks certainly were cold and hard. Even the moonlight was harsh tonight.

Hab Jones suddenly turned and began running up the Point.

. 36 . . .

He didn't have his gate key, so he scaled the fence, as he had used to do with John. He found a small kedge anchor and a length of rope, and pretty soon he was pushing out in the cat-schooner.

He knew he'd have to move fast, whatever he did.

For a moment, running, he had thought of going to John's house, waking him, warning him. This would be to give John at least a few hours' start. That it would make Hab himself an accessory after the fact did not occur to him then.

He discarded this idea before he had run far. John was by now in a deep alcoholic sleep, a stupor, the collapse after not an ordinary bam but several days of heavy drinking, and it would be impossible to awaken him, much less bring him to a realization of his danger.

Besides, Hab was not sure of what he himself might do if confronted with John Rellison again.

So he went to the yard instead.

He had thought the moonlight very beautiful a little while before, but now he cursed it. He was fully exposed when he approached the tip of the Point, which lay flat and white, all rocks, no shrubbery, not even any grass. There would be nothing unusual in the sight of the cat-schooner putting out at this hour: not having time in the day, Hab sometimes did go out in Deliverance I after dark, maybe to fish, more often to try some new idea in rig, occasionally just for fun. The danger tonight would be in getting a line to the body; for though the drop-away was sufficiently great and the cat-schooner's draft sufficiently slight to enable him to get right up to shore, because of the rocks he couldn't actually beach the craft, and on this incoming tide it was going to be difficult to do what he needed to do. If while doing it he was seen by somebody who just felt like strolling out for a chat, it would be unfortunate.

Suzanne bumped against unresponding rocks. She still tended hesitantly westward. Left alone, she would be down at the foot of the bay before the turn of the tide at sunup; in fact, she'd be somewhere near the Watts shipyard by that time—assuming that she hadn't previously been seen and fished out, which was assuming a great deal.

Hab shivered when he leaned over the stern. The prospect of getting very close to that thing, and especially those eyes, chilled him. Even in

332

death Suzanne was lovely, but—but—she *was* dead. Her skin would be very cold, it would be clammy. Her eyes strained without seeing anything. The crucifix still slid back and forth on that smooth ice-cold bosom.

Hab got the rope under one of her arms and leaned low to pass it beneath her back, reaching into the water for it. He had to push her arms a little away from her body to do this, and he had to lean very low, almost embracing her. His face was within a few inches of her face then, and he closed his eyes.

The rope slipped. He started to put it under the arm again, and a vagrant wind-pocket, a passing freak, took the boat away from shore. Suzanne, uninfluenced by the wind, bumped on, pitifully beseeching the rocks to give her refuge.

The boat had gone only a few yards, and rather than spread any canvas, which might make it more difficult to handle—the tide would keep it close to shore—he paddled back to Suzanne with his hands.

He glanced along the Point. Still nobody was in sight. It was very quiet, the air was quiet, and he could even hear the voices of those who drank at York's. But nobody came out.

Again he was close to the body. He didn't permit himself to shut his eyes this time as he passed the line around. The body smelled musty, rotten. The arms felt like they were resisting him—as though by means of some power of their own, some trace of their one-time muscularity, they were holding themselves in. Hab knew that this was sheer imagination; but it scared him all the same, and his hands trembled.

He had to get very close, both arms around the body, so that it was as though he was hugging and kissing her. Those eyes stared right at him. The lips, opened, seemed about to speak. Wavelets rocked the body so that the head went back and forth constantly, gently, and it was as if Suzanne were saying no, no, please don't. Hab's hair prickled at the roots.

Trying to get away from scary thoughts, he saw some bruises on the neck just under the chin. These were the only signs of struggle. He supposed that the bandanna covered others. He thought for a moment to take the bandanna off, but the knot had been swollen stiff by water. Anyway he didn't want to touch the body any more than he had to.

When he straightened, sobbing with relief, it was only immediately afterward to catch his breath at the sight of a man coming out of York's. The man looked back and forth, absently whistling, as though wondering whether to take a walk out to the tip of the Point. Hab crouched, holding his breath.

Crouching, then, he watched in fascination Suzanne's little ostrich plume atop the Rutland poke. (She'd been so proud of that Rutland poke!) The limp frivolous thing had been broken, and its upper half confusedly bobbed back and forth in the water, back and forth, back

333

and . . . It was a long while before Hab could tear his gaze from this, and raise his head.

The man outside the tavern was gone.

He made fast the line, leaving several yards, for he didn't want Suzanne too close. He hoisted sail and made generally for Wicopesset, off the east end of Fisher's.

The sound was huge with moonlight, and there were millions of stars. He had never felt so conspicuous.

He was not panicky, but he wasn't thinking too straight either. He forced himself to sit quiet at the tiller, not to look back but only to feel the line now and then in order to be sure that Suzanne followed, and not to look at the backs of his hands, wet with sweat rather than sea-water now. After a while he began to lay plans.

He would tow her out to the eastern end of the Race, and there weight her with the kedge anchor. He thought he could do this without looking at her again. The kedge anchor should be heavy enough to hold her down indefinitely, but even if it did break loose—after all, John, it seemed certain, must have weighted the body, which escaped from *that*—she would still, in all probability, be carried out to sea.

Coasting along Fisher's, Hab headed for the light on Little Gull. It was hard to do this. He itched to run away from lights now; and as he got nearer and nearer to Little Gull he felt with increased strength, like a pushing from inside his chest, the conviction that he was being watched, that everything he did, every little movement, was seen.

This was wrong, of course. His common sense told him that a man on Little Gull might be able to make out the boat, yes, and with a glass even identify it, but he never could see Hab himself or what he was do-ing—or what he was towing. However, his common-sense, tolerably strong in ordinary circumstances, was not working too well just then. Suzanne behind him, he thought (feeling that prickling of his scalp again as he thought it), would be swishing through the water large and bright. For all his promises to himself, he turned to have a look.

Maybe he screamed. He thought he did; but there were no echoes, out there where everything was water, to confirm this.

He looked at the light again. No, that was ridiculous! Even if he had screamed—and he wasn't sure—they could not have heard him at Little Gull. No, not at half that distance.

Unable to help himself, he looked back again.

It could have been some trick of the water, or rather of the current, strongish here, but more likely it was the way he had fastened the rope, which might have slipped underneath her breasts, though he'd tied it above them—but anyway Suzanne rode high and almost half out of the water. It was as though she were seated on something just a few inches beneath the surface, her back to him. Her arms were stretched before her, away from the rope and the boat, and the ribbons of her poke, well

334

above the water, and all but dry in the wind, flapped and snapped pettishly: Hab could even hear those ribbons snap, or thought he could. The shoulders and back were falling now right, now left, in the wake of Deliverance I, doing a wild weird dance, and the head, even worse, jiggled crazily to this side and that, sometimes jerked backward, sometimes slumping forward, so that the poke with its broken plume soared and swooped like a wounded gull.

He yanked the line; but that made it worse: that made Suzanne wobble more wildly and appear to try to lift herself clear out of the water. Frantic, he yanked the line again—and the line came free.

He handed it in. There was nothing on it. But Suzanne had subsided. He couldn't see her at all.

Well, he thought, I've done as much as I can.

He put the cat-schooner straight up into the wind and held the tiller, fighting it, the exercise helping him to think.

But there was no profit in thinking. He was past thinking. He knew that he should put about and find Suzanne and attach the kedge anchor, but he also knew that he wasn't strong enough to do that. He had never before been so shaken. He guessed he was a coward; but he was beyond the point where he could feel ashamed of himself. He only knew that he would never be able to look at that corpse again, no matter what happened.

Then reason, if it was reason, but anyway he thought it was, came to his aid. There wasn't any real need for the kedge anchor. If he knew anything about tides and currents at this end of the sound, Suzanne was caught up in the Race and would be carried far out. Adrift here, she sure wouldn't be washed up anywhere around Montauk. It was conceivable that in the course of a few days she might be washed up somewhere along the south shore of Long Island, though far from Montauk; but even if that happened it would be a long time before the news reached Stonington, supposing that the body was ever identified, and John would be gone by then. Ninety-nine chances out of a hundred, he told himself, were that she would be carried straight out to sea and never be picked up at all.

It was in this way that Hab argued with himself, easily convincing himself. He put the cat-schooner about and described a wide sweep outside, returning by way of the shoals near Napatree. He handled with elaborate care, concentrating. If he hadn't known these waters so well, and if Deliverance I had not been the boat it was, he would have grounded half a dozen times. He didn't ever get close to any place where Suzanne might be.

His wife asked him if he'd seen Captain Sheepshead, and he answered that he had and that the contract was all right. They wouldn't make as much as he'd hoped, he reported, but it was going to be all right. After prayers, and after she had gone to bed, he stayed up for a long time, just sitting, sometimes pretending to read to himself from the Book, but mostly just sitting. He was tired, but he wished to be more tired. He wished to go to sleep just as soon as he got into bed. He didn't want to wake up yammering, so that Deliverance would know.

Well, she knew anyway—knew at least that something was wrong. Deliverance was not stupid. Hab ate only three eggs at breakfast, and that in itself would tell her; but she didn't say anything.

He worked extra hard, and the day got past. He reckoned it was the hardest day he had ever known. Moreover, even at suppertime he wasn't right. He was very tired, and all his body ached, but he did not think he was going to sleep.

Through that day he had caught tag-ends and snippets of talk, and the next day he was to catch more, telling him that the village seethed. He stayed in the yard, minding his own business, but it was a small place, Stonington, and inevitably small things leaked through to him. Oh, he was John Rellison's friend, or the nearest thing to a friend John had these days, and because of this they were careful about speaking in his presence. But he didn't need to hear the words. He didn't need to see the faces. He could *feel* that the village was losing control of itself.

This was a terrible thing, which in Hab's memory had happened only once before. Judge Watts had been alive then. So had Red Ferguson, killed in the war. This time it would be worse. Joey Bludge was a man they hadn't truly hated, only despised. They hated John.

Late in the afternoon Hab Jones paused, unkinking his back. Had he ought to go to John now, and warn him? John had had a clear forty-eight hours in which to sleep off his bam. Was that enough? If Hab dallied, would *they* call on John instead?

It was at just this time, around five o'clock, that Suzanne returned.

That pathetic hip-bumping along the shore, that wistful request of a corpse to be taken out of the water, maybe it hadn't been all accident? Maybe Suzanne somehow had some will left in her poor sodden body? She'd slipped John Rellison's bonds and weights. It is a rash man who will predict the sea's behavior. John had been wrong, though John knew his tides. Even Hab Jones had been wrong. A fisherman coming in, with a so-so catch, had encountered Suzanne not more than three hundred yards off the tip of the Point, toward which she was floating.

Hab heard about this within minutes of the time the fisherman beached. In the excitement nobody weighed Hab's relationship to John Rellison. It could have been any of the workers in the yard, but it just happened to be Stubbs Houghton, an apprentice sawyer, who rushed up to him.

". . . Mr Rellison's kerchief too, right around her neck . . . Everybody's——"

Hab grabbed him by the shoulder as he started away.

"Now wait a minute! You can go there afterward. First I've got something for you to do for me."

Young Houghton kept wanting to go, but Hab held onto him.

"Now wait! What you're going to do is you're going to go up to my house and tell Mrs Jones that I may be a little late to supper. Understand? I may be a little late to supper. Afterwards you can do whatever you want."

He ran the whole distance to John's house.

It was a confused crowd, not more than fourteen-fifteen when he arrived, and with no organization, but it was growing. Men were coming singly and in pairs, never in groups. There were no women.

Gam Wallace was at the front door, shaking it, kicking it, rattling the knob, slamming the knocker, while he shouted for admittance. Others were at the back door. The windows were dark, and no sound came from the house.

Men walked around and around the house. Now and then somebody would climb to a window on somebody's shoulders, but the windows were locked.

More men kept coming all the time, and the newcomers cried out to smash the door in and why be so polite. Somebody threw a rock, breaking a window. Somebody cheered. But on the whole this was a quiet mob, which made it the more terrible. It felt its own strength; it didn't need to whip itself into a frenzy with shouts and curses and loud accusations. There wasn't a man there who questioned that John Rellison had killed his wife, and there wasn't one who doubted what they would do to him if they caught him.

There were no torches, but though the sun had set there was still light enough to see the faces, taut and pale with anger.

There was a mumble of thunder in the southwest, where the sky was waxing very dark; and the air began to smell like rain.

Three, Gam Wallace and two others, got some heavy rocks and smashed one of the panels of the front door. They reached in and threw the latch. Only for an instant they paused, and then they went on into the dim entranceway, and soon others plunged after them.

Hab Jones knew he was no Judge Watts to command attention with an orator's manner. He didn't try that. Instead he went hurriedly from man to man, pleading in broken tones, grasping elbows, being pushed away. Often he wasn't recognized, for these men had but one thought now; but even when he was recognized there was no anger directed against him. It was only John that they hated. They were sorry for Hab, who should ought to have better sense, but they didn't hold his misplaced loyalty against him.

However, if they did not find John here they'd look for him somewhere else, and what place more natural than the home of his friend, the house in which he himself had been brought up as a boy?

337

Hab got a little cold when he thought of the mob climbing to the Watts house. He ceased to grab elbows. He edged away.

It had begun to rain, large and languorous drops that hit with a soft sound.

The men inside had found but a single lamp, and they brought this to the violated doorway. They complained that they couldn't see anything inside there. The ones outside shouted that he wouldn't get away: they'd answer for that. The ones inside tore curtains, cushions, bedclothes, anything they could get their hands on, and wrapped strips of these around pieces of the shattered door panel, and dipped them in oil from the lamps, and lighted them; and in this way half a dozen torches were made. They glowed very bright, but uncertainly, coming and going at the windows like huge hellish fireflies. Indeed the whole scene was hellish. The figures of the men, black, two-dimensional, did not show human at the windows. Silhouetted in red, themselves black, they jiggled and danced, capering madly, appearing, waving their torches, disappearing.

"He'll never get off the Point" somebody yelled at Hab, not looking to see who Hab was. "We've got men watchin' the boats."

Hab nodded, and slipped away.

The rain which had started like a summer shower had changed quickly, in a matter of minutes, and now was a winter's rain. The drops came smaller, sharper. They were hard now, almost like hail, so that they stung the face.

The back door of the Watts house was open, and there was a light in the kitchen. Hab stopped, meaning only to arrange his clothes and wipe his face before entering, and it was while he stood there that he heard John Rellison's low urgent voice:

"Come on with me. I've still got a few dollars. We'll go out to the real country, God's country, like I told you about before, out to Ohio where folks ain't always——"

"Get out of this house! You've been after me for weeks, haven't even had the decency to leave me alone when I go to take care of my mother's and father's graves. I've spoke all I'm going to. Next thing I'll do if you keep this up is I'll tell Habakkuk, and then——"

"Listen, you gave yourself to me once, Deliverance. You must love me! Why not give yourself to me again, out where nobody'll know us? What've you got to lose? A home you're sick of, a money-grubbing husband who's always away working——"

Hab went into the house.

. 37 . . .

They were the other side of the table, and John stepped swiftly back and away from her, but Hab sensed rather than saw this, for he didn't glance at them. He said nothing. Walking neither fast nor slow, he went to the front of the house, and into the parlor, where he took down from over the fireplace the musket Jonathan Watts had used to squirrel with. He took down the horn and the mold box too. There was still powder in the horn, and when he stirred it with a finger he saw that it was dry: the Watts house was an exceptionally dry one. He cut a bullet with the mold. He tapped the gun against the floor, muzzle-down, in case there was any dust or dirt inside the barrel. Then he righted it, and poured in powder and dropped the bullet on top of this. He found in his breeches pocket a piece of paper on which he had charcoaled some calculations, figures of no significance now. This was the right size, and he crumpled it and tamped it home with the ramrod, as wadding.

When he had replaced the ramrod and banged the butt on the floor once or twice to be sure that some powder trickled out at the touchhole, he looked up and saw Deliverance in the doorway.

"You're going to kill him" she said.

He did not answer because he figured that it didn't need an answer, not being a question. He did nod. He pulled back the striker with both thumbs and heard it click into place. By that time he had started for the kitchen.

John was going out the kitchen door.

"Wait a minute" said Hab.

John stopped, and turned, and saw the musket. His face had been red, a dirty loose red like that of a cock's wattles, and now it went slowly gray. But his lips didn't tremble, and he didn't say anything. He kept looking at the musket.

Hab did not look at him—that is, at his face. Hab looked only at John's feet.

He got his rain hat from a nail and put it over his right hand to protect the priming: he was holding the musket high now, actually pointing it at John. He took down the key to the yard gate and slipped this into a pocket.

"All right, *now* we can go."

As he knew from the gun what was going to happen, so John must

339

have known from the key where it would be Walking slowly but not too slowly, his arms stiff at his sides, he descended to the gate of the yard. They met nobody. The men of the village were mostly back around John's house; the women, keeping the children quiet, were waiting at home—but not near windows, windows being good things to keep away from when an irresponsible citizenry's aflame. Anyway, though barely suppertime it was dark. Hab at first had to squint to keep John's shirt in sight. There was still a bumbling in the southwest, but this was slighter than before. There was no breeze. The rain was reduced to an even, icy, malicious drizzle.

With his left hand Hab held his hat over the touchhole. His right forefinger remained crooked around the trigger. He wasn't sweating or trembling. He didn't feel anything in particular.

They had gone less than halfway to the shore when the first little licking lights of red wavered on the grass before them, lights that shivered as though in ecstasy. These lights gained confidence, growing steadier as they grew brighter, until by the time John and Hab had reached the gate all the ground around them, and the gate itself, and the fence, were sprinkled with pink.

Each knew what that meant. John's house was on fire, back there over the brow of the hill, and low clouds reflected the blaze. Maybe a drunken man had dropped a still-smoldering torch. Maybe, exasperated by their failure to find John and still believing that he was in the house, they thought to burn him out. Most likely it was sheer rage.

Hab closed the gate and locked it. Still not looking up at John's face, he motioned with the barrel of the gun which way he wanted John to go.

It was a familiar route for these two. But this time they didn't go clear to the little dock. At the Black Pit, Hab called a halt.

John turned, and now his lips were twitching a little. His face was still gray. But his eyes, for those eyes lately, were curiously clear. He stood flabby, compared with what he had been, but erect. He had his back to the pit. He was pressing his elbows pretty hard against his sides.

"Turn around" said Hab.

The light of the burning house came slipping over the edge of the hill. It fell on everything. The whole world was reddish.

"No" said John. "You want to kill me, you can kill me this way."

Hab lifted the muzzle, putting his left hand under the barrel to support it. The hat slipped off, but he was holding the firing apparatus close to him and leaning over it so that the drizzle wouldn't reach it.

For the first time, he looked up.

John Rellison was beginning to smile. It wasn't bravado, it wasn't a sneer. John had not asked for mercy and wasn't asking for it now. He was, it looked like—well, he was sort of saying good-by. He was smiling for the last time at his friend.

340

It was a shy tilted smile at first, for John was scared, his muscles tight, his nerves tight. But as it caught on it started to run up his face from his mouth, and then the dark eyes too smiled.

Hab's heart quopped thickly.

"Well" he said.

He moved the muzzle to one side, so that the bullet would go into the Black Pit, and pulled the trigger. There was a sulphurous flash, a coughing sharp explosion. Then smoke wandered out of the muzzle.

John had closed his eyes in spite of himself, and when he opened them again he knew that he was alive, wasn't even hit. He went to his knees, almost tipping over into the pit after all. He wasn't praying, it didn't seem. He held both arms around his middle and was bending over low, as though he had a cramp: he might have been trying to vomit, or, more likely, trying to keep from vomiting.

Hab picked up his hat and put it on.

"All right. Get away and stay away."

How? Lifting his head, as the drumming cleared from his ears, he could hear the sound of the mob. John's house burned on, reluctant to burn out because of the drizzle and because of the green wood; but the mob had quitted it. As the reflection of the flames came over the rise of ground, so too did the sounds the mob made. They were tired of the fire already. They wanted blood.

John somehow got to his feet.

"I—I'll find a boat."

"They've got a guard on them. Got 'em all together."

Both of them knew what that meant. When the mob reached the line of the Watts house and the meetinghouse, which it must be near now, it had the whole Point blocked off. John was trapped. He might as well have been at the far end of a pier, with the mob at the land end.

But they wouldn't have taken——

No, they hadn't. Hab jerked his head toward the cat-schooner Deliverance I, which rocked gently at the dock.

"Go on!"

"Hab, it's yours. But I'll—I've got some money here—I'll send the boat back from New York——"

Hab had turned away, and when he felt a hand on his right shoulder he stiffened.

"Thanks . . . thank you, Hab."

Hab walked away from the hand, without turning.

He didn't turn, indeed, until he was almost up to the Watts house, and then he just looked back once, quickly, over a shoulder. Even that movement John Rellison must have seen, or guessed. John had Deliverance I under sail now, visible against the reddened water of the bay, and as Hab glanced back John, gay as ever, turned in the stern sheets and lifted a hand to wave. Hab went on, running.

They were coming in the back door as he went in the front. Deliverance stood in the kitchen to receive them, and she was very straight and even haughty.

"John Rellison in this house?"

"No."

"Where's your husband?"

"Right here" said Hab as he entered the kitchen from the front hall.

They were not badly drunk, not the ones who had crowded into the house, anyway, though some in the yard, from the sound of them, must have been pretty bad.

The ones in the kitchen were shamefaced, but all the same they were determined. Going after John Rellison, a wife-beater, a Guineaman, probably a pirate, certainly a murderer, was one thing. Talking rough to a man of Habakkuk Jones's standing, and in the presence of Judge Watts's daughter, was another.

Gam Wallace got himself pushed forward. Only a little older than Hab, and physically almost as big, he was respectful of manner, not truculent, but insistent.

"We aim to search this house, Hab, and you nor nobody else is going to stop us. We know we ain't got any right to, but we're going to do it all the same."

Hab nodded.

"Go ahead" he said.

It took them by surprise, who had steeled themselves against resistance. But in a moment they were organized. Only a few, six or seven, scattered to make the search. Several others stood at the doors. The greatest part of the crowd never even got to the house, though it was waiting nearby for the shout that would mean John Rellison had been uncovered. This was not a disorderly search, nor even a very noisy one.

Early, just after it had begun, Deliverance said quietly out of a corner of her mouth—she who on ordinary occasions spoke so levelly and directly when she spoke at all—"Did you kill him?"

"No. I let him go."

She was watching the men cut a candle into stumps and light these, and her face showed only disgust with their manners, distrust of their mission.

"I'm glad" she whispered. "I mean, for you. It's better."

The men tramped around, downstairs and upstairs and even into the muggs, but they didn't break or rip anything.

They all, like all those outside, had the same thing in mind, and their collective mind couldn't hold anything else, Hab reckoned. They sought John Rellison in this house, that was all. Not one thought to look out through a front window, from where, in the beginning of the search at least, John might have been visible. Not one remarked that Hab's head and shoulders were wet: even when he ran nervous fingers through his hair, and it skipped and snapped back into its previous disorder, they didn't observe the moisture. He thought sure that one of them would notice in the parlor that Judge Watts's musket no longer hung over the fireplace—Hab had left it in the yard—but none did.

Deliverance and Hab stood side by side in the kitchen, taking no part in the search, making no comment.

When the men came back they mumbled apologies, saying they hoped they hadn't disturbed anything. They made some attempt to straighten things, peeling up candle droppings as best they could, tossing the stumps into the trash box. Mr and Mrs Jones paid them no attention. One by one they backed out. Hab locked the back door after them.

Then he and Deliverance went over the whole house, inside. There wasn't much to be done. The men had been mighty careful, all things considered. The floors were muddy, of course, and they cleaned those; but the furniture, except that a piece had been pushed out of place here and there, and there were some candle drippings, was all right.

Deliverance had had supper ready long before, and after cleaning the house they sat down. They spoke very little. Once Hab said, as though just thinking of it, that John had saved his own life when he smiled. And Deliverance said yes, she understood; and she probably did, at that.

They were tired. They did the dishes rapidly, and Hab kept the prayers and reading short. The reading was from Jeremiah.

Afterward Deliverance went slowly upstairs; and Hab, standing at the front door, watched with great admiration until not only she but the last of her shadow had gone.

Deliberately then, with a deep sense of the solemn importance of this task, he shoved the bolt shut.

He lifted his candle and went upstairs after his wife.

www.ingramcontent.com/pod-product-compliance
Lightning Source LLC
Chambersburg PA
CBHW032234010726
47494CB00002B/491